PRAISE FOR MARTIN CLARK'S
THE JEZEBEL REMEDY

"The real pleasure here is the way [Clark] blends legal thriller with the more whimsical elements of a freewheeling, pica-resque novel."
—*The Boston Globe*

"A portrait of fine but flawed humans who find themselves unexpectedly thrust into the deep end of a system where the law can be either a life raft or a dead weight, depending on who gets to make the final judgment call. . . . Clark has a practiced ear for the subtlety and nuance of everyday existence."
—*BookPage*

"Thoroughly addictive. Part thriller, part legal procedural, it is also positively disarming as it posits that doing the right thing is really the only choice, no matter how much trouble doing the right thing sometimes is."
—*The Anniston Star* (Alabama)

"*The Jezebel Remedy* [is a] cure for summer doldrums."
—*The Charlotte Observer*

"Fast-paced and delightfully unpredictable. . . . Not only do the frequent plot twists keep the reader glued to the page, but Clark's depiction of life in rural Virginia and the depth and sensitivity of his character portrayals . . . make the book memorable for much more than its clever legal machinations."
—*Library Journal* (starred review)

MARTIN CLARK

THE JEZEBEL REMEDY

Martin Clark is a Virginia circuit court judge. His past novels have been chosen as a *New York Times* Notable Book, a *Washington Post Book World* Best Book of the Year, a *Bookmarks Magazine* Best Book of the Year, a finalist for the Stephen Crane First Fiction Award, and a Book-of-the-Month Club selection. His last novel, *The Legal Limit*, was the winner of the Library of Virginia's People's Choice Award and was called "a model of how to write a literary legal thriller" by *The Oregonian*. He lives in Patrick County, Virginia, with his wife, Deana.

www.martinclark.com

ALSO BY MARTIN CLARK

The Legal Limit

Plain Heathen Mischief

The Many Aspects of Mobile Home Living

THE JEZEBEL REMEDY

THE JEZEBEL REMEDY

MARTIN CLARK

VINTAGE CONTEMPORARIES | VINTAGE BOOKS
A DIVISION OF PENGUIN RANDOM HOUSE LLC | NEW YORK

FIRST VINTAGE CONTEMPORARIES EDITION, JUNE 2016

The Library of Congress has cataloged the Knopf edition as follows:
Clark, Martin.
The Jezebel remedy / Martin Clark.—First edition.
pages cm
1. Attorneys—Fiction.   2. Married people—Fiction.   3. Trials—Fiction.
4. Corporations—Corrupt practices—Fiction.   5. Suspense fiction.   I. Title.
PS36553.L2865J49 2015
813'.54—dc23   2014014401

Vintage Books Trade Paperback ISBN: 978-0-8041-7290-5
eBook ISBN: 978-0-385-35360-1

Book design by Maggie Hinders

www.anchorbooks.com

Printed in the United States of America
10 9 8 7 6 5 4 3 2 1

For Deana Clark

and

in memory of Mike Hubbard

I am guilty of a dreadful selfish crime
I had robbed myself of all my precious time

—ROBERT EARL KEEN, "Dreadful Selfish Crime"

THE JEZEBEL REMEDY

But...

Her husband, Joe Stone, was in his office at the opposite end of the building, a pair of matching Persian rugs and a long hallway of beaten oak boards distant, his door shut, their sweet cur dog, Brownie, probably dozing tail to snout on a chamois pad beside the heat vent, and Joe was no doubt explaining every boilerplate detail of the umpteenth will he'd prepared for his mercurial, crackpot client Lettie Pauline VanSandt, who, only a few minutes ago, had tracked red mud across the nice carpets and into his office, heedless as always. Nothing but a damn millstone, Lettie. For sure, neither she nor Joe would tend to the mud.

Lisa Agnes Kennedy Hotchkiss Stone and Joe had been married almost twenty years. She had five names, whereas he had only two, lacked anything in the middle. "NMN" was how it appeared on his driver's license. Joe NMN Stone. She and Joe had been law partners for practically all those years, just the two of them and their various secretaries, as well as an office manager they'd been able to afford once the money became consistent. This very November morning, watching him pour a cup of black coffee in their kitchen, she'd appreciated—again—what a graceful and handsome man he was: tall—right at six-three—but not gangly or a beanpole, thick hair that held its dark color and several waves at age forty-four, and a face full of fierce calm that was laid in deep and precise, difficult to budge. She loved him, absolutely she did, she loved her husband.

A Virginia Code volume was open on her desk, but she'd gotten sidetracked and wasn't reading it. A single page had cowlicked away from the rest, floating betwixt and between. Lately she'd felt a bit stuck, preoccupied with the flat patches in her life, mulling and noodling, flummoxed by how she seemed to have wandered across an insidious boundary and been shanghaied into a dull land of earth tones, Scrabble games, paint-by-number vacations, Cinemax replays of *A Star Is Born*, monthly potlucks, Lean Cuisines, cobwebs, dust bunnies, marital conversations retarded by a mumbled "Huh?" or a distracted "What, sweetie?," community center Zumba classes, flannel, mismatched silverware, lukewarm champagne and box steps every December 31, matted fleece bedroom slippers and sex so mission control she could count down the seconds between her husband biting her neck and squeezing her breast. She worried that her entire world, from alpha to omega, was nothing more than a stupefying loop, a big, whopping white-bread bonanza, comfort and familiarity their own worst enemies.

A sizable part of her delicate mood was rooted in the past summer, June and July, and its cause was obvious and easy to understand— she'd lost both her parents with no real warning, just unfair as hell. Her momma was killed by a monstrous clot and never woke up from a noon nap, the laundry still wooden-pinned to an outside line, a pound of shrimp thawing in the sink, a candy dish filled with pink, yellow and green butter mints on the dining room table, ready for Wednesday bridge club. Her darling dad was gone a month later, walloped by a massive stroke, so tough he'd held on for almost a week before he died, barely seventy, paralyzed and grimacing in a hospital bed and unable to speak, and it was impossible to sit through two sweltering Baptist funerals and not wonder when her day was coming, whether she was wasting her own precious time.

Also, and she *tried* not to be hateful about it, but bless his heart, some of Joe's quirks and habits had become a pain for her, and this wasn't helping her disposition, either. The charming cowboy boots she'd cottoned to back in law school now struck her as Henry County hayseed if he wore them off the farm. Naming their shaggy black puppy with the single white spot on his flank Brownie was genius, but then came Katrina and New Orleans and Joe hit his own endless jackpot, and every time . . . *every freaking time* . . . the mutt would roll over or shake hands or fetch his tennis ball, as predictable as a cuckoo clock at half-hour intervals, Joe would crucify her last nerve with the "heckuva job, Brownie" line, and yesterday, in 2010, he'd repeated it again, praising the dog for scratching at the kitchen door, the same slobbering ruckus every Wednesday, the pooch eager for the front yard, where he could bark and greet the garbage truck.

Joe would absolutely ignite and go Full Lewis—her term, after Jerry Lewis's spastic Nutty Professor—whenever he heard the opening riff of "Black Coffee in Bed" or Harold Melvin and the Blue Notes' "Bad Luck." No matter how many times he'd listened to the intro, no matter how dated and old-hat the songs.

At work, there was the trite shave-and-a-haircut knock despite her begging him not to do it ever again, please.

He would make her sit in his office and he'd "call the shareholders' meeting to order" and they'd vote on replacing the gutters or buying a new computer, even though *it was only them,* Joe and Lisa, husband and wife—they were the entire law firm.

She was weary of his corny "great googly moogly" and, at the other end of the spectrum, his crass, indiscriminate use of the word *fuck.*

Worst was his riding a motor scooter—not a motor*cycle,* mind you—to town in warm weather, this huge man putt-putting down Starling Avenue, an embarrassing big-ass helmet strapped underneath his chin so that he favored the Great Gazoo, the crazy cartoon alien from *The Flintstones,* and, yeah, of course he knew the whole deal was goofy, but she was unable to convince him that even a maximum dose of self-awareness and a tongue-in-cheek penumbra can't save some choices from coming off as idiotic.

To be fair about it, she realized that some of her failings had to bother him, especially how she often forgot to completely close the dresser drawers and occasionally spilled nail polish on the bathroom tile and never returned the living room phone to its base, and there were probably heaps of other irritations that he was too decent to mention. He kept things in check much better than she did.

She loved him though, she did, loved him in the fashion, she supposed, that you love a spouse hamstrung by two decades of marriage, loved him with most of the shiny paint scrubbed off, the gloss long ago weathered away, her affection down to the solid girders and nuts and bolts and sturdy welds, the steel guts of the arrangement.

But . . .

She stared at the taupe grass cloth they'd selected from a ritzy 1990 sample book as they finished refurbishing what had formerly been a hometown department store in the era of Perma-Prest and fancy petticoat displays. They'd not changed the walls since, and now the fragile threads and stiff, strawy weave were frayed and broken in places, especially at the corners and above the baseboards, and a few loose lengths of grass cocked out from their bindings like crippled insect legs. A vertical seam had separated, and Joe had tried to repair it with a specialty glue he'd discovered at Walmart, but the fix wasn't what it should've been, so there was a bulge not far from the ceiling, an obvious sag that needed attention.

Joe's voice came over her phone, very formally asking if she could walk down the hall and witness Lettie's will, his words sounding tinny and off-pitch through the speaker. "Sure," she said. She noticed the numbers on the phone's square metal buttons were getting harder and harder to see, eroded by thousands of pecks and taps, almost to the quick. "No problem."

She knocked and entered his office without pausing, and Brownie raised his head and thumped-thumped-thumped-thumped his tail, an arrhythmic beat that caught both cloth and the hardwood past the edge of his pad. The dog's welcome didn't last long, soon ended with a collapse and a sigh, a lazy tongue sloshing over his teeth and slight lips. The lips were black, matched his fur.

Lisa traced the muddy shoeprints to a chair where Joe's most persistent visitor sat. Fortyish and spectacularly tattooed, "Petty Lettie" VanSandt hadn't quit at simply inking her pale skin and matchstick limbs; she'd also gussied herself up with three nose rings and a gigantic gold front tooth just in case the needle painting needed accessorizing or wasn't overwrought and sideshow enough. As a final baroque flourish, she'd recently added a tongue piercing, a tiny silver barbell she could rattlesnake out from behind the fake tooth. Lettie claimed she'd done the job herself, with an ice cube and free-clinic hydrocodone tablets to numb the meat.

"My gracious," she exclaimed. "It's Della Street. The coffee made and plants watered and paper clips ordered?" There was a pet carrier beside her on the floor. A cat was inside.

"Don't start with Lisa," Joe warned her, his tone firm but mixed with a tiny undercurrent of amusement. "You know the rule." He was behind a video camera, a Stone and Stone Attorneys at Law acquisition that made possible his latest service, a no-frills recording of people as they read their wills aloud. The fifty extra dollars also purchased the chance to say your piece and have the last word; every syllable and cadence, whether praise or grievance, rebuke or forgiveness, was captured on a disc Joe placed in the client's file along with a copy of the signed final papers. Testators often came dressed to the nines and most took the event quite seriously, fashioning their sentences carefully and soberly, as if they were mouthing church creeds or the Pledge of Allegiance. More important, the DVD also memorialized the maker's competence and clear mind in case there were any challenges or questions later on, a genuine twofer, as Joe put it.

"Hello, Lettie," Lisa said coolly. "Is that a cat you've brought with you to our office?"

Lettie's three acres and ramshackle trailer were home to innumerable cats and dogs, strays and discards all, so many that anonymous do-gooders periodically called Lee Orr, the animal control officer, and asked him to check on the poor things' welfare, and he'd grumble and curse and drag out to her place, easing the county truck along her rutted dirt drive, and he *always* found every single creature well fed and kindly treated and granted free run of the premises, inside the double-wide even, bedroom, den, kitchen counters, it didn't seem to matter. But make no mistake, Lettie had her tolerances and kept her sanctuary reasonably clean, once using a broom to thwack a careless hound—right in front of the officer—when it commenced to squat and was too near the jackleg wooden deck.

"Yeah. So? You got a problem?" Oddly, Lettie grinned large and showed her gold tooth to full effect.

"Not really. What's the cat's name?" Lisa pasted on a phony smile. Maybe she could suffer through this.

"Why the hell would I name it, Della?" Lettie asked. "Huh? It's a damn cat; it don't speak English or understand nothing 'bout no name. Like every other animal, it just comes to my voice and knows the sound of a lid peelin' off a can of food. I suppose you'd give a name to a parakeet? Goldfish? A skunk?"

"That's twenty-five more added to your bill, Lettie," Joe intoned. He'd finished adjusting a tripod so the camera was aimed squarely at her.

"Yeah. And I been thinkin' about that, your little 'rule.' If it's twenty-five bucks to be insultin' to your secretary there, how much would it cost me to just slap the bejesus out of her?"

"Now you're at fifty. Lisa isn't my secretary. You know as much. I've told you a hundred times over. She's a lawyer. Probably a better lawyer than I am. She was law review at the University of Virginia. Meaning, Lettie, she's smart as a whip. Hey—look at how much money she's making for us right this instant. Fifty bucks in three minutes by merely walking down the hall."

For some reason, before she spoke, Lettie tapped her garish tooth with her index finger. Several of her nails were painted green. She wore rings with colored stones. She popped the barbell into view. Withdrew it. "Probably the only pay Della will collect the whole week," she remarked, giggling, her head bobbing atop an attenuated neck.

"Yeah," Lisa said, "now maybe I can finally afford that rose tattoo I've always wanted. Or a snazzy nose ring."

She and Lettie had gotten crosswise a couple years ago, when Lettie had inquired about obtaining a patent for "having trucks and bulldozers and whatnot beep when they go in reverse. A safety feature." Impatiently informed that this technology was already in place and had been for a long while, she threw a hissy fit because Lisa refused to help her "sue the bastards who stole my idea." Joe, though, always politely listened to her ramblings about perpetual motion machines, alchemy of every stripe and grade, poultices, miracle cures, inventions and contraptions. He'd set up a corporation for her and her nutty schemes, created pointless trusts and foundations, drafted a medical directive that she tinkered with almost monthly, prepared numerous limited liability companies and devoted hours to discussing her feuds with neighbors, magazine sweepstakes, the county landfill and the local board of supervisors, usually without charge, not so much as a penny, and his patience infuriated Lisa, this nitwit eccentric wasting Joe's time, he mollycoddling her for no rational reason. At least he really would ding her for the extra fifty.

"Wait. So how is it she can say any nasty insult to me for free?" Lettie complained. "She's makin' fun of me."

"I think you look great, Lettie," Lisa offered. "Primed for a star turn on the midway. Or to hoist the Jolly Roger above your very own ship."

"We're ready," Joe announced, almost before his wife finished.

He buzzed their secretaries, and they came in and stood against the wall, both saying cautious hellos to Lettie. She was cordial and asked Betty, the younger of the women, if her children were doing well. "Your littlest boy, Sammy, now he's a pistol," Lettie complimented her. "You tell him he's welcome to visit my trailer anytime and find himself a kitten or a pup."

"Okay, Lettie, the camera's running, so you can begin whenever you're comfortable," Joe told her. He handed the will to Betty, who passed it to Lettie. "First, though, I need to ask you a few questions. You know the drill." Joe addressed the camera: "Today is November eighteenth, 2010. The testator is Lettie VanSandt."

He had Lettie state her full name, her age, her birth date, her address, the extent of her assets and the names of her blood relatives. She noted she owned her mobile home and land and a savings account at BB&T Bank, notwithstanding the fact the bank had shorted her a time or two over the years. She kept a cash strongbox hidden at her trailer. She damn sure wasn't going to reveal her social security number, she informed Joe when he inquired; he had it on file and could dig it up if it was such a big deal. Without any prompting, she shed her sweater and stood—now wearing a ragtag V-neck T-shirt and Wrangler jeans—and read her will pretty as you please, almost theatrically, each word allotted its full due and properly pronounced, including the legal term *per stirpes*. She left her entire estate to her son, with the exception of a two-thousand-dollar gift to the Henry County SPCA. Joe was her executor, and Lisa cut her eyes at him upon hearing the news.

Lettie sat and signed the will, her seventh revision in 2010. After witnessing the signature and adding their own names to the document, the secretaries quietly exited Joe's office, their steps quick, relieved.

"Don't think I didn't see you makin' your pissy expression," Lettie said, still seated.

"What expression?" Lisa asked in a mocking tone.

"I wanted to leave Lawyer Joe somethin', but he wouldn't hear of it," Lettie said. "Make up for the torment his wife is to him."

"Maybe you could bequeath him your cauldron and list of spells," Lisa cooed.

Lettie laughed. "That's right funny. Gotta hand it to you. Pretty damn clever for the hired help."

"So why the cat?" Lisa asked, returning to the subject. "You know good and well Brownie's here nearly every day."

"I just wanted me some company on the ride in, okay? And this is a good pet who's had it rough. Wanted it to see the world. Special treatment." She cocked her head toward Brownie. "Me and Brownie get along fine. He knows I ain't tryin' to raise no sand with him. I could let this here cat go and neither one of 'em would so much as bat an eye. Me, I got a sense about animals."

"Leave the cat in the cage, please."

"Bet you the fifty, Della. Double or nothin'. Lion and lamb will lie down. Won't be no problem."

"We'll take the cash, thank you," Lisa told her.

"What say you, Mr. Stone?" Lettie asked, squinting across the desk at him.

He shrugged. "I'm with Lisa. I'm happy to have the easy money."

Lettie smiled. "Don't blame you. People realize I got a supernatural skill. With animals *and* humans."

"Right," Lisa cackled. "Hey, I'll tell you what: We'll wager the fifty, plus if I win you agree to address me as Attorney Lisa Stone for the rest of your life. And greet me with a little bow whenever we meet." She demonstrated, bending at the waist. "Make it interesting."

"Done," Lettie said instantly.

"Okay, well, count me in," Joe said. "But I'm rooting for my wife, Lettie. And against you." He checked the dog. "Don't be fooled by my man Brownie. He's pretty damn frisky for a nine-year-old. You're going to wind up owing us a hundred plus the regular bill."

"No I ain't," Lettie replied.

"Suit yourself," he warned her.

She walked to Brownie and knelt beside him, and the dog, affable and spoiled, rolled onto his back, smiling, legs akimbo, his tail drumming. There was a damp spot on the fabric where his jowl had rested. Lettie rubbed his chest and squeezed his paws and pushed in close to his face, bumped his muzzle with her nose. She tugged his collar until he sat upright on his rump, front legs extended, locked. Still on her knees and her eyes level with his, she said nothing but stared at him for so long that Lisa checked her watch, the office quiet, the phone ringing in the adjacent room, bits and pieces of Betty's voice filtering through the wall. "You understand?" Lettie finally said. Brownie lifted his ears. Tilted his head. Reached for her with a front paw that didn't touch her, a friendly jab.

She returned to her chair and removed a plump, brindled tabby from the carrier and cradled it in both arms. Immediately, the cat seemed terrified, a fur ridge raising across its spine, its eyes abuzz. Lettie carried it in Brownie's direction, where he remained just as she'd left him, mesmerized on his haunches, ears alert, his black head tipped slightly toward the high plaster ceiling. The cat was squirming. It spit and growled, the sound wet and feral, buried in its gullet. Lettie touched her open hand to the dog's nose, blocking him, then eased the cat to the floor, the animals separated by a matter of inches, their twitchy distrust inbred.

The tabby hunkered down, hugging the ground, hissed, and began retreating in deliberate backward slides, stopped. The moment Lettie lifted her hand, Brownie barked and lurched hell-bent after the cat, and it didn't quite get purchase on the polished wood at first, its legs whirligigging every which direction, its claws frantically scratching against the oak. Brownie rushed past Lettie and snapped at the cat, but it was able to dash away, crossed the room at full speed and somehow climbed straight up the far wall, nearly to the high crown molding, before it lost momentum and twisted and fell, landing on a table covered with files and law books. It made a beeline for the office door, swept around the corner and disappeared. As Brownie tried to shoot past her, Lisa grabbed his collar to end the chase, yanking him up onto two legs, momentarily choking him, his barks strangled in his throat, the last of them hoarse and breathless.

"That went well," she said, now holding the collar with both hands.

"You pick the wrong mojo, Lettie? Forget to turn in a circle after your incantation?" Lisa sounded agitated, but a sly smile was taking root.

Joe clapped sharply. He called the dog's name. He clapped again, and this seemed to tamp down much of Brownie's excitement. "Come here," he said, his voice stern. Lisa let go of the collar. The dog checked in the direction of the cat's quick departure, looked at Joe, relaxed, studied the empty doorway some more, bounced his ears and wagged his tail, barked once, then finally ambled toward his master.

Lettie remained beside the pad, crestfallen, every feature, every crinkle and crow's-foot, suddenly weighted. A permanent black tear was tattooed at the corner of her eye, and the dark drop seemed elongated. "I can't believe it," she mumbled. "My . . ." Her mouth was sprung open, the gold tooth more apparent than ever. She raised both hands and pressed her temples, the bottoms of her skinny biceps hanging toneless and feeble, slack below the divide of the bone.

She was so pitiful, so deflated, so shocked that even Lisa was sympathetic. "Hey, Lettie, nobody's perfect. I'm guessing Gunther Gebel-Williams probably had a dancing bear miss a beat or a lion forget a routine from time to time."

"Happens to the best of us," Joe added.

"Not to me," she replied, the answer freighted with disbelief, the flat-earther who'd sailed to the edge of her map and found an endless horizon, not dragons and sea beasts. "Lawyer Joe, you *know* I got a gift with animals. It's my callin'." The last word was soft, wispy. She was staring down as she spoke, focusing on Brownie's bed.

"Don't worry about it," Lisa said. "Tell you what: You can keep the money. You don't have to pay us the hundred."

"Oh no," Lettie answered. "Hell no. Lettie Pauline VanSandt pays what she owes. I ain't a welsher. You won and I lost."

"How about you donate the hundred to the SPCA?" Joe suggested.

"Uh-uh. I'll pay it when I leave." She collected her pet carrier and shuffled to the door, where she turned and slightly dipped her head and said, "Congratulations, Attorney Lisa Stone." She paused. "You lucky-ass bitch." She switched the carrier from one hand to the other. "*Adiós.*"

Lettie paid her bill in cash, the extra hundred included, then took her receipt and voodooed the cat lickety-split from beneath the lobby sofa and into the cage as if there were nothing to it. "Tell Lawyer Joe," she instructed Betty, "this crazy damn creature used to belong to the Cassidy girl, the teenager what was killed with her parents in the car crash last month. Those kinda circumstances queered it for me. I figured it out now. Otherwise I woulda won. You tell him, you hear?"

Two weeks and a day later, the Stones received the news about their screwball client, and when she heard the report, Lisa glanced up and noticed, for the first time, that Lettie's scared cat had clawed a tiny chunk out of the wall, this faint gouge nicked into the plaster, light playing through the window and setting the damage apart.

Not long after Lettie left, Lisa stuffed a file into her briefcase and began the drive to Roanoke for a doctor's deposition in a personal injury suit. Her client was a pleasant fellow who'd been broadsided by a bank president's kid at an intersection on King's Mountain Road. There was money to be made suing for car-wreck checks—large money, in fact—and there were any number of deserving folks who found themselves being scammed and cheated by slippery insurance companies and their unscrupulous adjusters, but after years and years of it she'd had a bellyful, enough, and, say what you might, no matter how much skill you brought to the courtroom and how ethical you were and how hefty the verdicts and how magnificently you could bewitch a jury, there was still something seamy about personal injury work, and though few in the legal trade actually gave voice to it, the blowhards on TV and the screaming billboards with mammoth head shots and audacious dollar signs pretty much spoke volumes, same as the local automobile hustlers or the state lottery, more Barnum than barrister, more Charles Ponzi than Antonin Scalia. She occasionally inquired of Joe if this was why the heck they'd gone to law school, why they'd memorized federal civil procedure and studied the Constitution, just so they could earn a buck off whiplashes, pain meds, soft collars and trips to physical therapy. She was sick and tired of putting chiropractors on the stand and leading them through the same dog-and-pony show, these half-doctors with degrees from suspect schools, always tutoring the jury with their chunk of prop spine, pointing to rubber vertebrae and declaiming mumbo jumbo about "treatment modalities" and, her favorite, so encased in irony, "manipulations."

She lit a cigarette and cracked the window. Hit the presets and, finding zilch, turned down the radio. She passed the old DuPont plant, forlorn and empty beside a deep bend in the Smith River, the asphalt parking lot starting to split and crumble, crabgrass, spindly weeds and declining paint insolent behind chain-link fence, the insides of the place eviscerated and hauled away, machine after machine carted off and sold as scrap for pennies on the dollar. Forty-five hundred people had once worked three shifts there, and in place of steady traffic lines every eight hours, the lunch pails, horseplay, paychecks, womanless-beauty-pageant fund-raisers, softball teams, break room gossip and casserole-and-congealed-salad company picnic was a dilapidated eyesore that would, inevitably, be razed and buried under red-clay dirt, rogue, random chemicals left to seep into the water table and haunt the community. Lisa stubbed out her Marlboro Ultra Light in the ashtray, even though there was plenty left. Then she flamed another. What the hell. The trees beside Route 220 had shed their leaves, stood skeletal and bored. The winter sky was listless.

Amidst snow showers and a swirling wind, she and Joe had cut the ribbon for their Martinsville, Virginia, office near the close of 1991, and in those go-go days textile wages rocket-fueled the community. Two decades ago, the area had supported multiple country clubs and a robust Main Street with a shoe store and haberdashery. Cabinets were full of Princess House collectibles, garages sheltered metal-flake speedboats, parents wrote checks for college tuition, credit union accounts were fat. These days, the plants and mills were closed except for a few furniture factories that hired minimum-wage illegals with patently forged papers, the country clubs had shut their dining rooms and abandoned their galas and formal dances, and Main Street was a sad run of deserted storefronts, nail parlors and doodad emporiums without proper signage, just stick-on block letters applied to the glass in a window or double door. The minor league baseball team was threatening a move to Tennessee. The Walk/Don't Walk signs hung broken on their uptown poles, no juice. Rumley's Restaurant and its homemade pies and cobblers were gone.

In Roanoke, she parked at the physician's building and took the stairs to the third floor, thinking the exercise might help cancel the smokes she'd had during the ride. A nicely mannered receptionist showed her to a conference room and asked if she'd care for bottled water or coffee, both of which she declined. She'd arrived a few minutes early, and she was surprised to see Brett Brooks seated at the table beside the young attorney who was representing the insurance company. A court reporter was stationed in the corner. Lisa had met Brooks only at cocktail parties and legal seminars, and he was regarded—rightfully so, by most measures—as one of the best in the state, a high-flyer with a degree from Yale and a flawless sense for the courtroom, perhaps an inheritance from his father, a flamboyant Montana con man who'd spent a portion of Brett's childhood in a federal pen—or so the scuttlebutt had it. He stood to greet her, and the other lawyer scrambled to his feet as well, banging his knee on the underside of the table as he rose.

"Lisa," Brooks said, "great to see you." He walked around to where she was and shook hands. "You know Chip Maxey, from Woods, Rogers?" He stood beside her and nodded in the direction of Maxey, who was stranded on the other side of the room.

"Hello, Mrs. Stone," Maxey said.

She'd checked, and Maxey had been with the firm almost three years. He was an eager young kid from a top-tier law school, just starting his career, sent over to do a routine deposition in a relatively minor case. "Hi, Mr. Maxey. Nice to finally meet you." They'd spoken on the phone several times.

"Same here," Maxey said.

"Looks like I'm about to be double-teamed," Lisa joshed. Addressing Brooks, she asked, "What in the world brings you to a run-of-the-mill personal injury dep?"

"Just here to watch the master do her magic," he replied, the modesty and compliment both sounding genuine. "I've already told my friend Chip he can expect a firefight." Everything about Brooks was impeccable—his pricey suit, his speech, the tidy tie knot that filled in around his collar. He was wearing a fancy belt, loaded with silver and turquoise.

"Ah," Lisa said, "I'm guessing you're here to watch over our young defendant."

"Bingo." Brooks smiled.

"We didn't even sue for the policy limits," Lisa remarked. "He doesn't have any exposure. This is totally Allstate's problem. Their check."

"I told him the same thing," Maxey said, still standing. "And I tried to convince my client's father there was no need to hire other counsel."

Brooks shrugged. "Do you know Miles Covington? Miles is very much his own man. He's also the president of one of the largest banks in the South; if he wants me to monitor the case, who am I to refuse?" He—very quickly, deftly—smoothed his lapel. "Though, believe me, I told him in no uncertain terms that Mr. Maxey could expertly handle this, and that he and his son were not at risk. They have a million in coverage. Your plaintiff sued for, what, seventy-five thousand?"

"Yeah," Lisa said. "Seventy-five."

"So"—Brooks grinned—"I'm simply here to watch and learn. Truth be told, I informed Mr. Covington he was wasting his money on me."

"A damn good gig if you can get it," Lisa replied.

"Yeah," Brooks said. "I'm not complaining."

Dr. Anthony Corbett came into the sparse conference room wearing his unbuttoned white physician's coat and carrying a thin file with numbers handwritten across the tab. A stethoscope was bunched in a commodious pocket at the bottom of the coat, and coils of black rubber spilled willy-nilly. His name was embroidered on the jacket, followed by the letters "M.D." Corbett was around fifty, with long limbs and kinetic eyes. His hair was thinning, he wore glasses, and like most physicians, he was not the least bit happy to be in the company of lawyers, about to be quizzed while under oath, especially since he had already sent a letter explaining the plaintiff's fairly routine injuries and prognosis to Lisa Stone.

Corbett was also grumpy because these self-important yakkers would no doubt exceed their scheduled time, and this nonsense would clog his waiting room and put him behind for the rest of the day. The attorneys would parse his every word, repeat questions ad nauseam and pepper him with legal jibber-jabber, all on account of a simple low back sprain and a broken arm that had fully healed without complication. And make no mistake, these sharks and their venal, bloodthirsty ilk were the very bastards who would sue *him* if they thought they could turn a profit, trial lawyers who kept his malpractice premiums through the roof, six figures every year thanks to their frivolous lawsuits and state-sanctioned extortion.

He said a curt "hello" and "good afternoon," took a seat, opened his file. Before being prompted, he raised his right hand and glanced at the court reporter. "I'm ready to start if everyone else is," he said, his tone leaking impatience. "I don't mean to rush, but I have a packed office today." For the first time, he paid attention to the other people in the room, and when he focused on Lisa Stone, he hesitated, couldn't help himself, blinked and ducked and wet his lips and aimlessly moved around his file, and his expression practically shouted "Wow!," and then he ineptly tried to play it off and made his gaffe even worse, more obvious.

Without uttering a syllable, Lisa had disarmed him. Brought the doctor over. Enlisted a convert. "Delicioused" him was Joe's colorful expression for her gift, a term he'd invented upon witnessing the effect for the very first time at a law school keg party. Watching Lisa sip a beer and immobilize a semicircle of men, he'd been reminded of his granddad Wilbur using a Barlow pocketknife to cut Golden Delicious apples into quarters and drop the pieces inside a rabbit gum. He'd take young Joe along with him on fall mornings to empty his traps, traps that were usually full of doomed, nose-twitching, grayish brown wild rabbits who'd chased the bait to a dead end, even though the creatures had to realize no meal could be worth pushing into a narrow plank box with a door curiously suspended above its entrance. Wilbur would kill and skin the rabbits on the spot, then carry them home for stew or to coat in flour and fry in a black skillet.

Not only was Lisa Stone smart as hell, but even in her forties she was also gorgeous, the beneficiary of a rarefied, finely fashioned perfection, her birthright a ceaseless allure, the va-va-voom craft of a very accomplished—and perhaps puckish—divine hand, as if she were Aphrodite's off-the-books project. Embedded in this loveliness was a profound streak of decency and an unmistakable kindness, and her hospitable heart was always present, too, just as apparent as her striking features and starlet's figure, so much so that very few people—men or women—ever resented her extraordinary looks, and she could convey it all, the whole delicious, rabbit-gum kit and caboodle, with as little as a smile or the set of her head.

"Thank you for your time," she said to the doctor. "I'm sorry we have to inconvenience you. I'm sure you're busy. We're all grateful and appreciate you disrupting your practice to see us."

"Okay," he replied, attempting to sound gruff, but clearly a reformed man now.

Lisa adeptly moved him through a series of questions, and she knew precisely how and where to nudge him toward a favorable answer, and when she was through with her examination it was clear the plaintiff had an unexpected ally, a jaded, experienced physician—not the usual hired gun—who was certain the case involved a permanent disability that would cause the unfortunate victim pain and suffering for years to come. Blindsided, Chip Maxey tried to impeach Dr. Corbett with a series of office notes and prior reports, directing the doc's attention to his own diagnosis and comments, none of which mentioned any long-term problems.

"Listen," Corbett finally told him, his tone contentious, "I'm the doctor here, okay? I know what my own notes mean. But just because everything healed doesn't mean it won't hinder him down the road. No one asked me about residual injury until today. Now that I've been asked, I'm telling you."

When the physician had departed and the three lawyers were left with the court reporter, Brooks glanced at Maxey and asked what his company was willing to spend. The younger lawyer was still miffed, almost punch-drunk, and he grunted and spread his hands, more bewildered than angry, and he finally mumbled, "We'll have to reevaluate our position, I guess."

"Very wise of you," Brooks encouraged him. There was no condescension in his voice. He was seated close to Maxey, and he patted him on the shoulder. "It happens to the best of us," he added. "Not much you can do if the doctor turns sour on you."

"Yeah," Maxey said.

"Nor is this Mrs. Stone's first rodeo. She certainly lives up to her advance billing." He looked at Lisa while he was speaking.

"Listen, gentlemen," she remarked, "this isn't a big case, and the truth is I caught a break with the doctor. We'd offered to settle for twenty-five thousand. Our position improved today, plus now I've got more time and money invested. I'll take fifty-five and be done with it if we can wrap this up by the end of the week. That's a fair number for everyone."

"I'll check with my client," Maxey said dismally.

Maxey was anxious to leave, and after he'd managed to regain a semblance of composure and shake hands, and after his briefcase—not properly snapped shut—spilled open, and after he'd collected his papers, files, cell phone, calculator, two energy bars, pen and a sailing magazine with the assistance of Lisa and Brooks, he finally was able to hoof it through the lobby and put the deposition and other attorneys behind him. The court reporter said her goodbyes and followed Maxey out, her equipment expertly stored and rolled away on a compact, two-wheeled cart.

"Nice kid," Brooks volunteered when he and Lisa were by themselves. "He has some skills."

"Yep," Lisa said. "I agree."

Brooks was standing, and he relaxed against the rounded corner of the conference table, crossed his legs at the ankles and fiddled with a shiny silver beast of a wristwatch. The attention to the watch seemed ordinary, not contrived or foppish. "It's close to quitting time. I'm on the verge of a scotch or cold beer. Haven't decided which yet. You're certainly welcome to bend an elbow with me." He began looking her in the eye roughly midway through, near the "haven't decided" part.

Because she'd spent a lifetime on the receiving end of men's overtures, some clumsy, some sophisticated, some raw, some pitifully pleading, some as practiced and delicate as Brooks's, and because she could X-ray the come-on right out of all the innocence, she immediately understood that Brett Brooks had a grander agenda than happy hour cocktails and a bowl of salty bar snacks, and damn—the recognition showed in a faint pull at the corners of her mouth—she was impressed he was skilled enough to drop the flirt virtually deadpan, tucked away in a rake's code and dispatched on a very private frequency, at once deniable and altogether unmistakable.

"Well, I'm surprised," she answered. She let the sentence hang, tweaking Brooks, sending back a confirmation instead of putting the kibosh on his mischief and thanking him just the same and declining as if nothing had happened.

He cocked an eyebrow, abandoned the watch. "Surprised?"

"I never would've pegged you as a man who drank before five. Or a beer guy."

"Noon's my bright line. You might be pleased to learn this means I've never bothered with a mimosa. No dog hair for me, either."

"Well, it's been a pretty grim week. Heck, it's been a pretty grim year. A drink would be a welcome perk. Let me give my husband a call so he won't be concerned." She put on her coat. "I'll yield to your local knowledge. Where should we go?"

Walking to her car, she used her BlackBerry to leave a message for Joe, told him the deposition went well and that she was stopping off for a meal on the way home, and then she followed Brooks to Metro!, a restaurant on Campbell Avenue, where they sat at the bend in the L-shaped bar, cater-cornered to each other. Brooks settled on scotch, she informed the barkeep in black pants and a white shirt she'd like a martini with lots of olives. She'd considered her order during the drive, what she'd drink . . . and what her choice would signal, another hint and cipher in their shadow conversation. She'd renewed her lipstick, but not too much, and checked herself in the rearview mirror.

She and Brooks talked shop and swapped funny legal stories and commiserated about how difficult and cutthroat their trade had become, and he asked the bartender to bring them a plate of the house sushi. After folding her arms across her chest and glancing at the art deco wall clock, Lisa agreed to another martini and Brooks pushed his glass toward hers and nodded for another drink as well. She debated a cigarette but thought better of it. He mentioned a recent client charged with killing his wife and described how the cops had seized this moron's computer and discovered hundreds of Google searches for "poison," "hit man," "overdose" and, of course, so there'd be no doubt, "how to kill your wife." The lamebrain had even adopted cats and dogs from the local pound so he could experiment with different poisons and doses, a twist that caused Brooks to breach the boundary between personal and professional and despise his own client.

She steered the conversation more personal after that, asked him whether he had pets, and he told her he didn't but wound up reciting all his great childhood purchases from Roses department store and the tiny-print ads in the backs of magazines: sea horses that materialized when a pouch was emptied into water, chameleons, iguanas, fighting fish, hamsters and painted turtles.

"Remember those turtles?" he said brightly. "They were so cool for a kid. You kept them in a plastic bowl. The bowl came with a raised center island and a flat green plastic tree that notched into the island. You filled the bowl with colored gravel flecks. I always seemed to get red or pink gravel."

"Yeah," she said, "and the turtles would usually somehow escape and you'd find them dead or dying, dry as a bone, smothered in carpet fibers." She laughed. "They were banned when I was really young, right?"

"I think so," Brooks said. "For sure, you don't see them these days. Haven't for a long time."

The gin was warming her cheeks and neck and bumping everything a tick toward the good, the bar noise and other people welcome, happy, Impressionist background, the give-and-take with Brett Brooks now past chatter about statutes and courtrooms. She rearranged herself on her stool, crossed her legs and slid closer to the bar. She sipped the drink, matter-of-factly ate a toothpicked olive and set the glass down, still a third full, her lips imprinted in red on the rim above the clear alcohol. "Do you smoke?" she asked him.

"No, never have. Took care of my mom in her last few years. She died of lung cancer. Would light up even when she was on oxygen. Horrible. The experience did away with any chance I might try it." He shrugged. "But feel free if you'd like."

"That's okay. It's hit and miss with me."

"I didn't mean to sound so negative." He smiled and flipped his hands open.

They ate all the sushi, but she left her drink unfinished. When she said she needed to leave, Brooks gestured for the bill, and she objected to him paying, reached in her purse and had her wallet ready before the tab made it to them. The bartender hesitated and diplomatically placed the brown leather folder smack in the middle between their glasses.

"Split it, then?" Brooks said.

"Fair enough."

"Come to think of it, maybe you ought to treat me—I'd say you had a far more profitable afternoon than I did."

"I did have a very nice afternoon," she said, but didn't look at him when she spoke, instead studied their bill and slid thirty dollars—her share—into the leather cover.

"I'm glad you decided to come. Enjoyed the company."

Brooks added his portion to their tab, gathered his topcoat from the stool beside him and went with her to the exit. Two women eating by themselves, salads and white wineglasses on their table, were watching him, and he had to sense their flattering stares, but he didn't acknowledge them, acted oblivious. It was dark now, and chilly, and he walked Lisa to her car and waited for her to unlock the door. He kept his distance, but after she'd cranked the engine and dialed the heater fan to its highest speed, he took hold of the door handle to shut her in, the interior light burning, her file haphazardly tossed into the passenger seat, the gauges and displays of her base-model Mercedes glowing white and amber. There were splashes of red in the dash, too, mostly in the warning symbols and letters that spelled out important cautions.

"Drive safely," he said, looking down at her. "Thanks again for the fun visit. I understand Gentry, Locke is sponsoring another seminar in a few weeks. A freebie and a great way to complete your CLE hours if you haven't already done them. They've lined up Judge Weckstein to speak. He's smart as hell and always entertaining. I think Justice Lemons is coming from the Supreme Court. I'll drop you an e-mail with the particulars."

"That would be great," Lisa answered.

"Give Joe my regards." He shut her door, and much of the light vanished.

She stopped a few miles later and bought a Blue Moon beer for the remainder of the trip, and when she pulled into their yard, the barn lights were burning and the winter sky was clear and flush with pin-point stars and she could see Joe in the breezeway, his sorrel horse, Sadie, cross-tied at one end, a saddle and blanket straddling the top rail of a stall gate. She shifted the car to Park but left the engine running, and she walked to where he was, toe-stepping to keep her heels from sinking into the pasture. Brownie trotted to meet her, his tail going great guns.

"Been riding?" she asked. She petted the dog.

"Yeah," Joe said. "I got your message. We did the trail down toward Snow Creek. Filled a flask and off we went." He was wearing a heavy jacket. His shirttail was loose on one side, untucked. "I'd forgotten how long it takes. We came home in the dark." He smiled. "Pretty deluxe, though. A nice ride."

"Want to go again?" she asked.

There was a slapstick instant before he understood exactly what she meant, and he half-turned and checked his horse—just for a second—and then he grinned and looked at her full on and said, "Hell yeah, I'll follow you to the house." He fished out his flask and had a pull of bourbon. Instead, she was waiting when he turned the corner, and she stopped him at her Mercedes and opened the door, and they had sex in the backseat, jammed in and wrapped around each other, struggling to fit, her hose and panties and fancy shoes on the floorboard, a DJ's patter and commercials and songs on the radio, the smell of perfume and brown liquor and quarter horse curling and roiling with the heat until they finished, her foot bottoms damp against the window glass, condensation everywhere.

"Lord," Joe declared. "Damn."

"Exactly," she said, and all of a sudden she snatched his thick canvas jacket and leapt from the car, giggling and shrieking, wiggling her arms into the coat sleeves as she dashed toward the house, almost naked, the cold air slapping her thighs and belly and face.

Joe switched off the engine and jumped out right behind her, all his clothes left behind as well, and he caught her near the brick sidewalk and grabbed her around the waist, then stooped and lifted her off the ground and onto his shoulder, her feet pedaling in front of him, her head pointed back at the barn, and he carried her to the door and spun so she could reach the knob and let them in, the both of them laughing. "I think we ought to keep this celebration rolling," he told her.

"Why not?" she said, standing in the foyer shivering.

Joe retrieved a bottle of grocery store chardonnay from the rear of the fridge, Lisa took a patchwork quilt from the blanket chest and moved the bathroom space heater to the den, and they buried themselves underneath the quilt and sat on the sofa in the heater's orange glow and passed the bottle, slowly warming.

"Hey," Joe said, finishing a swig and wiping his wrist across his lips, "since I'm spoiling you with cheap wine and Lord Byron–quality romance, how about we slay the bottle and then order up some TV jewelry? Should be a hoot with a buzz. I'll spring for a ring or a necklace from the jewelry channel. We'll call the 800 number and buy you a magnificent gift. Random and off the cuff, kind of crazy-love stuff. Not often you get four-wheel sex and then sprint around in the freezing dark with no clothes. We need to memorialize it."

"Seriously?"

"Yeah. Oh yeah. No doubt we'll land a great deal too. You'll be the owner of some gargantuan, freakishly colored, semisemiprecious stone that ends in *ite* and is about a grade away from polished riprap. The envy of your friends. I'll even make the effort to find the remote and bring you the phone."

"Only after the bottle's gone, okay? I want to make sure I don't squander the purchase by being too sober."

Forty minutes later, Joe phoned toll-free and bought a "stunning" six-carat tanzanite dinner ring—retail price $3,500—for $415, and soon after they slid longwise on the couch and fell asleep there, awakened by Brownie pawing the door around four in the morning. He'd been forgotten to spend the night in the barn but seemed no worse for it. At sunrise, they dressed and ate eggs and sausage and drank coffee, and Joe had to jump-start the Mercedes because he'd left a door ajar and the battery had drained, but they agreed it was a small price to pay for superior sex and tanzanite glory.

"Thanks for the effort," she told him. "You're a good husband."

"Effort? Huh? It was fun. My pleasure. What a weird thing to say."

CHAPTER TWO

The rollicking night buttressed Lisa's spirits for several days, but soon enough her mood dipped and things declined to mediocre and bloodless again, and when Joe brought the TV ring from the post office and stood beside her desk and opened the cardboard packaging, she teared up, simultaneously appreciative and disappointed. She thanked him, and meant every word, and raised slightly from her chair to kiss him, but even before he left her office, she was mad at herself, frustrated, ticked off because she felt selfish and whiny, unable—no matter how hard she tried—to pin down satisfaction for any length of time, less than content despite her excellent husband and damn-lucky circumstances, just another shrew with impossible demands and no cure in sight. "Don't be such a bitch," she mumbled to herself, the room empty now, the tanzanite blue and aggressive alongside her wedding band.

CHAPTER THREE

Traveling to work at the beginning of December, Lisa topped a knoll near several cracker-box brick houses and caught sight of three young girls, probably still in elementary school, prancing through a cheerleaders' routine while they waited for the bus, their spins and struts and hucklebucks and crisp steps and invisible pom-poms remarkably well synchronized, their winter coats in a casual heap alongside a narrow asphalt driveway, their expressions stitched with concentration. She passed a vase of faded plastic flowers next to a bridge where months earlier a teenager had wrecked his car and died on the spot, the concrete patch in the abutment brighter than all the dreary gray that bordered it. A rawboned man with a mechanical voice box was buying lottery tickets when she stopped for gas, and he told the clerk the numbers he wanted to bet, touched a black tube to his throat and spoke in a froggy, metallic monotone. He also had a tin of sardines and a breakfast malt liquor on the counter. The man was short a few cents, and Lisa made up the difference for him, discovered she knew his uncle, a retired bailiff named Garland Kinney.

At the office, she was antsy, easily diverted. She scanned the newspaper, played Bejeweled on her computer, put Brownie through his dog tricks and drank a diet soda. She cracked a window and lit a cigarette, then shoulder-propped against the window frame and watched a crew of city maintenance men as they decorated streetlight poles for Christmas, winding artificial holly from top to bottom. She read phone messages. Dictated a letter. Paid a credit card bill well before it was due. Joe was in neighboring Patrick County for a district court trial, and when he returned around noon she sat in his office and asked about the case, whether he'd won or lost.

"Not guilty for our defendant," he said. "I'm pleased to report that I helped bring justice to yet another roadhouse assault-and-battery brouhaha. By my math, I'm now four victories away from receiving my expert certification in redneck bar brawls. We'll have to get our cards reprinted to include my accomplishment."

"Same old stuff?" she asked.

"It was pretty much what you'd expect," he noted drily, "from a pair of drunk women in a boyfriend tussle. The usual cursing and spitting and hair pulling and eye scratching, plus the crowd-pleasing, shirt-rippin' topless grand finale. Of course, despite walking away scot-free, my client was pissed because her Sam's Club faux gold chain was broken and Judge Gendron wasn't of a mind to order restitution." Joe chuckled. "Gotta love this business, huh?" He put his feet on his desk, rubbed and squeezed the base of his neck. "Lunch? You hungry?" His tie was loose, his shirt unbuttoned at the collar.

"Yeah. Sounds good."

While they were deciding where to eat, Betty appeared to tell them the sheriff and a state police investigator were in the lobby and needed to speak with them. After almost two decades of practicing law, it was the kind of occurrence that raised their interest but didn't cause any particular alarm, and they continued to discuss diners, restaurants, fast food and blue plates until the cops arrived at the door. Joe and Lisa stood, and Joe gestured for them to come in.

Sheriff Lane Perry was a large, amiable man with close-cropped hair and a physicality that was pronounced and obvious but not threatening. The Stones considered him honest and conscientious, and he and Joe both enjoyed quarter horses and trout fishing, occasionally crossed paths at the saddle club or on the banks of the Smith River. The state police officer, Clay Hatcher, was younger, maybe thirty-five, a brash, noisy, spring-loaded hotshot who was, it seemed, always itching for a high-speed chase or a chance to bust into a house at 3:00 a.m. and scream commands as he brandished his pistol, though it was safe to assume he wouldn't be the first through a dangerous door, or even the second.

"Hey, Joe," the sheriff said. "I think you know Special Agent Hatcher from the state police."

"Yeah. Sure. Good to see you both."

Sheriff Perry then nodded at Lisa and said, "Mrs. Stone."

Hatcher had his hands on his hips and wore his silver badge on a chain around his neck. His weapon was apparent in a shoulder holster. "Nice to see you again, Mr. Stone," he said. "And pleased to meet you, ma'am."

"What brings you gents by?" Lisa asked. "Sit down if you'd like."

"We're fine," the sheriff replied. "Thanks just the same." He hooked a thumb into his patent leather gun belt. "I know you've been good to look after Lettie VanSandt," he said to Joe, "so I thought I'd tell you that we found her dead this morning. Out at her place."

"Oh no," Joe said. Everyone was still standing, and he'd walked back behind his desk and leaned against a credenza. "What—"

"Got fried cookin' meth," Hatcher interjected, eager to tell what he knew, no pity or concern in his tone. He smirked through the words.

"Meth?" Joe repeated. "Lettie's a lot of things, but she's not a druggie."

"Facts prove different," Hatcher remarked. He took his hands off his hips. "She was in a shack next to her house, and the damn place had the whole shebang, from the Coleman fuel to the matches to the boxes of cold medicines. Iodine. Burners. I've seen my share of methamphetamine outfits, and this lady was cooking crank. No doubt."

"It sure looks that way," Perry added. "Surprised me too. Lettie was a pain in the butt and as hateful as a striped snake, but I'd have never pegged her for a drug dealer, no sir, not me."

"So what happened?" Lisa asked.

"Well," Perry said, "it looks—"

"Meth is volatile," Hatcher interrupted, "and the fumes can be very flammable, and she screwed up and, boom, there's an explosion and a fire, and it's curtains. End of story. We bring in the feds to take these damn things apart—that's how serious it is. You brew this poison, bad things can happen to the chef."

"Thanks for the tutorial," Joe said.

"Poor lady," Lisa said. She sighed, raked a hank of hair behind her ear. "I never cared for her, but you have to hate it for the old kook."

"It wasn't pretty," Perry said. "We didn't find her for several days, and between the fire and all those animals, well, you get the picture." He peered at the floor for a moment.

"Ouch." Joe grimaced. "You guys certain it was her?"

"I mean, who else would it be, Joe?" Perry shifted his weight, and the hardwood boards creaked. "She's not around and hasn't been seen for well over a week, the remains—the little bit we can find—are in a shack on her property, the jewelry that didn't completely melt is similar to hers, and it's a female."

"How about dental?" Joe asked.

"We, well, a lot of her was either burned or destroyed or has gone missing. I'll check. But where would we find her records? She had the gold tooth when she moved here years ago from St. Louis, and I'd wager she's never darkened the door of a dentist's office since."

"Then you should run DNA." Joe was firm.

"There's a great idea," Hatcher said. "Let's waste time and taxpayers' money and clog a lab that's already months behind and can't get us what we need on *important* cases so we can confirm information we already know for certain." He narrowed his eyes. "The way I figure it, if she's not dead, we'll all know soon enough when she shows up at the grocery store or the Friday night square dance. Right?"

"Or the board of supervisors' meeting or my office or Delegate Armstrong's office or at the phone company to bitch about the static in her line," Perry cracked. "Joe, what more could there be to it?" he asked. "She was a mean old fruitcake who lived with a bunch of stray animals and could worry the horns off a brass billy goat. Nothing's missing so far as we can tell, nothing's hinky, and maybe a meth habit would explain why she was so contrary."

"People get killed in drug deals every day," Joe noted. "It's possible there *is* more to it."

"Like what?" Lisa asked. She was looking at her husband but noticed Agent Hatcher in the periphery, staring at her.

"I don't know. Maybe Lane's right. It's just a shock." Joe stood straighter, folded his arms across his chest. "I don't guess DNA would really tell us much, especially in light of the info you guys already have. It's ... well ... it's hard to believe, but it's hard to believe that friends you've known for decades are embezzlers or child molesters or wholesale alcoholics, and we see it happen again and again, don't we? The deacon at your church arrested for a DUI, the Rotary Club president in a trailer park buying dope from some skank. Nothing should surprise us in this business."

Perry nodded. "Right, you never know. But this seems clear to me. And to Agent Hatcher."

"She got blown up," Hatcher said curtly. "Fire and animals done the rest."

"How much does the DNA cost?" Joe asked. "If there's no rush?"

"For heaven's sake, Joe," Lisa scolded him. "Haven't we wasted enough time and money on Lettie VanSandt already? You especially."

Perry raised his hands, fingers gaped, palms uncovered. "Okay, Joe, sure, if it'll make you happy, we'll send the remains for an analysis. Whatever. I suppose if we can't make a visual ID, it's technically called for. We'll do it by the book."

"Appreciate it," Joe told him.

"I reckon you already know she left you everything and put you in charge of her affairs. You can ride out there with me first chance you have, and we'll collect her hairbrush and toothbrush. That's what they always request at the lab. I'll pull her prints from her concealed weapon application, but from what we saw, there won't be nothing they can do along those lines. I didn't see anything left that looked like fingers."

Joe glanced at his wife, then at the sheriff. "I'm her executor, but how do you know that?"

"We did a walk-through at her house," Perry answered, unperturbed. "Found her dead and burned, so it follows we'd investigate. Her will was wrote on a sheet of yellow legal paper. It was on a bedroom table. Left you everything and put you in charge." He smiled. "Quite a gift, huh? A pack of cur dogs and a bunch of starvin' cats. All yours now, Joe." The sheriff chuckled. "Plus her three or four acres and her run-down trailer. I don't envy you trying to administer that mess."

"Man, the place is just lousy with animals," Hatcher noted. He shook his head, amused. "I was expecting that Sarah McLachlan chick from the TV commercials to show up and start singing. That's how bad it is."

"You must've found an old will," Joe said, ignoring Hatcher. "We just did the paperwork here a couple weeks ago, and she left her estate to her son and the SPCA, not me."

"Well, this was all in her handwriting, and it . . . I took it with me, so you can have the original. Maybe it is old. I'll leave that to you folks with the legal degrees to solve."

"Was it dated?" Joe asked.

"Yeah," the sheriff answered. "But I don't recall the details. It was right recent, that much I remember."

Joe sawed his teeth across his bottom lip. He touched his temple with his index finger. "Odd."

"Why's it odd, Joe?" Lisa pressed him, clearly irritated. "Lettie was crazy as a loon, okay? She changed her will and rewrote all of her nonsensical corporate bylaws and tinkered with all the other assorted rubbish you drafted for her *every week*, like she was J. Paul Getty or Melinda Gates. Her life was *entirely* about signing meaningless documents and filing her own spite suits and harassing bag boys who didn't put her frozen hamburger and cans of white beans in the right sack. She was a legal hypochondriac. Jeez."

Hatcher grinned.

"You're probably right," Joe calmly said, but he didn't direct his answer to her or either of the men. His gaze was elsewhere, skipped everyone in the room. "But it is curious she'd suddenly do her own will when she loved to come in here and waste my time and thrived on the attention and the ceremony."

"So . . . I don't understand," Hatcher snapped. "What exactly is it you're gettin' at?"

"Yeah, Joe, what're you tryin' to say?" Perry frowned. "At first you were kinda hintin' maybe she was killed in a dope deal. Or suggestin' it wasn't her. Help me with this, but since she didn't leave a will to some stranger and then wind up dead, since she left her buddy Joe everything, why is that peculiar to you?"

Joe shrugged. "Who knows. Hey, thanks for doing the DNA. Like I said, I'm just a little shocked to hear the news, but drugs would go a long way in explaining her personality—"

"And her bizarre behavior and skin-and-bones appearance," Lisa interjected.

"When do you want to ride over there?" Perry asked Joe.

"Doesn't matter," Joe said. "Whatever's best for you."

"I might go too," Lisa added. "We've never seen where she lived. It'll be good to have a look at our grand inheritance. Assuming, of course, we're so fortunate." She walked to her husband and slid her arm around his waist so that the two of them were facing the policemen. "I've always wanted a summer home. And I understand she kept cash hidden. Probably three or four hundred dollars at the end of that rainbow."

Joe never grew tired of eating at Byrd's Store, and it was on the route to Lettie's, so they agreed to meet Sheriff Perry and Hatcher at the trailer around one-thirty and dropped by the store for lunch. The business was housed in a sprawling frame building and had been run by the Byrd family since the 1920s. A country emporium, it had stout shelves stocked with Vienna sausages, potted meat, green cans of Del Monte fruits and vegetables, Little Debbie cakes, cookies, chips, gum, candy, off-brand motor oil, antifreeze, fishing lures, bread, flour, sugar and cheap, flimsy toys, mostly race cars and six-shooters. A woodstove in the rear was surrounded by a couple rockers and some mismatched ladder-backs, and more often than not a picked-apart copy of *The Martinsville Bulletin* was lying on one of the chairs. The small grill served standard short-order food, but there was always homemade gravy for the morning, and pinto beans and corn bread at noon, and usually a stew during cold weather, and a fresh from-scratch pie early in the week.

They ate by the stove, their forks and spoons white plastic disposables, and when "Act Naturally" played on the radio—dialed to the local AM channel—Joe mentioned he was a fan of Buck Owens and liked the song but hadn't heard it since the 2004 Galax Fiddlers' Convention.

"It's okay, I guess," Lisa said. She was holding a bowl of Brunswick stew in one hand and spooning it with the other. Her Diet Coke was on the floor beside her chair.

"Buck's a dandy-fine musician. If you can survive *Hee Haw* and still have Dwight Yoakam cover you, that's pretty impressive."

Lisa wasn't interested. This was a minor variation of a set piece she'd heard Joe recite many times before. Soon would come a mention of Merle Haggard. She bit into a saltine she'd daubed with stew. "Most of those guys sound the same to me. No difference."

"It can be tricky, I'll grant you that. Buck Owens really is a talent and still holds up well, but poor old Porter Wagoner is an outright hick. A clodhopper extraordinaire. Conway Twitty will never be more than a sequined peckerwood with a hopeless name; Ferlin Husky's brilliant." He swallowed a mouthful of beans and sang a few lines of the song, the part about the movies and becoming a big star, patted his foot with the music. "Of course, there's no disputing that Merle Haggard's a minor deity. In the pantheon."

She watched him sitting there in his dark lawyer's suit against a backdrop of canned goods and dusty rural knickknacks, mouthing the refrain from a sixties novelty tune, filling up on pintos and yellow corn bread, the smell of food and burning kindling clouding around them, and she envied how damn content and satisfied he was with it all. "Yeah" was what she offered, a single mild syllable. She set her bowl on the floor beside the soda and didn't finish either of them.

He noticed she was distracted. "You okay?"

"Fine."

"You sure? You seem awfully quiet."

"A rough day," she said. "Plus I'm not looking forward to crazy Lettie VanSandt's nasty trailer."

Sheriff Perry and Hatcher were waiting for them at Lettie's, and after Perry unlocked the door they all filed into the trailer, everyone briefly silent as they entered, even Hatcher. The sheriff gave Joe Lettie's keys, the collection on a plain round ring along with a Food Lion shopper's card and a silver metal whistle. "Yours now," Perry told Joe. "They were hangin' on a nail beside the door when we first investigated."

The four of them walked to a tiny bathroom at the end of the hall. The sheriff went in, Joe and Lisa stood at the threshold and Hatcher peered over and around them as best he could. A section of discolored plywood, nailed down but not flush with the rest of the floor, covered an area in front of the shower. A kerosene heater was pushed into a corner. A bare ceiling bulb wired without a proper fixture was the only light, a worn red towel was draped across the shower rod, a razor and a toothbrush were in a recycled jelly jar beside the sink, generic baby shampoo sat on a small shower ledge and store-brand aspirin, rubbing alcohol and oodles of patent medicines—labels visible, organized by height—were crowded onto an unpainted pine shelf. Bottle after bottle of fingernail polish, the hues garish and bright—purple, chartreuse and scarlet—were meticulously lined along the counter, grouped by color and shade. The top was missing from the toilet tank and the sink mirror black-flecked with a crack arcing across the glass above the bottom edge.

"So you've never been here before?" Perry asked Joe.

"No."

"Pretty pitiful," the sheriff said. "She even has cardboard stuck in the den window." He squeezed his beefy hand into a latex glove, pinched the toothbrush between his thumb and first finger and dropped it into a plastic evidence bag. He placed the razor in another bag. He opened a drawer, inspected the contents, shut it, opened another, then removed a hairbrush with his protected hand. He held up the brush and they all could see strands of hair winding through the bristles. "That ought to do it," he said, sealing a third bag.

"Thanks again," Joe said. "Sorry for the trouble. For some reason, being here like this kind of drives home what's happened, though. Not much doubt how this'll turn out."

"No kidding," Hatcher groused.

Lisa stuck him with a hard look. "You know, the more I think about it, the more I agree with my husband: Joe's the executor, and he needs to be positive she's deceased. There's a correct way to do this." She kept glaring at the smart-ass cop. "I'm sure this case will find its appropriate place in the lab line, probably ahead of the extremely important analysis of a joint you seized at a sorority party or the examination of a Mason jar full of moonshine you guys raided from a still over in Woolwine. The woman's dead, Officer Hatcher. Dead is significant."

Before he could respond, Sheriff Perry spoke. "No problem. Joe's technically right. The rules say we should confirm if there's no visual ID."

"I still say it's a waste of time and money," Hatcher said stubbornly. "But the sheriff is goin' to do it your way, so you'll have your DNA."

"You wanna take a look at where the fire was?" Perry asked. "Where we found her?"

"Is there any problem with that?" Joe asked.

"Nope. We shot photos and a video, and we had the fire marshal do his investigation. We've collected some evidence, what little we could. Her remains are at the hospital. We're finished from a police stand-point. We soaked it real good, too, so the cinders won't kick up on us."

"Sure," Joe said. He looked at Lisa. "Okay with you?"

"Yeah. Fine."

"The sooner the better," Hatcher said. "It stinks of cat piss in here."

There wasn't much to see. The fire had left a charred rectangle dot-ted with debris and ashes and burned chunks of beams and posts, and the tin roof had collapsed into the blaze and later been dragged to one side by the police or firefighters. Cats and dogs wandered around, sev-eral approaching them. A fat black tomcat sat at the apex of the tin pile. The shed had been in a clearing, the ground around it worn to the bare red dirt by the strays, so the blaze hadn't spread. A blackened cinder-block foundation marked off the structure's dimensions. A few items were identifiable: a metal barrel, a scorched metal chair frame, sections of wire, beakers, the guts of a radio, a tablespoon, pliers and wrenches, a pair of car wheels wrapped in melted rubber.

"Damn," Joe said. "Ugly business."

"Where exactly was she when you found her?" Lisa asked.

"Well," Perry replied, "most of her, what we recovered, was at the far end over there." He pointed.

"Sad," Joe mumbled.

"Price you pay," Hatcher chirped.

Joe locked on to him. "Shut the fuck up. You've made your point, Agent Hatcher."

"Show some respect," Perry quickly added. "No reason you can't be professional."

"Hey, one less scourge making poison is the way I see it." Hatcher smirked, not the least chastised. "World's better off. You have your opinion, I'm entitled to mine. So, Mr. Stone, you can shut the fuck up.

You make your dollars helpin' criminals, I make mine puttin' them in jail."

Lisa had seen her husband walk into a barn stall and hold his own with a headstrong mare, and she'd seen him ejected from a Myrtle Beach bar for thrashing a letch who put his hands on her after twice being warned off. Joe possessed a big man's casual nature, was difficult to provoke and wasn't a tongue wagger, his size and build all the threat he needed in most instances, but once he was riled it came on him potent and feverish, and when he started to remove his coat and took a step toward Hatcher, Lisa realized it was serious, his dander genuine, and she jerked his arm, told him to knock it off, and Clay Hatcher's quick retreat toward the sheriff showed he realized there was no bluff in Joe's mood.

"Why're you so attached to the old shrew?" Lisa asked Joe as they were driving back to the office. "I've never understood it."

"Nothing more than I've told you before," Joe said. "She was a character, and the very first client to ever walk through my door. And there's a lot to be said for taking in stray animals, and hell, occasionally the shit she complained about deserved it. The world needs its agitators. Needs a few wasps and yellow jackets to keep things from going stale. As a bonus, you got the unvarnished truth from her— Lettie VanSandt was, if nothing else, a perfectly honest woman."

Lisa smiled. "Yeah, in the tradition of Savonarola or the Oracle at Delphi. Or the Wicked Witch. Probably most of those dogs and cats can fly."

CHAPTER FOUR

Margaret Jane Carter was called Pug as a child, a curious nickname that didn't suit either her appearance or her personality. Growing up in Henry County, she was a pretty enough girl, maybe even on the outskirts of beautiful, and an excellent student, even if she wasn't the absolute *very* brightest among her classmates. Her mom pulled second shift at the textile mill, and her dad drove a route truck for the Lance company, stocked Nabs and peanuts in vending machines and emptied trays of silver pocket change into a cloth bank bag, started his snack deliveries at dawn and did some nighttime mechanicing on the side, mostly brake and transmission repairs. Margaret graduated from Bassett High School and received a substantial scholarship to Ferrum College, where she earned magna cum laude grades, changed her hair color from brown to a modest blond and shed the name Pug for good, becoming Meg.

During her sophomore year at Ferrum, she met a Virginia Tech student named Alton Warner Gold IV, a handsome frat boy from a rich Delaware family, and they married in 1995, only a few months after they both finished college. The wedding was a six-figure spectacle, but the Golds were snotty to Meg's parents, snickering about her daddy's accent and her momma's Sunday-best church clothes. Meg and Alton settled in Arlington, Virginia, because she'd accepted a job at a health insurance company and he didn't care where they lived; geography was no restriction for a layabout's universal skills.

Three years later, Alton had spent all the money his parents and grandparents were willing to waste on him, he'd jacked up credit cards and bogged down equity lines, and he wouldn't work, hell no he wouldn't, though he did declare himself, at various times, a day trader, a financial adviser, a consultant, an entrepreneur, a freelance journalist, a life coach and a corporate troubleshooter. He printed impressive business cards and squandered money on office space. He leeched off Meg's paychecks and stole cash from the zippered slot inside her purse. His true gift was a passion for top-shelf highballs and Las Vegas, Tunica, Atlantic City and any cruise ship, backroom or Indian casino that offered green felt and a pair of dice. He stayed gone, rambling and carousing. He wrecked their car. He was arrested for shoplifting hair gel from a mall department store. He cheated on Meg. He charged a diner waitress's West Virginia abortion to their MasterCard and busted the account's credit limit, tacking on an extra thirty-five dollars and a collection call from the bank to the already dreadful insult.

Meg quickly moved into her own apartment and did all she could to salvage her finances and dump her no-count spouse. Still, untangling herself from a crybaby cad like Alton Gold was complicated. He'd surface at odd hours and pound on her door, sometimes penitent, sometimes enraged, occasionally promising rehab and religion but most often threatening to cut her throat or punch a screwdriver through her skull. She wouldn't even peep out at him, so he'd stand in the hall arguing with dead bolts and double locks until security arrived to remove him. Between disappearances with new druggie girlfriends and craps junkets financed by rubber checks, he'd ambush her in the parking garage at her job and insist—snarling, fussing, pleading—she owed him another chance, and he'd impulsively send flowers and, better still, store-bought cards with ponderous snatches from *The Prophet* printed across the front in fancy script. "Love, Alton," he'd usually scribble in red ink, a shaky, deformed heart drawn underneath.

She visited a lawyer, but most of her options were Byzantine and costly, and injunctions and protective orders meant time away from work, more lost wages and more contact with her dumb-ass husband, whose family, no matter how dismal his behavior, considered it a matter of status and clan pride to ensure he was utterly lawyered-up in any legal proceeding, even though they well understood he was a bum and a spendthrift. And all those court orders and official documents with seals and certifications were just sound and fury, little paper tigers that wouldn't mean diddly-squat to Alton Gold and would probably serve as a goad and a dare rather than any kind of effective restraint.

The worst of it came in March 2000, after she'd finally managed to pay an attorney for a divorce filing and the papers had been served on her husband. She arrived home to discover that Alton—drunk or high or both—had wormed inside her apartment and was waiting for her, and he rushed directly at her, grabbed her and rammed her hard against the wall, and her arm tangled in her purse strap and she lost her balance and twisted her ankle as she fell, and he was cursing and shouting and spit glommed on to every word coming out of his mouth. She smelled alcohol, stale cologne and a spike of rancid breath. He tore her blouse and jammed a knee into her thigh, making a red impression that turned blue, black and yellow in the days that followed. She tried to roll and twist and squirm away, and she pushed against his chest with both elbows, and she screamed, screamed again, and this only made him more combative. When he finally fought her pants down and then her panties, he couldn't have sex, humped her limp-dicked and slithered and ground and clawed her shoulders and scratched her neck, bit her nipple, drew blood. He was furious, enraged, and he slapped her and blubbered and caterwauled and said more than once, "Look what you've done to me, you bitch."

He wrestled her into the bedroom and crashed down on top of her. Muttering and groping her, he soon passed out, his dead, worthless weight smothering her, and when he awakened, his wife, bruised and with a cracked rib and two broken fingers, wearing a pair of sweat-pants, barefoot, still in her ripped blouse, was standing above him resting a .38 caliber Taurus revolver against his lips. The gun was a gift from her daddy. Big-city protection.

"Alton," she said, calm as could be, "I'm done with this."

He was groggy and sluggish. He closed his eyes. She inserted the short barrel of the gun into his mouth, felt the steel bump against his front teeth. He blinked, grunted, began to focus.

"Here's how this is going to work," she said in the same deliberate voice. "We both know I'm not going to kill you, though you deserve it, and I could pull it off pretty easy. The cops would take a look at me, talk to whoever you bribed to let you in and discover you're full of dope and liquor. It'd be self-defense."

"Whoaammm, uh, lisnnn." The sounds stuck mostly in his throat, clogged there. "Lissn."

"No. You listen." She glared at him. He appeared to be rejoining her, his expression starting to animate. "First off, you're going to apologize. Say you're sorry." She raised the gun slightly.

"Am. I am."

"And next you are going to humiliate yourself, just like you've humiliated me."

He narrowed his eyes, unsure. His lips twitched.

"You and your shriveled little penis are goin' to say, 'I'm a piece of shit and a failure as a man.'"

He stared up at her. She noticed he was breathing through his mouth.

"Right now."

"Ha. Uh-uh. No."

"I'll ask you once more."

"You won't do anything." His hair was oily, messy, every which direction. One thin black strand stuck against his forehead and reached to his eyebrow, as if a fissure had begun, a dark split. He still had on socks and a shirt, which was mostly unfastened. She noticed he was tan to the middle of his groin, then pallid, then tan again, the different hues born of years spent lounging around in various tanning salons, a vanity he never neglected and bought with fraud and slick lies.

"Last chance."

He flickered a grin, smug and spiteful, then lurched toward her, and in a smooth, quicksilver sweep she swung the gun sideways, set it at an angle against the thick of his biceps and pulled the trigger, bang, and she felt relief and satisfaction and a wicked, tit-for-tat joy, and it was a chore to stop at the single shot. Alton screamed and clutched his arm and blood started to color the bed, and it seemed to her the harsh explosion from the .38 stayed with them in the room for several seconds, loud, lingering, echoing, commanding.

"Alton, I'll shoot you again."

He was whimpering and cursing, saliva dribbling from the corner of his mouth.

"Come on, Alton: 'I'm a piece of shit and a failure as a man.' Easy to say. And oh so true."

"I hate you, you awful whore," he shouted, but for the first time ever the words were puny and inert, their menace waning.

"The sooner you finish, the sooner I can call for help. For all I know, you might bleed to death."

"I swear to god, you'll pay for this," he yelled. He partially sat up, still holding his arm. Blood leaked from between his fingers. Crimson streaks and splatters stained a white pillowcase.

"I'm sure I will, Alton. I've paid for everything else." She was standing, her knees at the edge of the mattress. She aimed at his leg, gripping the gun with both hands, dramatically closing an eye as she peered through the sight.

"I'm a piece of shit," he recited. "And a failure as a man."

"Say it again. Slower. Listen to yourself. Let it sink in."

He repeated the words, and she called 911, told them she'd been attacked and was injured and had been forced to shoot her husband. "Please help me," she sobbed to the operator, the hurt in her voice completely genuine and heartfelt, the catharsis so deep that no cop or attorney or juror could ever doubt her circumstances.

Alton located his pants in the den. Holding them as best he could with a bullet hole bored into his flesh, he hopped and wiggled them on but wasn't able to hook the clasp at his waist, and with the cuffs still below his heels and his shoes left behind, he scrambled through the door, realizing there wasn't much hope of explaining away his battered, beaten wife, especially when he was full of booze and had brazenly lied to the building's new manager to get inside Meg's apartment. She told the police he'd tried to rape her and, somehow, thank the Lord above, she'd been able to grab her pistol from the nightstand drawer and wound him in the arm. As simple and horrific as that. His partial handprint was visible on her cheek when the cops interviewed her, a lowlife's pink abuse.

Despite the fervent urgings of well-intentioned volunteers and the warnings from a slew of professional advocates with catchy acronyms—S.T.O.P., CAFV, WEAVE, NOW—on their business cards, Meg declined to cooperate with her husband's prosecution. "I have my reasons," she informed an assistant commonwealth's attorney in Alexandria.

The attorney, an office veteran named Andy Minchew, removed his glasses and twirled them a time or two and didn't show any emotion. "Your decision," he said. "We can still go to trial, you understand. We can subpoena you and call you as a witness. Put you under oath and make you testify. I'd do that if I thought it was the wisest choice. If I thought it was in your interest."

Meg scooted her chair forward. The gray, public-servant carpet snagged one of the legs, so she ended up closer to the desk but slightly crooked. "Alton Gold," she said firmly, "is a bastard who has beat me and threatened me and stolen my money. He's a drunk. A womanizer. He used our credit card to pay for another woman's abortion. Ruined years of my life. He views legal proceedings, this whole world of yours, Mr. Minchew, as a chance to manipulate me. To prolong these awful things. To have me badgered by his high-priced lawyers. In a strange way, he'd probably enjoy court. Might even make him—how to say it?—more determined. He's not afraid of lawyers and judges—he has nothing to lose." She leaned in Minchew's direction. She put her elbows on his desk. She laced her fingers, touched her chin with her thumbs. "But right now, sir, he's afraid of me." She bent her neck enough to talk around her hands. "I don't want that to change. And I don't really want to spend a lot of time on the details of, you know, *how* he was shot." She untangled her hands but kept leaning toward Minchew. She never quit looking at him, never broke off.

Minchew returned his glasses to the bridge of his nose and closed a file on his desk. "Good for you, ma'am. I see your point. Good for you. Well handled. Best of luck to you."

She didn't say anything else, nor did he. He sent her a wink when she hesitated at his door to thank him, and she rode an elevator to the ground floor and walked the full length of a bright hallway, through the chatter and commerce and ordinary bustle of the courthouse building, her fingers splinted but the harsh ache in her ribs healing, breaths coming easier.

Two weeks later, Meg returned home to Henry County, and that's where she met Lisa Stone for the first time, went to see her about completing the divorce and recovering some of her money. "The truth is," Meg confessed after they'd discussed her horrendous marriage, "I can't pay you, and I don't want to ask my parents for help. But when I'm on my feet, I'll see that you get every penny you're owed. I promise you." Meg said it without tears and without begging. She'd made an appointment and sat there—not even thirty years old—dressed in the clothes she used to wear to her job.

Lisa nodded, smiled. She stood and reached across the desk to shake hands. "Fair enough. Deal. No worries. I believe you."

Immediately, she called Alton's highfalutin, prick attorney in Washington, and his secretary left her stranded on hold listening to looping Brahms and finally reported that Mr. Broaddus was "too engaged" to accept her call but would try to find a moment for her later. Lisa waited three days, heard nothing, then filed a dense, explicit, firebomb lawsuit against Alton *and* his parents for assault and battery, breach of contract and intentional infliction of emotional harm. She filed it in Alexandria but hired a seedy Delaware process server to deliver the papers during Mr. and Mrs. Gold's cocktail hour at their country club. Broaddus called within hours of the suit hitting, and she ignored him, and he and his minions flooded her with motions and interrogatories and threats and bluster and forty-page faxes, and she enlisted Joe and they stayed late at their office and kept the coffeepot busy and drafted reams of their own bullshit, didn't flinch or buckle, and soon the case filled two entire boxes in the clerk's office.

When she finally decided to talk with Broaddus, he was full of piss and vinegar and began by warning her that not only would she and her client lose their case but also he'd see to it that she'd forfeit her law license.

She listened but didn't respond. Broaddus raged and bullied, and she kept quiet until there was an empty, vacuous silence on the line. In several minutes, she'd uttered a total of five words: "Hello, this is Lisa Stone."

"Are you still there?" Broaddus was forced to ask.

"Yes."

"Do you understand, Mrs. Stone, that filing a frivolous lawsuit against Mr. and Mrs. Gold is going to land you in a very undesirable place? I promise you the considerable weight of my firm will be dedicated to this case. You need to realize this isn't some hick dispute about cows and chickens that we'll pitty-pat around in general district court on Wednesday afternoon. If you persist in this, I'll pulverize both you and your client. You damn well know you have no valid claim against Alton's parents."

"Well, Oscar," she said, using Broaddus's familiar name, "we pittypat around the livestock cases on Tuesdays, not Wednesdays. Item next: I was law review at Virginia; you were evidently a middling student at a middling school. And lastly, the case is sound. Alton's selfishly enabling parents promised my client they'd enroll their son in rehab if she would stay with him and not embarrass the family. They would ensure he received help. Twice they made that commitment. His mother put it in a letter to my client. Wrote it on expensive lavender stationery. Instead, they did nothing. Nothing, Oscar, not a damn thing. Didn't even hand their shiftless boy a brochure or a hotline number. Nope—they gave him cash when they knew he would use it to buy drugs and alcohol and further abuse his wife. That's a contract, Oscar. Offer, acceptance, consideration. Next we have a breach by Mr. and Mrs. Gold. His trying to rape her and ruining her credit, we call those damages, Oscar. The damages come from their failing to honor their agreement."

"No chance that'll ever fly. None. This is a gross shakedown."

"We'll see." Lisa paused. "But you may be correct about venue as to Alton's parents. I think I might concede that. We may just go ahead and agree to your motion. We'll move the case to Rehoboth. I'm sure it would serve as a great topic while their friends are watching sailboats and playing croquet and swigging their gin. Might even make the local newspapers."

It took longer than she expected, but seven months later Lisa received a check for $155,000 and a final divorce decree. Sitting in Lisa's office, Meg cried and dabbed her eyes with a knot of tissue from her purse. She paid Lisa for ninety-three billable hours, a total of $11,625.00, and reimbursed Stone and Stone for $1,097.96 in expenses. The balance was hers. As Meg's father put it, Lisa Stone had miraculously gotten blood from a turnip, had somehow figured a way to extract a tidy payoff from a penniless loser.

Living at her parents' home in the same bedroom she'd forever abandoned to attend college, the Prince and Bon Jovi posters still thumbtacked to the wall, her high school trophies and awards still crowning her dresser, Meg had accepted the first job she could find after fleeing Northern Virginia. A week after returning to Henry County, she took work selling construction equipment for Ingersoll Rand, drove her Honda Civic to Greensboro at 4:30 a.m., then climbed into a company dual-axle with a utility trailer and hauled and hawked Bobcats, hammers and attachments across three states, her region's only woman rep, wading into construction sites in heels and skirts and quickly learning the ropes and impressing her buyers, hopping behind the controls of her machines if need be, her girl's shoes on the pedals, her skirt adjusted, undeniably high on her thigh, but every man watching understood the bargain was for the equipment and nothing else—"Meg's legs" were her giveaway, her promotion, her gimmick. She occasionally slept in her truck, and she burned through boxes of blue and black shoes from Payless and Walmart, but she enjoyed the hours traveling alone in the big cab, she was honest with her clients, and soon she was banking sizable commissions and winning bonus contests, earning more than any other employee in the East. The cash from Alton's family was a big boost as well.

Years later, she'd emerged from another chrysalis and was M. J. Gold, and before forty she was rich, rich, rich, damn rich, rich enough to be as erratic as she chose to be, she was fond of saying, the owner of beaucoup construction equipment franchises, a shopping center, apartment complexes and nine radio stations. By now, her story had been honed and amended to do her success justice, and it was gospel that M. J. Gold once shot a man in Northern Virginia over a contract dispute and then forced him to urinate in his own cocky fedora, and everybody knew she'd earned her first wad of cash by bearding a tough-as-nails waste disposal family from the Northeast.

Her attorney, Lisa Stone, as much as confirmed the accuracy of Miss Gold's colorful business history when she cryptically told a reporter from *The Atlanta Journal-Constitution* that "M. J. Gold has never been formally arrested for shooting a business associate, and standing up to shady operators who think they can steamroll you because you are a small-town woman is simply an admirable and commonsense choice." M. J. Gold became a minor celebrity, and Alton Gold wilted into an obscure, mutating memory for his former wife: First he was Fool's Gold, then Mr. Pyrite, then simply the Craps Pirate.

Despite their minor age difference, Lisa and M.J. became friends, close, dear, lip-gloss-sharing, spa-tripping, pot-sneaking, martinis-at-lunch friends, tight as kin. They occasionally traveled together, talked and texted and e-mailed and saw each other frequently, especially when M.J. was passing through to visit her parents. She now lived in Raleigh but had bought a small farm outside of Stuart, just up the road from Martinsville, so she could be near her folks and enjoy a respite from the city and her work's grueling pace.

She'd never remarried. She adored men, though, no mistaking her tastes there, but her courtships were invariably her own stylized, checklist productions. Her "beaus" were attractive, athletic, attentive, well mannered and poor enough to be beholden to her. They were always younger, though never too much so, no more than six years her junior—that was a Gold rule. Six years was believable and not altogether obvious; past that, she had once noted to Lisa, making her point with a cigarette vised between her second and third fingers, her elbow planted on a restaurant table, the Marlboro Ultra Light level with her ear, smoke ribboning toward the ceiling, and you come off as fucking Cher. Or frightful Norma Desmond. A joke. Snickers when you leave the Caribbean front desk for your suite. Even worse, if you reach beyond a decade's difference, probably the best you'll do is Larry Fortensky or some wet-behind-the-ears backup dancer.

Ten days after her trip to Lettie's trailer, Lisa drove to Winston-Salem and met M.J. at the bar of a restaurant called Bleu. They sat at a table against a wall and ordered pomegranate mojitos and an appetizer sampler. M.J. showed Lisa a new jeweled watch she'd purchased on a trip to Miami and invited her to the Raleigh coliseum for the Royal Lipizzaner Stallions show. M.J. was the queen of offbeat entertainment: She'd load up her boyfriend and bottles of champagne into a limo and off she'd go to see Holiday on Ice, where—suitably buzzed—she'd cheer every salchow and triple lutz. She was a devotee of Yanni, cruise-ship magic shows, the professional bowling tour, ventriloquists, every Vegas permutation of Cirque du Soleil, and Riverdance as well as its many frenetic spawn.

"Thanks," Lisa laughed. "But no thanks."

"Suit yourself. It's a fun evening. Beautiful horses."

Lisa took hold of her fork and pushed a shrimp tail across a small plate. She rested the fork on the rim of the plate, sipped her drink. She slid a bright blue napkin over a dot of spilled sauce. "Listen," she said, "I want to ask you a question. Ask your opinion."

"Sure," M.J. said.

"In strict confidence. No exceptions." She lowered her head. "This is serious."

"Absolutely," M.J. replied.

"Your blood oath?"

"Yes. Of course. Tell me."

"Well, it involves Joe. And my marriage. I haven't gone too far yet, but . . ." She trailed off. "I need some advice. And . . ." She checked to see if anyone was close by. "I might, maybe, be thinking about . . . sort of seeing another guy. Not leaving Joe or—"

M.J. interrupted, waving her hand, and she was suddenly, visibly different, the dancing show horses and country-girl indulgences chased from her demeanor. "Wait a minute," she said, still agitated. "Here's my advice before I even hear the rest of this craziness. Joe Stone is a gem. You're lucky. I'd tell you otherwise, right? I'm your best friend. Don't trifle with your marriage. Don't risk it. Heck, if you're tired of Joe, maybe we can agree on a swap. I'd even break my rules." M.J. smiled with half her mouth, turning up a corner. "Easy decision for me already. I'd trade all the bimboys and all the sex and all the—" She caught herself. "Not to say you're in a deficit. With sex, I mean."

CHAPTER FIVE

Even if she'd made up her mind—and she definitely hadn't—there was no way Lisa would have sex with Brett Brooks so soon and rashly swap her birthright for a bowl of porridge and a few downtown martinis on the sly, but she nevertheless set to preparing for this absolute impossibility, got ready in fine style, starting with a week-early hair appointment, a spa facial and a manicure from the masked, yip-yapping Koreans at the mall and finishing with a trip to Winston-Salem for new crimson underwear that matched and was patterned for show and low-slung tease, not comfort or eight-hour slogs at a law office. She loved the extravagant prelude to her pretend first date, had a ball splurging on hair and nails and clean, scrubbed, treated skin, the reclamation nearly bone deep. She also bought new shoes, a pair with a higher heel than her normal.

A week after Dr. Corbett's deposition and the evening at Metro! Brett—as promised—had sent her a short e-mail, confirming the details of the seminar. She'd replied the same day. When she arrived in Roanoke for the program, lawyers were milling around, drinking coffee and nibbling free bakery pastry, everyone talkative. Brett wasn't there, and he didn't appear until fifteen minutes into the first lecture. She'd tried to keep an empty seat beside her, but another Martinsville lawyer had spotted her and taken the chair, pleased to see a colleague from home. He immediately smothered her with a dry narrative about a land dispute he was handling, warring hillbillies squabbling over a worthless acre of Henry County dirt.

She and Brett met at the ten o'clock break, and he casually stretched an arm around her so they were touching at the hip, his trunk twisted slightly away from her, and he gave her the kind of brief, social hug that a garrulous character like Brett Brooks would give any woman he'd met at least once.

"I can't believe you didn't save me a seat," he said, pretending to be upset.

"You were late." She smiled.

"Damn. You look like a million bucks." He was facing her now. "Glad you could come."

"Thanks. I appreciate your telling me about this. I'll almost satisfy my CLE hours for the year."

"Sure. My pleasure." He laid his hand in the center of her back and left it there, his palm and fingers pressed into her so she could feel the push, the directness, and he slipped closer, just for an instant. "Maybe we'll be able to visit when this is over. See what the afternoon brings." He kept his eyes on her point-blank as he took his hand away. "Last time was fun. Hope we can get together again."

Somewhere, she realized, every flirt and two-step has to either stall or grab traction and bull ahead, to cross its own particular Rubicon, because you can only dally and dip and dance and double-entendre for so long, and now Brett was blunt and clear. This was his offer, a plain overture to fuck and fool around and live louche and veer down a route with corrupt sex and catch-as-catch-can trysts and a do-not-disturb placard hung from a hotel door handle while the two of them were twisting free of their clothes—pants kicked off here, a skirt tossed there—and she was jazzed by the temptation, wired, excited by the prospect of what was at stake, tiptoeing toward lovely vice and happy as much as anything to be, well, so happy.

"Yeah." She paused, and without meaning to she recalled stealing a bottle of sweet grape wine from the grocery store when she was seventeen and drinking it in a friend's basement, screwing off the metal cap and pouring her virgin taste of alcohol into a paper cup with foldout cardboard handles, the purple almost over the brim. She quickly ran through the memory, and she shifted so she rubbed against Brett's shoulder. She was wearing perfume. Two buttons from the top, there was a small gap in her blouse. "Last time *was* fun. I'm betting today will be even better."

After the seminar ended, they drove separately and met in the Hotel

Roanoke's Pine Room and sat side by side at a square table underneath a framed photograph of a locomotive. A bearded man was nursing a dark beer at the bar and another couple was eating sandwiches and gabbing up a storm near the middle of the room. It was closing in on four-thirty and cold outside, the January day already dimming, shades of common gray curtaining off bright blue and white. Brett ordered a scotch but wasn't fussy about it, asking for "whatever's good and single malt." Lisa picked a merlot from a list the waitress brought.

More people came to the bar, the speaker music changed to rhythm and blues and the waitress announced a dollar-draft special. Lisa and Brett drank and chatted and told stories and laughed and shared a bowl of pretzels, then left their heavy coats across a chair and carried their second round into the adjacent room and played pool at a table with red felt and woven leather pockets. During the first game, Lisa leaned over to reach the cue ball and take the measure of a difficult shot, and Brett let her see him staring at her, her hair pitched forward and almost touching the felt, the stick slowly sawing through a finger bridge as she tried to solve the angle. Her thigh was mashed against the table. Chandelier light bounced off a thick silver bracelet. She flicked her eyes away from the game and toward him and then missed the shot by a fraction, almost sank it. "Nice," he said. He grinned. "Good try, I mean."

The last rack they played nine-ball, and despite having lost all the games before, Lisa wagered dinner.

"And drinks," Brett added. "The whole package."

"Absolutely."

He broke and never allowed her a turn, finished matters on his fourth shot, running in the winner with a long combination. He stayed bent over and peered up at her as the balls kissed, was studying her, not the pocket, when the nine fell and clicked against the other ball already there. His expression let on that he realized his no-look trick was cheesy, a flash of courtship swagger and preening tail feathers, and she laughed at how he was showing off for her. A younger man wearing a sweater and slouching against the bar's broad doorway complimented Brett's skill.

"I'll call a cab," Brett said. "So we can ride together and not worry about how much we drink."

"Meet you in the lobby. I need to find the restroom."

She peed and washed her hands and dried them on a small cloth towel she tossed in a wicker basket. She wet another towel and rubbed a blue pool-chalk wisp from her sleeve. Still at the sink, she phoned her house and left Joe a message that the seminar had ended and she was going shopping downtown, then to the mall, where she'd probably grab a food-court meal. For him, there was baked chicken to warm and a salad she'd made that morning. She was lying about her plans, but it was a faint lie without any serious impact or consequences, a dry-run untruth, a practice deception, a little baby distortion that would for certain prove to be meaningless.

It was Wednesday, so Joe was at the gym, lifting weights and exercising. Strong and fit, he could bench-press three hundred pounds multiple times and do a hundred sit-ups in under three minutes. Comically though, he began every session with toe touches and oafish jumping jacks, like he was a sixth-grade PE student from 1953, and he simply couldn't remember to bring white athletic socks and often worked out in tennis shoes and his dress socks—blue or black, whatever he'd put on for the office. Occasionally, he skipped the socks altogether and popped off the spastic jumping jacks with reddish, elastic imprints ringing his calves. She still found *this* hopeless quirk endearing, and she'd usually grin and wisecrack and needle him if he wore his colored socks and old Nikes home from the gym.

She tasted the wine in her mouth, but there wasn't very much saliva along with the merlot, and the bathroom seemed hot, the heat stagnant and sweetened by chemical scents. The alcohol and anticipation pinched her stomach. She wasn't about to focus on the mirror and mire down in her own thoughts and reflection, had no interest in taking the clichéd inventory where she'd stare at her failings and dither and fret and face a whorish adulterer taunting her from the glass. As she was heading for the door, she did sneak a sidelong glance, couldn't help peeking, and watched herself until the mirror ended and the tile started and her image disappeared.

They both got full-tilt drunk at a pricey steak house, ordering a bottle of champagne and then another, and never made it to an entrée, just picked appetizer plates on a whim and didn't finish any of them. Brett emptied the second bottle into their glasses, dunked it upside down in its silver pail, told her there were several bands nearby and asked her if she wanted to hear some music.

"Talking seriously about music," she said, her words lush, fulsome, lavish, "with a single man out on the town"—she lifted the last of the champagne but didn't raise it to her mouth—"is pretty much a first cousin to discussing sex, don't you think?"

Brett smiled, his expression happy and cockeyed. "I like that. Probably true. Kind of like sex's envoy or placeholder. Special trade representative or some such."

"Ambassador at large, maybe."

He stretched his neck forward, rested his elbow on the table, set his hand underneath his chin. "So what do you like?"

"I like it all, except, well, I don't care for . . . well, I really can't stand rap, and I hate to say this, living here in this part of the world, but I'm not a fan of the high mountain sound either, you know, hardscrabble bluegrass, Ralph Stanley and all the primitive wailing. Nothing personal, it's just not for me. Truth be told, Joe's more into music than I am. Well, more into it kind of clinically, dissecting it, studying it, cutting it to shreds." She swallowed champagne until none was left. "I'm about tipsy," she declared. "Wow. I usually don't drink this much. But, yeah, right, let's do go somewhere else. I don't care. You choose. No need to waste this hard-earned buzz."

"Great. I agree." He moved his hand, changed his posture and folded his arms across his chest. "There's a good jazz band in town. I've heard them a couple times."

"Oh damn, we don't have a car. How long will the cab take?"

Brett winked at her. "I had him wait. He's here."

"Clever. Nice. I like that. Big spender." She touched her ear, worried she'd lost an earring. She felt it still there. "So you like listenin' to jazz? Listening. I forget the ends of my words if I'm too liquored."

"I really like Dave Brubeck. Beats rap and banjo hoedowns, right?"

Lisa insisted that she honor their wager, but Brett asked the server for their check, and while they were waiting for the bill, Lisa's cell phone went off with "Hey Joe," and even though she knew the ring tone was her husband's, she fished and fumbled through her purse and found the phone and saw his name in stark black letters against a luminous background.

"Speaking of music," Brett said. "I'll ... I'll track down our waitress and give you some privacy," he offered, standing as he spoke. He bumped the edge of their table, causing a water glass to spill. He quickly set it upright. A pile of ice remained, cubes dumped beside a dirty plate.

"No, it's okay. Don't worry about it. I'm not goin' to answer it." She sat back, slumped a little. "What would I say?" She dropped the phone into her purse.

She scooted only to the middle of the cab's seat, didn't completely cross the carpeted ridge above the transmission, and Brett eased in beside her, closing the door as he came. The car accelerated onto a wide avenue. It was dark now, the city candled by streetlights, traffic signals, bar signs with burning neon script and the plodding glow of various window displays, their bulbs illuminating travel posters, antiques, pawned saxophones and guitars, and mannequins wrapped by layers of trendy woolen clothes.

"You know," Brett said, "if you don't want to go to a bar, I have a little pied-à-terre not far from here."

Lisa laughed, snorted and gulped air and leaned into him and dipped her head and kept laughing and wiped at her eyes. "How was it you pronounced it? It's one of those words you see a lot but never really learn how to say. At least, I've never heard it said out loud. It's crossword fodder. Brett Brooks has a crossword lair. A fancy-pants den. A French apartment. Suave." She laughed some more, but there was no barb in it, nothing mean-spirited.

Brett repeated it. "Pied-à-terre." The alcohol caused him to slow down the syllables.

"Once more." She elbowed him.

"Now you're just making fun of me," he said, but he was grinning, playing along.

"Yep. I am. Damn right." She dabbed at the corners of her eyes. "Oh, gosh. I can't remember the last time I laughed so much." She glanced at him and then went on another jag. "Tell you what," she said when she'd composed herself, "you've got some serious bullshit in your bag. You're a pro. I get the feelin' maybe you've done this before."

"Nah. No kidding, Lisa, I haven't had a date in months." He leaned away so he could see her complete face. "And what would you prefer?

What would be a better term? Crib? Bachelor pad? Love nest? One-bedroom apartment with a tiny balcony?"

"A date, huh? We're datin'? At any rate, at least you didn't say you *keep* a little pied-à-terre. That would be about candy-ass and prissy." She frowned, thought for a moment. "Wow, I sure am cursin' a lot. So, uh, no, I won't be visiting your apartment tonight, but you didn't blow it for eternity."

"Glad to hear it."

"I wanna go see the Chairmen of the Board. I've changed my mind. The hell with the jazz; that'll be too slow and earnest. Where were the Chairmen playin'? They make me think of college and summer. I love 'Give Me Just a Little More Time.' Is General Johnson still with 'em? We'll kick winter to the curb. Banish all this blah. Yeah, let's do that."

"No problem."

At the show, Lisa continued to drink—a beer, a daiquiri in honor of beaches and warm weather, another beer—and she and Brett made a path through the crowd to the front of the stage, where they sang—yelled, actually—the parts of the songs they knew and danced in place and brushed and bumped against other people and held their bottles high over their heads when the lyrics mentioned "ice cold beer." There were a few people their age at the show, but not many. They stayed until the band finished and the houselights came on harsh and jarring and a bouncer circled the room telling everyone it was closing time, to kill the alcohol or throw it in the trash. Glass banged and clanked in garbage bags behind the bar, a young man in a knit cap pushed a wide janitor's broom over the floor.

Brett took Lisa's hand, and they walked outside into the frigid air. Shivering, she pulled her coat tight around her neck. The same cab was there, the engine running, cozy for them.

"What now?" Brett asked as they were climbing in. He was holding the door for her. He shut the tail of his topcoat in the door and had to open it, pull the fabric free and then shut it again.

"Well, for once in my life, I really didn't plan ahead, so, hell, hmmm, that's a brilliant question. It was nice just to go somewhere off the clock and not worry about missing a court deadline or whether or not I had enough friggin' eggs for a recipe. But I'd say I've got a travel dilemma."

"Yeah, there's no chance I'm letting you drive. And I'm way too tanked to take you anywhere myself. We'd probably blow a fifty or so combined."

"I'm call . . . I'll just find a room back at the hotel. I'll call Joe from there. Me. I'm gonna rent a room for me. By myself. Alone. A-lone."

"Sad news about staying alone, but understandable." Brett told the cabbie to take them to the Hotel Roanoke. It was after two in the morning.

During the trip there, he pushed up the hem of her skirt and touched the inside of her thigh, but he wasn't sloppy, wasn't rushed, wasn't clumsy, didn't paw or grope, just rubbed his hand a few inches in different directions, his flat palm up and down and sideways against her hose, a thin, stretched nylon separation between her skin and his. "I figure we should go ahead and kiss good night now—take all the awkwardness out of it," he said. "I don't want to be standing there freezing in a damn parking lot, floundering and stuttering. Wondering and so forth." He kissed her, and when they finished, he kissed her some more, and she relaxed into the seat, and the side of his hand hit higher on her leg and didn't quit, brushed against her crotch, and she bent her leg, but not entirely, hinted it toward him and shut her eyes, felt him underneath her skirt, the alcohol framing and concentrating it all.

She opened her eyes and glanced in the mirror because the driver would have to be aware of what was happening. He was watching the road, discreet. Anyway, it was dark in the car, and there were coats and shadows concealing them. When the car slowed and the driver flipped the blinker for the turn into the hotel, they stopped kissing and Brett slid his hand to her knee, let it rest.

"Whew," she said. She adjusted her skirt but didn't bother with anything else. "No denying that." She sat up straighter.

"You want me to have him take us back to the bar and we can do the same trip again?"

"No," she laughed.

The cab pulled up next to Lisa's Mercedes, and Brett gave the driver a handful of bills, a hundred obvious on top.

"A pleasure doin' business with you, Mr. Brooks," the man said.

"Appreciate the tip. You got my number. Ya'll be careful. Ain't no problem for me to carry the lady direct to the front entrance."

"Thanks. We're okay."

The cab circled the lot and headed away, the only vehicle in sight on the road, and Brett wrapped both his arms around her at her waist, facing her. "Do you need anything out of your car?"

"No."

He walked with her to the lobby, where he sat in a leather chair near the entrance while she paid for a night's stay. She dropped her wallet and several charge cards spilled onto the floor, and the clerk had to tell her twice where to initial the paperwork. She squinted at the room rate and informed the lady behind the desk she'd been drinking and couldn't drive home. The clerk, a wiry woman with short gray hair, told her avoiding the highway was a smart decision, though she sounded sour and strict when she spoke.

The clerk peered at Brett. "Will your husband be staying?"

"Oh, no. No. He's not my husband. I had too much drinks . . . to drink . . . at a business celebration, and he was kind enough to bring me here. My husband's home." Lisa leaned across the counter and whispered, "Now, well, uh, he probably would *like* to. We all know how that goes." The words were thick, the pace of her speech off-kilter.

"I hope you sleep well," the clerk said. "I imagine you will." She wrote a room number on a small cardboard folder and underlined the four digits, the felt-tip line drawn with a quick, prim swipe. "Would you care for one of our signature warm cookies?"

Lisa cocked her head, collected her purse. "Yeah. Hell, yeah. Sure. Why not?" So what, she thought while she waited for her chocolate chip. Screw her and her bitchy attitude.

"You set?" Brett asked from his chair in the main lobby.

She swung toward him and blew him kisses with both hands, her purse sliding down to her wrist, her cookie and room card jammed between her fingers, very nearly slipping free. "Thank you, Brett Brooks. Sweet dreams. You were nice to take care of me. See you around." He stood, but she was walking and didn't wait or linger or offer him any possibilities, went zipping into an open elevator. She pressed her floor number, watched the doors seal, slumped against the wall and stared at the glowing button as she rose through the building to her level. By the time the elevator *tinged* to a stop and the doors rolled away, she was sitting on the parquet floor and looking out at colorful carpet, fresh flowers on a hallway table and a framed black-and-white print of the city from bygone days: horses, wagons, wooden buildings and muddy streets.

Joe was alarmed and still awake when she reached him. "Where have you been? Are you okay?" There was no separation between the questions. The sentences piled into each other.

"I'm drunk," she said. She giggled. "Oh, Joe."

"Why didn't you call me?"

"I did. I did call," she said. She was sitting on her hotel bed. She bit into the cookie and considered the minibar. "Sure did."

"You called at, like, five o'clock. It's almost three in the morning now. I've been worried to death. I called Gentry, Locke and couldn't catch anyone after hours. Checked with the cops in both Roanoke and Salem. Wore your cell out. Jeez."

"No. I called around ten. Ten at night."

"No, you didn't," Joe said. He sounded more befuddled than angry.

"Yep I did. From a bar. To tell you I couldn't make it home. Not to be worried."

"Well, I didn't—"

"I've got the proof here. I do, Attorney Joe Stone. On my phone. On Recent Calls." She waited a beat. "Uh-oh. Joe, I'm so sorry. I called the office. Damn." She had, in fact, called from the bar around ten-thirty and intentionally left a message at their office.

"The office? *Our* office?"

"I've been drinkin'. I made a mistake." She sighed. "Do you forgive me? I wonder if this little fridgey thing has champagne? Or Baileys? Baileys would be a treasure." She crossed the room to the minibar.

Joe chuckled. "So you somehow wound up drunk and now you're in a hotel? Safe and sound? How could you confuse the messages here and at work?"

"It was loud, okay? I just hit, uh, the preset on my phone and waited for the beep. Punched the wrong one. My bad. My error. I apologize."

"What hotel?"

"The Hotel Roanoke," she said. "And Conference Center," she added nonsensically.

"And you're okay? Drunk but okay?"

"Yep." She opened the minibar and looked inside.

"Who did you go to a bar with? How'd that happen?" His voice changed, not much, but enough for her to notice the edge. "Last I heard you were headed to the food court. Helluva detour."

"Well, sorry, but I just fell in with bad companions, Joe. It was fun. Spur of the moment." She located a small bottle of Baileys and cracked it open. She took a draw from the miniature opening. "Believe it or not, Brett Brooks was our guide. He and his girlfriend, in case you might worry—"

"Brett Brooks? Brett Brooks is a hound of the very first rank and—"

She interrupted. "His freakin' girlfriend was there, Joe. And a wonderful lawyer who was visitin' here by the name of Sarah. She went too. Sarah."

"Well, I doubt that would slow him down. Just more birds in the covey for him."

"He is quite the operator," she said. "Handsome too."

"Handsome like a copperhead. Did he—"

"He was a gentlemen . . . gentleman, I mean. Nice as you'd ever want. And his girlfriend's a sweetheart."

"I'm sure she is, Lisa. It was probably like attending a world-hunger summit with Marc Anthony and Jennifer Lopez. Nothing but goodwill and beneficence."

"Marc Anthony? Huh?"

"How did you wind up at the Hotel Roanoke? Surely you didn't drive, drunk as you are."

"Sarah and I took a cab. She went home after here. It's so cute you're jealous." She opened her mouth and let the bottle drain in until she had a full swallow. Some of the Baileys hit her lips and trickled onto her neck and blouse. "Damn, I just poured brown on my new top."

"What?"

"I'm having problems with my nightcap." She giggled again. "So, anyway, I'm safe and here where I am, and I love you and I'm goin' to bed, okay? Okay? Oh . . . oh. You need to cancel my appointments tomorrow or cover for me. Please?"

"Yeah. Do I need to come and get you or anything?"

"Why? No. I'm *fine*, Joe. I allowed myself one night to let my hair down and be silly, and it's been years since I was irresponsible and it's not like . . . like I'm callin' you from Paris high with . . . on heroin from some soccer star's pied-à-terre. I'm an hour away, in a classy hotel."

"I'm just glad you're okay. I was worried sick." He sighed. "I can't believe you fouled up the message. Imagine if I'd done this—you'd kill me. But it's good you had such a big time. You've been kind of subdued lately, so I suppose you're owed some fun."

"Good night, Joe."

She'd dozed off wearing her clothes and with her makeup still in place, propped against the dresser next to the minibar, its door not closed, rich candies and stunted rows of booze lining its racks, and there was knocking from out in the hall and a hotel security officer announced loudly that Mr. Joe Stone had sent him to check on her and make sure she was safe. Could she give him a "visual confirmation"? She told him to leave, but evidently he didn't hear her, and when he peeked past the safety chain and saw her sprawled there on the floor, he offered to help, and she told him, from behind a pointed finger with a brightly painted nail, to leave her the hell alone and shut her damn door and that she was a lawyer, understand, and she'd sue him and his polyester-blend blazer and walkie-talkie into infinity.

She awoke on the floor to a window blasting winter daylight, sick, her fingers and blouse stained by the cookie and the Baileys, the carpet weave unpleasant and rough against her cheek, unsure for several seconds where she was. She made it to the bed and lay down and pulled a pillow from underneath the fold in the counterpane and didn't leave until noon, ignoring the maid and the ringing phone, twice rolling toward the mattress's edge to gag and spit and puke into a leather wastebasket.

Joe was kind enough when she returned home, though he made her detail her lies and embellishments a second time, and he frowned at each mention of Brett Brooks, girlfriend or not, and because she was still sickly and disabled on the couch at dinner, he grilled a cheese sandwich in the frying pan and brought it to her, along with a bowl of canned vegetable soup, and he sat next to her while she ate and said, with a sincere half smile, that he was tickled to see she had the instincts of a party girl left in her. Maybe they should give some thought to a trip to Hawaii or Mexico, where it was warm and they *both* could cut loose. Maybe they'd cancel the house at Emerald Isle they'd rented since 1993 and try a new vacation, though it sure would be tough to break their streak of beach Scrabble and a shrimpburger lunch at the Big Oak Drive-In. Might jinx them, too.

The residue of the alcohol's pernicious claim crept into Friday as well, but Lisa, frazzled and woozy, nevertheless left the office early and drove to Mt. Olivet Elementary School for her volunteer tutor's gig, same as she'd been doing for the past eleven years, and she met this year's student, a bony girl-child—eyeglasses crooked, a tooth chipped—at the door to a classroom. The child, a fifth-grader named Montana Triplett, snatched Lisa's hand and right away commenced prattling, gushed run-on fragments about her teacher and a report card and the several free throws she'd scored during her basketball game and a prankster who'd toted a live guinea pig to school in his backpack.

They spent almost an hour at the city library sorting through school assignments and selecting a new book for Montana to read, then finished off the evening at McDonald's, the girl wasting most of her burger, scarcely interested in food. Before they married, Lisa and Joe had decided they weren't suited for raising children, and they'd never seriously regretted their choice, no more than an occasional specula-tion at Christmas or a generous envy when moms and dads e-mailed photos of a darling newborn. Still, Lisa had filled a lot of gaps caused by shiftless parents. She'd bought her fair share of tennis shoes and fashionable mall jeans and always shuffled appointments and trials if she could help chaperone a field trip. She enjoyed her commitment, appreciated the chance to ride shotgun on exuberance and shining possibility, to witness it firsthand and tap into it around the margins, never once put off by the realization that many of the kids' deficits were so unruly that they wouldn't be tamed by a few hours a month with a pretty lawyer-lady volunteer.

"You look tired, Mrs. Stone," Montana informed her as they were stacking their wrappers and tall cups onto a tray, ready for the garbage.

"Really? You think so?"

"Uh-huh."

"Well, sweetie," Lisa told her, "I can promise you this: You'll leave me better than you found me. Seeing you pepped me up. Made my day. Thanks. It's nice to have you as a friend, you know?"

Soon afterward, around seven-thirty on a Sunday morning, she found Joe in the kitchen with Brownie, and as she came past the pantry Joe told her to stop where she was. To emphasize the request, he straightened a traffic-cop arm in her direction. He was wearing striped flannel house pants and a ratty T-shirt, standing near the stove, the dog sitting on his black haunches. "Check this, Lisa. Old dog, very new trick."

He slowly lowered a piece of bacon toward Brownie, and the dog's tail quivered and he Gatling-gun sniffed and he keened his head, but he stayed rooted to the floor, didn't lunge or snap at the food. Joe kept closing the distance and placed the bacon squarely on the animal's nose, and remarkably, Brownie—amped, drooling, excited—didn't budge, didn't gulp it down until Joe said "Eat," and then the dog ducked his snout and grabbed the meat straight out of the air, snatching it so rapidly it was as if he'd never moved.

"Damn right. Smart boy," Joe praised him. "How about that, Lisa? Cool, huh?" He knelt and rubbed and patted and scratched Brownie, who soon tumbled over onto his back, all four legs pointing at the ceiling.

"Don't say it," Lisa muttered, too late.

"Heckuva job, Brownie," Joe said. He glanced up at her. "Say what?"

"I've told you a million times I hate the 'heckuva job' line. It's so annoying. Same as how you think it's hilarious to blow the horn and startle me whenever I'm anywhere close to the front of the car."

"It's part of my impish charm," Joe replied, unfazed. "Makes me the unique, lovable rascal you married. You'd miss it if I quit."

"I'm willing to take the chance," she said. "It's so stupid."

"And Brownie loves it, don't you, boy?" Joe stood, and the dog rearranged himself on the kitchen tile. An oval of tepid dog spit had dampened the floor. Joe ignored it and poured himself some coffee. "Want a cup?" he asked cheerfully. "It's fresh. I had it ground at the coffee shop on the way home yesterday."

"Yeah, sure, thanks. I hope it's not the Colombian—that's too strong."

"Nope. It's the blend you like so much: Jamaica Me Crazy. Bought it just for you."

CHAPTER SIX

A month into 2011, on a dreary February morning, Neal VanSandt, Lettie's son, was seated in Joe's office, waiting for Lisa to join them, his winter gloves resting one atop the other on his lap. While his mother came off as a clamorous and flamboyant human carnival, Neal was so ordinary as to almost not be there. He was around five-eight, with thinning brown hair and nondescript glasses that slid slightly down his nose and were never adjusted. He was neither heavy nor thin. His clothes fit him well enough but were dull, humdrum. He was cautious, quiet, polite, skittish, almost a vapor. Brownie had scarcely stirred when he entered.

For the past six years, he'd worked at a pest control company in Atlanta, a desk job, scheduling appointments so the technicians could kill roaches and termites and fog whole homes with strong chemicals. According to the last report from Lettie, he'd been dating a woman he met at a flea market booth, a "clean lady with a reliable car." Truth be told, though, Lettie had never mentioned him all that often.

He tucked his gloves under an arm and stood and shook Lisa's hand when she came in. "Hi, Mrs. Stone," he said, briefly meeting her eyes. He simultaneously broke their clasp and began withdrawing into his chair.

"Neal." Lisa nodded at him. "Sorry to see you under these circumstances. Hope your trip was tolerable." They'd exchanged a few words at Lettie's memorial service, which only six people attended, including the preacher. Lisa had also met Neal in 2007, when Lettie was sick with pneumonia and he was staying at her trailer to watch over her horde of animals and tend to her while she recovered.

"Thanks," he replied. A glove fell to the floor, and he bent down and retrieved it.

"Well, I'm glad you were finally able to make it to Martinsville so we can take care of your mom's affairs," Joe noted. "I was getting worried."

"Yeah, I'm sorry I took, uh, a . . ." He'd confirmed and rescheduled three other appointments. "Busy at work, you know. A tough drive too. Holidays. Thanks for bein' so understandin'." He had a noticeable southern accent, blurred and mashed the last syllables of several words.

"No problem," Joe told him. "Again, we're so sorry about Lettie."

"She thought the world of you, Mr. Stone," Neal quickly added. "'You can always count on Joe Stone' was how she put it."

"She was quite the lady," Joe said. He paused for a moment, then found a paper clip on his desk and began bending it straight. "As for the business part of things, Neal, like I told you—"

"Do you think it would be okay if I had the reports about Mom? The DNA? Do you have them? The actual papers showin' it was her who died?"

"I do. Absolutely. We'll give you a copy."

"Great. It's just, well, it's just the kind of stuff I guess a person should have if it involves your mom."

"Of course," Joe said.

"I don't mean to be a nuisance."

"You're not," Lisa assured him. "We understand."

Joe had twisted the clip into a straight silver line with two tiny kinks that wouldn't disappear. "As I was saying, I don't have any interest in claiming Lettie's estate. None. The holographic will—the handwritten paper Sheriff Perry found—was created a few days before the date the coroner set for her death. Technically and legally, it's valid and her last will. It specifically states it trumps the document I prepared for her here in the office. I admitted it to probate because it's a legitimate legal document and because someone needed the authority to manage her affairs and pay her debts. That said, I don't intend to accept any benefit or cause any complications for you concerning her property."

"Thank you," Neal said. "Awful decent of you."

"Maybe, maybe not."

"There're a lot of strays," Lisa remarked.

"Yeah," Neal answered. "A bunch."

"Have you thought about what you're going to do with them?" Lisa asked.

"Sort of."

"I've been able to find homes for about half the dogs," Joe informed him. "The cats are a tougher sell, and despite our best efforts we've had a couple unexpected litters." He smiled; he and Lisa were planning to take a pair of rambunctious tuxedo kittens to patrol their barn. "The folks from PAWS in Patrick County are going to remove a few more dogs as soon as space opens. In the end, though, you're looking at a serious problem. There are eighteen dogs left, and most of them are old or surly, and several are crippled or missing a leg or some such. One hound mix is blind as can be. Not what the average happy family dropping by in the minivan is looking to adopt. The damn cats seem impossible to place. We've unloaded most of the kittens for you, but there're probably thirty adults still there."

"Lettie was insistent they be taken care of," Lisa told him. "You can't dump them or haul them to the pound to catch a needle." She pinned him with a long stare until he acknowledged her. "Okay?"

"I'm pretty sure I've found a spot in Florida, a rescue kinda deal, and they said they have room. It's called the Ross Sanctuary." He tipped to his right, reached into his front pocket and removed a folded sheet, printed from the Internet. "I contacted them, and they say they'll help. They'll even come and pick everything up." He reached forward and offered Joe the paper. "It's in Bradenton. A man named Ross donated the money."

Joe dropped the paper clip and unfolded the single page and read for several seconds. "Great. This seems perfect. And you've actually talked to them?"

"Yeah."

"And they'll drive all the way to Virginia to make this happen?" Lisa asked.

"I have to give 'em five hundred dollars for expenses. Fuel and so forth." Neal glanced at Lisa, then Joe. He jammed his hands together, palm to palm, and began churning and twining them. His fingertips colored red with blood, some underneath his nails. "I'd sorta planned to use the cash in her bank account to pay 'em."

"Well, Neal, that's just fine; it's your cash." Joe folded the paper in half and laid it on his desk. "But you understand we've spent down the money to feed these animals and pay the funeral home and Lettie's last bills? I sent you an accounting. Of the original six thousand dollars, there's only around seventeen hundred left."

While Joe and Neal were discussing Lettie's bank account, Lisa had swiveled toward Brownie and made rapid, damp, clicking sounds, her tongue soft-tapping against the roof of her mouth, and he'd ambled to her from his pad beside the heat vent. He was parked on his hind legs, and she was raking the black fur all along his neck. "Speaking of assets and money, Neal, we were never able to locate Lettie's strongbox. There might be several hundred dollars hidden in the trailer."

"I hope I can find it," Neal said. "Boy, would that ever be nice."

"So let me know the details," Joe said, "and we'll help load the animals for this Ross place, and the moment that's done I'll sign a document and renounce my interest. That's the legal term: *renounce*. If there's no will, she would be deemed intestate, and her estate would go to you as her only heir at law."

"Okay. Yeah. You mentioned how it all works at her service. Thanks for, uh, explainin' it again."

"Then, it'll be yours," Lisa added. "The house, the land, her money, her personal property. Together with whatever else she might have." She stopped rubbing and scratching Brownie, who glanced up, his ears perked, his mouth opened slightly. "Is something the matter, Neal? You seem really uncomfortable."

"Yeah . . . yes, ma'am, lawyers make me jumpy. Legal stuff, bein' here. I never had to visit a lawyer before. Not ever. This whole situation makes me right smart nervous." He licked his lips, then wiped a wrist across his mouth, part shirt cuff, part skin. The lenses of his glasses distorted his eyes, caused them to appear a size or two out of scale.

"No need to worry or be nervous," Joe told him. "Everything's settled and on track. We're almost at the end."

"Thanks." Neal was standing as he spoke. "Thank you both. For now and for your kind help in the past."

"Are you aware of any other assets?" Lisa asked him. "Anything Joe's giving up that I haven't mentioned?"

"Uh, no. No. Why?" He hesitated and lowered himself back into his chair, tugging at his collar.

"Just curious. Covering the bases. I'm a lawyer, Neal. It's what I spent three years in law school learning to do. Nothing personal."

"*Is* there something else, Lisa?" Joe asked impatiently. "Do you know something we don't?"

"No. As far as I'm aware, there's nothing else. I'm not trying to be a jerk, but this is Contracts 101. Basic. I figured I should ask." Her voice was muted, almost meek. "Who knows, maybe Lettie won the lottery before she died. Or has a famous, expensive dog among her collection of curs and strays. Or used her considerable intellect to concoct a potion that will cure whatever ails us. Perhaps there's buried treasure under the mobile home or a long-lost share of a family fortune you're throwing away without even being aware of it. Or . . . well, you get the picture."

"Since I handled most of Lettie's business, I have a fairly good idea of what she owned." Joe twisted his mouth to the side. "But, sure, okay, I suppose we should check. Do you know of anything not on the list I sent you, Neal?"

"No, Mr. Stone. No. The list is right. I don't have any idea about other belongings beyond what you told me she had. There's nothin' else. Nothin'. You know more than I do probably." He wouldn't look at either Joe or Lisa for very long. "I want to be honest with you." He gripped the gloves, twisted them as if he were wringing them dry. "The trailer and land and her bank account. Her vehicle. That's it."

"There you go," Joe remarked. "I'm sorry if we've upset you. Lisa's simply looking after me. Nothing against you. You calm down and catch your breath, and we'll have this finished and behind us as soon as the animals are taken care of." Joe stood. "Come on, I'll walk you to the door." He reached for the sheet with the sanctuary details so he could return it to Neal.

"My apologies as well, Neal," Lisa said. "I'm sorry you lost your mother and sorry if I seemed pushy. I hope you understand. Joe can occasionally be a little too casual, and I'm very protective of my husband. He's always had a blind spot where Lettie's concerned." She stood and took a step toward Neal, rested a hand on his shoulder. "I hope you're not cross with me." Her tone was gentle, soothing. She smiled at him and quit touching his shoulder. He remained in his seat, uneasy about standing with her so close.

"Let's get you out of here," Joe said. He came around his desk and inserted himself in front of Lisa and walked with Neal down the hall, wished him safe travels and watched as he skedaddled to a small, gray Chevrolet with Georgia plates.

"Damn, Lisa," he upbraided her when he returned, "the guy's scared of his shadow, a fucking milquetoast, and you decide to grill him. For no reason other than you disliked his daffy mother."

"Grill him?" she said. "Hardly. I couldn't have been any less con-frontational, could I? Seriously? I didn't intend to upset him. I was almost whispering." She turned her head, briefly glanced off. "I had no idea he'd be so sensitive. And, for sure, I did need to check, right? Ask a few basic questions? Heck, I don't want you suing me for malpractice because I let you give away the store." She grinned at him.

"I guess so." They were standing at the threshold to her office, nobody else within earshot. "I appreciate the concern. But what did you expect—can you imagine being reared by Lettie? He's lucky he's as functional as he is."

"Well, I should've given you a heads-up so we'd have been on the same page, instead of just asking him and blindsiding you. My bad." She shrugged. "At any rate, at least we'll soon be rid of everything VanSandt. Hallelujah." She took his hand, swayed into him. "You're a good man, Joe Stone. Somebody has to take care of the simpletons and nuts and cast-off animals." She kissed his cheek.

"We'll still have the kittens to remind you of Lettie and the good old days. They'll probably despise you," he joked. "Hiss and spit at you and plague your ankles with sharp claws."

"Or bow when they see me."

"Just one damn time," Joe was saying to Harlowe Fain, "I wish I could come in here to buy my groceries and cold beer and not be pounced on by some club selling brooms or cookies or gigantic, seven-dollar candy bars. Or the fire department pushing raffle tickets for a shotgun or a curio cabinet, whatever the hell that is. Or a church group hawk-ing tracts and begging money for the 'youth group's missionary trip to Orlando.' Could I please, just once, walk into Food Lion and not get pestered like I'm a tourist in Bangladesh? I swear, you have to factor in an extra five panhandle bucks for every trip to the store."

"My favorite," Harlowe drawled, "is the clubs what sell the damn Krispy Kremes for two dollars a box more than you can pick 'em up inside off the shelf. Why in the world they let all these people pitch camp right at the entrance is beyond me. I've mentioned it to Dudley, and he always says, 'Corporate makes the call, not me.' Even though he's the store manager, he can't politely tell the cup shakers and crusaders to leave folks the hell alone. My wife's constantly buying chances for those baskets—'Longburgers,' or some crap like that—they dragoon the schoolkids into hustling. Try to shame your ass if you don't come across with the cash. What a racket."

Joe and Harlowe were leaning on shopping carts in front of the meat counter. It was near the middle of February, and several grimy mounds of snow were in the corners of the parking lot, the remnants of ferocious weather the week before. Students had missed school for three consecutive days, and the weight of the snow and ice had brought down so many power lines that most of Henry County had been without electricity the better part of a week, houses heated by kerosene and firewood, lit by candles and Coleman lanterns. Still, people were accustomed to it and made do. The Stones owned a generator that allowed them running water and an oven, and Joe kept their woodstove and fireplace hot, burning oak and poplar he'd split with an ax and a maul and stacked chest-high back in September.

"How's your son making out at Tech?" Joe asked. "What's this, his second year?"

"He's a senior," Harlowe answered. "Hard to believe, huh?"

"Yeah, jeez, where does the time go?"

"He's doin' fine. He'll graduate on schedule, and he ain't been in no trouble that me and his mom know about. I figure that's 'bout all you can expect." Harlowe smiled, proud. He traced his bush of a mustache, ran his thumb down one side, his index finger down the other. "He wants to get into this green-energy deal. They say there's money in it. Damn sure ain't nothin' for him here."

"Good for him. Tell him I asked after him."

"He remembers how you helped him with that bullshit marijuana charge over in juvenile court. A clean record means a lot to him now."

"Glad to do it," Joe said. "He's a great kid."

"Yeah. Thanks."

"You guys busy at work? Keeping things straight?"

"Same crap, new day." Harlowe was the 911 director for the county. Until the plant closed, he'd been a dress-shirt-and-khakis supervisor at DuPont, drew a paycheck almost double the size of his current salary. "Of course, I have to say our traffic's down considerably since we lost your girlfriend, Miss VanSandt. She was truly a pain in the ass. Can't say I miss her. Old bitch cursed me once 'cause I wouldn't listen to her complaints on her ice cream. She was bonkers because it was out of sequence. The three-color package. Neapolitan. According to her, it was supposed to be strawberry first, then vanilla, then chocolate. Hers was different, so she figures the smart decision is to bother us. She called 911 and the sheriff's office like we was the damn morning chatterbox show on WHEE or her own private consumer hotline."

Benny the butcher appeared and handed Joe a package of steaks. The meat was on a white Styrofoam tray, wrapped in tight plastic. "Two nice strips, my friend," he said. "Hope you enjoy them. Send my regards to your wife."

"Appreciate it." Joe set his steaks in the foldout kid's seat and aimed the cart toward the beer cooler. "Well, I'm sure Lettie was a handful," he said to Harlowe. "Probably a lot of that was just because she was alone."

"To her credit, her last call was a doozy. She went out in a blaze. Crazy as a shithouse rat."

"Really?"

"Yep. She was claiming it was end-times and other nonsense. Yelling and carryin' on about Mystery Babylon and a woman in purple come to do her harm. She was positively biblical. Threatenin' to kill people. It was a real A-plus performance, even for her. I'd award it a blue ribbon, and she set a damn high standard."

That night, Lisa met M. J. Gold at the Dutch Inn Lounge, a hotel bar that had been jerry-rigged and ventilated to accommodate smokers after Virginia restricted indoor cigarettes. The bar was located in the top section of a huge fake windmill, and the two of them were sipping mediocre margaritas made from a jug mix and house tequila and enjoying a fresh pack of Marlboro Ultra Lights. It was Thursday, so a couple of plump, oblivious women who fancied themselves talents took turns doing karaoke tunes, both of them comically average, mangling an occasional note, screeching the refrain of "Dream On" and oversinging—eyes shut, chin quivering—the shopworn standards like "Crazy" and "Wind Beneath My Wings." The younger of the two, whose name was Clarisse, had recorded her own CD she sold from her table and at several local convenience stores. A drunk welder with a longneck beer and his lanky brother sang "Brick House," were much more entertaining than the women and earned cheers and applause from M.J. and Lisa.

Lisa didn't care for the lounge, but M.J. liked it because it was the only place in Henry County where she could both smoke and drink, and she still felt at ease with men who burned their names into their belt leather and didn't change out of their Red Wings and blue shirts before stopping for the cheese-sticks-and-draft special on the way home from Wimbash's Garage or the Kendall Lumberyard. There were some Main Street regulars there, too, an off-duty bailiff from general district court, an insurance agent eating a burger with his gin and tonic, a dental hygienist with blond extensions and circus breasts and a Caché top who'd been married and divorced more than once, the first go-round to a local boy with a dab of coin. The hygienist flipped her hair and stared at them. Lisa gave it straight back to her.

M.J. was subdued. She was also soon a full drink ahead of Lisa. In the last month, she'd had to fire several employees from her equipment businesses. "This shit is getting dire," she said. "The economy's a mess."

"Are you okay?" Lisa asked. "Moneywise, I mean?"

"Yeah, sure. We're just hunkering down and riding it out. Me, I've got years and years of profit salted away." She hit her Marlboro and blew smoke toward the ceiling. "And we're full at the apartments. People losing their houses . . ."

"Maybe it'll turn around."

"It might if we didn't have a bunch of moronic pimps managing the government. I swear to god, Lisa, I'd rather have the mafia in charge. I would. With them, you at least get what you pay for, some degree of competency, and the shakedowns are predictable and the costs reasonable. I say let's tar and feather the whole bunch of politicians and send them home and hire a competent CEO and let her run the show for a year or two. Seriously, look at who we have in charge. That guy Harry Reid should be the substitute weekend weatherman for Channel 10, that would be about at the top of his skill level, and the Republican clown, what's his name? Boner?"

"Boehner," Lisa corrected her.

"Yeah, that tool's an obvious sot who looks like the Grinch's tropical island cousin. And poor Barack is your brother-in-law the dentist, right down to the mommy jeans and know-it-all lectures."

Lisa laughed. She sipped her drink, set it on a waterlogged napkin and started laughing again. "But you're not in any trouble?" she finally asked.

"Still rich. Rich enough to be erratic and not suffer because of it."

"Good."

As M.J. was reaching for their pack of smokes, a tall man wearing a wool blazer and dark slacks walked to their table, and his stilted, static smile and his slightly tucked chin and the casual way he dangled his beer bottle all signaled his intentions, and he stopped next to them and nodded, said hello. "I'm Paul Rourke," he announced. "Nice to meet you."

Lisa shook his hand, her expression noncommittal.

M.J. had worked a cigarette free from the pack, and as she raised it, he bent toward her with a blue plastic Bic and she leaned slightly sideways to meet the flame. The union was quick and precise, the Marlboro's tip burning orange in a second, the lighter extinguished, a smoke trail languishing, nowhere to go, unable to rise in the dense air. "Thanks," she said. She also shook his hand.

"I hope I'm not bothering you ladies," he told them. "Just thought I'd come over and meet you."

"Where're you from?" M.J. asked.

"Dayton. I'm here on business." He was still standing, closer to M.J. than to Lisa.

"What business?" M.J. wanted to know.

"Wholesale lumber. Bassett Furniture's a customer."

"Used to be nothing but furniture plants here," M.J. said. "Pretty slim pickings nowadays."

Rourke shrugged. "I hear you." He switched his beer from one hand to the other but didn't drink. "Mind if I ask your names?"

"I'm Lisa, Lisa Stone." She was pleasant. Paul Rourke seemed nice enough, and she could tell M.J. wasn't aggravated by his being there.

"I'm M. J. Gold. From Raleigh."

Rourke slanted his head, touched his chin. "The business lady? Heavy equipment, right?"

"Yep." M.J. poked around in her margarita with a thin red stir stick, jabbing ice toward the bottom of her glass.

"I read a piece on you not long ago. In one of the trade magazines. 'Everything Turns to Gold,' it was called. Or something like that."

"I remember it. It was a nice article."

"It's a pleasure to meet you." Rourke's tone had changed, and his words were rushed, clipped. He took an awkward half-step away from the women, probably wasn't aware he'd done it. He transferred the bottle again, then swallowed some beer. "I was going to offer to buy you a drink, but I might be out of my depth with you ladies."

"Not at all," M.J. told him. "I appreciate the courtesy. My friend Lisa's married, so don't waste the money on her. Tell you what—why don't you send me another margarita, and your next beer will be on us."

Rourke seemed relieved. "Sounds fair."

Lisa noticed the three companions at his table, watching bug-eyed, grinning, one of them elbowing the other. She recognized Joel Hammond, a vice president at Bassett. She'd represented his first wife in their divorce. He was now on number four.

"I take it you're single?" M.J. said.

"Divorced about a year. Married for sixteen. It's a new world for me, I can promise you that much. Still gettin' the hang of it."

"Ah. Well, you're a nice-looking man. Very charming. I doubt you'll be on the market too long. Makes me wish I weren't dating someone." She took an elaborately engraved case from her purse, then stood and handed Rourke a calling card. "My contact information and my telephone number. Like I said, I have a steady boyfriend, but it was nice of you to make the effort to come over and visit us." She sat again. "And if you ever need any equipment or radio advertising, let me know."

"Yeah, I sure will." He dug his wallet from his hip pocket and handed her his card. It was dog-eared at both top corners. "I'll order your drink. Lisa's too. Even though she's married."

"Thanks."

"Yeah, thanks," Lisa echoed.

"Okay, then. Great. Pleased to meet you." He returned to his table and huddled and talked with the three men there, and they all did a poor job of attempting to appear casual and less than fascinated.

"Paul Rourke seems like a good egg," M.J. said.

"True, I suppose, but why'd you give him your phone number?"

"Hell, Lisa, it's my business phone. It's not like I sit in the lobby at the reception desk and answer the calls myself. Plus, how hard is it to find my numbers? And why not, huh? Nice guy, not creepy. Not pushy. Why be a bitch because he thought we were attractive enough to hit on? Good for him, I say. And I didn't want to castrate him in front of his buddies, now did I?"

"He did have a pleasant vibe." Lisa glanced at Rourke's table, then at the karaoke machine. A spotlight was trained on the small stage. A row of colored bulbs was also burning, the reds, yellows and blues mingling with the smoke and blending the hues near the machine. A man was playing a video trivia game at the bar. "Still, it must be sad to live on the road like that, traveling and selling and drinking with people—especially shit-heels like Joel Hammond—you're kind of acquainted with in hopes of moving a few more units or hitting your quota."

"Well, not necessarily, and I should know, shouldn't I? You sure are grim and pessimistic recently. I'd rather think he just landed a big sale and is enjoying free drinks on a corporate expense account. Chatting up pretty girls like us." A waitress brought two margaritas, and they raised them in Rourke's direction. He replied by lifting his beer. "I tell you what's sad: Some laid-off banker or fired teacher at a mall kiosk, pushing miracle cleaner or nail buffers or log-home kits or cell-phone accessories or time-share deeds. A kiosk, not even a real store, mind you, just an aisle shanty. *That's* down in the heels. I can't even look at them. I hate it for 'em. Hurts."

"Funny you should mention cell phones. I need to borrow yours."

"Now?" M.J. reached for her purse. "Who're you calling? Joe?" She rested her cigarette in an ashtray notch, the filter tipped up. "Or your boyfriend."

"I don't have a boyfriend."

"Right."

"I don't," Lisa repeated.

"Whatever."

"I need to use it for a few days, please. Around the first of March. You can leave it with me, and I'll FedEx it back to you."

"I have three. Which do you want? Equipment, radio or personal?"

"If the personal shows your name, I'd prefer that one."

"I'll just bet you would." M.J. pursed her lips. "Where are we supposedly going, you and me?"

"The Bahamas. Paradise Island. The Ocean Club. You might want to mention it on your Facebook page. What a great time we're having, sent from your laptop while we're there. Joe's your Facebook friend, isn't he?"

"Can I have sex with Joe after he divorces you? What's the dear-friend waiting period on that?" M.J. was bent over her purse, sorting through her phones.

"No."

"Can I go too? I mean *really* go? I'd bring my beau, Brian, and we'd tour the island in style. My treat. I hear the Ocean Club's swank as hell. And I'd like to get a look at this Brett Brooks character."

"I think we'll do better by ourselves."

"How many times have you seen this guy? Besides your big night in Roanoke? A suitcase date is not too far below the hundred-dollar, diamond-chip, preengagement ring."

"We had a nice sober lunch in Salem and a quick cocktail at a bar in Greensboro. Bowling and beers one night, which was a blast. Neither of us had ever bowled. Plus phone calls and e-mails. Brett's a handsome man, really hot, and good company, smart as hell, too, but you and I both realize a big part of this is just the timing, sort of where I was in my life when he asked me to have a drink."

"I mean, wow, how do you go from twenty years of model marriage and a dog by the fireplace to flitting off to the Caribbean with a guy you've known for a few hours? If you ask me, it seems too quick and half-baked. One day you're here, the next day you're in the Bahamas. Soon you'll be flying to California to screw a man you met on the Internet."

"Brett Brooks has been around forever—he's not some con-artist loser sending me a bus ticket to shack up in his mom's basement. I've spent time with him. And I want it to be spontaneous. I want it to be off the cuff and sudden. Crazy. Romantic, with all the ribbons and curlicues, not some motor court in Danville. That's the point. That's exactly what I'm missing in my plodding life."

"A happy house and a straight, faithful, employed, handsome, smart, funny man without needle tracks or a liquor demon are damn near priceless. Trust me on that."

"True, but here's something I can tell you from a couple decades in the domestic-relations business: Crock-Pots and comfortable couches are the killers. The middle of the road often leads to a lawyer's office."

"Well, even though I'm against this in principle, you know I'll cover for you and lie and scheme and do whatever it is accomplices are supposed to when their friend has a fling." M.J. laid a cell phone on the table and slid it toward Lisa. "It has to be exciting, for all kinds of reasons. I get that part." She leaned in and smiled mischievously. "The first of it, the front end, the start of a romance, nothing can compare." She brought her margarita to the middle of their table and encircled the glass with both hands. "Nothing can top *new*. As my batty Uncle Luther used to say: 'It's better than hard liquor and White Owl cigars.'"

"I mean, I love Joe, absolutely, no doubt, but I've had so much fun lately it doesn't seem fair that I can't . . . do this and not feel guilty or damage my marriage. There's no going back, either. If Brett and I have sex, there's no way to cordon off adultery. Even if you stay with your husband, it's not the same. Big ugly scar. You're a cheater. You can't really patch it so it's repaired. There's a major difference between 'I've always been faithful' and 'I've only screwed around with one other man.' And if I start seeing Brett, I'm thinking, well, how long would it continue? I'm sure not planning to leave Joe."

"Listen, marriage was a nightmare for me. Talk about scars." M.J. was briefly somber. She tapped a phone's screen for no reason. "I'm hardly the person to give advice on the subject. But years and years with the same guy, no matter how handsome, how perfect he is, well, I don't know if . . ."

"The worst of it is that I feel like a total ingrate and harpy. I *should* be happy with my situation. Who wouldn't be, right? Of course, you can't help how you feel. Not much I can do there."

"Ha. Now we're talkin'. Next comes the other monster cliché of adulterers and slip-arounds: 'It's not him, it's me.' I'm waiting for you to trot out that beaut. Or the classic 'I love him, I'm just not *in love* with him.'" M.J. grinned at her, almost smirked. "And you're all ornery because he praises the dog and does a stupid little knock on your office door—stuff a lot of us would see as *personality*." She paused, and they were both silent for a moment. "But fun is fun, and life is short," she noted sincerely, "and nobody should be waking up miserable if there's a reasonable alternative."

"Listen, you lose your mom and then watch your invincible daddy die on a rubber sheet with IV dope drips pouring straight into his blood, and you learn real damn quick how short life is. Okay? You wind up waiting by a sickbed, watching the suffering and indignities firsthand, and you can make the case that shit is just cruel and random and there's no honest scorecard at the end, so, hey, we all ought to have some leeway before we hit the line for our own heart caths or radiation treatments. You school yourself not to brood about all this, and after a while you stop talking about it, but *my* act one is finished and the curtain's dropped, and every single day I realize there's only so much left."

"I'm sorry, Lisa. It had to be awful, especially your daddy."

"White Owls? Aren't they called blunts now? The cheap cigars you fill with pot or more serious dope? At least that's what we see in court."

"Yeah, well maybe crazy Uncle Luther was ahead of his time."

"Could be," Lisa replied, distracted. She was pointlessly tearing strips from a cocktail napkin and scattering white shreds in front of her.

"I remember you had your Tampa Nuggets and Swisher Sweets too. But the Owls were the aces in his world."

"It's also possible," Lisa said, "that brown booze and a filling-station cigar aren't really all they're cracked up to be."

CHAPTER SEVEN

A partially peeled banana with a bite missing, a black-stubbed cigarette and its ashes near the center of a bread plate, a tourist coffee mug from Niagara Falls, a saltshaker, a scrap of toast and a streak of grape jelly, a butter knife tipped purple with the jelly, a lighter and a wadded paper napkin were Lisa's accessories at the kitchen table the following morning, a Friday. She was awake at dawn, early for her, before Joe, and was lolling in a wooden chair when he and Brownie appeared, the dog in the lead, four sets of hooked nails clicking against the floor. Joe scooped dry food from a tin container and dumped it into the dog's bowl, then opened a Pedigree can and spooned half the wet meat over the kibble. He covered the can with foil and set it on the counter, next to the sink, the remainder saved until Brownie's supper.

"What's your schedule today?" he asked, bent into the fridge, shuffling cartons and bottles and Tupperware so he could get the orange juice from the top shelf. He wasn't looking at her when he spoke, was turned completely away, the words vanishing into the cold air and leftovers.

"Hmmm?" she said, though she had understood him.

"What're you doing today?" He had the juice now and was pouring himself a glass. He joined her at the table. He neglected the juice carton, left it beside the dog food, its white plastic top on the other side of the sink, dropped there as soon as it had been unscrewed.

"District court in the morning. Hair this afternoon. I've told you twice about my appointment." She rearranged herself in the chair, no longer slouching.

"Oh," he said. "What kind of case?"

"Do you think I should wear my hair shorter?"

"Sure," he said. "If you want to." There was no inflection in his voice.

"I thought you liked it this length," she said.

"I do."

"Then why do you want me to cut it?"

"I didn't say I wanted you to cut it," he told her. "DUI? Is your case a DUI?"

"Why are you ignoring me?" she demanded.

"I'm not."

"So you don't like my hair this length?"

"I honestly like every style you've ever worn," he said, practically begging to be let alone. "If I don't, I'll tell you."

"So if I cut it, you'll be okay with that?"

"Yep. Fine."

"I might just tell her to trim the ends and try to grow it longer."

Joe didn't reply.

"Maybe I should try some new color. Add some pizzazz. I'm so tired of the same bourgeois helmet. It's starting to look like crap. More and more gray to battle."

"You have gorgeous hair."

"So you think I shouldn't color it? Maybe some highlights? Could you please give me a little input?"

"I have," he said. He sipped his juice, lowered his gaze. "We've plowed this field a million times, Lisa. Your hair's great—long or short or medium. You're beautiful. You are. I promise you are."

"I should leave it alone?"

"I'm not sure I have a lot to add."

"Maybe I'll just have her shave my head and dye my eyebrows green. How would that be?"

"Different, for sure." Joe stood up. The dog was crunching the dry food, the occasional brown chunk falling back into the bowl.

"For sure," she repeated. "It's like you have zero interest in my appearance."

"Sorry, but you always choose well. I'm easy to please."

"How about you declare long or short? Could you at least do that much and stop being so damn passive-aggressive?"

"Listen," he said, pique etching his voice, "we have this same conversation every month. Same predictable, tedious discussion, and there's no good answer for me, is there? Even worse, no matter how your hair looks, even if Vidal Sassoon himself manned the scissors, I can guarantee that when you get home from the beauty parlor—or whatever you call it—you'll be pissed about the results and snap at me and be grouchy for at least a day. It would be great if you'd simply leave me out of it, make a choice, skip the harangue and be happy about the hundred bucks you've spent."

She glared at him.

"No offense intended." He put his glass in the sink, next to a pot of last night's shoepeg corn, the kernels covered over by oily scum.

"Thanks, Joe. Thanks so much. You're a champ. The best. Brilliant. You and Vidal Sassoon both."

"Fine, okay. I'm an ogre and a stooge. You're a minor deity. Far be it from me to offer advice that might actually be worthwhile."

She scowled at him. "And please make certain you leave the juice right where it is with the cap off so I can deal with it, okay? Leave it there on the counter like always. Talk about predictable."

She did, by god, correct her hair, stomped into the Hairport Salon still nettled and exasperated and anxious about Nassau to boot, and she told her gal Melanie, even before the cape was in place, that something had to give. "I swear," Lisa groused, "I look like a cross between the Cowardly Lion and a guest-star hussy from *Knots Landing*." Three hours later, she walked to her car with her hair styled dramatically shorter and its color noticeably softer, satisfied and pleased with her choice, snips, strands and thick brunette chunks ringing the chair, sliced from their roots, waiting for the broom and dustpan.

To his credit, Joe made it a point to compliment her, not when she came home on Friday, the both of them still miffed, but the next morning at the bathroom vanity, where he told her the changes were truly an improvement, very original and sexy. "Great googly moogly," he unfortunately added as she stood, clad in nothing but her underwear, a handheld mirror put away in a drawer before she left to dress.

"Thanks," she said.

．　　．　　．

The following Sunday, they met Neal VanSandt at his mother's property. Neal was already at Lettie's trailer, ahead of their three o'clock meeting time. A white cargo truck was parked parallel to the porch, its rear door rolled open and wire cages stacked inside. A tall, muscular man, conspicuously tanned and groomed, was standing with Neal. "Ross Sanctuary" was woven into the fabric above the left pocket of his short-sleeve shirt, "Don" was embroidered above the right. He was not wearing a jacket, even though it was forty degrees at best.

Neal was his usual skittish, incomplete self, a collection of shuffles and tentative handshakes and scattershot glances. Don from the Ross Sanctuary introduced himself and thanked Joe and Lisa for coming to help with the rescues. He seemed bullish and clumsy chasing down the cats and dogs, but persistent. He cursed a cat that was nimble and difficult to trap. Neal took forever to cage even the friendliest dogs, appeared timid and halting, reluctant to shut the wire door on any of the animals. They needed over an hour to gather all of Lettie's remaining creatures and load them into the truck.

"How long will it take you to get to Bradenton?" Joe asked as Don was fastening the cargo door.

"It's a serious haul. Near twelve hours."

"What about the animals?" Lisa quizzed him. "Certainly they can't stay jammed in a dark cargo area for that long."

"I'll stop at a motel tonight. Too far for me to make it home today. I'll set 'em all out in the parking lot, feed and water them, and make sure everybody's safe and sound." He finished securing the door, pulled a lever tight, metal against metal. "I'm not supposed to, but depending on the weather sometimes I'll carry a bunch of the littlest ones with me and let them stay in my room. Dogs, mostly they'll be okay in the truck. I'll have the whole gang at the shelter for the vet to check by noon tomorrow."

"That's quite a ring you got there," Lisa noted. Don was wearing a garish gold ring, chunky and bright, the surface almost the size of a quarter. "Very nice."

"Gift from my wife. Thanks." Neal was standing beside him, silent, toeing into the dirt drive with tiny staccato kicks.

"Hope we didn't cause you too much trouble," Joe said.

"Believe me, it wasn't so bad." He grinned and offered his hand to Joe. "I need to hit it if I'm goin' to make any kind of schedule."

"Safe travels," Lisa told him. They shook hands as well, then she covered her mouth for an instant. "Oh, I didn't notice your manicure. I hope you didn't ruin your nails chasing these varmints through the mud and bramble."

Don held his meaty brown hands in front him, at chest level, and ran his eyes across all ten fingers. "Nah, I'm good. No problem. Wouldn't be the worst that's ever happened to me in this line of business. Least nobody was bit."

"How long you been working at the shelter?" Joe asked.

"A while. Several years. Started in 2004. Promoted to the office in 2008. Air-conditioning and a desk sure as heck beats shoveling the pens." He chuckled. "Thanks again. And thank you, Mr. VanSandt." He placed his emphasis altogether on the first syllable. *Van*Sandt. "We're glad we could arrange this." He patted Neal's shoulder.

"Okay," Neal replied. "Me too. Thanks for comin'."

"The paperwork's at the office," Joe told Neal. "How about you swing by, and I'll sign everything and turn over your mom's keys and checkbook to you? It'll all be yours from here on out."

"I'll, uh, follow you," he said.

The Ross Sanctuary truck left first, straddling ruts and gullies, slowly weaving a path to the hardtop, its brake lights flashing red for most of Lettie's driveway. The Stones came next, trailed by Neal.

"Are you getting some weird vibe from this?" Joe asked Lisa as he eased them toward the state road. "I have pretty dull antennae, so it takes a lot to register with me, but did you sense something peculiar? Maybe it was just being at Lettie's, her being burned to death, the finality of it, and Neal's a fucking basket case, so you toss his general strangeness into the mix, and maybe that's it, maybe it simply is what it is."

"Yeah, the whole deal struck me as off-center. Can't say why either. For me, Neal is creepy. Bell-tower-and-sniper-rifle creepy, so maybe that explains it. I'm glad to be finished with him. Delighted to put this behind us. Especially since we've done this pretty much for free, Joe."

A scrawny cat, yellow with fixed round eyes, appeared on the side of the drive, ramrod perched on a red-clay bank, in the midst of quartz rocks and wan winter weeds, and stared at the caravan departing Lettie's.

"Damn it," Joe exclaimed. "We missed one."

"Huh?"

Joe pointed. "There. A cat."

"Well, stop," Lisa told him. "What a pitiful little thing."

He pressed the brake pedal and shifted to Park, but as soon as Lisa opened the door, the cat was gone, slipping through a thicket into deep woods, so quiet not a leaf rustled or a twig sounded, away from Lisa and Joe and help and steady, store-bought food and clean water in a silver metal bowl. Lisa climbed the bank and searched several paces into the trees, called "kitty, kitty, kitty," in a sweetly inviting voice, but nothing came of it.

They waited for Neal outside their office, and then Lisa and Neal stood alongside Joe while he sorted through his mess of keys, the three of them silent, not even small talk. Joe inserted an old key and jiggled and coaxed the balky dead bolt until it finally clunked open. He flipped on the waiting room light, and they walked down the hall into his office. Joe sat behind his desk, Lisa leaned against the wall and Neal kept standing, hovering at the corner of the desk, at loose ends as always.

Joe removed a sheet of paper from a drawer and reached toward Neal with it. "Here's the document I've prepared renouncing any interest in your mom's estate. I'm resigning as executor and transferring everything to you."

"Thank you, Mr. Stone." He took the paper but didn't examine it.

"I've already signed it, and I had it notarized on Friday since I knew you'd be here when our secretaries are off. Lettie's estate is now yours, free and clear."

Neal inhaled so hard that it was audible, mouth-sucked a breath like a spelling-bee child about to embark on an obscure word, and he banged against the desk leg with a telltale shoe, and he fumbled through one front trouser pocket, then the other, until his search finally made it to an inside coat pocket, and he pulled out a folded sheet of paper and spread it to full size. "Mr. Stone, I, uh, you know, if you do your own legal work, then you're your own fool, so I thought I should have my separate lawyer draw up the papers. I hope you don't think it's because I don't trust you, or I don't appreciate everything you've done."

"Pardon?" Joe frowned, more befuddled than irritated.

"I, uh, figured it was my responsibility to get the papers written, and since it's legal business and you're a lawyer and I'm not a lawyer, I kinda went ahead and had the official stuff done elsewhere. Not because I didn't trust you or Mrs. Stone. I just thought I should. Thought it was required. Thought it was best." He jigged his eyes in Lisa's direction.

"Well, sure, okay." Joe slanted forward. "Could I see what you have there?" He took the paper from Neal and read it. "Neal, if you compare these, you'll see they're virtually identical. Word for word the same, okay? Most of this stuff comes straight out of a form book. All lawyers use basically the same template. I'd be happy to sign your version instead, if that would make you happy. Doesn't matter to me."

"May I see it?" Lisa asked. She stepped to the desk and took Neal's paper from her husband. "Right from the book," she said, but her voice was strained, the nonchalance forced. "Same form we use." She shrugged, the beat between the rise and drop of her shoulders overplayed.

"Well, now I guess I don't know what to do," Neal said. "Can I see 'em both?" He arranged the papers side by side on Joe's desk and finger-read each copy, mouthing and mumbling phrases as he went. "Yeah, okay, yeah, they seem totally alike to me." He smiled, relieved. "And yours is already signed and notarized and mine isn't, and it's a Sunday, so there's a definite problem, so if it's legal and okay by you, I'll use yours and be on my way."

"Whatever suits you," Joe told him. "If you want, you can take ours and I'll execute yours and send it along to Atlanta. You can have a duplicate."

"No need," Neal assured him. "Since they aren't any different. I'm sorry for the trouble."

"I wish you'd asked me about this before you paid a lawyer," Joe said. "We could've saved you some money."

"No problem," Neal said. "I didn't mean to, uh, upset you or act like I don't trust you."

"No, actually, Neal, I'm glad you ran it through your own counsel," Lisa replied. "We probably should've mentioned it."

"So I reckon we're finished," Neal said. "I can't thank you both enough. On my behalf and my mom's. Don't know what to say."

Lisa moved so she was in front of Neal. "I'll bet a silk-stocking lawyer like Brett Brooks cost a pretty penny, huh?" She'd spotted Brooks's firm name and address at the lower-left corner of the stationery, embossed in conservative black letters.

"Two hundred fifty dollars. It cost me two hundred fifty," Neal said, the answer quick, hasty. "Yep, two hundred and fifty."

"Huh," she grunted. "That *is* steep."

"Brett has a solid reputation," Joe said. He cut his eyes to Lisa. "Of course Lisa's better acquainted with him than I am." He flickered a sardonic grin at her.

"Uh, I just picked him from the Internet. Off the Internet. He's in Roanoke."

"Good luck to you," Joe said, standing as he spoke. "Stay in touch, and give me a call if I can ever do anything else for you or your mom's estate. She'll be missed. Henry County's a much more ordinary place with her gone."

"Amen to that," Lisa added.

They waited quietly—each understanding the other's silence—until they saw Neal's car pass by the office window, made certain they were alone before they spoke, lest they be overheard discussing business best kept to themselves. Joe typed in a Google search for "Ross Sanctuary" while they were killing time.

"Website says Don Beverly is their chief fund-raiser and serves as their treasurer. Maybe that explains the fancy nails. He owns a rescue papillon and a Lab. Plays golf. Married. Originally from Michigan." Joe peeked over the computer screen at Lisa, then returned to Don Beverly's biography. "Huh . . . says here he's been with the organization since its founding in 1997."

"Not exactly what he told us, but who knows, maybe he was just a volunteer or some such and they're counting his service prior to being hired. Or maybe the info's wrong. Half the stuff online is inaccurate anyhow."

"Yeah." Joe continued to explore the site.

"For damn sure, I plan to check with Brett Brooks in the morning and see if I can discover anything there."

There was a small grain of unease in her tone that registered with a husband's ear. Joe stopped sliding and clicking his mouse and studied her. "Okay," he said. "Let me know what you turn up."

The next morning, she phoned Brett on her cell as she was driving to work. She veered into a Hardee's parking lot while the call was connecting, kept the Mercedes idling so she'd stay warm. A woman in a muddy Chevy LUV pickup spied her and blew the horn and waved. She looked familiar, probably a former client. The Chevy joined the other vehicles in the breakfast line, the truck's exhaust a steady, persistent cloud owing to the February cold.

"Brett?" she said when he answered his own cell.

"Yes?"

"Good morning. It's Lisa Stone."

"Morning." Brett was cagey. His voice gave away nothing.

"Are you where you can talk?"

"I am," he said, still very formal. "Hope you're doing well." He could've been speaking to his tailor or an insurance agent.

"Alone?" she asked.

"Yes." He paused. "Just left the diner. A morning ritual. Everything okay with you?"

"Fine. I'm in a Hardee's parking lot. By myself."

"Excellent. Hard to top the bacon, egg and cheese, though I avoid their burgers." He chuckled.

"Listen. Do you know a Neal VanSandt?"

"Say what? Who?"

"Last name is VanSandt. First is Neal. You recently did an estate waiver for him. Joe, my husband, renounced any interest in Neal's mom's estate. Her name was Lettie. Lettie VanSandt."

"No." Brett was emphatic. "Doesn't ring a bell, and it's the kind of name I'd recall."

"You're positive?" Lisa pressed him. "The document was on your firm's stationery."

"Yeah. Why? I thought you were calling about our most important case, the Bahamian . . . affair."

"It's this weird, loopy family, and we recently spent a red-flag afternoon with Neal and a Florida gent wearing tacky jewelry."

"Huh. Sorry, this is news to me. If we did it, something simple as that, I'm guessing one of the associates handled it. Want me to check?"

"Please. Yeah."

"What is it you need to know exactly?" Brett asked. The reception broke for an instant, caused a word to divide. "Did it go south on you? I'm not sure what you're after."

Lisa watched the woman in the Chevy collect her order, an arm, shoulder and part of a visored head stretching out from the restaurant's rectangular pickup window with a bag and then a large cup. "I'd like to discover everything you can ethically tell me, Brett."

"Okay. How come?"

The truck disappeared behind the building, came into sight again, and stopped near the Mercedes, separated by a sidewalk. A woman in jeans, black leather tennis shoes and a hooded down jacket got out and started toward Lisa. The woman was waving again, her hand held high and pistoning sideways as she walked, her smile tentative but friendly, her approach cautious, almost on tiptoes.

"Shit," Lisa said. "Hang on." She rolled down the window. She recognized the woman but couldn't recall her first name. She was a Fulcher, from Fieldale.

"Hi, Mrs. Stone."

"Good morning," Lisa said.

"I just wanted to tell you how much I appreciate all you done for me in my custody case. It's really turned out good. Them tutoring sessions has been a big boost for Odell, Jr., and my child support's comin' regular. Can't thank you enough. Not many lawyers woulda let me pay over time, either." The woman had a lazy eye that wouldn't lock; it languished and drooped and sulked.

"Oh, great, I'm glad to hear it. I am. It's kind of you to mention it." Lisa held the phone away from her face.

"Okay. Well, I hadn't run into you in a while, and I wanted to speak. My cousin was askin' about a lawyer a few weeks ago, and I told her you was at the top of the list."

"Thanks."

"I can see you're on the phone, and I don't want to be no bother. Gotta get to work. Thanks again."

"Sure. You were at Stanley Furniture? Am I remembering correctly, Mrs. Fulcher?" Lisa concentrated on her healthy eye.

"Yeah, still there. Don't know for how long in this economy. 'Bout everybody I know is laid off. Everybody drawin' unemployment or goin' to the community college on the Trade Act. Gettin' retrained." She laughed. "I reckon Henry County's gonna be full of fifty-year-old paralegals and computer programmers. Shame there ain't no jobs for 'em."

"I'm glad you're still okay," Lisa said sincerely. "Great news about your son too."

"You have a blessed day. And I told you before you can call me Cassie."

"Take care," Lisa said. She waited for her to leave and returned to the conversation with Brooks.

"Wow," he said. "That ought to make your morning, Lisa. Impressive. Not many of my clients track me down to offer attaboys."

"It was very generous of her," Lisa said. "So find out what you can about this case and the VanSandts, please. It's really spooked me."

"Why? It was routine, right?"

"The timing's just too ticklish for me, with Nassau and everything. Plus Neal VanSandt gives me the willies, and his mother's been a thorn in my side forever. I want to be certain how this fits and that I'm not missing something important."

"I'll check and call you as soon as I learn the details."

"Use my cell, please," Lisa instructed him.

Thirty minutes later, he informed her it was a simple, everyday transaction at Brett Brooks and Associates. "Bess Reed, one of the new lawyers here, handled it from start to finish. According to her, we were contacted by Mr. VanSandt himself, and he provided Bess the particulars over the phone. Very basic undertaking. Precisely as you suggested, he asked that we prepare a renouncement involving Joe Stone and this guy's mother. We did. Hell, you just print out the form and fill in the blanks. We mailed it to him in Atlanta. He paid us promptly by personal check. Which cleared."

"Too freaky, too much coincidence." She was sitting at her office desk, the door closed.

"It is odd," Brett said. "But I see it as a warm-weather, pool-drinks-and-romance, stars-aligned charm: There you are slogging through yet another drab case, and who should appear but your buddy Brett with a sly valentine at the bottom of a will disclaimer. Not every suitor could pull that off."

Lisa laughed. "You are so full of shit." She hesitated, deadened her voice. "So there's nothing to this, Brett? Happenstance before a trip? A fluke? You give me your word? Because Lettie VanSandt has been my personal albatross for years, and everything about Neal and his hiring a lawyer is suspicious to me. I'm of a mind there might be more to this than a routine dab of paperwork."

"Lisa, I swear, my hand over my heart, I don't have the first clue about these people, don't work for them, won't work for them, and I'm not part of any conspiracy, okay? From my end, there's no KGB in this, no Mickey Finns and trench coats. If I were orchestrating something sinister, why the heck would I send a guy to you with my name in neon on the paperwork? All I want to do is catch some sun and visit with you for a weekend and see where we go from there. Maybe try the fried lobster down at Arawak Cay. A cold Kalik beer. That's my only agenda."

"Okay," she said, still wary. "See you soon. I suppose."

Shortly before shipping the remainder of Lettie's animals to Florida, Lisa and Joe had brought home their two cats and made a place for them in the barn. They'd put two oval fleece beds in the tack room, along with a feeder full of kitten chow and water bowls and several toys, mostly fabric balls and vaguely avian contraptions with colorful feathers and yarn legs. The cats were probably six months old when they arrived at the farm, two lads, Pancho and Lefty, all leaps and hisses and feints and bluffs and paws batting at everything, from flecks of dust to hayseeds to the occasional ladybug, their battles usually ending with full-throttle scampers through the stalls or pop-eyed dashes up a four-by-four post.

As Lisa was leaving early on a Friday morning for the airport, Joe under the impression that she and M.J. were taking a quick girls' trip to the Bahamas, she noticed only a single cat, Pancho, roaming next to the barn, and she stopped the car, concerned because she couldn't spot his brother, and she waited without any luck for him to appear and impatiently stepped out of the car and called his name but couldn't raise him, though Pancho interrupted his lark and stared at her, crouched, his tail twitching. "Shit," she said, and despite realizing Lefty was probably in the loft, she traipsed from the Mercedes through the pasture, with its manure and muddy booby traps, her elegant, spindly heels sinking into the ground a time or two, until she located the missing cat sunning himself on a window ledge, doing as he pleased, ignoring her, and she was relieved to find him in good shape, and also relieved she wasn't traveling under a bad omen, some warning or obvious message that would compel her to stay home and scotch her plans, providence putting her to the test. She'd wash and wipe the shoes in the airport sink and be on her way.

CHAPTER EIGHT

That same Friday, Joe was at his desk revising a timber contract for a third-generation Henry County sawmiller when Betty appeared in his doorway and told him she was sorry to distract him, but there was an unusual man in the lobby who claimed he had an emergency and needed five minutes to explain his problem. He didn't have an appointment. She didn't know him from Adam. He was alone.

"Ah, let me put on the turban," Joe joshed. "It's Friday afternoon, and I'm ready to go home and enjoy the bachelor life for a weekend, so I'm guessing this is some doofus with zero money and a frivolous child visitation complaint, or it's also possible we have the classic late Friday 'urgent' driveway easement feud and running gun battle that commenced around 1975 and will continue unabated until the Rapture." He smiled and touched his temple with his forefinger. "How'd I do?"

"Well, Mr. Stone," she answered, "I have to say he's a very odd fellow." She raised her hand and cupped one side of her mouth and hushed her voice. "A little off mentally, maybe. He wouldn't tell me why he wants to see you."

"Huh. Nice. So a *crazy* man with no money and a secret emergency. You know, unless he wants to tell you what's what, I don't really feel like spending an hour listening to a lunatic's ramblings. Tell him I'm busy and set him a scheduled appointment."

"Okay."

"Did he even give you a name? He's not a regular client's relative or something? A referral?"

"No sir, he didn't. I asked more than once. I don't think he's from around here."

"Good enough. Send him along with our best wishes. If it's important, he'll keep the appointment."

Betty returned quickly, rapping on Joe's open door even though he'd already peered up from his paperwork and was looking at her. "Well, he claims he's a friend of Lettie VanSandt. Or was, I suppose you'd say."

"Ah. Now the crazy part makes sense. Has he decided to tell us what the emergency is, or are we still Ouija-boarding on that front?"

"No sir. He mentioned Lettie. He didn't tell me more. He's kind of pitiful, really."

"Wonderful. Okay, just bring him back here. We'll spend more time debating it than it'll take me to deal with him." Joe pushed the timber contract toward the middle of his desk, dropped the ballpoint he was using to make corrections.

Moments later, Betty ushered in a thin man wearing a paisley tie and a dark suit that was too large in the jacket, too snug and short in the trousers. His shoes were brown, his socks white, his hair mostly gray and buzz-cut to his skull. He appeared much younger than the gray hair suggested, his skin smooth, no trace of a beard or stubble. "This is the gentleman with the emergency," Betty announced.

Joe stood and faced the stranger, unspooling slowly and purposefully to his full height. He flipped his hand at an empty chair. "Have a seat," he said. He looked at Betty and thanked her and she took the cue and departed the office. Joe waited for the man to sit, then did the same. Brownie had shifted on his pad so he could inspect the visitor. The dog lifted his head, tightened his lips, appeared on the verge of a growl, seemed unusually alert.

"Thank you so much, Mr. Stone," the man blurted. "I understand I didn't have an appointment. Thank you." He twisted and corkscrewed in the chair, but his face and features and aspect were almost serene. "I'm sorry I couldn't schedule a time in advance." His mouth twitched on the left side when he finished his sentence, the slight corner of his lips jerking toward his ear.

"No problem," Joe assured him.

Brownie sighed, relaxed, lost interest.

"I don't want to waste my five minutes." He sounded sincere, no irony or sarcasm. "I, I—"

"Let's begin," Joe interrupted him, "by you telling me your name. Who you are."

The man swiveled to check in the direction of the door, then searched the entire room with his eyes, tracing an obvious square as he surveyed the ceiling, the last place he inspected. He made no bones about what he was doing, didn't attempt to conceal it, though his face remained calm and satisfied as he scanned corners and walls and crown molding and ducked to peek around the desk in front of him. "I realize I couldn't see the tricks if they were hidden. But you already know that. My name is Steven Downs. Dr. Steven Downs. A degree in biochemistry from UCLA." His lips twitched again, the tic evidently chronic.

"Okay," Joe said. "Nice to meet you, Dr. Downs."

"Thank you. Is the dog safe? A known quantity?"

"Uh, yeah. His name's Brownie. I've had him for years. I'll vouch for him." Joe kept a .38 Ruger in his desk. He discreetly cracked the drawer. "I understand you mentioned Lettie VanSandt. You realize she's deceased?"

"Yes. You bet I do." His voice was animated, almost a yelp, but his expression held, stayed curiously tranquil.

"Okay. So how did you know Lettie?"

"We met on the Internet. At Token Rock."

"I'm not familiar with it," Joe said. "Pot and music?"

"No. There's a great deal of numerology information there."

"Right. Why am I not surprised? Though Lettie didn't own a computer. I'm fairly sure she didn't."

"She used the library."

"So what brings you here today, Dr. Downs? Late on a Friday afternoon?"

"I know you think numerology is a farce. It might be in some applications. But Pythagoras believed much of the world can be explained mathematically. I enjoy it; so did Lettie. I have an advanced degree in a hard science, so—"

"Fair enough." Joe folded his arms across his chest.

"To complicate things, you'll discover I've been institutionalized for psychological concerns. I can't deny it. So you're aware. Full disclosure."

"I appreciate the candor."

Downs took a breath. He was silent while he eye-checked the room again. "Lettie was murdered." His expression showed no distress.

"By, uh, whom? Count von Count?"

"No. For goodness' sake. I'm trying to be helpful. I'm not a fool, Mr. Stone. Making light of me and my efforts gains us nothing. Just because I have a facial tic and have suffered with some issues doesn't mean I'm not reliable."

"I'm sorry. So who killed Lettie?"

"I suspect a smart fellow like you found her death puzzling. Am I correct?"

Joe shrugged. "Lettie was odd. We checked it out. She was cooking meth and her lab exploded. Hard to locate any motives elsewhere."

Downs smiled. "Lettie was different. No doubt. But surely you don't really think she was a dope dealer. Lettie?"

"So what's your theory, Dr. Downs?" Joe unfolded his arms, leaned forward and rested his elbows on his desk.

"Before I was unfairly and illegally discharged, I was employed by Benecorp. I'm certain you've heard of this corporate beast?"

"Sure. Of course. Pharmaceuticals. Tedious TV ads during every sitcom and football game. They are, what, right up there with Merck and Pfizer?"

"Not quite as big as Pfizer. But well ahead of Merck. Fifty-five billion a year."

"Okay. And they fired you. And this is connected to Lettie . . . how?" Joe leaned away from the desk and rested his head against the back of his chair.

"Yeah, I know. Give me just a minute to explain. So Lettie sent me a compound. To test for her. I'm a genius in the lab. You can ask anybody. I actually hold three equipment patents. The compound was an epidermal regeneration formulary. As I understood its mechanism, it operated via the transforming growth factor alpha. A wound-healing salve, in plain terms. One of my specialties. That's why she sent it to me and I agreed to shake a beaker for her. I have other specialties too." His expression changed for the first time, became earnest and emphatic. "I did not run it on Benecorp's time. Though that's my job, right, to do research? I did it on a Saturday. I was a conscientious employee. I was wrongly fired." His point made, the emphasis in his features vanished, the creases around his eyes flattened out and disappeared. "Maybe we could discuss that, too, how I was treated."

"I don't practice employment law," Joe said brusquely. "Plus, I'm assuming your termination occurred in another state. I'm only licensed here in Virginia."

"Sorry. Yeah, I'm letting myself get sidetracked. Wasting my appointment. But you already know that."

"Let me see if I can anticipate a few things and move us along. Lettie discovered you on a numerology website and sent you one of her thousands of wacky poultices. It was supposed to promote wound healing or wound care. Did it work?"

Downs clapped his hands together in front of his chest and kept them clasped there. "My gracious, no. Might have made a good solvent. That's an old lab saying." His mouth pulled left twice.

"Figures. No big surprise."

"But you see, Mr. Stone, all Benecorp lab data is stored and some is processed and analyzed and compared blindly, automatically, Hail Marys and cold hits. A clever program called MissFit Matrix. A separate department. Actually takes a sample of your compound and applies it to other projects, the big stuff like certain cancers. AIDS. The money-makers. It's a brilliant technology. The magic is being able to replicate the control subject cheaply and accurately. Make it cost effective to create thousands of petri dishes, is how I describe it. Benecorp can. Pretty incredible. Anyhow, Lettie was in the system, and the system is always scanning. Hunting. People introducing Lettie VanSandt's failed concoction to everything under the MissFit sun. Other employees who still have jobs often didn't follow procedure and didn't enter their compounds into the system. It's a little extra effort. I always did. But I was fired, not them."

"Sounds like remarkable science."

"Indeed. We dummy into a lot. Fleming accidentally discovered penicillin. But you already know that. The microwave oven—luck.

LSD, even Viagra. All were happenstance. Outside the trials and protocols. Fahlberg discovered saccharin while experimenting with coal tar."

"Lettie's medicine was a failure for its intended purpose but was effective in some other area?" Joe slid forward in his chair. He scrutinized Downs.

Downs finally dropped his hands. "Correct."

"Okay, I'll bite. What does it do?"

Downs commenced his searching again. He made several square trips around the ceiling. He locked on to Brownie, who ignored him. "Don't have any idea," he said. His lips tracked left, and he swiped the corner of his mouth with a fingertip.

"Huh?"

"I only know it was something worthwhile. Very, very valuable."

"And this formula with its unknown use, if I'm following your theory, Dr. Downs, somehow got her killed?"

"For certain."

"For certain," Joe repeated, practically mocking him. "And how, pray tell, do you know this?"

"My supervisor contacted me and asked about the composition. History, trials, origin. My Grand Pooh-Bah supervisor. His name is Anton Pichler. No scientist at all. Guess what degree he holds?"

"Couldn't say," Joe answered.

"Guess," Downs insisted.

"You're wasting your five minutes."

Downs's expression remained serene. "Yes, but I imagine you'll at least let me finish before you kick me to the curb."

"Depends on how long it takes," Joe said.

"MBA. He has an MBA. Studied basic chemistry at Ole Miss. Two whole semesters in their vaunted, world-renowned department. Wowee. Moron couldn't even light a Bunsen burner. He's my boss. He's with a big cheese from MissFit, a woman, Mrs. Meade, and those people are top-notch. They're rude and aloof, but I give them their due. I immediately add up what's happened. No reason not to tell them the facts. Lettie's miss with me is a fit elsewhere. Or at least there's some promise. There are plenty of false starts with the program."

"Sounds good so far."

"Indeed. Ah, but you knew our girl Lettie. I offer Pichler my results and the basics. I truly am not privy to the precise composition of 'VanSandt's Velvet Number 108.' That was her designation. Silly, huh? 'VV 108.' It was topical, by the way. Not oral. They asked me to call her."

"Okay."

"And I did." Downs's grin segued into a snicker. "Lettie flew hot. Was furious. I told her VV 108 was a failure for its intended purpose. The good news was that it evidently had utility to Benecorp and some interesting properties and a promising application. Not what she wanted to hear."

Joe smiled as well. "Oh, damn," he said. "I can imagine the conversation."

"She thought highly of you, Mr. Stone. You obviously have a sense of her personality. She was angry because I suggested it couldn't do what she said it would, and that was the extent of her perspective. She was positive it was a viable wound compound. I was certain it was not. She took it poorly. We'd been friends—well, correspondents, you might say—for many years. We'd even met at some numerology conventions. Broken bread together."

"Classic," Joe said. "Just perfect. You truly could tell Lettie she'd accidentally stumbled onto the cure for death itself, but if it didn't fit with her exact plan, she'd argue with you until she was blue in the face."

"Yes. Worse, not only are you telling her that her brainchild is a failure, but you're also telling her you nonetheless want it. For purposes that are secret. Purposes you will not share with her. Ha! Many people who aren't as suspicious and quirky as our friend Lettie would be reluctant, don't you agree?"

"Perhaps. No doubt it would cause Lettie to go paranoid, I'll grant you that much."

"Did she mention this project to you? VV 108?"

"Listen. Lettie had so many balls in the air, so many grievances, so many complaints, so many inventions and concoctions, so many stupid legal jihads that I guess she might have, but I didn't keep a list of all the windmills she and Sancho were trying to slay. But, now that I think about it, I do recall her, a few days before she died, wanting to sue a drug company because it was trying to steal something or other. She lit into me as I was headed to lunch. Of course, thousands of corporations had already stolen thousands of her other inventions over the years. It was a never-ending battle for her. I heard it monthly, if not weekly."

"She brought it to your attention. Confirms my story."

"Not with any specificity, and like I just told you, she'd pestered me with a zillion variations on this tale."

"At any rate," Downs continued, "Pichler blames me. I can't deliver the goods. Can't persuade Lettie to so much as accept his phone call. She threatens lawyers in an e-mail to me and Pichler. You were probably the lawyer. Pichler is livid and scrambling. MissFit really wants this. Around the same time, Mr. Seth Garrison, the man himself, was on site. Mr. G. The G-Man. He's almost invisible, but there's a rumor he's there. I saw him board a helicopter. He's very famous and powerful, Mr. Stone. But you already know that. Rarely seen. He *is* Benecorp. Among other things."

"Why not just take it? Lettie's a loon living in a backwoods trailer. It would be a piece of cake to have some scientist—Pichler, for instance—stand over a counter and stare at a test tube and scream 'Eureka!' and claim he'd suddenly invented a great new medicine. Benecorp is huge. They could grind her down for years. They could build a lab record and show their experiments and pass her off as an eccentric phony, which in fact she was to some degree."

"They could. Yes. But remember they still have me as a problem, and they still have her, and she's a squeaky wheel and a talker and a happy litigator and a gadfly, and no matter what, my notes and my entries are in the system."

"Yeah, your notes say it was a failure. How would anyone ever know it was this formula, Lettie's Velvet, that wound up hitting the jackpot?"

"Well, if you discredit me and purge the system, and MissFit and Pichler and Meade elect to be dishonest, they're home free except for poor Lettie—and how, ladies and gentlemen of the jury, could she know the detailed and secret composition of a drug they claim to have created? Make no mistake, despite her oddities, I liked her. She took care of neglected creatures. But you already know that."

"Do you have anything at all beyond your speculation? Any evidence that would make this more than a colorful hunch?"

"Of course you would ask me. Understand I'm fighting the leviathan here. So I've tried to prepare our case. First: I'm not sure even Benecorp can erase phone records. If they tried, it would be a battle of a big powerful corporation—Benecorp—versus a big powerful *incompetent* corporation—the phone company. Hard to whip incompetence. For sure Pichler called her from his number."

"Easy to explain. He was responding to her question or her threat to sue his company or your request to explain the failure of her latest juju. A phone call is a phone call. Next?" Joe's one-word demand was professional, objective. He wasn't rude to Downs.

"I have an e-mail from Lettie. We talked too. On the phone. They sent 'negotiators' here, right here to Martinsville, Virginia. Under the radar. Hush-hush. They threatened her. Warned her. She was spooked. Afraid." Downs ended with another tic, and his eyes shut simultaneously with the lip spasm.

"Unfortunately, Lettie isn't around to confirm any of this."

"But I have the smoking gun, Mr. Stone. Lettie gave me the plate number for their car."

"Uh, Doctor, I'm afraid that's hardly 'smoking.'"

"You can trace the license plate. Listen, it's not going to belong to Mr. Garrison. But you already know that. Or Pichler. Pichler probably couldn't pass the test to get a learner's permit. But I bet if you check, it will be irregular. What would you lose? The car was at Lettie's around September second or third or fourth or fifth. Early September. She sent me the e-mail on the fifth and said they'd just been there."

"It'll probably come back to a rental company. Big deal. And I doubt they'd give me any information about the rental particulars. And so what if the car was in fact registered to Benecorp?"

Downs's face remained placid. He leaned forward to Joe's desk and raised a legal pad and a file and another file, peered underneath them, always searching. "Well, if the plate isn't kosher, at least it might make you consider the possibility of power in numbers. Numerology." Downs summoned a smile, and he came off, momentarily, as quite sane and composed, his inflection, features, demeanor and message all briefly in sync. He reached into his inside coat pocket and withdrew a partial fist, stood and hunched over and deposited a matchbox on the desk. "The number," he said, "is inside." He glanced at the ceiling, examined the window. "The technology is such, Mr. Stone, even the basic technology, that a satellite could read every number I've written. Clear as a bell. They'd see it better than you can. Be careful. But you already know that."

Joe made no effort to camouflage his skepticism, his amusement. He laughed at Downs, dismissively. "Yeah, sure, I know that. And tell me again why it matters, especially given that *they* already have the number, right? It was their rental. Hardly a secret to them."

Downs began sawing his chin with his thumb. "A warning for future reference. And believe you me, Benecorp is watching and listening. Listening and watching. To me. You too now."

Joe didn't reply. He got up and thanked Downs for his concern and shook his hand and escorted him all the way through the waiting room to the exit door, trailing a few feet behind him at a steady pace to ensure that the scientist kept moving and didn't stray. Joe thanked him again for his interest in Lettie, and Downs, dispirited, his frail shoulders sagging, faced Joe and met him eye to eye and begged him to please at least check the license plate. Downs also warned him again to be cautious, told him, in a close whisper, that he'd be in contact by e-mail, using the alias Robert Culp.

Despite Downs's obvious peculiarities and his fantastical tale, Joe decided to open the small cardboard box on his desk. He had nagging concerns about what might actually be inside, so he stopped by the toilet and took a pair of yellow rubber gloves off the lip of a cleaning pail and returned to his desk. Wearing the gloves, he palmed the box, gauging its weight, then slid it apart and dumped out a scrap of notebook paper that had been accordion-folded to a fraction of its full size. It was only a few inches long but wouldn't rest flat, zigzagged from crease to crease. Joe slipped the gloves off and spread the paper and saw "VA ZZB-4132" was typed onto it. For the heck of it, he checked the ceiling, traced the same perimeter Downs had scanned a few minutes earlier, hesitating at the cat gouge from Lettie's final visit. He considered calling Lisa in Nassau. According to his wristwatch, it was

4:20. March 4. He smiled, shook his head. Hell, even if the number was registered to Seth Garrison himself, so what? "A snipe hunt with a witch doctor as my guide," he muttered to the empty room. "You ready, Brownie?"

Joe drove an older Jeep Wrangler with a hardtop, and he was almost to the vehicle, finished for the week and headed home, when he spotted Toliver Jackson, a spindly, balding black man on the cusp of going to seed across his belly. Jackson was a Henry County investigator, a bright, solid guy who could be counted on to testify truthfully and not take it personally and sulk and fume just because he had to answer a few aggressive questions about a Miranda waiver or chain of custody.

"Hey, Toliver," Joe called, opening the door and tossing his briefcase into the passenger seat. "You keeping crime under control and the county safe for us?" He snapped his fingers, and Brownie crouched and jumped and wiggled through the Jeep and took his spot on the rear seat, near the middle, behind the gearshift.

"You know it, Joe. Course we might be better at it if we didn't have to deal with slick lawyers scammin' Judge Gendron into freein' the guilty." Jackson smiled. The jab was friendly, Friday afternoon banter between middle-aged men who'd crossed paths in the same system for years and never hoodooed each other, never cheated or cut corners.

"Our goal is to improve your job skills. Keep you sharp."

"I got your bill for my divorce, and I wanted to say thanks again. I appreciate the hard work and the damn fair results. You didn't have to give me a discount, though. It was a long fight. I never expected it to end as well as it did."

"Glad to help. And we give all our law enforcement clients a discount. Even the rogues like you."

"Well, all kiddin' aside, I appreciate it. Sure do. Let me know if I can ever return the favor."

Joe paused, looked off. Three blocks down, he noticed Steve Draper leaving from his clothing store. The street was mostly empty, a smattering of cars, a few people. "Huh," he said, turning back to the cop, "come to think of it, your timing is pretty good. It's a long shot from an iffy character, but could you track a tag number for me? A rental, probably."

"How come you want it?"

"It's connected to Lettie VanSandt. Her estate. I'd decided not to fool with it, but I figure I'll never use the favor otherwise and you showing up right now is awfully coincidental. So yeah, if you could chase it down, I'd be grateful."

"Lettie was crazy as a bedbug. Can't say she is too much missed by those of us at the sheriff's department." Jackson pocketed both hands and studied Joe. "You're not leadin' me into anything, are you? Nothin' I can't take care of?"

"As far as I know, you're just tying off a huge, improbable loose end, okay? If that changes, I'll tell you. I'm only asking for a plate number, Toliver, not a wiretap or grand jury testimony or Daniel Ellsberg's file. Hell, I could probably locate the tag information on the Internet if I wanted to spend the time on it."

"What's the number?"

"I'll have to get it from the trash can in my office. That ought to give you a clue just how remote the possibilities are."

"Okay. Then I got to head to Figsboro. Ollie Akers's Mexicans are back for the tobacco season, and they've had some kinda cuttin' ruckus."

"You usually don't hear a peep from that bunch," Joe said. He and Jackson had started for his office, Brownie, unloaded and leashed, right with them. It was a clear, cold day, no hint of spring, and they both were still wearing winter coats.

"Same group's been comin' for twenty years or so. This is the first scrape we've had." The two men were side by side as they walked. "It'd chafe my butt if I lived in Texas or Arizona and had the illegals hikin' through my yard and cloggin' my schools and suckin' down social services dollars and refusing to *hablo* any English everywhere you go. But Ollie's crew, they're mostly here to work. You won't be findin' very many Henry County types who want to prime tobacco or pick apples or dig a ditch for Fulton Lester. Least the Mexicans aren't afraid of an honest day's work."

"Can't argue with you," Joe said, "on either point."

"Only problem I have with the Mexicans bein' here is you can't find an eight-hundred-dollar pickup or a two-hundred-pound white girl. All taken during the farming season." Jackson glanced at Joe and grinned.

"Only you," Joe said, "could cram two offensive stereotypes into such a short sentence. Didn't the sheriff send you to some kind of diversity training?"

"Nobody has a sense of humor about anything these days," Jackson griped.

"Yeah, well, Sinbad, while you're honing your comedy routines, I'd also like you to discover to whom the car was leased if it is in fact a rental. And the total mileage, the odometer when it left and when it returned."

"You won't find that shit on the Internet, huh? I'll see what I can do. So how about a good lawyer joke? Or are those off-limits too?"

"Have at it," Joe said.

"Okay. So what happens to a lawyer when he dies?"

They were almost at Joe's building. "His chances of becoming a Henry County cop increase?"

"Nope," Toliver replied. "He lies still." The officer paused for effect. "And that would apply to Mexican lawyers, Greek lawyers, English lawyers, black, white, yellow, man, woman, old, young. It's what we in the police business call race neutral."

CHAPTER NINE

Brett and Lisa's suite at the Ocean Club opened out onto a ground-level patio and a sweeping view of the ocean, and when the porter inserted their plastic key card and sidestepped away from the entrance and Lisa saw where they'd be staying, she was still wearing her Virginia clothes, and she dropped her purse and wool jacket on a counter and left Brett behind, sailed across the room, past the elaborate bowl of fruit and bottle of champagne, right through the patio doors, and she didn't stop until she hit the water, the air warm and salted, the sun close enough to do her some good, the blue and turquoise and the long horizon and lollygagging heat a sublime improvement on the dregs of a Henry County winter. A Jet Ski banged over waves, chatter from the hotel's bar meandered down the beach, a swell nudged in and rose to her knees, soaking her slacks. Her shoes were kicked off on the sand, neither of them upright, separated and pointed in different directions.

Brett waited on the patio, drinking a Kalik beer, dressed for Nassau—flip-flops, a wrinkled linen shirt—since he'd boarded a plane in Roanoke. She returned after a while and used the tub spigot to wash her feet and changed clothes in the bathroom, and she and Brett walked to the bar, which was built on a bluff's edge and caught the tail end of a trade wind, just enough breeze to register. They sat at an outside table, both of them facing the ocean. She had no plans, nowhere to be, no more ambition than to finish her drink, a tourist piña colada, and why not, she told the waiter, she was a tourist and it was the Bahamas and what could be better?

The Ocean Club was elegant and polished, a tile and mahogany showcase with British trimmings. The pool was beside a terraced garden populated by classical statues: a stone gathering of satyrs, a Hellenistic Zeus, a bare-breasted demigoddess and flitting cherubs eager to spread Bacchus's wisdom. Oddly enough, a marble FDR and Napoleon had also joined the party. Unlike her last Caribbean vacation, there was nary a T-shirt salesman or hair braider in sight, no teenagers hawking trinkets on the beach, no touts for the banana boat and booze cruise, no all-you-can-eat buffets. Their suite came with a butler, and shiny electric golf carts navigated paved trails to deliver guests to their various accommodations, the carts' only sound the brake pedal springing free as the driver started forward.

After Lisa had finished a second drink and been brought another, Brett asked if she wanted to leave and visit the casino at Atlantis, maybe shoot dice or play baccarat or try her luck at blackjack, but she told him she was happy where she was, and she scooted her chair closer to him and rested her hand above his knee, her flat palm intimate and frankly carnal against his leg.

"I don't really know, uh, what interests you," Brett said. "I guess that sounds kind of strange given our current circumstances. But tell me, okay? I hope you will."

"Hard to beat this," she answered.

"No kidding." He covered her hand with his.

It didn't take long for the alcohol to affect them, but they were high and loose, not obliterated like they'd been in Roanoke, and Lisa asked for a glass of water and a plate of fruit, had to think for a moment because the waiter inquired if she wanted her water plain or with gas. "Plain will be fine," she told him. As it slipped away in increments, the sun put on a nonchalant soiree, illustrating the sky and Technicoloring the clouds and water, and a group of gulls casually glided and dipped over the ocean, the boldest ones landing on a wooden railing at the bar to plead and screech for scraps, their heads herky-jerking, bobbing.

"Let's walk back to the room," Lisa suggested, "and watch the last of this."

"You want to take anything to drink? Should I order a traveler?"

"I saw the bottle of champagne. I think that'll be perfect."

While Brett was paying the waiter, an elderly couple passed their table, and the woman, immaculate and sweetly proper, her hat fastened with fabric strips that knotted beneath her chin, paused to speak to them and told them they were a lovely pair. Such pretty people. "And you both look so happy," she said. Her husband nodded, agreed. He was carrying a cane with a carved knob but didn't seem to need it, appeared able to stand and move around on his own. "How long have you been married?" she asked Lisa. "My Gary and I have been together for fifty-three wonderful years," she quickly added.

Lisa instinctively lifted and spread her fingers. She'd seen no reason to remove her wedding ring. She was married, and Brett knew she was married, and she was planning to stay married, and taking her ring off struck her as both pointless and naïve, akin to pretending the last two decades could be quarantined in a velveteen jeweler's box. "Twenty years this summer," she said. "My husband and I have quite a ways to go to catch you and Gary."

The lady beamed. "Are you in the movies? You're so attractive. We hear a lot of famous people vacation here. We really don't follow the culture as much as we should."

"She does look like a movie star, doesn't she?" Brett said. Jovial and relaxed, he didn't appear at all upset by Lisa's reply.

"Well, honey, you're no slouch yourself," the lady told Brett, a harmless flirt from a woman who'd no doubt been a beauty in her time. Pushing eighty, she still delivered the line stylishly.

Brett and Lisa didn't make it to the champagne, not immediately. They began kissing a step or so inside the open patio doors, slightly under roof but still a part of the lawn and ocean and the epilogue hues—blues, oranges, pinkish reds—saturating the sky. Buzzed and light-headed, she hardened her choice there, divided off her house and dog and mom-and-pop law practice, ditched the threadbare routines and millstone schedules for a needle full of passion, flew toward an obviously pernicious flame, chose a two-day jolt over her for-as-long-as-I-live promise, decided for real what she'd already decided in theory before leaving the farm, and the fact the affair was corrupt and off-limits only added to the lure, notched it higher.

Soon they were twined together on the king bed, and the run-up to sex was completely unmapped, all the particulars a glorious blank, each button or zipper or hook deliberate and joyous, every squeeze and rub loaded, nothing wasted, nothing overlooked, nothing discounted. It had been years and years since she was seventeen in a car's backseat or upstairs in a sneaked bedroom during a sorority bash, forever since she'd wanted to have sex and knew she would but had no idea what the details might bring. The sensations, touches, rhythms, all of it was foreign, erotic, the strange cologne, the unfamiliar skin, how he pieced into her. They spent half an hour taking off clothes, unwrapping, side by side, Lisa on top, Brett on top, and he removed her modest emerald-and-diamond necklace and then asked if he could put it back on her, pinched the clasp and encircled her neck after she collected her hair to keep it from interfering.

"Birth control?" he asked.

"Pills."

With the doors still apart and the curtains gathered so she could see the beach, and the night scents hinting and thickening and electric lights turning on around the property, she rolled to the edge of the bed and, naked except for her bikini panties, paraded across to the champagne and fetched it for them, and Brett uncorked it and they took pulls straight from the bottle, and while she was drinking, taking her turn, he kissed her neck and her breasts and before long he slipped his hand inside her underwear and she lay back against a bank of pillows, half-ass tried to set the bottle on the floor but didn't, so that the Dom Pérignon spilled on the covers and quickly lost its chill and wet the duvet and sheets, dampened the mattress.

They'd tracked sand into the bed, and those fine grains were wet, too, and all of a sudden the sand was underneath her calves and ankles, and she couldn't get rid of it, and it started bothering her, just a little irritating at first, then a drumbeat problem, bad enough that she thought about getting up for a towel, or maybe pulling the duvet off the bed, and she shifted and wiggled and caused Brett to accidentally nick her with his watchband. The metal bit into the soft skin high on her rib cage and distracted her more, and she lost her place and sort of had to start over, and then her conscience wasn't so smothered, resurfaced, and she began thinking and worrying and fretting, her own voice magpie-chattering in her head, no damn good for sex. Twenty years. A *vow*.

She couldn't settle her mind, couldn't cut herself free, wasn't so sure she should keep to her choice, and she decided she needed to wait, almost felt panicked. There were still two days left, plenty of time, and now she mostly wanted to be finished with what they were doing and put on warm-weather clothes and leave the room, so when Brett slid his finger inside her again, she reached down and touched him and rubbed and spit on her hand and kept rubbing and working until he was done. A ceiling fan circled above her, a tasteful lamp shone on a nightstand, a wisp of sea air curled through the curtains, and the crystal in an unused champagne flute trapped the lamplight and prismed it into low, subtle color.

"Are you okay?" he asked her. "I think we lost a little ground after the champagne spilled. Sorry."

"I'm fine," she said. "It's just . . . a lot. Even perfect, even here, it's not going to be easy. I'm, well . . . let's not dwell on it. It was exactly where I needed to be. Not too much." She caught herself wondering about an earlier flight home, the fee to change her ticket. "But I can't help . . . the guilt."

"I understand. We can move at your pace. No pressure. I'm for sure not complaining about a pretty amazing evening, but I feel bad. That was kind of one-sided. You sure there's nothing I can do for you?"

"Not for now." She was on her back, watching the fan. It moved slowly enough that she could see the four blades clearly. "Other than taking me somewhere to eat." She turned toward him. "I probably should be apologizing to you. I know we didn't come here for me to deal with my issues on your vacation." She smiled. "Let's get out of here and have some fun." She picked up the Dom bottle and there was a sip that hadn't been lost, and she downed the very bottom of the champagne, sitting there naked except for her necklace.

They showered and dressed and hopped into the resort's Range Rover, and an affable fellow wearing a pressed tropical shirt drove them to Atlantis. It was almost ten o'clock when they finally ate a meal, and they kept right on drinking, ordered a bottle of wine with their dinner. Afterward, they spotted a sign and followed an arrow and strolled on a labyrinthine path past wall after wall of huge aquariums filled with fish, eels, sharks, rays and sea turtles. The rooms were kept dim, the aquariums, some nearly as big as a city bus, were brightly lit. Lisa and Brett held hands and occasionally stopped to watch the goings-on in the tanks.

The walkway wound them back to the casino floor, where they posed for a cheesy photo seated together in an oversize prop throne, the king and queen of this gaudy paradise. They both laughed at the picture and bought it from the hotel vendor, who asked them, while he was fitting it into a cardboard frame, if they had any children and if they were enjoying their vacation on the island.

As they were leaving, Lisa was waylaid by a Wheel of Fortune slot machine. She studied it and squinted at the payout lines, and Brett asked if she wanted to give it a try.

"Yes. Do you have a dollar?" She set her cosmopolitan on a ledge in front of the machine.

"I do, but you need to bet all three lines. If you were to hit a jackpot, a buck wouldn't win you the best money."

"I'm not sure I completely understand, but I'll take your advice," she said.

"Here's a twenty." Brett handed her a bill.

"I want to pull the handle," she remarked. "That's half the fun."

"It'll be a test for us," Brett said, "to see if we're lucky together."

She fed the twenty into the slot. "We'll probably win a car or a humongous check and have to pose for a publicity photo in order to claim it." She grinned at him. "So I push this button?" she asked.

"Yep. Hit Bet Max."

The third time she played, she landed on the Spin-the-Wheel gimmick, and a recorded audience singsonged "Wheel of Fortune" through the machine's tiny speaker. Brett had her mash another button, and a colorful wheel of chance on top whirled around and slowed and the pointer barely ticked into a three-hundred-dollar space, and she shrieked "Oh, damn, Brett, we won three hundred dollars." The same fake audience clapped and cheered from inside the machine.

"Yeah. More important, we evidently have some pretty prime luck operating for us."

To her amazement, they returned to a dry, repaired bed with fresh linens and chocolates on the pillows. They kissed some more, and he took off her top and bra, but it was uncomfortable when he touched between her legs and she made him quit. Then they fell asleep half-naked and drunk, with her makeup still in place, the photograph from the casino set nearby on the nightstand, their jackpot—three crisp hundred-dollar bills—folded in half and tossed beside the goof of a picture, the paper money and silly throne shot the last image she recalled before shutting her eyes.

Regardless of how late she went to sleep, Lisa usually awoke at the same time, no clock or alarm needed, and she was up at six-thirty the next morning, the day just starting to take shape, the sky still bland and listless, the light subdued. She felt sketchy. The sides of her head ached. Her mouth was dry and stale. The coffeemaker was far too involved and complicated in the murky room, so she drank some bottled water and scrubbed her face with a white washcloth and brushed her teeth.

Yesterday, she'd called Joe from the airport while waiting in the immigration line, and an hour later she'd phoned to let him know she'd arrived safely at the hotel, the room under her name if he needed her for an emergency. She finished the water and checked her messages, discovered he'd left a voice mail at 10:33 last night, telling her to have fun and sleep well. She walked outside and shut the patio doors and used M.J.'s cell to call the farm. Brett was sleeping, his cheek flush against a pillow, his hair in a riot, still wearing the dress shirt he'd put on for their evening at Atlantis.

"What's the word, M.J.?" Joe said when he answered, his voice alert and chipper despite the hour. "You're up and at 'em awfully early for a girl on vacation."

"It's me, Joe," Lisa said. "My stupid cell is on the fritz. I'm using M.J.'s. She's still sleeping."

"Oh," he said, "even better. How's my wife?"

"Fine," she answered. "How are things there?"

"My man Brownie and I are in total command. We watched some pro hoops and busted out *Zombieland*. Polished off the spaghetti you left for me. Probably the gym and a horse ride today. I might try to replace that bad sheet of tin on the barn roof too. How are the Bahamas?"

"Fun. It's warm and sunny, and that counts for a lot. We had a nice dinner and a few drinks. Went to the casino. By the way, *Zombieland* was made for stoners and teenage boys."

"Well, I'm neither, but I have to find movies Brownie can enjoy."

Lisa laughed. "Of course."

"The casino, huh? Don't get tangled up with some high roller and run away on a yacht, okay? I imagine you and M.J. strolling through a gambling hall at night probably set off alarms and turned more than a few heads. Especially since I'm guessing M.J. was very short-skirted and you were the hottest woman in the joint."

"That's sweet," she told him and suddenly felt very affectionate toward him. She was wearing her white hotel robe and cloth slippers. The sun was rising, the ocean stirring. "But as best I can tell, we didn't attract any admirers."

"Oh, yeah, damn, I do have one gripe. I hate that friggin' Pampered Chef can opener. It's worthless. I thought you were going to buy a normal one, one I could use."

"I showed you how it works, okay? It's actually an improvement. Neat as a pin."

"Could be. But it's not an improvement over my pocketknife, which is what I used to gouge open a can of pears last night."

She laughed again. "I'm headed to find some coffee."

"Hang on. Wait a minute." She heard him moving through their house. "Now we're ready. Speak, Brownie, speak!"

The dog barked, stopped, barked some more. "You guys be careful and steer clear of shady Rasta men and time-share hucksters," Joe said when he came back on the phone. "Hey—remember when we were, what, a year out of law school and suffered through that condo presentation in Mexico so we could earn a free extra night and a breakfast coupon?"

"Yeah," she said. "The good old days."

"See you soon. I love you."

"I love you too. Give the mutt a hug for me."

She felt melancholy after she ended the call, a bit *too* unencumbered and rootless, hungover in another country, an honest to god adulterer of sorts, her companion a charming, handsome man with whom she shared a casino visit and a bar show in Roanoke as her main common denominators, but she'd struck that bargain and understood there'd be a Saturday morning with far less luster than the night before, and she hadn't traveled to Nassau to be even more pensive and gloomy than she already was in Henry County, and yesterday was textbook blue-sky romance, exactly why she'd flown away to the Bahamas, so she papered over the second thoughts and misgivings, smiled at the vast ocean and the swath of perfect green yard and the palm trees and hibiscus hedges, raised her hands as high as she could and stretched out the kinks, sins and booze-aches into surroundings that seemed quite capable of absorbing them, no problem.

She slipped back inside, checked to make certain Brett was still asleep, carefully picked and sorted through her suitcase, found her hat and sunglasses, and scrawled a note to him, wrote that she was hunting for coffee and then planning on some beachcombing; she'd see him later. She glanced at her watch before she left. The sky was lit now, and the beach was vacant, the sand smooth, not a single footprint.

She stayed gone until around nine-thirty. She and Brett had room service bring them breakfast on the patio, and even at the beginning of his morning, diminished by a night of steady carousing, he was talkative and attentive. After the young man from the hotel had set their plates and poured their coffee, Brett courteously pulled a chair from the table so she could take a seat, and he told her he wished they had more days together. She said the hotel was beautiful and thanked him for making the arrangements and mentioned that the pineapple looked like it had just been picked. He smiled and teased her about taking such a long beach walk; she'd been away for nearly three hours.

They spent the morning at the pool, and she ordered a mimosa for lunch, Brett a rum and Coke. They took a cab into Nassau and toured the town and stopped for an early dinner in the Fish Fry area, sat on a balcony and spent an hour drinking and sharing a plate of conch, fried grouper and homemade coleslaw. As they were leaving the restaurant, they laughed off a couple local drug dealers and a guy in a Toyota with tinted windows who wanted, at barely six o'clock, to take them to "the most happening club in the Caribbean." They returned to the resort, swam in the ocean and sat on the sand shivering under towels for a few brief moments until they dried.

"So what comes next?" Brett asked.

"This might sound dull, but I wonder if we could drag chairs down here and have them bring us a bottle of wine? Put on some dry clothes and sit at the edge of the water."

"I'm all for it," Brett said. "I'll start to work on the chairs." He stared out at the ocean, wasn't looking at her. There was still daylight left. "To tell the truth, I was kind of referring to longer-term plans. If that doesn't ruin the evening for you. Fine with me if we just take the rest of Nassau as it comes and worry with the details later."

"Yeah," she said, and she didn't focus on him, either. "Let's not complicate such a nice vacation."

"Sure," he told her. "Okay. But let me say one thing: I want you to understand I wouldn't jump in the middle of a twenty-year marriage for a quick party trip, even with the amazing Lisa Stone. I've never, ever been with a married woman. You're a spectacular lady—I'm guessing you've heard that for most of your life—and I wouldn't be doing this if I wasn't thinking about more than a weekend. Of course, who the hell can predict how things will or could turn out for us, and I don't want to sound like some infatuated teenager, but I realize how much you have invested. I've had a great time so far, and you're better than I imagined you'd be . . . and I had large, high expectations. So there you go. For what it's worth, I'd like to think we can manage to keep seeing each other."

"Thank you," she answered. "You're sweet to say all that. I don't guess I planned to dump twenty years for a weekend, either. But I'd rather not start exploring that road, trying to see around the bend, not here, not now." She felt another stab of remorse, and it was harder to tamp down, especially since she had only this last night remaining before her plane boarded and she'd be returned to Martinsville and her permanent address and a much sterner landscape, the butlers, fresh flowers, pool drinks, high tides and gorgeous vistas utterly and completely gone, behind her, not even saved and tucked away in snapshots.

.   .   .

Three, three, three. 3:33. The digital red numbers on the clock all matched, and when Lisa awoke several hours later and saw them, she was addled, disoriented, and for a moment there were echoes of the slot machines and casino games, and it was as if the wheels had spun to another winner and she was due a jackpot, triples in the pay window, all lined up. But there was also something spooky about the sequence, the row of fiery threes—they almost menaced the unfamiliar room, like Lucifer's signature at half strength. She rubbed her eyes. Blinked. The end number flashed to a 4.

As she came to herself and faded into her surroundings, she had to pee, that's why she wasn't sleeping, and damn if it wasn't pressing and urgent, and she realized right then it was going to sting and her bladder would vex her for at least a week, and the Azo pills and cranberry juice probably wouldn't be heavy-duty enough to remedy the infection, so she'd have to visit the women's health center in Roanoke and endure the PA's clipboard questions and Marcus Welby shtick, a steep price for a simple prescription. She scurried to the restroom and sat on the toilet, didn't bother with the light, closed her eyes and bit her lip as the urine streamed into the bowl.

The next morning, first thing, Brett slid off the bed, went to his suitcase and cartoonishly shuffled and windmilled clothes until he finally located a piece of paper. "Ah. Found it. Here you go: My last try on the last day. My eleventh-hour petition. I had the whole panel done last week. All negative for embarrassing diseases. Because we're lawyers, I brought the proof with me in case I needed it. I thought maybe that's why you're avoiding sex with me." He grinned, folded the paper into a haphazard plane and tossed it toward her. It rose quickly, a nose-up burst, then lost height and momentum and pitched to the left and augured into a pillow on the side of the bed opposite her. "Consider it evidence of my bona fides where you're concerned. You realize I literally had to give blood for the test? How about some bonus points and gold stars for the effort? A glowing letter in my permanent file? A morning of serious romance?"

"All that for me, huh? Pretty darn selfless. And what could be more romantic than STD results?" She unfolded the report and glanced at it.

"Sad to say, I woke up with a . . . well, anyhow, a problem. I'm not used to so much sex—well, so much, you know, sex like we had, with, uh, your hands. The infernal sand, maybe. And drinking. All the drinking couldn't help."

"Seriously? Are you all right?"

"It's just, uh, cystitis. If you have to know. You're mostly to blame." She'd hoped to come off as glib and droll, but didn't. "Not really. I'm only kidding, okay?"

"Sorry." He sat on the foot of the mattress. "Bummer. I'm guessing this doesn't bode well for my remaining prospects. Our last few hours here too."

They took separate flights in Atlanta, Lisa to Greensboro, Brett to Roanoke, and by the time they left each other, she was sick and glum and her crotch pained her even more, the hurt an emphatic rebuke, and she really didn't know what to say to Brett when he kissed her goodbye, right there in the busy airport amidst the hurry and swirl of strangers. The light was harsh and indifferent. The trapped air smelled of too many scents at once.

"Thank you," she said.

"You're welcome." He slid his arm around her waist. "Are you going to be able to manage? Want me to walk with you to your gate?"

"You're a sweetheart. I'll be fine. I'm just worn out."

"How should I get in touch?" Brett asked. "I'll probably have wicked withdrawal. The DTs for a couple days."

"E-mail," she said, not facing him, distracted, already heading in another direction, anxious for the shuttle and a different concourse and the flight home, rolling her small suitcase along with her, the bag poorly packed and lopsided, a threat to tip over even on the smooth, level floor. She fell in with the foot traffic and never looked back over her shoulder, never considered turning around.

Five miles from her farm, Lisa eased the Mercedes onto the shoulder of the road and switched off the ignition. She bowed her forehead until it rested against the arc of the steering wheel. Stopped there near a scrub sourwood tree and a clump of briar bushes, she wept, the regret and remorse she'd numbed on Saturday morning now raging and febrile, almost to the point she was disabled, an invalid. She cried and cried and wiped snot on her bare wrist, and when she finally gathered herself enough to consider traveling to her house, she looked through the windshield and noticed she'd pulled over beside a pasture, several acres enclosed by rusty strands of barbed wire, the brown wire sagging and lackadaisical and tacked to mismatched fence poles, the first spring weeds starting to sprout at the bases of the poles.

A black and white cow and her calf stood along the fence watching her. Two kids on Japanese motorcycles sped by. Lisa lowered the car window and inhaled fresh air. A minivan passed, followed by a tractor-trailer. The cows continued to stare, occasionally flipping their tails, the mother jawing a fescue cud, simple, contented beasts with no more than a handful of thoughts and instincts in their docile skulls.

She didn't know how she would walk through the door and face Joe. She had reasoned out her decision as much as was possible, and she understood the aftermath would be difficult. She'd tried to imagine it, dissected it in her mind, weighed and assayed, debated it for weeks, but the choice now seemed plainly foolish, her cure and fabulous antidote not even quality snake oil, her grand escape a dumb-ass detour, and she felt like a fucking dunce and an idiot and, worse, a tired, implacable cliché, because, sitting there on the side of the road, sobbing and sick, she wanted the weekend erased, realized she loved her husband and her small-potatoes hick life and all her mundane altars, and she was afraid she could never fully correct her mistake and reclaim the substantial marriage she'd bartered for a flash-in-the-pan pittance. At least she hadn't screwed Brett. At least she'd realized her error early, had mostly escaped the high-roller champagne and beautiful ocean view and kept the damage to a minimum.

Short term, the best she could accomplish was to quit bawling and snubbing and drive home and act as if she had some sense and vow to treat Joe extremely well, so that's what she did, except he was gone when she arrived. There was no note or explanation, even though she'd called before leaving the Bahamas to let him know her flight schedule. Now a cool, prickly sweat was coating her. She was worried Joe had somehow discovered her adultery and packed his bags. Her hands trembled. A streak of sunburn on her calf seared her leg. She yelled for the dog, then hurried outside and shouted his name. Searched the barn and found only the cats. Brownie was missing, too. Inside the house again, she called Joe's cell and heard it ring in the den. She peed and it stung, worse than several hours ago.

There was nothing else to do—she lit a smoke and sat miserable at the kitchen table, too frazzled and distraught to cry anymore, picking apart possibilities, flicking ashes into an empty glass, mired, speculating, hog-tied by her own reckless choices.

I deserve every last bit of this, she thought. And then some.

CHAPTER TEN

The cigarette was almost down to the filter when Lisa's BlackBerry played the chorus of "I Wanna Be Rich," and she snatched the cell off the kitchen table and clicked on, rushed a "Hey, M.J." before the phone reached her ear.

"Welcome back," M.J. said. "How come you didn't answer my call while you were gone? Saturday morning? I left you a message. Must mean either really good news or really bad news."

Lisa stubbed out the butt on the inside of the glass and dropped it into the dead ashes at the bottom. "Listen, I'm sick over this. I'm at the farm, and even before I left the Bahamas I knew I'd screwed up, and now I can't find Joe." Her voice ruptured on the last few words. She was barely able to finish her husband's name. "I got home, and he and Brownie are missing."

"Seriously?"

"Yeah."

"So what happened in Nassau? Was the guy an ogre or something? A gherkin penis? Cheapskate? Ghoulish yellow toenails? Toupee you hadn't uncovered? What?"

Lisa laughed and cried at the same time. "No. No, Brett is top-drawer all the way around. You'd be hard-pressed to find a better man." She hunted up another smoke from her purse. "But I never should've done it. It was a huge mistake. Awful. Plus I've got cystitis and ache like a two-buck hooker. I'm just miserable because of the whole stupid decision, and, I mean, you know, certainly Joe couldn't have found out, right?"

"I don't see how."

"Just idiotic," she sobbed. "I'm so angry at myself."

"Well, I kinda tried to warn you," M.J. chided her.

"No you didn't. You let me borrow your phone." She lit the cigarette.

"That's my job, right? Part of my best-friend duties once the decision is made. But, yeah, I guess I wasn't exactly trying to confiscate your passport. You seemed so blue and sad."

"The worst of it is that I thought it through and planned it. How could I have misjudged things so severely? It was great at first, but the regret sort of starting creeping in, I kind of knew, and by the time we left each other in Atlanta, I mean, jeez . . ."

"At my company, the equipment business, we call it Two Pieces With Harland. I actually write 'TPWH' on memos and loser proposals. Sooner or later, everybody falls for it in some fashion. You absolutely know how it'll end up, but you talk yourself into dinner at KFC, because, heck, it's chicken, white meat, and how unhealthy can it be, and it tastes wonderful for the first few bites, really delicious in its own greasy way, and you've added an order of the whipped potatoes with gravy, the sweet tea, and like I said, it's tasty until you eat down to about the first bone, about midway through the regular recipe breast, and then you start feeling a little full, and by the end you've got a D10 Cat dozer excavating your stomach and you're nauseous and regretting it. Two months later you sure enough do the same crazy thing again, knowing your two pieces with Harland will turn on you in the long run, but ready to endure it for the few good bites at the start. It's the same as spending too much money on a grand opening or a corporate Christmas party. Or a spring Kate Spade purse in electric lavender."

"This is a little more significant than a chicken leg and a bellyache, okay?"

"Just trying to make you feel better. It's a similar principle on a different scale. That's my point."

"I can't imagine where Joe and the dog are."

"I'm sorry, sweetie. It's probably nothing. Maybe they're out for a walk."

"His truck isn't here, M.J. Joe would've left me a note. He's very considerate like that. And he wouldn't normally leave here with me traveling. Especially since I've been gone for the entire weekend."

"Well, look at the bright side: Now you know. You realize you love Joe. You won't be moping around and wondering. Black-clouding your friends. This, in a certain sense, made your marriage better. Showed you how valuable it is to you. It's a net positive. My advice is to drink lots of cranberry juice and start taking great care of Mr. Stone. Put it behind you. Bury it. Lesson learned. Valuable instruction."

Lisa exhaled a jet of smoke. "No wonder you sold all those backhoes and chain saws."

"Never sold a chain saw."

"Don't you dare breathe a word of this to anyone. Ever."

"Duh."

"And so we're clear, we never had complete sex. No intercourse."

"Hardly seems fair—if you're going to feel this guilty and sick, you should've at least gotten to enjoy the full crime."

"I'll mail your phone to . . . oh, wait, damn, Joe's truck is pulling in the drive. Gotta go."

CHAPTER ELEVEN

Immediately, Lisa could tell Joe was distressed. Tense. Bothered. His face was ratcheted tight, and his movements—stepping from the truck's cab, closing the door—were precise and determined. She was quickly through the hall, den and mudroom but stopped well short of her husband, stood a few feet outside the entrance to their house, tentative, her thoughts mush, her bare arms folded across her chest, no coat or sweater.

"Are you okay?" she asked. He had pivoted toward the pickup's bed. "What's the matter?"

"Brownie's sick, Lisa." Joe was striding toward the tailgate. "I had to take him to Greensboro. The emergency-fucking-room for animals. Not a single damn person you can raise in Henry County on a Sunday. I tried every vet here and in Stuart, and all you get is a recording telling you to take your emergency to the twenty-four-seven hospital in Greensboro. I even called Dr. Withers at home, but he didn't answer. So I loaded Brownie in the farm truck and off we went. I didn't have any other choice. Sorry I wasn't here." He gestured at the bed. "Can you help me?"

Lisa teared up and both hands reflexively covered her mouth. She started walking with her fingers still guarding her lips. Already enervated and jumbled and sickly, she swayed into the side of the truck, briefly lost her balance and brushed a fender before she reached Joe, and when she dropped her hands, her lungs were misfiring, needed two or three pulls to suck down an effective breath. "Oh god, Joe. What happened?" She leaned across the tailgate, inspected the dog. "Is he alive?"

The dog was flat and listless on a quilt, a white bedsheet draping him and secured at the edges with strips of silver duct tape so it wouldn't blow away during the ride. Brownie's neck and head were curved at an extreme angle, stretched abnormally, the muscles and tendons flaccid, as if he'd turned to rubber and was somehow stuck in the midst of a big, heavenly howl.

"He was when I left Greensboro. I stopped and checked twice, and he was hanging on." Joe jerked the handle and lowered the gate. "I heard this awful racket coming from the back porch, something beating against the house, and I go out there and poor Brownie was slobbering and convulsing. He was on his feet, but he was having a seizure. At first I thought he was rabid, that's how it seemed, especially because he wasn't able to focus. He didn't recognize me or act like I was there. He was glassy-eyed. He collapsed but finally came around. Seemed better. Recognized me. Even though I knew different, I hoped maybe it was something he'd eaten or just a passing moment. Then it started again." Joe clambered into the truck and pulled away the sheet. Brownie didn't move or respond.

"What's wrong with him?" she asked, looking at Joe.

"He either has a brain tumor or liver complications. His blood tests showed very bad liver readings, so that's most likely the problem. We need to take him to our vet in the morning. The doc in Greensboro sedated him so he'd quit thrashing and suffering."

The dog weighed at least eighty pounds, but Joe knelt and forked his forearms underneath him and effortlessly scooped up the deadweight. A single stride put him at the end of the tailgate, Brownie utterly limp, his head dangling from the crook of Joe's elbow, his paws slack and purposeless. Joe crouched down from the truck, awkwardly extending one boot and then the other onto the ground, encumbered by the dog the whole time. Lisa scrambled to gather the quilt and sheet and trailed them into the den, where she made a pallet on the floor and Joe laid their pet near the center of the bedding.

As soon as Joe was finished and upright, Lisa hugged him and pressed the side of her face into him, felt the hard jut of his clavicle, and she cried and sobbed and said "This is terrible" and "I hate this" and "I shouldn't have ever left you two."

He patted and kneaded her back and assured her it wasn't her fault.

"Brownie's a tough old *hombre*," he told her while she was buried in his chest. "Let's see what Dr. Withers has to say in the morning."

Lisa sat down beside the dog, her weight on her butt, her legs straight in front of her and rigid. She rubbed his muzzle, neck and belly and repeated his name in a gentle voice and told him he'd be fine, better than new. She watched his slow breathing, could see the shape of his smaller ribs through his fur when he exhaled and flattened out. He sighed and opened a filmy eye for a second, licked his lips but lost his tongue so that it lolled pink and dry from the side of his mouth.

Joe brought in a kitchen chair and joined her. She told him the trip to Nassau had been mediocre, and she wished she'd stayed home, especially now. She thanked him for taking such good care of her and Brownie. She told him she loved him and had since she'd first met him. She rested her head on his thigh and knee and said she was lucky to have such a remarkable man, almost cried again but didn't. She inquired about fixing them a meal. "Maybe it's antifreeze or some poison," she added clumsily and too quickly after asking about supper, no transition at all. "Did they check for that?"

She realized her husband of two decades sensed there was more in the mix than simply Brownie's poor health. He didn't mention it or try to coax the other, mysterious disturbances to the surface, but she knew he was aware her grief was unnatural, a slot too high on the scale, her haggard expression and worried, red eyes too deep-set and entrenched to have been so recently birthed.

"Yeah. They checked." Joe peered at her. "Are *you* okay?"

"Sure."

She spent the night there beside the dog, sharing his quilt and the hardwood floor underneath, and around midnight rolled and dragged him to a different spot and sopped up a damp circle of urine that had leaked from him. At daybreak he was more alert and able to stand, and he ate a raw Jesse Jones frank for breakfast, but soon after he looked at Lisa and canted his head and wobbled slightly—an unbalanced hop he clearly didn't anticipate—and seized up again, his jaws spasmed wide open, his gaze congealed and distant, his legs locked and forced stiff and fast away from him as if every bone were expanding by several inches, his skeleton bulling its way free through skin and fur. He fell onto the kitchen floor, his full weight slamming the tile. Wet, choking sounds formed at the rear of his mouth and wouldn't quit. Lisa was scared and heartbroken, even afraid he might bite her, but she knelt and stayed beside him while spit dripped from his mouth and puddled near her painted toes.

Together, they drove him to the vet's office. Usually, Brownie barked and scuffled and dug in fierce with his front paws and hunkered low and doggedly resisted the threshold to the clinic, but he was so spent and so infirm that Joe had to carry him into the waiting room, where he lay on the floor wrapped in a clean new blanket, eyes closed, his head and bushy tail poking from opposite ends of the cloth cocoon. An elderly woman clutching a solid white cat and a man with a stitched and bandaged basset hound were also waiting.

Dr. Matthew Withers was a lean, happy-go-lucky man with a devilish, graying Vandyke beard. He was thorough and compassionate with his animal patients. After he helped Joe guide Brownie onto a silver metal examination table, he shook his hand and told them he was sorry about Brownie's circumstances. He put on pale latex gloves and started looking the dog over.

"Dr. Dubois from Greensboro has already faxed me the tests from yesterday," Withers said while he was pushing up Brownie's black lips to expose his gums. "I got your message this morning and went ahead and called Greensboro so I wouldn't be behind."

"Thanks," Joe said.

"Absolutely," he replied. He was looking at Joe and Lisa, two fingers gently scratching behind the dog's ears.

"What do you think?" Lisa asked.

"Well, I'm going to run his blood again, but it seems pretty clear Brownie has a significant liver abnormality."

"Not a brain tumor?" Joe inquired.

"I seriously doubt it. You'd see many of the same symptoms, but with these numbers in his blood work, it's a safe bet we're dealing with the liver." A blaring overhead light illuminated the table, and some of the fluorescence blanched the vet's face and shirt. "So this isn't the worst news, okay?"

"Well, I mean, what're his chances if it's liver failure?" Lisa asked.

The lighting bleached Withers so much he seemed drained and powdered, like a black-and-white-movie actor cooking up experiments in his madman's laboratory. "Will he be okay?"

"Yeah, I'm optimistic we can give him a really good quality of life."

"Damn," Joe said. "That doesn't sound promising. *Quality of life* usually means boatloads of intravenous narcotics and making sure your power of attorney is notarized."

"No, no, no. Not at all. He's just going to require daily medication and some extra attention from you and Lisa, and he'll be chasing squirrels again." Withers moved away from the table and the electric light, and the color returned to his features and clothing. "Now, honestly, it's probably a progressive disease, but we can arrest it, treat it, and he'll perhaps have several healthy years left. That's what I meant to explain. He might very well die of something else."

"Or he might not," Joe said quietly.

"True, but let's see what we can do," Withers answered.

He summoned a round-faced girl in a festive smock, and she shaved a small patch on the dog's front leg. She tied a blue band tight just above the patch and the vet drew blood into a tube. Brownie lifted his head and yelped when the needle pierced him. Lisa couldn't help thinking of Brett Brooks and his gold stars and bonus points.

As they were leaving the room, Joe paused at the door. "We want to do everything possible for him," he said solemnly. "Please make sure he gets the absolute best."

Driving them from the vet's to their office, Joe mentioned the bizarre visit by Dr. Downs, though he didn't let on to Lisa that he'd enlisted his pal Toliver Jackson to investigate the matchbox plate number.

"Seriously?" she replied when he finished. "Interesting. And this Downs character was loony?"

"Yeah, he has some issues. Probably a genius and very sincere, but obviously touched." Joe looked across the bench seat at his wife. "Still, I . . ." He slowed for a poking car they'd caught.

"Still what?" Lisa asked.

"Nothing. I doubt we'll hear from him again. No big surprise there were some genuine characters in Lettie's orbit."

"I suppose." Lisa studied the car creeping along in their lane. "How could Benecorp be involved in killing Lettie? You don't think there's anything to it, do you?"

"No."

"Joe?"

"No. Why would I?"

They returned for Brownie after work, around five, and Withers repeated what he'd told them earlier, assured them there was every reason to believe the dog would gain strength, and he gave them two prescriptions, one to treat the liver disease, the other—phenobarbital—to keep the seizures in check. It required several wretched days of trial and error, but they fine-tuned the correct amount of medicine to use, enough to suppress Brownie's horrible seizures, not so much that he was zonked and virtually unconscious. Twice a day, they fed him a pill and three-quarters of another hidden inside a ball of Kraft cheese or a wad of bologna. Sure enough, as Dr. Withers promised, Brownie recovered, to the extent he seemed mostly normal, and by the time the buttercups popped through the dirt and the trees budded, he was healthy enough to dart into the pasture and bluff and bark at the horse's hooves and then scamper away, hugging the ground as he belly-wiggled an exit underneath the lowest fence board, same as he'd done since he was a pup.

CHAPTER TWELVE

The first deluxe, bells-and-whistles spring day hit in early April. By midmorning it was almost seventy degrees. Infant leaves swarmed the oak and maple branches, Bradford pears were stacked with white blossoms and dogwoods were ready to unfold their Good Book crosses. The forsythia was gaudy yellow. Croaks, chirrs, flutters, squeaks, trills, whirs, clicks and screeches had once again started kicking up around sunset, animating the hollows. Pond frogs had emerged from the mud. Hummingbirds were scouring the vines and new flowers with their needled beaks. Ladybug hordes crawled on windowsills. Hornets and wasps and bees appeared. Moths had begun their spry jigs around outdoor bulbs. Deer were everywhere. The creeks were full and vigorous, undercutting their own banks.

Driving to work, Joe cracked the Jeep's window so Brownie could ride with his head poked out, and the dog loved it, occasionally barking into the wind just for the hell of it, exuberant. Joe left his office soon after arriving and began walking to the Daily Grind for a cup of coffee. He made the trip more to enjoy the spring surroundings than to buy coffee, so he was wandering along, hands in his pockets, his tie already loosened, no jacket. Even uptown Martinsville, with its vacant storefronts and destitute streets, seemed briefly enlivened. Near the barbershop, he heard someone call his name. He stopped and checked over his shoulder and waited for Toliver Jackson to catch up with him. Toliver didn't hurry, continued walking normally until he reached Joe.

"What in the world do you have on?" Joe asked his friend.

"A suit," Toliver answered. He was wearing a dark blue suit, a white carnation in the lapel.

"No shit. I see that. Why the flower?"

"Why not, Joe? It's spring, and I'm in a fine-and-dandy frame of mind. Pages have turned."

"You look like a pallbearer. Carnations are for funerals. I hope somebody didn't die. Then I'd feel bad about making fun of you."

"You should feel bad anyway. You're a damn killjoy. Here I am celebratin' for no reason, just because, lovin' life, and you're poor-mouthing me." He smiled.

"Seriously?"

"Yeah," Toliver replied. "Adding a little flair. A little cheer. Simple as that."

"More power to you."

"So I got your car information." Toliver pulled a small, wire-bound pad from his coat pocket. He flipped through several pages.

"I have to admit, Toliver, I'm still impressed by the midget's note-book. Nice and old school. I'll bet it really unsettles the criminals, especially when you flick it open with extra policeman's emphasis."

"Remember your punk client Sherm Duggan? Two-day jury trial, and you badgered me about my notes and his statement and how accurate my investigation was? Ring a bell? And who was the boss of that case, Esquire? I seem to recall me and my notebook got him found guilty and a nice, fat penitentiary sentence. I put an ass whippin' on you like you were Hamilton Burger."

"Even the blind hog finds an occasional acorn." Joe smiled. "What about my plate?"

"Yeah, sorry I took a while to check it. I had some actual police business to do. Okay: The plate belongs to a Hertz rental. A Nissan Altima, red in color. September of last year, relevant to your dates, it was checked out from the Roanoke airport counter. September third, to be exact. Rented to a lady by the name of Jane M. Rousch. Because I'm good at my job, I tracked down a little more for you. The clerk's fairly sure the renter had a man with her. I got an operator's license photo of the Rousch lady. I checked, and she has no entries in the criminal records exchange."

"Where's she from?"

"Wisconsin. Or so her license says." Toliver made a show of shutting his pad, thumbing back through every page until he reached the blue cardboard cover. "See, the license is bogus, my friend. When I ran the DMV on it, Wisconsin tells me the identifiers all belong to some lady by the name of Jane Pendry, who looks nothin' like our woman at the airport. Basically, somebody pasted the Rousch photo on this other license."

Joe and Toliver were blocking the newspaper racks and had to crab several steps toward the barbershop entrance so a burly man could buy a *Martinsville Bulletin*. They both apologized to him while he was inserting his coins.

"Does the Jane Rousch name produce anything at all?" Joe asked.

Toliver frowned. "Nope. Not a thing."

"So the lady who rented the car using the name Rousch isn't in fact Rousch or even Jane Pendry, and we have no idea who she is, just a picture?"

"Correct. And the picture's sorry even by DMV standards. She paid cash money for the rental. Gave them a credit card with the same Jane Rousch name for the security deposit."

"Huh," Joe said. "I'll be damned."

"Definitely some trickeration in play," Toliver noted.

"How about the mileage?"

"Car was checked out in the morning, odometer showed it traveled a hundred and sixteen miles, returned later the same day."

"Which is pretty close to round trip from the airport to here."

"Yep."

"Great googly moogly," Joe said.

"Did you know I have the highest clearance rate in the department? Third best in the state?"

"I didn't realize the state kept rankings."

"Well," Toliver replied, "I researched it and calculated it myself."

"Now there's a surprise. Hardly like you to showboat and wave your own self-promoting banner."

"Well, here's another surprise for you, courtesy of some exceptional Toliver Jackson sleuthin': Records show our Miss Rousch was in Roanoke for another rental on November twenty-second, right before Thanksgiving. She was supposed to return the car like she did before, okay? The same day. This time it's a white Ford."

"And?"

"She doesn't. In fact, she never brings it back to the airport. Nine days later, the cops find the car in Charlotte."

"Is it wrecked or anything? Damaged?"

"Nope. Abandoned in a commercial parkin' deck. The attendant noticed it didn't have a proper sticker and hadn't paid the fee, so he called the cops. Virginia had it in the computer as stolen, reported missin' by Hertz in Roanoke."

"How about evidence of a crime? You know, blood or signs of a fight or whatnot?"

"Signs of a fight? Like, oh yeah, people leave notes sayin' 'We've been scuffling here, please excuse the damage to the upholstery'? Nothin' strange that anyone recalls, but the report came in as an abandoned vehicle, so there wasn't much focus on the car as a crime scene."

"You have any theories?"

"I don't. Usually an airport rental car and a fictitious identification mean obvious drug deal. But these people flew to Roanoke; your dealers and mules, they rent the car then drive the wheels off to make the delivery. Savvy criminals don't risk airport security and try to hide dope in their luggage or undershorts. If it was a drug deal, I'd expect a Florida or West Coast rental, then a long-ass trip. Not one hundred and sixteen puny miles. Still, I wouldn't rule out narcotics."

"Yeah. I agree."

"But I can give you a last, showboatin' puzzle piece. Hertz was paid for the extra days. Penalties, mileage, the full tab."

"By whom?" Joe asked.

Toliver toyed with a grin. He adjusted his flower. "By Jane Rousch, naturally. She sent a money order."

"Too strange."

"You think?" Toliver teased him. "Of course, right now there's really no crime and nobody's been ripped off or injured. Worst I see is a Mickey Mouse identity theft, but it'd be a bitch to put the pieces together for a prosecution, and we'd still have to locate our buddy Miss Rousch. Like I say, no harm, no foul. She used a fake ID but paid the bill, so Roanoke ain't gonna waste resources pursuing this, especially with no victim complainin'."

"Thanks, Toliver. All kidding aside, I appreciate it. Damn thorough investigation."

"You mentioned a connection with Lettie," Toliver reminded him.

"Yeah. This certainly gives some support to my tip." Joe noticed a nondescript bird land on top of a mildewed awning across the street. The bird didn't stay long, touched down for an instant and then fluttered off.

"You want to share this valuable nugget with your police pal who busted his hump and traded favors on your behalf?"

"No more than to say that my source is not too stable. I will tell you there's a theory that Lettie's death wasn't accidental." Joe looked at Toliver, moved closer and lowered his voice. "You'll keep that between us? Confidential?"

"Okay," Toliver promised. "Unless and until we open a case, this is just me and you shootin' the shit on a pretty spring day."

"Thanks," Joe told him.

"Well, it's mostly for my own protection and sanity. Can you imagine the number of suspects, right from the drop, I'd have to interview if Lettie didn't actually blow herself to smithereens? Can you? Who in Henry County didn't carry a grudge where she was concerned? Hell, right before she died, I got dispatched out to the convenience store on Spruce Street, and she's in a fracas with the clerk, raisin' holy hell. Lettie claimed she'd been cheated at the gas pump. That there was gas still in the hose, gas she'd paid for but wasn't allowed to take. She'd bought three whole bucks' worth of unleaded but wanted them to allow her another quarter's worth to drain the hose. I'll never forget it, long as I live. She was threatenin' the clerk with an electric carving knife. Wavin' it around. One of those monstrosities your parents had way back in the seventies to slice the Christmas ham. She'd push the button and the blades would take off. Zzzzzzzzz." Toliver mimicked the sound and waved an imaginary knife. "The clerk wanted her gone but didn't want to press charges. Who the hell totes around an ancient electric knife in your purse?"

"Huh. I hadn't considered that. Is there still gas in the hose? You could argue that it's been run through the pump and registered against your total but is stranded in the hose."

Toliver snorted. "Yeah, well, why don't you grab your electric knife and go investigate it?"

Two days later, on a cloudy Friday, M.J. was in Martinsville for business. She was buying another apartment building, and no matter what the deal involved or where it took place, she always had Lisa review every jot and tittle of the contract. After they'd discussed a thirty-four-page draft agreement between M.J.'s company, Goldbricks, Inc., and the struggling, cash-strapped owner of the South Carolina apartments, and after Lisa had spotted and corrected a mistake M.J.'s silk-stocking South Carolina lawyers had missed, they left the office for a late lunch at the Binding Time Café. They drove separately, Lisa leading.

They sat at a corner table, and the waitress brought their water and wrote down their orders. The café was quiet, a few stragglers still finishing lunch. M.J. mentioned that she'd joined a new gym, and that she'd had to fire a lazy assistant at her equipment business. Lisa listened and sipped ice water and asked how old the assistant was. "I'm worried about you," M.J. finally said. "The new eye shadow and Stepford smile aren't fooling me. You going to be okay?"

"Well," Lisa sighed, "not any time soon. The Caribbean thing."

"Yeah, I assumed that was it. I could've faxed the contract to you, but—"

"Thanks," Lisa said. She sipped some more water.

"I can tell it's still upsetting you. You've been awful quiet lately." Since the Nassau trip, with the exception of their first frantic exchange, Lisa's e-mails and phone calls to M.J. had been short and blasé, cordial enough, but so bland they telegraphed a much bigger message, the relative silence a second language easily understood between friends.

"I don't know what to do," Lisa told her.

"Can we smoke in here? We can't, can we?"

"Of course not," Lisa said.

"It's a café, right? By definition, it ought to be allowed."

"Anyway, I'm miserable. Ashamed." Lisa hesitated. Their waitress, a young girl with frizzy red hair, approached the table and brought them soupspoons. "I'm afraid there's no answer," Lisa said once the girl was gone. "No remedy. I'd hoped a few weeks might make it better, the 'time heals all wounds' theory, but I have a tumor, not a paper cut, and I feel worse and worse every day. Sometimes it completely saturates me, like the flu—I physically feel icky and achy."

"At least you're still able to do your job. Thanks again for the sharp eye on the apartment deal."

"Work is a wonderful distraction. I'm glad I could help. It's a great buy. I'm happy for you." Lisa pushed her water glass to the side. It left a wide, wet path.

"Maybe, just maybe, you're overreacting to some heavy petting and a hand job. Wouldn't this be a misdemeanor and not a felony?" M.J. glanced toward the door, where a gaggle of elderly ladies was leaving, most of them carrying purses and wearing Alfred Dunner wind suits.

"You can go to jail for either. I'm just so pissed at myself and not sure how to fix my mess."

"You think you should tell Joe?" M.J. asked.

"I'd certainly like to. I'd feel better about myself. He's entitled to know, and a confession would sort of wipe the slate clean. But, god, the risk. I don't think he'd take it well, and I don't want to lose my husband and my marriage. The bottom line is I cheated on him. If it was only the drunk night in Roanoke he might get past it, but the Bahamas is so calculated, so plotted, and he'll probably never believe I didn't screw Brett."

"Only two choices. Like I already suggested, bury it deep and be happy with what you've learned. Then forget it. You validated your marriage. Went to a dream spot with a hot new guy and Joe was still king. Or—second option—tell him. There's some marketplace value in letting him know. Maybe if he understands there's competition, he'll up his game and appreciate how fortunate he is. The realization you were restless might make him clip some nose hair or *ixnay* his dorky motor scooter. Make him a better Joe. There're men who would work extra hard to hold on to you and ensure you're happy. He might try to improve to keep you around."

Lisa dropped her head, twisted her mouth into a grimace, locked her eyes and stared at her friend. "Maybe on the Lifetime channel's movie of the week. Or if we were Tristan and Isolde and King Marke, and we all sang our parts. Somehow, I don't quite see Joe doing that math."

"You're probably right. I'm just brainstorming. At any rate, I'm not convinced I'd want a jolly cuckold around, regardless of how much effort he was investing in me. Doormat guys aren't attractive over the long haul." She shifted in her chair, leaned forward and rested her forearms flat against the table. "So if you confess and he stays . . ." She changed positions again, slumped slightly and folded her arms across her chest. "There's not really a helpful business model for adultery."

The waitress returned with turkey wraps and homemade tomato soup. Lisa and M.J. both thanked her and told her they didn't need anything else. The wraps were held together with toothpicks; each bowl of soup was garnished with a basil leaf. The women neglected the food and kept talking. It was approaching three o'clock, and they were now the only customers.

"I'd actually thought about seeing a . . . counselor or, who knows, a minister or priest. This should be well within their field of expertise."

"As for the counselor, I'd only consider a psychiatrist. If I'm going to suffer all the jibber-jabber, I'd like the words to have some pharmacological backup. The pills pay the bills, not the chitchat. I had a counselor for a while when I was married to the Craps Pirate, and it was okay, I suppose, but it didn't solve the first thing. It was nice to have the sympathetic lady with the master's in social work to commiserate with, but I was still married and he was still a piece of shit, and all her solemn nods and calm advice didn't change that. The miracle of prescription dope might've at least given me a few nights away from the stress."

Lisa chuckled. "There's the issue of this being Martinsville too. I know all the counselors, and Art Prillaman's the only psychologist in town, so it would be terribly awkward. Yikes. Ugh. We're friends. He's my friend and Joe's friend."

"You'd have to make an appointment in another city."

"Plus," Lisa said, "even though he's honest and very professional and wouldn't do it on purpose, I worry about news of my mistake leaking into the community gossip. A busybody sees you there at the counselor's office, or a fired employee blabs, or hell, it's a small town and it's like spontaneous combustion the way your private concerns just, poof, become public at the Chatmoss pool or Snow's lunch counter."

"True. Exactly. I grew up here, remember?"

"I wish I knew a solid minister. But Joe and I have never really gone to church."

"Happy hunting, Lisa." M.J. shook her head. She stirred her soup but still didn't eat any. "Last place I'd look for help, especially in Henry County."

"I said a solid minister."

"I gave the whole religion gig a big try, right? Wednesday night Bible study? The cruise to the Holy Land? As best I can tell, no one's nailed it for sure yet. Take your pick. There's Scientology, Haile Selassie, Wicca or the Mormon guy, Joseph Smith. You can unlock the secrets of Xenu, or smoke pot, or learn cool chants, or marry lots of young girls, all in the name of some god or another. You can be a Christian or a Jew—bet either black or red on the roulette wheel. Not much middle ground there. Or put your money on the Pope. Or buy a Vishnu ticket. Quarrel about grape juice versus wine, debtors versus trespassers. After years of struggling to sort through it, I decided I'd just begin my praying with 'to whom it may concern.'"

"There're tons of great people in the churches," Lisa said. "Far more good than bad. You're using fringe examples. Most everyone understands there's a god, a creator."

"Imagine my surprise when my new Baptist 'church family' in Raleigh informed me I was disqualified from every godly office because I was divorced. Huh? Excuse me? That's my fault? I mean, damn, come on."

"I'd just be curious to hear another opinion. There're preachers who are college-trained, who went to legit seminaries. Part of their job is counseling people and keeping confidences. You don't necessarily have to buy into all the theology for them to help you."

"For me, same as the counselors. I'm having none of it unless this preacher can write me a prescription." M.J. picked up her fork and pointed it at her friend, jabbing the air as she spoke. "Religion is like fashion, but with a much longer shelf life. Your mainstream Baptists and Methodists are the spiritual little black dress—they've managed to hang around for centuries. The fly-by-night folks, they'd be your caftans or cowl-necks or stonewashed jeans. Your apple-green trouser suits."

"Okay already. Calm down." Grim as she was, Lisa couldn't help but laugh. "I didn't mean to get you started. I understand the topic pisses you off. But the minister's for me, not you, and I'm willing to try whatever, anything, hypnotism or colonics or acupuncture, if there's even a remote possibility. So far, I'm not curing this on my own."

"Sorry." M.J. laid the fork on the table. "I'm sorry. But it sticks in my craw. I still volunteer at the food pantry my old church sponsors, so it wasn't a total loss. But, yeah, we have to fix this for you. We need to stay on track. So have you cut ties with boyfriend Brett?"

"Completely. I called him the next Monday."

"How'd that go?"

"He was a gentleman. He sent some roses disguised as a gift from a title company and tried to persuade me otherwise, but he's left me alone. We were on the phone for an hour, and he sounded sad at the end. Oh—he did send me a long e-mail several days later. It was sweet. But he's not a groveler or a stalker. I think he kind of had a huge clue before we left, so it didn't sucker punch him."

"Thank heavens. That would be a nasty complication."

"At any rate, I—"

"I met a guy," M.J. interrupted, "at my aunt's funeral." She still pronounced it "ant," the Southside way. "My mom's sister. The preacher did a nice job with the service, and I spoke to him afterwards in the church basement. Cute little round fellow, bald, tearing up a paper plate full of deviled eggs, ham biscuits and macaroni salad. He was from Louisiana, and lo and behold, I discover he has an MBA from LSU and quit his family's business to become a minister. He was close to forty when he enrolled in the seminary. Kind of a different route— evidently, he was hauling in some serious jack, but left it behind to preach. Usually it's the reverse. Plus, he had a dash of Cajun in him and was fun to talk to. My parents were upset he'd been invited to preach the funeral because he and his wife drink an occasional beer or glass of wine. The Carter family is strict Pentecostal, as you'll recall. Of course, I liked him even better for it."

"Huh. Where's he from?"

"Patrick County. Stuart, I think. Bucky was his first name. Last name was odd. German sounding. He's Presbyterian. Shouldn't be hard to track him down if you really are convinced it's worth a shot. He seemed reasonable and normal, which is about the best you can hope for from that bunch."

"Maybe. Sounds as if he's what I'm looking for. I might check into it."

The waitress was wiping a nearby table, and M.J. asked her if she could pop their soup in the microwave for a few seconds. "We were gabbing so much, we let it get cold," she said apologetically.

While waiting for the soup, they each took a bite of the wraps, and M.J. noticed the giant blue TV ring on Lisa's finger.

"I don't mean to change the subject again, but I like your ring. I've never seen it."

"Thanks. Seriously? It seems a little tacky and over the top to me. I don't wear it too often."

"Tanzanite. Nothing wrong with it, in my opinion. It's a lovely shade of blue. Snooty bitches pooh-pooh it because you can buy it on the shopping shows. So what? Who cares? I own some, and I damn sure can afford Tiffany's or the typical stuff, diamonds and emeralds." M.J. grinned. "But I also adore Pigeon Forge and a Catskills hot tub, so I'm not sure how much my vote is worth. When did you get it?"

The waitress returned with the soup bowls. "John poured out the old instead of rewarming it," she informed them. "He wanted me to tell you."

"Oh. Well, we appreciate it," Lisa replied. "He didn't have to do that."

"Sorry to be a nuisance," M.J. added.

Lisa told M.J. how she'd come to own the ring. M.J. ate and listened. She was silent for a moment after Lisa finished. "Yeah," M.J. said, "this is worse than I thought. You really stepped in it. Twenty years together, and he's drinking wine with you on a weeknight and buying you jewelry off the TV? As a bonus, he's wearing his cowboy clothes before you two have car sex? Sheesh."

"Thanks for reminding me."

"I told you before: This was a Two Pieces With Harland choice." M.J. shrugged. "My final advice would be to keep your mouth shut, realize

what you've learned and spoil Lawyer Joe like there's no tomorrow."
She raised her index finger. "But not so much he senses it's restitution
and catches on you've cheated."

The waitress interrupted with their ticket, and M.J. apologized for
being a difficult table and arriving late for lunch, and she handed her a
hundred-dollar bill as a tip.

"For me?" the girl said, stunned.

"Yes. I hope you can use it."

The girl's pale neck and cheeks colored. "Oh, oh . . . yes. The water
pump in my car's broke, and I didn't have no idea how I could afford to
fix it. Thank you, ma'am. I can't believe it. Thank you so much."

"My pleasure," M.J. replied.

"John made me promise not to bother you, but I know who you
are," she told M.J.

"Oh?"

"Miss Gold," the girl said. "You came and did a speech at the high
school years ago. I was in tenth grade. They said you were sort of a
female Donald Trump."

"Ha!" M.J. cackled. "Not hardly. I've never filed for bankruptcy, and
I don't feel compelled to stencil my name on every building and plane
and doodad I buy."

"You have your own personal airplane?" the girl asked.

"Yeah. A Citation Ultra. And I can fly it too. I have my pilot's license."

"Awesome."

"Listen, sweetie. You take your car down to Sirt's Auto Repair and
tell Mike to replace the water pump. A new one, not something sal-
vaged or rebuilt. Tell him to send the bill to Mrs. Lisa Stone here, my
attorney, and I'll see that he's paid. You keep the hundred and buy a
treat for your kid."

"How'd you know I have a little boy?" The girl's mouth stayed open
after she asked the question.

"Same way I wound up with my own plane," M.J. told her, and the
words, despite their smart-ass swagger, came off as generous and amiable, without any hint of condescension.

"You're a piece of work, aren't you?" Lisa said to M.J. while the waitress was walking away but still within earshot.

CHAPTER THIRTEEN

Inasmuch as he wasn't eager for a double-barrel, twelve-gauge blast of scolding, Joe understood he needed more evidence—hell, he needed *some* evidence—before he mentioned the name VanSandt to his wife again and revisited Dr. Downs's contention that Lettie had been assassinated by a multinational pharmaceutical company because her madwoman's quackery was actually useful and mysteriously valuable. Joe decided that Neal would be the easiest, softest source to explore, so for a couple days after his meeting with Toliver Jackson, he mulled strategies and plans and then cold-called Neal early on a Thursday, nine o'clock sharp, at the Atlanta pest control service where he worked.

"Neal, good morning. It's Joe Stone. How're things down your way?" Joe was seated behind his office desk, still wearing his suit jacket. Brownie was torpid on his chamois pad. He'd suffered a seizure at breakfast, trembling and gagging and jerking in the kitchen, and Joe had given him extra medicine, half a pill more than normal.

"Attorney Stone? From Martinsville?"

"Exactly," Joe said enthusiastically. Neal sounded as meek and scattered as ever. Joe envisioned him hunched over a computer, scheduling appointments and entering them on an electronic calendar, his dingy coffee mug beside the keyboard, his brown-bag lunch and pudding-cup snack in the common-area fridge.

"Well, yeah, right, hello. Hi. I didn't expect you to be calling."

"Hope I'm not bothering you."

"No. Not really. But we are busy today." Neal sniffed, coughed. "And we're not supposed to have personal conversations during work hours."

"I'll be quick," Joe told him. "I'm afraid we have a loose end we need to discuss."

"Okay," Neal said warily, stretching the word.

"Here's the problem, and most likely it's no big deal. Before she died, your mother created several trusts. Do you know what I mean by that, a trust?"

"Kinda."

"A trust holds assets and distributes them to the object of the trust, who's called a beneficiary. The trust has to follow very specific rules as to how it pays the beneficiary. Lettie established a number of foundations, too, basically the same principle."

"Uh-huh."

"Well, when we settled her estate and I signed the renouncement giving you her assets, I didn't consider the trusts. Didn't even think about them." This was true. Joe was careful not to lie. Lettie was constantly setting up trusts and foundations, none of which was ever funded, none of which had ever paid out a single dime. They existed entirely on paper, Lettie's grandiose, pipe-dream plans to provide food for stray cats in Thailand or award scholarships for high school girls who wanted to study the haints and apparitions that bedeviled Turkeycock Mountain. "I'm concerned about potential trust holdings, things that were left in the trusts or foundations when she died."

"Oh. Like what? What . . . uh . . . do you think could be there?"

"Money. Cash."

"Okay. How much? And how would you find it?" Neal coughed again. "Sorry. I have a sinus infection," he noted. "Drainage."

"Good question. Do you have any papers or account numbers other than the information I gave you?"

"No," Neal said. "I just went by what you told me. I have boxes and boxes of her files that I took from her place, but I never paid them any mind. They're in my basement."

"It might be worth the effort to investigate the local banks and see if there are any accounts in the names of the trusts and foundations."

"Okay. Yeah. Thanks."

"You want me to send you the various names?" Joe asked. "I can pull the files."

"Sure. Thank you, Mr. Stone."

Joe let the conversation stall for a moment. The line was completely quiet, miles and miles of separation in their connection. "Oh," he said after the break, "this probably won't matter, but Lettie was always talking about funding the trusts with her inventions and creations. I can't imagine why it would be an issue since none of her various schemes ever amounted to a hill of beans." He chuckled. "No offense to her. Not long before she passed away, she had me draw up a trust to provide seed money for a rebellion against the Henry County Zoning Board. Month prior to that, it was a foundation to tackle cheating in the state lottery. She actually paid to have both of those filed in Richmond with the SCC." He made it a point to sound wistful, nostalgic for his quirky client.

"Mom had lots and lots of ideas, no doubt."

"She mentioned dedicating the profits from—oh, what was it?— VanSandt's Wound Velvet Medicine and her shingles remedy to start the zoning rebellion. She was also kicking in the earnings from her project to copyright the sounds of certain birds, beginning with whip-poor-wills and barn owls. She liked to remind me that the true owners probably weren't in a position to sue her." He chuckled again. "I don't know if she ever actually transferred anything or not, but I gave her the paperwork with fill-in blanks to use, and Lettie being Lettie, and as much as she enjoyed shuffling legal papers around and keeping company with notary publics, she certainly could have."

"Wait. What're you sayin'?" Neal almost shrieked.

"Reminiscing makes me realize how much I miss your mom," Joe said, deliberately ignoring his distress. "She was irreplaceable. Eccentric as hell too. There'll never be another. I'm sorry—you were asking me a question?"

"The trusts and so forth. So what if she did? Put the Velvet . . . put, well, you know, an *invention* in one of these trusts?"

"It wouldn't matter, Neal. As far as I can tell, all her inventions and formulas are worthless. You just need to make certain there's no cash money in any account. If there is, you could simply donate it to the cause Lettie had picked, or to a similar and legitimate organization, assuming such a thing exists. Many of Lettie's beneficiaries were unique, to say the least."

"Can I . . . can I . . . get whatever's there out? Would I own it as your son? As her son, I meant to say. Darn." His voice spiked on several of the words.

"No. Nope." Joe's tone was smooth and lawyerly. "But who cares, Neal? And I doubt there's any cash floating around, but I'll pull the names of all her foundations and trusts and send them to you so you can inquire at the banks here. I'll have Betty include the telephone numbers for the banks. Save you some trouble."

"So, but, yeah, okay, yeah. Thanks. Yeah. How would I find if she put stuff besides money into her trusts? A foundation? How would a person know?"

"You'd have to search her papers and files, which you have. Most of the time she'd drop a copy by here too. She was meticulous when it came to her business. I have huge boxes of papers, letters and forms she left with Betty over the years. But it would take forever to sort through them, and there's no need."

"Would you do it?" Neal hastily asked. "Check and see? Please?"

"I guess we can. We'd have to charge you, though, and I hate to waste your money. What possible difference could it make? Her thousands of creations and ideas are all claptrap. It doesn't matter who or what owns the rights."

"I'm willing to pay," Neal said. "I . . . Well, you, uh, called me, right? So there you are, it must be legally important." He sounded more composed, despite the stammering.

"Only if a chunk of money happens to be deposited in a bank account. Even then, you'd only be cleaning up her affairs. Housekeeping, really. Any money belongs to the trust, not you."

"True, true, yeah," Neal agreed. "But I probably should investigate so I can protect these people, uh, the people Mom wanted to take, uh, care of and, oh, what if someday one of her things really worked and wasn't a crazy joke? Then I'd need to know for positive if I owned it."

"I guess, Neal. It's your choice. I'll have Betty start searching when she has a chance. And what exactly do you want? Do you want to know all the assets she assigned to every trust and foundation? That could take a while and dip fairly deep into your wallet."

"Oh, crap. Huh. I suppose some are . . . But, right, yeah, I need to know what each trust has, I guess. How many of these things did she set up, Mr. Stone?"

"Lord only knows," Joe said solemnly. "At least fifty, maybe more."

"But if you don't find a certain invention put in some trust or foundation, then it would be mine, right?"

"Absolutely," Joe assured him.

As soon as Joe finished the call, he swiveled his chair toward the dog. "Heckuva job, Brownie. Fucking great googly moogly." The mutt recognized his name and thumped the floor with his tail, a single lethargic stroke, up and down.

Lisa heard Joe tramp the entire hall, walk in her office and push the door shut. She could see his blur at the margins of her vision and could sense that he'd turned toward her while the door was still swinging closed and was planted there beneath the high ceiling and its 1970s department store, fluorescent-tube lighting. She was scribbling notes across the front of a file and didn't immediately look up or acknowledge him. She'd barely finished her appointment with a petty larceny client and his grandmother when Joe shot in, no doubt crowding past the elderly woman and her shiftless grandkid as they left.

"You won't be happy with what I have to say," he announced.

"How come?" she asked, still writing. She finally focused on him enough to register his expression and see his gaze leveled at her, and her gut shrunk and her face and neck tingled and she wondered if this was it, if he'd discovered she'd cheated on him, oh shit, and she quit her writing in the middle of a word, went limp and dead as if she'd been unplugged, the pen's tip still touching the off-white file cover, halted halfway through a cursive *l*'s loop.

"It's not the end of the world, Lisa," he said. "I didn't mean to scare you to death. They haven't banned Bejeweled or Plants vs. Zombies from the Internet yet. You sure have been jumpified lately. On edge."

"Well, Joe, your preface was fairly serious." She dropped the pen. It hit the file and rolled off catawampus. "What did you expect?" She hated living with such a wicked secret, her mistake lurking and festering in its dungeon, occasionally breaking free and ruining her days, transforming every phone ring, or door knock, or deliveryman, or suspicious e-mail, or post office trip, or conversation with her husband into a potential catastrophe.

"Your neck's red." He kept standing. He narrowed his eyes, then released the tension.

"Yeah, so? You barrel in here all grim and ominous and tell me you have bad news. How am I supposed to react?"

"I never said it was bad news."

"Okay. Technically, you didn't."

"At any rate, here's the story, which I didn't bother you with till I had more to go on, because I realize it's not your favorite subject. I fully anticipate I'll receive the standard lecture about keeping things from you, but in my defense, it's a tough balance to strike, especially given how often you've said you're relieved to be shed of Lettie VanSandt and you despise—what was your phrase?—my 'stupid fascination' with her."

Lisa slowly shook her head from side to side. "I never, ever used the word *despise*."

Joe reminded her of Dr. Downs's visit to Martinsville and the doc's theory that Lettie's death wasn't as it appeared. He lowered his eyes and cleared his throat and added that he'd asked Toliver to investigate Downs's license plate number as a favor. Sure enough, the rental car arrangements were crooked, and the car's mileage matched a trip to Henry County. He detailed the shenanigans with Jane Rousch, the second rental abandoned in a parking garage, the money-order payment. But the tipping point—for him—had come when he spoke with Neal five minutes ago, and Neal panicked and freaked out when he learned he perhaps didn't own the rights to the Wound Velvet.

"Damn," Lisa said after Joe finished, "that *would* make you think twice. You and Toliver have been busy lads." She arched an eyebrow.

"Yeah."

"Where to next?" she asked. "What do you think we ought to do?"

"If you keep holding that cynical high note, there's a chance you'll shatter the window glass. I could've kept this to myself."

"I'm not being cynical," she said. "I promise. The fake license combined with Lettie's e-mail sounds odd. Of course I'm not sure you can get a meaningful read from a fruitcake like Neal, so I'm inclined to discount that part a bit."

"Seriously?" Joe asked.

"Seriously," she repeated. "I've had a weird feeling since that dog guy was here. But more to the point, you're my husband, and if it's important to you, it's important to me. Count me in. I'm happy to help."

Joe leaned against the wall. He accidentally brushed the light switch and extinguished the overhead. "Do I need to make an appointment with an exorcist?" he joshed as he was flipping on the switch again. "There must be a crafty demon in possession of my wife's soul. This is Lettie VanSandt we're discussing. I've been wasting time and burning favors to track down leads I got from Dr. Strangelove. Worse, I'm just now telling you all about it."

"We need to get a handle on this. I have an open mind. Based on my history with Lettie, you waited till you thought it wise to tell me. I can appreciate that. No worries. I'm not ten years old, Joe." She said it pleasantly, without sarcasm. "What do you think happened? Or maybe happened?"

He slid into a chair. "Connecting the dots," he said eagerly, "it seems plausible that a man and woman from Benecorp came to visit Lettie about her wound formula. On September third, they traveled from Roanoke to Henry County in the rental. The mileage fits. We can certainly infer they were trying to conceal their identities. Lettie's e-mail puts them at her trailer. They cajole and threaten her, which would've been like trying to train a deaf mule. No results. They return in roughly the same time frame as her death. She's killed. But something goes south. There's no way they wanted this rental car to turn up bright and blipping on the radar. I think perhaps tough old Lettie injured one of them. If she did, they can't visit our local ER, and they damn sure can't return to the Roanoke airport. I checked, and there's a hospital a block away from where the car turned up."

"Makes sense," Lisa said. "Though there're closer hospitals. How serious can it be if you travel two, two and a half hours?"

"If we can somehow manage to pull the string, I'd love to see the ER records."

"Possibly worth a shot," Lisa said. "But good luck with all the HIPAA bullshit. You'll need a court order with gold seals and special ribbons. I'd wait awhile. I wouldn't go to so much trouble yet. You said the car was paid off?"

"Yes, by the mysterious Jane Rousch."

"Who, so far, is a complete dead end."

"Correct," Joe said. "Also, ask yourself why the hell Neal kept rescheduling appointments and took so long to come here and settle Lettie's small estate. Was he in negotiations with our pals at Benecorp? Or were they pressuring him and the arm-twisting required several months? Or were they rehearsing him so he could meet with us and not screw up? From his reaction, either he sold somebody the Wound Velvet formula or he still has it and knows it's an extremely hot item."

"Now that I'm hearing this, here's another red-flag tidbit for you: Soon after your sweetheart died, a call came in from a collection agency, asking about the terms of her will and potential assets."

"Right, yeah. I remember. I forwarded the info to Neal."

"And I had Betty advise them that you were the beneficiary but planned to disclaim any interest. The more I think about it, and in light of what you're telling me, I think it was bogus. Lettie didn't owe anybody a dime. She was tight as a tick. I think somebody was fishing, trying to discover where her assets were heading. Or maybe confirming information they'd received from Neal."

"Could be. Damn. I wonder if we still have the number for the collection company?"

"I'm sure we do," Lisa said. "Betty has the message from the first client who ever called us."

They went together to their secretary's desk, and she located the number for them, and when they dialed it using the speakerphone, they heard a three-part electronic tone and a woman's scratchy, recorded voice informing them the number was no longer in service.

"Okay," Joe said. He focused on Betty, who reflexively opened her steno pad and gripped a pencil. "If my wife and law partner agrees, I vote we wait a day or so and then have you contact Neal VanSandt in Atlanta and inform him that we think we might've located copies of the paperwork. Tell him it's possible his mother's most recent directions left all her inventions to the rebellion trust. Make sure you emphasize the words *think* and *might*. And say there's no charge for the research."

"Do I need to pull a file for you, Mr. Stone?" Betty inquired as she jotted shorthand notes. "Or search the VanSandt boxes in storage?"

"That would be a waste of time," Joe said. "At one time or another, I've read every paper in those boxes; you can't find something that doesn't exist." He looked at Lisa. "Let's see if we raise anybody to take a peek at our bait."

CHAPTER FOURTEEN

Even though she wasn't able to cure the hard lump in her conscience, by early May, Lisa felt slightly better and the pangs and assaults were at least manageable, incorporated into her life like a bum leg or arthritic joint or insulin imbalance, something to compensate for and tolerate until the discomfort became routine, the hurt mitigated simply because of its dreary persistence. The Monday following a spur-of-the-moment, early-anniversary, weekend trip to Primland Resort for a prix fixe meal and extravagant wine and a stay in a hotel room twice as large as their own den, Lisa was frantically fetched to Joe's office by Betty, who scurried down the hall several paces ahead, chattering as she went, arms chugging. Joe was seated at his desk, an ear trained on his boxy 1990s phone. As soon as Lisa walked through the door, he gestured excitedly at the phone and mouthed something she wasn't able to decipher. A man was talking to him through the speaker.

Joe bent toward the phone and interrupted. "Mr. Champoux, sorry to break in, but my wife just arrived." When he used the speaker, Joe had a habit of bobbing closer to the base each time he spoke and then rocking straight again after he was finished.

"Ah. Excellent. Mrs. Stone, my name is Matt Champoux, and I've already introduced myself to your husband. I understand you two are partners, and he wanted you present for our exchange. Good morning to you, ma'am. We were discussing the Red Sox's prospects for the year while we waited. Your husband and I are fans."

"Good morning." Lisa walked behind the desk and stood next to Joe's chair. "I hope he's not in too much trouble."

Champoux laughed politely. "Oh, no. I'm afraid I'm the one with a problem. You see, my firm represents a client who purchased assets from the . . . let me make sure I read this correctly . . . the Lettie Pauline VanSandt estate. We took title from her son, a Mr. Neal VanSandt. We now understand there might be a problem with title and our ownership. A possibility that the late Miss VanSandt had transferred certain assets into trust before she passed away. I've already given your husband an overview; he wanted me to highlight my issues for you as well."

"Who's your client?" Lisa asked.

"I'm sorry, but that's confidential. I hope you can appreciate our position."

Joe leaned toward the phone. "That brings us to a bit of an impasse, doesn't it? I don't feel comfortable discussing Neal's business without his consent. Moreover, assuming for the sake of argument that a trust or a foundation holds the rights to certain of Miss VanSandt's assets, we can't give you any details or information unless we have approval of the trustees."

"I understand. As we speak, you should be receiving a fax copy of Mr. VanSandt's consent and waiver. He has no problems whatsoever with you discussing the estate with us. In fact, I'd be glad to wait while you confirm this with him on another line."

"He doesn't like to be bothered at work," Joe said. "And I usually prefer to set my own agenda."

"I didn't mean to suggest otherwise." Champoux tried to sound deferential but wasn't able to mask his impatience.

"Exactly which asset is it you're concerned about?" Joe asked. He slanted toward the phone to talk and bounced upright when he was through, reminded Lisa of a glass-bodied novelty bird, perpetually dipping its beak in and out of a water glass.

"A fair question," Champoux said. "My client purchased the rights to all of Miss VanSandt's formulas, medicines and inventions, lock, stock and barrel. Everything. Or so they thought."

"How about VanSandt's Velvet, a wound salve?" Joe asked.

"This may or may not surprise you, Mr. Stone," Champoux said tersely, "but I have no idea about any of the particulars. I simply handle the acquisitions and secure the rights. No more, no less."

"That must hamstring you," Lisa told him. "It would seem to make your job complicated."

"I'm not sure I follow you," Champoux said. "However, I'd appreciate it if you would check with whoever needs to be contacted, and if there is indeed a flaw in our title, or we do not own what we think we do, please let us know what needs to happen to correct the oversight."

"Meaning?" Joe asked.

"Meaning, Mr. Stone, that we still wish to purchase the assets and stand willing to make a fair offer to put this to bed."

"That's curious. As far as we know, Lettie's inventions are nothing but humbug. Worthless." Joe remained bent over the phone this time, didn't bounce back.

"Mr. and Mrs. Stone," Champoux replied, now more exasperated than irked, "I promise you I truly don't know the small details. I simply want to acquire the rights we thought we had gained from her heir, this Neal VanSandt. I would think it makes your decision easier if the items are of little value."

"Perhaps," Joe said into the speakerphone, his voice full, almost loud. "But here's our take on this: I'm on the board of every single trust and foundation Lettie ever created. Usually it was Lettie, myself and, occasionally, Lettie's friend du jour, and that could be anyone from a clerk at the convenience store to Homer Lockhart, who delivered her mail. Ultimately, this will be my call, and I plan to be very prudent. Very circumspect."

"Of course," Champoux said. "Don't blame you. But the good news is that you'll have the authority to negotiate with me, correct?"

"Not exactly. I'd like to do my negotiating with Benecorp. Directly. I *am* very interested in the small details, you see. No offense to you, but I want to hear from Anton Pichler. Tell him to give me a call, and we'll see what we can do."

"I'm not at liberty to—"

"Mr. Champoux, I'm not interested in smoke and mirrors and posturing and what you can or can't do. If Benecorp wants the Wound Velvet, they're going to have to show up at the table and quit ducking and hiding behind lawyers and tell the truth for a few minutes. Simple as that."

"Well, Mr. Stone"—Champoux was gruff, didn't want to appear cowed—"you're in no position—"

Joe cut him off again. "The Sox overpaid for Lackey. He'll prove to be a chump. Theo Epstein's an idiot and should be embarrassed. Mark my words. And you tell Anton I'm expecting his call." He pressed the button to disconnect them, and Matt Champoux was gone.

"Damn," Lisa said. "This is really getting interesting. Evidently, at least one of Lettie's bizarre inventions is actually valuable. You think we'll hear from Pichler?"

"Yeah, now I do."

"I wish we could locate Dr. Downs. It would be helpful to talk to him again." Lisa looked at the phone, then at Joe. "I hope nothing happens to him."

"I had the exact same thought."

"This is starting to seem huge and serious," she said. "I mean, of course we don't need to jump to the wrong conclusions, but this truly is strange. Hard to imagine. This Byzantine conspiracy here in our small town. Major corporate intrigue. Like we won the upside-down lottery."

"Everything has to happen somewhere," Joe mused. Almost immediately, he laughed at himself. "Good to know you can count on me for that kind of fatuous insight if things turn dicey, huh?"

Lisa had a general district court case in Stuart the next morning, and she knew where the road was that led to the Presbyterian church, and she detoured toward it after she finished her trial, didn't turn for Martinsville. It couldn't hurt to drive by and see the place, a windshield gander, and maybe she'd stop or maybe she wouldn't, and who knew if the preacher, this Bucky guy, would even be there, and she was learning to live with her sin as it was, so maybe that was her best bet, but there was nothing to lose by taking a peek and seeing what struck her as she eased down Staples Avenue, wandering, undecided.

The church was small and older, brick with a white steeple, and two vehicles were parked in a gravel lot, a Toyota sedan and a dusty

Ford Explorer. A positive sign, Lisa thought. No Cadillac STS, no Lincoln with a personalized preacher's plate and an NRA sticker, nothing black and apocalyptic. She slowed and considered pulling in, almost stopped, then accelerated past the church and turned around at an elementary school and retraced her route. She parked beside the Explorer and crunched across the gravel to a sidewalk, then hurried for the door with her head tucked and shy, the way she'd seen people dart into the liquor store at the mall or the off-track-betting parlor over in Ridgeway. She entered an empty office that connected to another office, and she knuckle-rapped a wall and tentatively called "Hello?" She heard a wood-against-wood scrape, and then brisk footsteps from the next room. A man appeared and stood underneath the doorway between the rooms.

She'd already decided that hair product of any kind, veneers, French cuffs, monogrammed shirts, pocket squares and tie clasps were immediate and lethal disqualifiers, so she was relieved to see a bald man— clipped gray on the sides—wearing khaki slacks and a lightweight, crewneck sweater standing across from her.

"Hey," he said. "Oh. Well, hello. Nice to see you, Mrs. Stone. Welcome to Stuart Presbyterian."

"Huh? How...?" she stammered, flabbergasted. "How do you know my name?"

He laughed. "No holy magic, I promise. The heavenly hotline doesn't work quite that quickly. We met several years ago. I went to court with a member of our church family, a lady named Ashley Forbes. Ashley had a tough drug problem that led to her writing bad checks and stealing. You were her lawyer. She was poor, so the court appointed you. I remember you gave her your best efforts, despite the circumstances. You helped her a lot. I testified as a character witness."

"Oh, okay. You sort of stunned me there for a minute. Sorry I didn't remember you."

"No worries. I'm sure you have contact with hundreds of people." He smiled. "Recalling names and situations is a big part of my job." His face was intelligent and cherubic in equal measures, hospitable and smart, but a tad too impish to reach beatific, the countenance of a man who just might've veered off for a few colorful furloughs and side trips along the way to the Sunday pulpit. "Can I help you with anything?" he asked. "You're from Martinsville, right?"

"Yes. Am I interrupting you?" Lisa asked. "There're two cars in the lot."

"Oh no. Not at all. That's Wendy's car. She's our secretary. She's downstairs, trying to organize seven file cabinets of old records."

"We have the same problem at our office. So much paper."

"Computers and discs sure make it easier," he said.

"So, actually, if it's not an imposition, and if you wouldn't mind, yeah, I'd appreciate a few minutes of your time. You're Bucky, right? The pastor here? I suppose we need to clear that up."

"I am. Bucky Hunsicker," he said warmly. "Come in." He beckoned her into his office. The sign taped to his door was the size of a playing card, a piece of plain white paper with "Reverend Hunsicker" typed across the middle. "Makes it easy for them to send me packing," he said when he noticed her studying it. "And easy for me to go if I need to."

"Oh," she said. "Probably wise for both sides."

Hunsicker's modest office was dominated by a large, L-shaped executive's desk that was too formidable for the space and hogged the room. The desk was filled with a jumble of books, papers, knick-knacks, Bibles, photographs and a model car kit—a Corvette—still in the box, wrapped in plastic. The wall to Lisa's right was loaded with framed diplomas.

"Where'd you go to school?" she asked. She was seated in front of the behemoth cherry desk.

"Undergrad at LSU and my MBA there as well. A master's from the University of Chicago. A doctorate in religious studies from Wheaton College."

"Wow."

"I'm a latecomer to the ministry." Hunsicker smiled. "I was in the family business for several years. Hardware wholesale."

"How long have you been here, in Stuart?"

"Fourteen years now," he answered. "Can I get you some coffee or a soft drink?"

"No. Thanks, though."

"Let me know if you change your mind."

"I will." Lisa looked at him and was quiet. The silence didn't seem to bother him or make him uneasy. He waited for her, didn't force the conversation or clutter matters with chitchat or press her with some trite reassurance. "Well, I . . ." Her mouth was grainy and sandpaper dry. Her tongue was mutinous. She caught herself twisting her rings, tapping her foot. "I have a question, I suppose." She sighed. "I was just wondering if you—your church I mean—might be able to let my clients, especially the juveniles, work off their community-service hours here. It's getting harder and harder to find places that will help."

"Oh, well, certainly. Depending on the charge and the person, we'd be very open to it."

"I'd do my best to screen them," Lisa said.

"Sure. Just let me know. We have plenty of work we need done."

"Thanks," Lisa said, her mouth still dry. She'd pop a Tic Tac as soon as she got to the car.

"And that's what you wanted to ask me?" Hunsicker slanted his head slightly.

"Yes. That's it. I'm grateful." She could hear her own breathing. Looking down, she noticed the bottom of the desk was nicked and scratched. "I'll be in touch. I appreciate your speaking with me."

When she returned to the office after a lunch in Stuart, Joe made a production of knocking on her closed door, five rhythmic beats followed by the "two-bits" coda, and instead of pissing her off, it made her grin, and he smiled as soon as he saw her reaction and said, "See, I knew you secretly, deep down, liked it. Next, you'll finally admit *Black Swan* was a ninety-minute gulag. An utter failure as a date movie, despite the girl-on-girl hook for husbands on a forced march."

"I like you. The knock remains obnoxious. The movie won awards. So what's up, Joe Stone?"

"Two things. I took your intuition seriously and called my law school buddy, Paul Yarbrough, in Florida. He was kind enough to send a paralegal to check out the Ross Sanctuary. It's real and legitimate. Big-ass place, saves hundreds of animals every year. Yarbrough's guy asked if they'd gotten the donation from Neal. They did. He sent them a check."

"Clean so far," she said.

"So far." Joe put his hands in his pants pockets. She noticed his belt buckle wasn't centered, was stuck behind the first loop. "But guess what? They never received a single animal from Virginia in our time frame. Nothing from Neal, nothing under Lettie's name, zilch."

"I knew that whole freaking production was fishy. It didn't make any sense why it would be, but I damn well knew it. Still, why would anybody go to the effort to collect all of Lettie's curs and strays? What possible gain or advantage could there be?"

Joe answered quickly. "It had to happen to make the deal go down. I wasn't going to sign the estate over to Neal unless he made arrangements for the animals."

"I guess," she said. "But why not just go ahead and take them there? It's not the donation or the cost—Neal paid for that."

"Beats the hell out of me." He took his hands from his pockets. "Here's the more interesting tidbit. When I went to their website to find the address and so forth, I checked on our friend Don Beverly, and—how should I put it?—he's gone missing."

"What?"

"The same bio, but a different picture now. A completely different man. Sort of similar, but clearly different."

"Huh?"

"See for yourself," he said.

She put on her reading glasses and typed in the Web address. "Yeah, you're right. This definitely isn't the guy we met." She removed the glasses and set them on a stack of files. "Do you think we're at the point where we need to alert the cops?"

"We don't have much of value—legal value—to tell them. If we don't hear from Benecorp, I'll try to prod them some more. Item number two: On the Dr. Downs front, I sent him a coded message on Token Rock. We'll see if anything comes of it. Short term, I can't think of any other options."

"Short term," she said, "I have an idea."

"Okay."

She stood and walked past him and locked the door to her office, and he watched her pass by him and tracked her as she returned to where he was standing instead of her desk chair, his expression quizzical the whole time.

"You want to sit or stand?" she asked, the words slow and languid. She cocked a hip so that her skirt tightened around her thigh, more than enough to communicate the remainder of the question to her husband.

"No shit? Seriously?"

She took hold of his belt buckle and tugged the leather free from the metal pin. She put her lips against his neck, pulled his shirt loose, separated the clasp at the top of his pants.

He stepped sideways and dipped into a chair, settling mostly against its rounded edge. "What did I do to deserve this?"

"Consider it a preanniversary gift."

"Thanks," he said. "You think you could take your top off while you're doing it? Really ring the bell?"

CHAPTER FIFTEEN

Joe was not at the law office on the final day of spring turkey season. Instead, he was in the reborn woods trying to coax gobblers toward his position behind the lip of a small swale so that he could blast them with a shotgun. He'd left the house before sunrise, dressed in camouflage, carrying a thermos of black coffee and a bacon biscuit wrapped in wax paper, the paper's folds and creases etched white. For months he'd been practicing his turkey calls, at home, at work, in the car, using a box-scrape to imitate the bird's sounds. Lisa would hear him from the kitchen while she was cooking a meal. At the office, he'd show off yelps, cutts, purrs and kee-kees for his clients who also hunted. He reminded her that any fool could kill a deer—the newspaper ran pictures of twelve-year-old girls posing with high-powered rifles and stiff, dumb-ass bucks—but your turkeys are smart and wily as hell.

Every year, he'd spend most May mornings in the woods and hollows, tricking the birds with his bogus talk while the sun sopped up the early mists and the sky came into focus. He'd wait until almost his last legal chance, barely under the wire, before he'd finally return to the farm with a huge dead turkey. He'd fetch Lisa out to the tailgate of his Jeep and comment on the tom's beard and impressive fan and oddly iridescent feathers, then clean and skin it and cook it in a special fryer he'd bought from Cabela's, and they'd eat it for dinner that very evening, along with sliced tomatoes and cowboy beans.

When Anton Pichler phoned, he first asked for Mr. Stone but informed Betty that Mrs. Stone would do just fine if he was unavailable. Lisa was with a client, a scruffy layabout from Figsboro who was explaining that the pot and cocaine the cops had found in his pocket weren't his, you see, because he'd by mistake put on his cousin's jeans before moseying over to the Eagles Club for darts and a pizza. She was just letting him fib, taking in his wide, dramatic eyes and the occasional "I swear" and, somewhere near the middle of his spiel, the obligatory "I know this sounds hard to believe, but . . ." After Betty buzzed to tell her who was on the phone, she stood and announced that she had to leave for a moment. "While I'm gone, please reconsider your story," she said forcefully. "Judge Gendron has heard this fiction before—several times, in fact. He'll be insulted you think he's so stupid, and he'll jack your punishment because of it. Try to compose a more creative lie, or give some thought to telling me the truth. Okay?"

She walked down the hall to Joe's office and took the call there, the door closed.

"I appreciate you interrupting your meeting," Pichler said. "Thank you."

"Sure. No problem."

"I imagine you already know why I'm contacting you and your husband." Pichler spoke in a contrived, mechanical voice, very restrained. He sounded like HAL the computer from *2001: A Space Odyssey*, a few of the accents vaguely British, and Lisa surmised he was the kind of man who never lost his temper in public, never ranted and screamed, but bullied and intimidated his underlings by speaking more and more softly, all menacing whispers and bullshit Zen.

"Lettie VanSandt," she replied.

"Yes," Pichler answered. "Miss VanSandt." He briefly hesitated but didn't give Lisa a chance to talk. "I don't intend to waste your time, so let me see if I can take us to the bottom line. I work for Benecorp. You're evidently already aware of this. Additionally, you now know we were—and are—interested in a compound connected with Miss VanSandt."

"All true," Lisa agreed. She was standing. Brownie's pad was empty. She'd left him at the farm.

"I also assume you've been in touch with Dr. Steven Downs. I regret that."

"Why?" she asked. "Why would you assume we've spoken to Dr. Steven Downs?"

"Because it's how he operates. He's contacted numerous individuals and agencies about Miss VanSandt, and they've alerted us. He's filed reports with the Virginia State Police and the police here in Dade County."

"And they in turn called you?"

"Mrs. Stone, Dr. Downs is mentally ill. Truly. So you'll understand, I'm having a series of documents overnighted to you and your husband. Reciting his entire history would take too long, but here are the highlights: He has been hospitalized for psychological problems on three occasions in the last seven years. By court order, he is barred from entering our property or having any contact with us. In the past, he has accused this company, me and his co-workers of criminal behavior. Because of Dr. Downs, we have been needlessly investigated on several occasions for everything from attempting to poison him to stealing his nonexistent inventions. We have been subjected to inquiry from local law enforcement, the FBI and the EEOC. I'm sending you the results of those investigations along with telephone numbers for the state and federal agents involved. Both the reports and the investigators will tell you that he is unstable, untruthful and unreliable. He is paranoid and, well, quite crazy."

"You have a valid court order barring him—"

"From any and all contact with us or our employees," Pichler finished. "Absolutely. Entered three months ago by the court here in Miami. It'll all be in your hands by tomorrow, and I hope it resolves any doubts you might have. If you spent any amount of time with Downs, you should have a sense of how fragile he is. If you have questions, please contact our local sheriff or Agent Bev Larson with the FBI. I'll include their numbers."

"Fair enough. But I suppose he's a bit peripheral to the reason for your call."

"True," Pichler said, "but I worry his bizarre accusations might complicate our business. Do you mind telling me what he is saying about us? I am correct that you've heard from him?"

"My husband spoke with him, so I only know the generalities. I understand you and Benecorp are interested in Lettie's estate, particularly a wound medicine. Of course, your lawyer was very mysterious about his client. We simply assumed it was Benecorp." She debated revealing more but decided to see what this might tease from Pichler. "And erratic as Downs might be, he was working for you as recently as last year."

"Yes. But try to discharge an employee because he or she has a mental 'sickness.' Not the easiest task in the business world. We attempted to assist him until it became impossible. Our owner and founder has a soft spot for him."

"Okay," Lisa answered noncommittally.

"But yes, we're interested in Miss VanSandt's compound. Before we leave the subject, please also understand that Downs is not the stereotypical cuddly genius with a few quirky habits. He was simply a low-level chemist here, average at best and, not to beat a dead horse, certifiably mad."

"Of course, at least a portion of his information is accurate—you guys do want the wound medicine, obviously."

"My only point is that we didn't steal it from him, or discover it by testing it on kidnapped teens, or murder Miss VanSandt, or whatever else he might be peddling from his roster of wild accusations. Once we discharged him from our company, he upped the ante in his vendetta against us."

"What exactly does Lettie's concoction do?" Lisa asked.

"We consider that proprietary information. Am I to understand that she placed the rights to this creation in some kind of trust before her death? Legal tells me we might not own it."

"Well, my husband would know more about those particulars than I do. I heard him talking to his assistant the other day about Lettie's files, and I know he was trying to track down whether this Wound Velvet belonged to her or one of her trusts. He'd spoken to her son, Neal, and there was some question."

"Neal told us. Yes."

"But you have to realize, Mr. Pichler, that we would never sell or transfer any of Lettie's assets until we know precisely why you want them. We'd be complete idiots to do otherwise. Especially when you begin this dialogue by having your lawyer treat us like we're a couple of pinheads."

"Yes," he answered, his voice lower, almost a hiss. "A temporary impasse."

"Did you say 'impasse'?" she asked, even though she'd understood him. "I'm having trouble hearing you. Could you speak up?"

"Yes, an impasse. If in fact we don't own the rights already. When do you think you or Mr. Stone could either confirm or deny the holdings of these trusts? Legal tells me they've searched Virginia records and did find a few corporations associated with Miss VanSandt, but that most of them have lapsed."

"Why would we tell you anything, sir? We're wasting each other's time. Joe is on the board of every trust or foundation Lettie ever created. There's no chance he'll give you any information, and an even smaller chance he'll sell you the rights unless he knows the value of what the trust has. If you won't tell us what it is that we own, we certainly won't sell it to you."

"I see. You're not being unreasonable there. Yes. Well, how about this: We have a standard confidentiality agreement we use to cover any number of situations. I'll have our lawyers fill in the blanks and include it with my package. Once you and Mr. Stone review and sign it, we can discuss Miss VanSandt's formula in more detail. Fair enough?" He intoned almost every word without inflection or emotion.

"Sure. We'll take a look at it."

"Mrs. Stone, I hope you understand we're doing our best to be ethical and transparent. You must realize it would be easy for us to avoid this rigamarole and use Miss VanSandt's creations and no one would ever be the wiser. You and the rest of the world would never know the difference. We're simply doing everything in our power to be a good corporate citizen. I *can* tell you that the application for the VanSandt formula is rather minimal and completely internal."

"Really? It seems inconsistent, then, that you'd twice dispatch people up here to knock on Lettie's door and badger her about her invention."

"Pardon?"

"If this is so insignificant, and you're just being charitable with us, then why did Benecorp send people here to strong-arm Lettie?"

"Ma'am, I promise you this is news to me. We did not send anyone to . . . to impose on Miss VanSandt." The jagged jump between his words reminded Lisa of a skip in a Victrola record. "I myself talked with her on two occasions, and I can promise you the conversation from my end was polite and professional. She was rude, but I was as pleasant as any human could possibly be under the circumstances. She was highly profane. Irrational too." Pichler began to speak even more softly. "We never had any other contact with her. We never had any further discussion about her property until she died and we located her son."

"Huh." Lisa had spent twenty years in courtrooms and earned a living from gauging the truth of people's claims, protests, promises, assurances, denials, stories and oaths, and she was surprised that Pichler sounded so genuine and honest, so convincing. "You didn't send people to Henry County to lean on her?"

"No."

"Is it possible that you have competitors who know about Lettie's invention?"

"I hope not."

"Interesting," Lisa mused.

"Why do you think Benecorp sent people to visit Miss VanSandt? When is this supposed to have happened? Did Downs tell you this?"

"I would consider that proprietary information, Mr. Pichler." She said it flatly, without any spite or smugness. "Joe and I will review your package and get back in touch. I don't see why we can't settle this on terms we're mutually comfortable with. I'm all for selling it to you if we can establish what's what and if your company offers a fair price. Why wouldn't we?"

"Thank you. I'll look forward to hearing from you and Mr. Stone. I appreciate your willingness to negotiate with us."

The package arrived the next morning, shortly before noon, and after she and Joe perused the court orders and law enforcement reports and confirmed the number for FBI Special Agent Bev Larson and spoke with her, Lisa asked if he still believed Dr. Downs. They were in her office, both seated on the client side of her desk.

"Well, I believe he's not your average bear. But there was never much doubt about that, was there? Doesn't mean he's wrong or telling us a lie or hallucinating the whole scenario."

"I agree," she said. "Right now, I'm positive of several things. First, I'm positive that the e-mail from Lettie to Downs is authentic. Why would he go to the trouble to fabricate an e-mail? Second, the people who visited her were Benecorpers—the sketchy car rental info matches up. Third, she mentioned this feud with a drug company to you near the time she died. She—"

"Let's not go overboard," he interrupted. "She complained about hundreds of companies stealing her ideas. For all I know, this was another in a long line of fanciful gripes, and she never specifically named Benecorp."

"Still, it's a tiny piece, and they start to add up." Lisa pursed her lips, shifted in her seat. "I have to say, though, that Pichler seemed truly surprised when I told him we knew his henchmen had been here to goon-squad Lettie. I'd bet the farm he was being honest with me."

"You're usually right. Your instincts are a helluva lot better than mine. So I'm assuming he's telling the truth."

"I say we sign the confidentiality agreements and see what they'll give us."

Joe smiled. "Nothing to lose. I'm guessing Mr. Pichler won't be too thrilled when we finally admit there's no transfer to any trust or foundation, and he and Benecorp owned everything from the drop."

"Honest mistake," she said. "We'll sincerely apologize."

"You sure are invested in this," Joe said. "Gung-ho."

"Why wouldn't I be? The evidence is there."

"Yeah. But I wish Downs didn't have an ax to grind. That's a red flag, Lisa."

"Take him out of the equation and there's still a lot we can confirm. More to the point, ask yourself: Why is this major corporation going to such elaborate lengths to discredit him? Over what they claim is a trivial matter? We absolutely should stick with this. If nothing else, it beats the heck out of prepping another reckless driving case or filling in child support guidelines. I'm glad you got the ball rolling."

Joe nodded. "Just to be safe, I'm going to see if Toliver can obtain the e-mail records from the library. It's still possible that Downs manufactured Lettie's note to him."

"I guess he also pulled numbers from thin air and hit a license plate that belonged to a hugely suspicious car with fraudulent renters? A car whose mileage would corroborate the e-mail?"

"I'm the cautious Stone, remember?" Joe was holding an incident report from the Miami Police Department. He laid it on his wife's desk. "I think I'll also pay Harlowe Fain a visit. A while back, he told me about Lettie's spectacular last call to her dear friends at the 911 center. The tapes might have something worthwhile. I'll listen to her last few conversations and see what was on her agenda."

"That could take several months," Lisa joked. "She was their most loyal customer."

"Beyond that," Joe said, "I'm not sure where we go next. Pretty soon, the jig'll be up with Benecorp, and it's not like we have much more than good old-fashioned suspicion."

Lettie's last call to Henry County 911 was a complaint about Clackers, the obnoxious balls-and-string toy from the 1970s. Harlowe Fain had compiled her greatest hits onto a CD. It wasn't easy to winnow down the list, he told Joe, given the oodles of rich material from which to choose. He'd included the Clackers piece simply because it was her final report to 911. "Lord, I love not having to deal with her contrary ass," he declared.

"Clackers?" Joe asked. He was standing in a hallway adjacent to Harlowe's office.

"I shit you not," Harlowe said.

"I don't understand."

"Why would you? Why would any rational person?"

"What did she want?" Joe asked.

"She'd bought a set of Clackers at a flea market and evidently the damn things busted. Can't you just picture her, sitting there at her trailer with her gold tooth, wild-eyed, up to her neck in cats and dogs, probably juiced on meth, banging them balls together fast as she can go until they shatter? Lovely. Perfectly lovely."

Joe laughed. "Oh, damn. I remember she had them in our waiting room once. Lisa came out and told her to quit it, and they had one of their many rows."

"Well, she called us to report the problem and insisted we send the police to her place so they could 'investigate.'"

"Investigate what?"

"Who the hell knows, Joe? My point exactly."

"I thought you told me at the grocery store her last call was really memorable. Something about Babylon?"

"Did I? Well, if I did, I was mistaken. The Babylon call came earlier. It's not on the CD. I'm checking with the city attorney to see if I can sell 'em, her crazy-ass calls, like a bloopers record. She's dead, and it's public record, so I don't see any reason I shouldn't be able to do it. Some of the exchanges are hysterical."

"I'd be curious about any calls around September third of last year. Twenty ten."

"I'll pull them for you."

"So she called that day?" Joe asked.

"Hell, Joe, she called almost *every* day. Why should September third be any different?"

Harlowe left and went into the control room and returned with numbers scribbled on a yellow Post-it. "She checked in with us for sure. Big surprise. Brenda's locatin' it for us right now. Do you want a copy, or just to listen?"

"Just a listen should be okay for now," Joe told him. "Thanks."

They went into the control room and stood behind Brenda Farmer's computer and listened to Lettie and a weary operator as the recording of the call began.

"Oh, man, does that bring back bad memories," Harlowe said.

"Tell me about it," Brenda added without taking her eyes off the screen. She was wearing drugstore reading glasses. She clicked a mouse to increase the volume.

"Oh, yeah, yeah, here you go. You're right, Joe. I did mention it. It's not her last, but it was kinda different for her. Actually a little scary, even for Lettie."

On the screen, a red line in a display marked "audio" bounced and rose and plummeted with the voices, creating peaks with sharp, pointed tips. Lettie interrupted the operator almost immediately. "You know, Betina Kirby, who the hell this is and where the hell I live, and I ain't got the time to waste playin' your little ten-questions game. Right now there's a serious problem here at my place. A woman dressed in purple and scarlet means to do me harm, and I want protection. Do you know your Bible, Betina, or are you a heathen? Book of Revelation, Chapter Seventeen. You and everybody else needs to damn well be on notice that I just saw Mystery Babylon herself, standin' right on my stoop, wearing her wicked gold and pearls, the Great Whore, and I'm sure you and all them other overpaid county employees sittin' there half-asleep and drinkin' coffee on the taxpayers' nickel will make sport of me and gossip 'bout how crazy Lettie VanSandt is, but I want this on the record, don't you dare erase it, 'cause when it all comes tumblin' down, you been warned, and if I'm in fear of my life, you better believe I know my rights, and I won't hesitate to defend me or my property. So are you goin' to dispatch me an investigator, and not that scrawny Pritchett kid they sent last week, who wouldn't know baby crap from apple butter? How'd he get hired, anyway?"

"Ma'am, Miss VanSandt," the operator said, "I'm not sure I understand your complaint tonight."

"Little smart-ass, aren't you, Betina? 'Tonight,' huh? I catch your sarcasm. Fine. Send me a cop, or go screw yourself."

"Is there a person with you now?" the operator asked, exasperated.

"Long gone, sweetie. I'm lookin' down the road. The future."

"And what's the emergency?"

"I already told you, you little ditz. You're Wallace Underwood's daughter, ain't you? You're as thick as your daddy. Who're you goin' to send to investigate?"

"Miss VanSandt, I'll relay all your information to the police, and they can make a decision what to do. And I don't appreciate you talking ugly about my daddy. I don't have to listen to it. Do you have anything else to report tonight?"

"'Do you have anything else to report tonight?'" Lettie mocked her. "You'll see soon enough, Betina *Underwood*."

"Goodbye, Miss VanSandt. Least my daddy doesn't live with a million dogs. Probably the only creatures that can abide bein' around you."

Joe shook his head. "Jeez, she was abusive. I never saw much of that side in the office. Did you ever prosecute her, Harlowe? There's a statute on—"

"One try cured me of the notion," Harlowe interrupted. "We can waste ten minutes on the phone with her, or we can waste hours sittin' in court, then more time when she appeals to high court. It took darn near forever answering her subpoenas and making copies of calls for trial and complying with her ridiculous requests, which the judge had to allow. She represented herself. I guess you was otherwise busy. We simply considered it an occupational hazard. Take the relative short pain over the phone rather than hours of unproductive torture with the courts. Then there were the suits and FOIA requests she was always filing against *us*. I'd wager she spent as much time in court as you did."

"Did she ever raise the Babylon topic again? What was her next call?"

"Not that I'm aware, but I didn't listen to every conversation."

"Well, I hate to be a nuisance, but could you make me a CD of all her calls following this one? No huge hurry, and I'd be glad to pay you for the research and copying."

Harlowe smoothed his bush of a mustache, grinned through the thick whiskers. "Sure, so long as you aren't plannin' to tread on my material and steal my CD plans."

Joe laughed. "You have my word, Harlowe."

"I can get it done for you in a week or so," Brenda told him. "Unless it takes longer than I expect, there won't be a charge."

"Appreciate it," Joe said. "Were her complaints usually so ominous?"

"She covered a lot of ground over the years, Joe," Harlowe said. "The weird deal here was how she's worried with something happenin' to her and asking for protection. Ninety-nine percent of the time, it's Lettie who's planning on dishing out the ass whippin'."

"Yeah, I noticed," Joe replied. "When people talk about their rights and defending their life in the same breath, it often doesn't end well. Especially if you have Mystery Babylon all dressed up and knocking on your trailer door."

CHAPTER SIXTEEN

Joe went home after stopping by the 911 office, but Lisa had to work late, almost until ten, putting together exhibits and sorting through depositions for a daylong equitable distribution hearing, and it was dark when she finally made it to the farm, and she rushed into the house and located Joe watching a black-and-white western, and she started talking over the movie, loud and excited, still holding her purse. "Joe, listen, you'll never believe this, it's crazy, but fifteen minutes ago I was cranking my car, and I heard a woman's voice call my name, call it twice, 'Lisa Stone, Lisa Stone,' and I realized someone was in the backseat, directly behind me. It was completely horrific, every woman's slasher-movie nightmare, and it was even worse when I turned and looked and it wasn't a woman, but instead was this gross man with a beard and a leprechaun's bowler hat. I freaked and grabbed for the door handle, but the safety belt and shoulder harness tangled me up, and I thought, Oh shit, this is it, and my purse was zipped so I couldn't get to my Mace even if that would've helped."

"Are you okay?" Joe stood and used the remote to mute the TV. He started toward her, and she could see he was alarmed, but she took a step away and pushed in his direction with both hands.

"Yeah, yeah. Let me finish. I'm fine now; I'm not hurt or anything. You don't need to worry with consoling me and all that. Just listen."

"Okay," he said, puzzled. He stopped beside the sofa.

"Guess who it was? Guess who was sitting there in the car?" She barely paused. "Lettie. Lettie VanSandt."

"Say again, please."

"Lettie," Lisa repeated, still energized.

"Lettie's dead, Lisa. What're you talking about?"

"Evidently she's not."

"I saw the burned shed, the sheriff collected the remains and the DNA matched. She hasn't been around in months. Are you fucking with me?"

"I am not," Lisa said.

"So walk through this with me. Slow down. You finish work and leave the office. You get in your car. It's dark. Before you start the engine, you hear a woman's voice—"

"Say my name. Twice."

"It sounds like a woman," Joe continued, "but when you turn and look, it's a giant friggin' leprechaun sitting behind you."

"Close," Lisa said. "It's Lettie. In a disguise. A fake beard. A hat. A man's jacket."

"Okay, I'll bite: What does the ghost of Lettie want from you?"

"It wasn't a ghost, Joe. It was Lettie. She tells me she's alive—obviously. She tells me Garrison tried to kill her—which is no surprise. She says she's scared and hiding. And she hands me this." Lisa reached into her purse and removed a small rectangle of cardboard—pinched it at the top corner—and gave it to Joe. "Be careful with it. We don't want to lose any prints. She said she'd split the Wound Velvet with us sixty-forty if we can help her get the better of Benecorp and figure out what the formula actually does."

Joe read out loud: "60LPV 40LS on VV 108 IF!" The note was written in black ink. The cardboard section was irregularly torn from a box—a partial circle was imprinted on it, the weight of a can. "Not the clearest contract I've ever seen. We'd play hell collecting on that, though Lettie's damn honest when it comes to keeping her word."

"I was completely floored." Lisa was calmer. "Frightened to death, then shocked."

"Where is she now?" Joe asked.

"She left. She wasn't there more than a minute. She cut through our lot and headed down the alley by the sandwich shop. She told me she'd be in touch on a site called Number One Chat Avenue. I'm supposed to check at nine every Thursday night. The message will be from Roberto100."

"You just let her go? Stroll away?"

"I was scared and stunned, Joe. It was a sneak attack. I barely could breathe, much less wrestle her to the ground."

"And that's it?" Joe asked. "Are you sure it was her?"

"Yes. I'm sure."

"How sure?"

"Well, Joe, pretty damn sure. It was Lettie. Who else could it've been?"

"Give me a number, please," Joe said. "How certain are you?"

"I don't know—ninety-five percent. More, probably."

Joe sat on the sofa's arm. "We just turn up the heat on Pichler and Benecorp and, holy cow, a dead woman miraculously appears, at night, in a disguise, and recruits you, Della Street, her sworn enemy, to join her crusade against Seth Garrison. You're stressed, thinking you're about to be robbed or raped or killed, and it's pitch dark. Why am I hugely skeptical and unconvinced? I'm not sure where the bear trap is, but this is a put-up job, Lisa. Lettie's dead. This is somebody screwing with us."

"I don't think so. If I'm wrong, then this was the best fake ever." Lisa jiggled the collar of her blouse, fanning air around her neck. "Let me pour a glass of wine and change clothes and we'll pick it apart."

"Well, one thing's for certain. This doesn't leave here. We need to lock this down and keep quiet until we can solve what happened. Agreed?"

"Agreed. That's easy. Anyway, who would I tell?"

They sat at the kitchen table for half an hour, speculating as to how Lettie could be alive and why Benecorp—or anyone else—might try to trick Lisa with an impostor. They talked and swapped ideas and Lisa drank her glass of wine and Joe jotted possibilities on a junk mail envelope. They decided there was an obvious starting point, so the next morning Joe called the state lab and spoke with the assistant director, and she pulled the VanSandt file and informed him the test showed a clean and unequivocal match. There was nothing unusual or irregular. Special Agent Clay Hatcher personally delivered the six items. The scientist who did the analysis was a meticulous eleven-year veteran, whose work was double-checked by his supervisor. "To put this in layman's language," the lab lady noted, "it's a no-brainer. The three exemplars from Lettie VanSandt have the same DNA profile as the three tissue samples collected from the deceased."

"Absolutely nothing even the slightest bit odd?" Joe pressed.

"Nope. Though I will say it seems to be a popular case recently. We had another lawyer, a Mr. Champoux, inquiring a few days ago."

"Would you please let me know if anything pops up?" he asked.

On Thursday night, Lisa registered as Della Street, and she and Joe sat in front of the computer in their living room and the screen automatically scrolled through babble and idiotic drivel and slang combinations they didn't understand and relentless ads for webcams and "1000's of hot and sexy girls," but they didn't see anything from Lettie or Roberto100 and gave up after an hour. "This is bullshit," he said when they closed the site.

"It was her, Joe. It was. You still don't believe me?"

"I believe there was someone in your car, okay? But how the hell does a tattooed, loudmouth troublemaker stay invisible for months? How? And why does this reborn Lettie come out of hiding only to tell you she's hiding and offer you a fat payday? Why doesn't she simply contact the police or ask us to protect her?"

"Hell, if she acted rationally or made a lick of sense, then I really would be suspicious—it's Lettie VanSandt we're dealing with. Think about this: If this is a plant or a scam, why didn't they follow through online and keep the story going? Keep stringing us along? Why contact me and then disappear?"

"Let's make sure we keep the note darn safe so we can check it for prints if we ever get to that point," Joe said.

"So what next?" Lisa asked.

"We don't go off half-cocked, and we don't panic. We do exactly what we're trained to do: We treat every possibility seriously, and we examine every plausible alternative. In other words, we assume she's alive and we assume she's dead, and we bust ass on both theories. We walk two different roads as best we can. And if one day we hear she's in Limbo, we add that to the list and bust ass there too."

"Thanks for all the faith in me, Joe." She wasn't bitchy or strident. She nearly smiled. "Glad you at least trust your wife enough to consider my eyewitness account plausible. I understand why you're skeptical, but I saw Lettie, okay? She's alive. This completely whipsaws everything."

CHAPTER SEVENTEEN

"I'm on my way to Stuart to meet some clients for a guardianship hearing," Lisa said into her BlackBerry. She was driving the Mercedes, traveling on Route 58, talking to M.J. "They're always sad cases. Ancient people in Velcro shoes and huge diapers who don't know where the hell they are."

"That'll be us one of these days," M.J. said. "At least we won't be accusing our kids of stealing from us or poisoning the Ensure."

"I don't even want to think about it. Ugh. I've had my fill of dying this last year."

"How'd it go with the preacher?" M.J. asked.

"He was pleasant and friendly. Very genuine. I liked him, but I just couldn't go through with it. I basically chickened out. I didn't want to be put to death by stoning or banished to the wilderness to perish or whatever else the Old Testament requires, plus talking to a complete stranger about my marriage was just too weird, especially since religion hasn't been my cup of tea. Makes me wish it were to some extent—it'd be nice to have something to rely on. I'm starting to believe that there is no Jezebel remedy. There's no conscience chemo. No pill for cheating. No therapeutic number of Hail Marys or blow jobs or home-cooked meals or good-wife deeds."

"Sorry it didn't help."

"Oh, wow," Lisa said, "you have to love Henry County. I just passed a guy spray-painting his pickup. Blue freaking spray paint. There were, like, ten empties on the ground, and he's just going to town, spraying up a storm. The truck was parked next to the great big fake-rock well cover, and he's sporting the classic bibs with no shirt on underneath."

"The denim tuxedo," M.J. replied. "Pointer Brand formal. Ah, I miss home."

"Yeah. Damn, now there's some lunatic woman about to run me over. She's on my bumper in a minivan."

"I always slow down to a crawl and make them even madder. I can't stand ignorant drivers."

"Oh, wait. She's passing me on a double solid."

"Just let her go," M.J. said.

"I am. If I thought they'd catch her, I'd phone in her license to the police. What a moron."

"She'll probably turn in about a hundred feet. With no signal. Hey, did I tell you I found an amazing deal on Vegas tickets for Garth Brooks? I wonder if he still flies during the show."

"Damn, and now she's blocking me from the front." Lisa pressed the brake pedal.

"Do you know her?" M.J. asked. "Or recognize the van?"

"No. It's a Virginia plate. She's got the flashers on, like she wants me to stop."

"Don't," M.J. said.

"Okay . . . so she's motioning to me from the window."

"Is she alone?"

"As best I can tell," Lisa said.

"Maybe it's a client."

"She's pulling into the Old Country Store."

"I say keep driving, fast as you can," M.J. urged her. "Your number's in the book if it's that important."

"I'm going to nose in behind her. There're plenty of people in the parking lot and at the pumps. You stay on with me. I've got my Mace."

"Big whoop. Lot of good it'll do against a bullet. Read me the plate number, just in case."

"Green minivan, a 'My Child Is an Honor Roll Student at Spotswood Elementary' sticker, license is Virginia GBF-1289. I'm pulling past her, closer to the entrance."

"Okay," M.J. said. "I've written everything down."

"She's stopped and motioning to me again."

"Don't get out."

"No worries there," Lisa said.

"So?"

"She's just sitting in the minivan. Straight, shoulder-length hair. It looks red. Very red. I've never seen her before. The view's not the best in a mirror, but I have no clue who she is."

"You stay put, Lisa."

"Oh, okay. Problem solved. Joe's buddy Elbert Hodges just came out of the store. I'll switch you to speaker, but he can handle it."

"Be careful," M.J. told her.

Lisa yelled for Elbert, and he walked over to her window. He was a foreman at the concrete plant and had served on the school board for three terms. "Hey, Lisa," he said. He was average height, but burly and broad-chested. "Looks like the weather's finally turned."

"It does," Lisa said. "Listen, Elbert, there's a strange woman behind me in that green minivan. She has red hair, and she sort of followed me here. I don't recognize her, and I don't know what she wants. Do you think you could go back there and find out why she's so interested in me? I'm a little concerned about doing it myself."

"My pleasure, Lisa," he answered, calm and stolid, no bluster.

"Be careful. Maybe I should call the police?"

"No need."

"I'll have to admit there're advantages to Henry County," M.J. said from the phone, which was lying in the passenger seat. "Good luck finding a man you can count on to confront your creepy stalker in Raleigh. Tell Elbert I said hello. He was a year ahead of me in high school."

"Yeah. Shhhh." Lisa powered her window completely down.

Elbert walked to his truck, in no hurry, and she saw him lean in across the seat and disappear from sight and then straighten up, his shirttail draped over his pants when he emerged, and he went behind the truck and pretended to look at something in the bed. Lisa twisted around so she could see without using the mirror, watched him directly, and she heard a loud knocking on the car's window, the passenger side, and it startled her, caused her to gulp a breath and blurt "Oh crap."

A man with short gray hair was standing beside her car, bent over so his face was next to the glass. "It's me. Culp. Robert Culp."

"What's happening?" M.J. asked from the phone. "Lisa?"

"Damn," she said. She checked behind her. The minivan was empty.

"Are you okay?" M.J. asked.

"Yeah. I'm going to cut you off and call you later." Lisa looked at the man and cracked the window so she could hear him better. "Who was your boss at Benecorp? What's Anton's last name?"

"Pichler," he said. "Please let me in before your friend attacks me."

Elbert had bolted from the pickup and was quickly at Lisa's door. "This guy came outta the minivan on the passenger side," Elbert told her. "It ain't a woman. It's him." Elbert pointed. "He was wearing a wig. A disguise."

"It's okay, Elbert. Everything's fine. We're good. No problem. But thank you so much. I'm sorry to have involved you. This is Mr. Culp. It's just a misunderstanding."

"Who the hell is he?" Elbert asked. "Why's he wearing a wig? And stalking you? You sure you're all right?"

"He's Mr. Culp, a friend of Joe's. A client. He's harmless. I'm so sorry I put you to the trouble. Thank you. He's, uh, doing some undercover work for the cops and didn't want to be seen with lawyers, and I didn't recognize him in his disguise and, well, you can see why I was concerned, but we're fine. He was just trying to meet me without anyone discovering it, and now I've probably caused him to be at risk. The sooner we break this up, the better. I don't want to blow his cover."

"Not the disguise I would pick," Elbert said.

"Anyway, I'm grateful to you," Lisa said. "Sorry I overreacted. I owe you one."

"Pleased to help," Elbert assured her. "I'd be spooked too, if I had a dude in a wig bird-dogging me down the road." He glared across the car roof at the man on the other side. "I don't know where you're from, but around here dumb stunts like what you were doing will get you shot. Clear?"

"Clear. Sorry."

"Tell my pal Joe I sent my regards," Elbert said. "I hear he killed a beast of a turkey this year."

"He did," Lisa said. "And, Elbert, please, the fewer people who hear about Mr. Culp . . . Understand? He really is doing important work for the police, and Joe will also confirm he's a solid person. We need to do all we can to keep drug dealers off the streets."

"Yeah," Elbert agreed. He raised a hand toward his forehead to touch the bill of an invisible hat. Turning to leave, he glowered at Mr. Culp again but didn't say anything, didn't break stride.

Lisa gestured for her visitor to get in the car, then raised both windows. "So you're Dr. Downs?"

"Yes. I am."

She glared at him. "How dumb can you be? Have you lost your mind? Have you?"

"Yes. Yes. And then found it again. More than once."

"That whole production was stupid beyond belief," she said. Blocked by other vehicles and an obese woman poking along in a Rascal scooter, Lisa was clicking the shifter into Reverse while she spoke.

"So sorry."

She peered at Downs, started with his brown lace-up shoes and made her way to his pinballing eyes. She drove to the side of the building and backed into a lined space so she was facing the gas pumps and the highway. Her purse was gapped open on the console, the Mace handy. "I'm already late for an appointment in Stuart."

"Oh, goodness. Please, I can't leave my sister's van. It might get damaged. Or stolen. But don't you worry, Mrs. Stone. I'm no threat. I'm your ally."

"At least you're not wearing makeup. That would trigger all the alarms."

He flickered a smile and glanced away, and Lisa was relieved his reaction was normal, slightly embarrassed, chagrined, like when she caught Joe sinking his cheeks and flexing his arm muscles in front of the bathroom mirror. "I'm being followed," Downs said. "I sneaked out from my sister's. She has red hair, so I wore a long coat and the wig. Mr. Stone sent me a message on Token Rock. I could always hope for a part in *Some Like It Hot* if this went poorly for me. Tony Curtis, Jack Lemmon, 1959. One hundred twenty minutes running time, one Oscar, number twenty-two on the AFI best movies list. A little joke. But you already know that."

"Should I call Joe and have him meet us?"

"No! I'm sure they're listening to your phones." His mouth ticced left.

"How about I tell him I've had car trouble? Who would ever know you're here?"

Downs scratched his head, near the crown, ten nervous fingers scouring gray stubble. "They still might be on his trail."

"Is that why you're following me instead of Joe?"

"Exactly. But you already know that." He quit with his fingers and rested his hands in his lap. He checked the highway, the store's entrance, the seat behind him. "How much has Mr. Stone told you?"

"He . . ." Lisa stopped and stared at him, waiting for him to harness his eyes and pay attention to her. He kept at his vigil, even scrunched lower so he could gain a view of the building's roof. "He told me a lot, Dr. Downs. But the important thing is I believe you, okay? I think Lettie invented something very valuable, I know Benecorp wants it, I know they came here to force her to sell and I know they returned later with bad intentions toward her. I also believe they've treated you unfairly."

"Yes. Thank you." The reassurance failed to halt Downs's agitation and constant surveillance. He was transfixed by a black car cutting diagonally through the lot.

"Dr. Downs," she said, touching his arm, "look at me. We're okay. Safe. The villains wouldn't be following you in a shiny black Lincoln."

"I'm listening. Don't be fooled. We can't drop our guard."

"Calm down. Take a deep breath. Are you sure I shouldn't call Joe?"

"No, don't. Not yet." His lips ticced again.

"Do you have any new information?"

"I still have a contact at Benecorp. A mole. I call them Malcorp. *Mal* is the Latin root meaning bad. But you already know that." He almost whispered the sentences. "There are a few people there who realize Malcorp wronged me and is an evil operation. But there's nothing new to report."

"So what does the Wound Velvet do? We're back to square one."

"Do you recognize the people in that car? The black car?"

"I don't," she said. "But it has a Henry County sticker. It's local, not Benecorp."

"They're cunning."

"If they were cunning, Doctor, they wouldn't roll in here with a big black car."

"Counterintuitive. Hiding in plain sight."

"We've heard from Benecorp that the Wound Velvet's use is internal and minor, whatever that means."

"Ha!" Downs slapped his thigh with his palm. "Silly talk. Listen to me. Seth Garrison doesn't fly there for routine tweaks and refinements. Pichler doesn't bully me. But most certainly, MissFit Matrix is geared to match with very specific goals. They've hit one of the grails."

"So the MissFit program wouldn't produce what they're claiming?" Lisa asked.

"No. They would have you believe they were ocean fishing for a whale and caught a field mouse. It's that incongruous. I'll bet dimwit Pichler told you this nonsense. He's a hateful man and a joke scientist."

"But you have no more information as to any details?"

"Mr. G has been on campus several times recently. He doesn't just come because there's a retirement party or for employee appreciation day. He's reclusive. He visits one point seven times per annum."

"Anything else you can tell us, no matter how small?"

Downs pointed at her. "I'm being watched. Okay, yes, I'm paranoid, but my sister will confirm it. It's obvious. They're sending me a message. I'm afraid."

Lisa touched his shoulder. "I believe you," she said. "And I'm sorry. Is there anything Joe and I can do?"

"Crack this case." He sounded normal, composed, his tics and peculiarities momentarily suppressed. "These people want to kill me too, Mrs. Stone. This isn't a Keystone Kops outfit. Money rules, and huge money rules like Stalin. Show trials and no prisoners."

"You might be safer here. Joe and I have a strong relationship with the police. We'd be glad to arrange protection for you."

"Lettie was safer here too?" He began his watch again: the road, the parking lot, the store, its roof, the area behind him.

"Lettie was surprised. You won't be. Why don't you let Joe and me put you in a secure place? Please. I really wish you would. At least for the short term, we could have an off-duty deputy stay with you. We'd handle everything."

"I'll consider it. But they'd find me."

"You do need to be careful. I'm convinced these are dangerous people. The best choice is to let us help, Dr. Downs."

"You certainly are eager." He strayed off his routine to examine her. "I just can't say. It's so hard to make decisions."

"You can trust us," Lisa promised him.

"Mr. Stone, yes. Lettie didn't care much for you. But you already know that. No offense meant. Only another fact for me to consider."

"I understand," she said. "But I think Joe would give you the same advice."

"Probably. It's not as if I have many good options. We are smack up against it, Mrs. Stone."

"Do you recall what elements or ingredients are in VV 108?"

"Some. But not all and not the precise formulary. Nothing exact. Why?"

"You can't match the ingredients with any known disease or use?"

"No. That's what MissFit does. MissFit is genius. Mr. Garrison pioneered it. Despite everything, I admire him as a scientist."

"Well, how many diseases are plugged into MissFit?"

"Over a hundred would be my guess. For instance, there are many different variations of cancer."

"Huh. I guess that's a big fat dead end." She sighed.

"Mr. G knows what Lettie's compound does. A few others."

"Could there be any connection to animals? Cats and dogs? Lettie's have gone missing under very strange circumstances."

"Nope. None I can see. Benecorp does people only."

"This is so frustrating," she said. "We're absolutely stymied. Damn it. Why'd you risk coming here if you don't have anything else to tell us?"

"Mr. Stone asked. He sent me a message. We're partners in this. He was Lettie's counselor. I did provide you new information. Benecorp is lying about this being internal—new."

"May I ask you a question?"

"Yes." Resolutely focused on the highway, Downs scratched his head again.

"Are you barred from having contact with Benecorp? Did a court enter an order?"

"Yes."

"How many times have you been hospitalized for psychological issues?" she asked.

"Total? I couldn't count. It's the one number I choose to forget."

Lisa smiled at him. "At least three in the last several years?"

He nodded. "Yep." He sawed his thumb across his chin. "But my work has always been superior. I'm proud of that."

"Well, I guess it's a good thing I believe you're correct about Lettie, huh? Otherwise I might think you were unreliable and crazy."

"Yes," he said. "You're very kind. I appreciate it."

She turned and looked behind them. "Still clear in this direction," she said. "Would you allow me to at least let a police officer follow you to your sister's and make sure you're safe?"

"I'm not positive that's where I'll go. I don't know if that's smart. Right now I have an advantage—a head start. But I need to return her van. I—" Downs broke off and violently rocked toward the door. He dropped to the floorboard, balling himself into the space under the dash. "It's them! From my sister's!"

Lisa watched a tan Ford sedan with a Maryland tag enter the lot. The car hesitated after making a left turn from Route 58, then moved toward the minivan and stopped alongside it. After a few stationary moments, the car began patrolling through the lot, passing in front of Lisa and Downs, the passenger hunting, scanning, staring at her, the eye contact direct and bold, the vehicle slowing while he checked her and the Mercedes, the man's expression professionally belligerent, as if he had a license to do as he pleased, no matter how coarse or intrusive. The car parked, and he went into the store. He was tall, impressive, crisply dressed, creases in his trousers.

"I'm calling the police," Lisa said. "And Joe too."

"Now might be the time for it," Downs agreed.

Lisa told the dispatcher she had an emergency. She asked if there were any cops nearby, and the dispatcher inquired if she was Mrs. Stone, the lawyer.

"Yes, it's Lisa Stone. Who's close?"

"I think Car One is. Sheriff Perry. He's on Carver Road."

"Great. Excellent."

"Wait, okay, yeah, and Trooper Wilkinson just marked on. He's en route too, Mrs. Stone. Are you hurt? In danger?"

"Not yet. Just tell them to hurry."

Harold Wilkinson was at the store in minutes, lights strobing, his car's siren wailing, the nose of his blue and gray state police cruiser floating skyward when he crested a hill at over a hundred and came into view, the tires seeming to tiptoe on the blacktop. He drove straight to Lisa and Downs, braked. He adjusted his hat as he strode toward her. Sheriff Perry arrived seconds behind him and sprinted for the Mercedes.

"Are you all right, Lisa?" Wilkinson asked. A few months short of sixty and retirement, he loved to spin hilarious stories about chasing 1970s bootleggers, backwoods characters who fashioned their stills from copper and never gave him a speck of trouble if he got the better of them in a fair pursuit. He was still agile and trim, his uniform squared away. Lisa stepped out and shut the door and stood beside him. As usual, he smelled of grocery store aftershave, the sweet, slap-on, watery variety that contained pure alcohol and had to sting like the dickens if it found a nick or scrape, a bygone scent that suited him perfectly and gave Lisa a quick sense of well-being. "What's happening?"

"Thanks for coming so fast. Here's my problem. The man in the car with me is a client of Joe's, Dr. Steven Downs. He's hiding because he's scared. See that car?" She pointed at the tan Ford. "We're fairly sure those guys are tracking him. We also think they might be a danger to him." She saw Joe arrive, in a rush like the others.

"Joe," the trooper shouted, "you stay with your wife while the sheriff and I check the car."

"Oh shit," Joe exclaimed when he reached Lisa and spied Downs. The doctor was still hiding, remained mostly on the car's floor.

"Hello, Mr. Stone," he said meekly after unrolling and stretching to crack the door. He gave Joe a choppy, harried wave. "I got your message. Sorry for all the fuss I brought with me."

"So, either I'm as paranoid as the good doc," Lisa said, "or two fairly threatening men followed him here. The driver's still sitting in the car. He's been wearing out his rearview mirror looking at me. His buddy went inside."

"How in creation did you meet him?" Joe asked, gesturing at Downs.

"Yeah, well, that's another tale completely. Suffice it to say, we are indebted to Elbert Hodges."

"Why? How's that?" Joe asked.

"I'll tell you later. I want to see who these guys are. And if they're here for Dr. Downs."

At the trooper's direction, the driver was soon standing beside the Ford, the door swung wide open, the key reminder buzzing. He was squat, without any discernible transition between the back of his head and his meaty neck. His head was shaved bald. He was wearing a blue blazer, and he seemed pugnacious, his legs spread, his hands on his hips, his shoulders shot forward. Lisa could hear Trooper Wilkinson telling him something. She walked closer, Joe right with her and slightly in the lead, clutching her elbow.

"Minding my own business at a convenience store is a crime in these parts?" the bald man said.

"Nope. But tailing people and menacing a local lawyer might be. All we need is some ID and some answers."

"If by 'local lawyer,'" the man replied, "you mean Lisa Stone over there, I hardly think driving past her constitutes any kind of offense."

Hearing his wife's name in the conversation, Joe released her arm and pointed at her, his finger almost touching her nose. "You stay here. Do not budge." The tan car was maybe thirty feet from him, and he exploded through the distance to confront the bald man. Simultaneously, the stranger's companion pushed through the store's smeared glass doors. The companion didn't hurry or rush or appear concerned, simply joined the other four men. "Good morning, Officers," he said genially. "What has Saul done this time?"

"He evidently has an issue with my wife," Joe said. "And I plan to find out just what his issue is." Even in a lawyer's suit, striped tie and scuffed black wingtips, Joe was formidable, imposing, and it registered with Saul, caused him to reset his shoulders and soften his posture. "Who the hell are you?" Joe demanded, taking off his jacket and draping it across his forearm.

"Easy, Joe," Wilkinson said. "He was gettin' ready to tell us."

The man who'd come from the store raised both hands to signal that he wasn't spoiling for a fight, at least not right now. "No worries, boss." He was speaking to Joe. "Our apologies." He had thick black hair clipped high and tight and a reptile's unpredictable eyes, cold-blooded and cagey. Unlike Saul, he didn't seem fazed by Joe's size and anger. He lowered his hands. "I'm Dillon Atkins. If the sheriff and the trooper permit me, I'll reach into my pocket and provide you with my ID. My friend Saul will do the same."

"Please," the trooper said.

"Okay," Sheriff Perry agreed.

Atkins quickly located two laminated rectangles and handed them to the trooper. Saul tugged his wallet free from his hip, then fumbled through the compartments and leather slits with brute fingers until he found his driver's license. He dropped the license, muttered "Damn it," grimaced, crouched, recovered it, stood up again and unhappily thrust it at Wilkinson.

"To speed us along, Trooper, uh"—Atkins leaned forward and angled for a closer view of the officer's nameplate—"Trooper Wilkinson, we're both private security, employed by Aegis Alpha, a global company with our domestic headquarters in Washington."

"Yeah, okay, I've heard of you people," the sheriff offered. "You ex-military?"

"Affirmative, sir. Ten years army. Three years with the FBI after that."

"Can I see the IDs, Harold?" Perry asked.

"Yeah." Wilkinson handed him the three cards.

"So what brings you gents to Henry County?" the sheriff asked. "And what business do you have with Mrs. Stone?"

"No business with her or her husband. Again, we apologize for upsetting you both." Atkins had a salesman's honey in his voice. He briefly humbled his head, broke eye contact with the other men. "Saul knows her name—and so do I—because she's associated with Dr. Steven Downs, who I'm speculating is probably hiding in Mrs. Stone's Mercedes, which is, of course, completely her prerogative. Not my concern."

"What's your interest in Mr. Downs?" Perry asked.

"Strictly professional. Our client wants him watched and wants to know his movements. Our client has verifiable reasons to believe that Dr. Downs is dangerous and an active threat. We monitor him twenty-four-seven and report. He left his sister's home in Harrison-burg, Virginia, earlier today wearing a disguise. Soon as we realized he was missing, we followed him here."

"How?" Joe pressed. "How'd you locate him?"

"We have state-of-the-art techniques, Mr. Stone," Atkins answered. "But with all due respect, that's our business, not yours." His tone was politely antagonistic. "To finish my report to the officers, let me make clear that we're simply tracking Dr. Downs at a professional distance. We don't speak to him, impede him, bother him or inter-fere with him in any form or fashion. I don't think there's anything illegal in our surveillance coverage. We're well trained to respect his autonomy."

"What makes you think he's a danger to your client?" Wilkinson asked. "You have some proof?"

"Proof?" Saul sneered. "In spades. He's lucky all he's lookin' at is a couple babysitters."

"Saul makes a valid point. If you'd allow me, I'll show you our paper-work. It's in the car."

"Yeah, I'd like to see it," Wilkinson said.

"It's Benecorp, right?" Joe interrupted. "Benecorp hired you?"

"As a matter of protocol, we usually don't reveal the identities of our clients. In this case, though, it's no secret that your very unstable acquaintance, Dr. Downs, has threatened Benecorp and its CEO, Seth Garrison. So, yes, absolutely, sir, we are here on behalf of Mr. Garrison and his company." Atkins nodded toward the tan Ford. "May I?"

"Go ahead," Wilkinson told him.

Atkins walked to the passenger door, opened it and retrieved a file. He removed the key to stop the warning racket. He returned to Trooper Wilkinson. "The first document is an e-mail sent to several Benecorp employees on April seventeenth, just last month. In it, Dr. Downs states that my client, Seth Garrison, 'must be eliminated at any and all cost.' He adds seven exclamation points to that very direct threat. A variation of this attack on Mr. Garrison was posted on a website called Token Rock a few days later. Though the poster used an alias, we have proof it was Downs. This all comes on the heels of a court order entered against Dr. Downs because of repeated threatening conduct. He is barred from any contact with Mr. Garrison or Benecorp. You are also welcome to check Dr. Downs's history with Dade County and the FBI." Atkins made a production of handing several documents to the trooper, highlighting what each set of papers contained.

"Is this Downs fellow with you, Lisa?" Sheriff Perry asked.

Lisa started for her husband. "Yes. He's hiding in my car because he's afraid of these two for-pay bullies."

"Ought to be the other way around," Saul suggested. "We aren't the people on the wrong end of an official court order."

"You might find yourself on the wrong end of more than a court order," Joe snapped.

Wilkinson returned the documents to Atkins.

"Hey, wait a minute," Saul complained. "You didn't even read 'em."

"Read all I needed to," the trooper told him. The response was pleasant, measured. "Read the very first line, which is typed in all capital letters. It says 'Circuit Court of Florida.'"

"So?" Saul's mouth remained rounded after he spoke the word.

"This is Virginia, sir," Wilkinson noted. "Henry County, Virginia. Not Miami, Florida."

"Hey, an order's an order," Saul argued. "You sayin' you ain't even going to read it? It'll tell you all you need to learn about this Downs character."

"I'm not sure we need to learn much of anything," the sheriff said. "He's here, not bothering anyone, visiting with two respected lawyers."

"Exactly," Atkins said. "We have no problem with him being here, and we certainly share your respect for the Stones. My only point is we are simply doing our job and have a legitimate reason to be watching Dr. Downs." He locked on to the sheriff. "You would agree, I assume, that we're free to continue our work." He drilled the word *agree*. He didn't blink while he was speaking. Lisa noticed crinkles form—two delicate lines—at the corner of each eye.

"You might want to be mindful of the difference between proper surveillance and stalking here in the commonwealth," the sheriff warned him.

"Code section 18.2-60.3," Atkins replied. "Saul and I are well aware of it. I actually have testified before the Virginia legislature about proposed amendments to the statute, so we'll be on top of it, don't you worry. More importantly, we are exempted from its terms since we're licensed as private investigators."

"You're planning to sit here until Downs leaves and then follow him day and night?" Lisa asked, now shoulder to shoulder with Joe.

"Yes. At a respectful distance."

"There he is," Saul interrupted. "In the Mercedes." Downs's head and neck were visible above the car's dash, like a newborn bird peeking from its nest.

"We always want to work in conjunction with local agencies, Sheriff Perry. Here's a card for you. Trooper Wilkinson too." He gave them each a small white card with a shiny, embossed logo. "Now, Saul and I are planning to create a comfortable buffer between us and our subject and wait for him to begin travel. We'll drive to the opposite end of the building, as far away as anyone could want."

"We don't have to tell you jack, not really," Saul bitched at Joe. "We could have our people on this like white on rice. It'd be no contest against you Hooterville chumps."

"I'd welcome that, Saul." Joe glared at him. "Here's some more Hooterville for you: You ever bother my wife again, and I'll stomp a mud hole through your bald little ass."

"That's a threat, isn't it? These officers heard it too."

"They'll hear this as well: You're a pussy, Saul. I can spot your type a mile away. I'm holding you responsible for anything bad that happens to Downs."

"Joe," the trooper cautioned. "Let it alone."

"Sorry, Harold."

"If we're done here," Atkins said, "Saul and I will leave you gents be."

"We have no reason to stop you," Perry said.

Saul started the car and drove them to a far corner of the lot.

"What kind of doctor is your guy?" the sheriff asked.

"Scientist," Lisa said.

"Oh, okay. Not a medical doctor?"

"Nope." She checked the car, and Downs had disappeared again. "Thank you both for coming."

"Glad to," Trooper Wilkinson said. "Someone had to be here to keep Joe from committin' a felony."

"Both of those guys just reek," Joe added. "Nothing but high-priced trouble."

"I agree," Perry said. "One is way too rough, the other way too smooth. Crooked as a barrel of fishhooks, but they're not breaking any law. You think this guy, the doctor, really intends to hurt their employer?"

"Maybe," Lisa said. "But there's no chance a heavy hitter like Seth Garrison is truly worried he's at risk. They have other reasons for making Downs's life miserable."

"Which would be?"

"That's where we come in," she said. "Generally speaking, it's a business dispute."

"Must be a big deal to warrant hiring these fellows," the sheriff said.

"Big enough," Lisa replied. "And thanks again for looking after us."

"Yeah, we appreciate it." Joe shook Wilkinson's hand.

"Mind your temper, Joe, you hear?" the trooper told him. "And you both be careful."

The sheriff and Wilkinson left, and Joe and Lisa went to the passenger side of the Mercedes, and Joe opened the door. "Okay, Doc, you can sit up now."

"Where're the Benecorp thugs?"

"Still here, unfortunately," Joe said.

"Oh, my heavens. Can't the police help?"

"Technically," he answered, "Saul the Neanderthal and his handler Atkins aren't breaking any law. They're licensed private detectives from a reputable agency. They have a legitimate reason for their surveillance, especially since you composed a threatening e-mail and sent it to Benecorp. You did that, yes?"

"It seems I might have," Downs admitted. "It was a warning and an alert, not a threat. There's a difference."

"I see," Joe said sourly. "Great."

"What in the world am I going to do?" Downs asked.

"Damn good question," Joe said. He was still carrying his suit jacket. The weather was pleasant, so he didn't bother putting it on again. "What brings you to Henry County?"

"Your message. Plus, I have important information to share."

"Yeah," Lisa said. "Helpful blockbusters such as Seth Garrison has visited the business he founded and owns. Very valuable insight. Also, Dr. Downs is being followed. More big news for us."

"Yes. But we can't talk here." Downs put his index finger over his lips. "Shhhh. I'm sure they are eavesdropping. Easy to do from a mere few feet away. I do have very critical facts for you, Mr. Stone. We need to talk."

"I thought you didn't have anything else for us," Lisa said. She scowled at Downs. "Other than the Wound Velvet is a big discovery, not a minor tweak. Why'd you follow me if you weren't planning to tell me anything?"

Downs wouldn't look at her. "Ad hoc for me. Making choices as I go along. Mr. Stone was Lettie's counselor-at-law. Lettie trusted him. But you already know that. No offense. My report is a secret for him."

"Sure, Doctor," Lisa said. "Whatever."

"Where do you want to go?" Joe asked.

"Let's do this," Downs replied. "We'll leave in your vehicle and drive around, then you can bring me back here. I have to return my sister's van. She's a parent. A mom. Two kids. Returning it is primary, no matter what." His lip twitched and stayed stretched for an instant, hung.

"You understand those men will follow you all the way to Harrisonburg?" Lisa said.

"They will follow me wherever," Downs said. "I don't have a chance."

"You're truly welcome to stay here," Lisa reminded him. "We'll hire security for you."

"Thank you, Mrs. Stone. I have to leave. Thank you very much, but I've decided."

"Dr. Downs," Joe said, "you have to realize I'll tell Lisa whatever you tell me."

"Your choice, sir." He shrugged. "Lettie trusted you. You can do as you please. It'll be on your head. Your actions, not mine."

Joe put on his jacket. He tugged his white shirt cuffs into view from beneath the jacket's sleeves. "In that case, she can simply come with us."

"Fine," Downs said quietly. "On your authority, not mine."

They all loaded into the Jeep, Downs in the front, and the doc told Joe to find a clear station and play it loud, loud as the speakers would bear, and with Saul and Atkins keeping pace behind them on Route 58, a mile from the store Downs slipped Joe a sheet of paper and leaned into his ear, their cheeks almost touching. "E-mail," Downs confided. "Pichler to Mr. G."

Joe drove and read: "Mr. Garrison—Per conversation with Lettie VanSandt attorney, maybe we have competition for MissFit project. Realize project is absolute priority, so wanted to alert you and legal. Who else is interested? A. Pichler."

"The same day he spoke to Lisa," Joe said. "I'll be damned."

Downs was half-sitting, half-squatting, still crowding against Joe. "'Absolute priority' for Seth Garrison. It's a monster, Mr. Stone. A grand slam." He continued to keep his voice hushed.

Joe nudged Downs with an elbow to separate them and handed the page back to his wife. "How do you happen to have your old boss's e-mail?" Joe asked. He pushed against Downs again. "Get off me, Doctor. Lord. I can't drive with you in my lap."

"Hacked it. Child's play, if you know the IP address. Don't need it, though. Pichler's password is Mr. Nobel. His secretary told everybody at our Christmas party. She was drinking. She despises him also."

"Well, if there was ever any doubt," Lisa said, "this puts it to rest."

Downs had returned to the passenger seat. He checked behind him, where Saul and Atkins continued their tail. "I can't let them wreck me in my sister's van. I should've never used it. What a stupid imbecile I am. Or if they shoot it or shoot a tire or shoot *me* and ruin the interior."

Lisa noticed Joe canting his head, and she met his reflection in the rearview, matched eyes. "How frigging far is Harrisonburg?" he grumbled. "Three hours? I'll follow you home, Dr. Downs, though I seriously doubt they'll do anything now that they're exposed and as obvious as tits on a boar to the police. It would be far too untidy for Benecorp. But, yeah, I'll follow you to your sister's."

"Thanks a million, partner," Downs said. "Sorry for the trouble."

"You want me to ride with you?" Lisa asked.

"No need," Joe said. He'd left the mirror and was watching the highway. "And if something happened, I'd rather you be here and safe." He switched the radio station and turned the volume lower.

"Thanks a million," Downs repeated.

"Keep your cell on and call me, okay?" Lisa leaned into the front so she was between them. "I'll be worried until you come home."

"They can track us by the phone," Downs exclaimed. "If you call."

"No shit," Joe said. "They might even find us and a hire a couple minions to follow us."

Downs touched his temple with a forefinger, bobbing his head rapidly. "Yes. Exactly. I wasn't thinking clearly. Just be careful not to mention anything you don't want intercepted. But you already know that."

"By the way," Joe said, "when was the last time you heard from Lettie? Or had any contact with her?"

"Oh, gracious, let me think ... probably about two weeks before I learned she was dead."

"Nothing since then?" Joe asked. "Nothing more recent?" He glanced at Downs.

"No. Of course not, Mr. Stone." His mouth ticced. Ticced again. "Are you testing me? I haven't broken with reality just yet. How would I talk to her if she's dead? That's crazy, even by my standards."

CHAPTER EIGHTEEN

Lisa stood near a pallet of fertilizer sacks and watched as Dr. Downs, Joe and the hired dicks departed the Old Country Store and caravanned toward Harrisonburg, Downs in the lead, Joe next, Saul and Atkins skulking behind. She checked the time and decided to finish her trip to Stuart for her appointment, but she lit a cigarette and smoked it to the filter before actually cranking the Mercedes, sat there with the window lowered while customers pumped gasoline and scratched lottery tickets on car hoods and gobbled hot dogs, burgers and barbecue sandwiches from the grill as they walked out of the building, the food nested in thin, white-paper wraps. She phoned Joe, and he promised her everything was fine so far, except that Downs was creeping along at forty on the bypass, where the limit was sixty-five and the cops wouldn't bother you at seventy. "Be careful," she told him. "I love you."

Even with the new cell tower in Spencer, service was spotty for most of her drive, so she waited until she was a few miles east of Stuart to call M.J., who answered immediately.

"Tell me what happened," M.J. said anxiously. "You okay?"

Lisa recounted the episode with Downs, Saul and Atkins, and the police. She was smoking another cigarette, held it pinched and erect with the fingers of her steering hand, and she had to trap the BlackBerry between her cheek and shoulder and switch her grip whenever she thumped ashes through a slight window crack. Some of the ashes would suck back into the interior, and as she was accelerating away from the stoplight at Walmart, a dead gray chunk broke off prematurely and hit the floor mat, quickly scattered, *pfffft*.

"Amazing," M.J. said. "Hired guns and secret formulas. Damn."

"This will be ginormous if we can figure how to beat these people. The e-mail from Pichler confirms we're dealing with a huge payoff."

"Yeah, that Joe gave away, right?" M.J.'s tone wasn't mocking or cruel. "Isn't that where you're at?"

"As of today. For sure, we have a major complication. But we'll be okay. No matter what, Benecorp needs to be exposed."

"Take care of yourself," M.J. said solemnly. "Joe too."

"I will," Lisa said. "It's at the point of being scary."

"Especially if they have ex-military apes on the payroll."

"Our best protection," Lisa said, "is how much of this is now in the open. The sheriff's alerted. The state police."

"I'm not sure that's really the kind of firewall I'd prefer. Me, I'd feel better about something a little less abstract."

"Joe's no slouch, either," Lisa added. "He could've kicked Saul's butt back to Northern Virginia. Thank god, I'm not married to a wimp."

"Well, listen, while you've been busy solving mysteries with Scooby-Doo and Shaggy, I've run into a snag of my own."

"Oh, sorry," Lisa said. "I didn't mean to hog the conversation. Business or personal?"

"Both, unfortunately. My latest beau—"

"Brian," Lisa interjected. "From California. The Reiki guy with almost enough credits for a junior college diploma in hospitality management."

"Quit it. When you shorthand his résumé, it makes me look even stupider. He's gorgeous, completely selfless in bed and blessed with one of the biggest penises on the planet. Those would be his most important qualifications."

"How would you know exactly? About how big he is compared to other guys? Unless you have an accurate database or have done a thorough marketplace sampling? The latter would make you convincing and reliable but also a slut."

"I saw the *Pirates* movie, okay? The X-rated knockoff of the Johnny Depp adventures. Ramona Hough showed it at her bachelorette party. It was cheaper than a stripper, and you can fast-forward it when everyone gets bored. Those guys are professionals. Brian would have no problem with the casting specs. How's that?"

Lisa laughed. "I'd say you're qualified to testify as an expert." She laughed some more and coughed as she was exhaling an Ultra Light draw. Her eyes watered and she had to shoulder-squeeze the phone again so she could dab at the wetness. "Anyway, you were telling me about your woes."

"The romance with Brian was going great and, lo and behold, I discover he's a plushie."

"Huh? A what?"

"A plushie, Lisa. He's been really generous and willing no matter what sex I want or how I want it, so for fun, I asked what I could do for him. *His* fantasy. I'm expecting, you know, a French maid outfit or a cheerleader skirt or a Zorro mask and a bullwhip. Maybe a public quickie in a storeroom at the mall. Handcuffs. The threesome would be a no, of course, unless I'm in the minority. Anyway, he tells me he wants us to dress up like big stuffed animals. In human-size costumes."

"Really? Seriously?" Lisa couldn't help but giggle.

"No joke."

"Did you? Did you do it? What were you? Which animal?"

"I gave it a good faith effort. I was a giant squirrel. Just so you'll know for future reference, the costume wasn't cheap, and I'm sitting in a hotel room sweating and suffocating inside it, especially the head, which was hot as an oven and made me claustrophobic."

Lisa howled. "I'd give anything for a photo. Did you wear normal shoes or did you have paws?"

"Paws. Big furry paws with skid pads on the bottom."

"What was he?" Lisa asked. "So you have the romantic rendezvous with him, all squirrel-girl and sweating, and he gallantly arrives in his costume? Or did he dress in the bathroom and pounce out on you?"

"Oh, no," M.J. said. She stretched the "oh," and Lisa imagined her rolling her eyes as she spoke. "Nope, he proudly sashayed down the hall to our suite fully in character. His *fursona* is how they describe it. He's basically a teddy bear character, in the mold of Dancing Bear from the Captain Kangaroo show if you can remember back that far. But with a long tail. I think the tail was his own after-market addition. It was more of a lion's tail."

"Oh, M.J. How hysterical."

"Yeah."

"Did you go through with it?" Lisa asked. She'd finished her cigarette and sealed the window. "How can you have sex in the fur suits?"

"Easy enough for him—he has a fly at the front of his and big enough equipment to easily make it through the interference. But first, you groom each other, like monkeys or something. Plushie foreplay. While he's picking at me, he's doing these squeaks and trilling noises, which makes no sense if he's supposed to be a bear, okay? There's also this kind of modified dutty wine dance that goes along with the flea picking. Finally, I have to drop my costume bottom and he stays in his outfit and bends me over the bed. Unfortunately, I'm still stuck in the gigantic head and a hot-as-hades top."

"A question, M.J.: Exactly how much walking-around money are you giving him each month? I know 'allowance' isn't the proper term, but how much did this cost you? Prorated over a thirty-day period?"

"In the larger scheme of things, it's harmless and completely his business. It's not like he wanted me to do something dangerous or illegal. I'm a live-and-let-live type. As long as it doesn't affect me, more power to you. Problem is, once you've been groomed and squeaked at by a man in a bear suit with thick polyester fur, any kind of decent sex afterwards is impossible with him. You can't do it. No matter how handsome he is, you're thinking grown man with his dong poking out of a bear costume. It's not an image you can erase, ever."

"Yeah, it would have to be, uh, unbearable," Lisa said.

"Very funny. So, I had to cut Brian loose. I ended our relationship."

"Sorry to hear it. I am."

"He didn't take it well," M.J. said.

"Did you end it or just ... *pause* for a while." Lisa was tee-heeing through every syllable. "He'll probably be tough to fur-get."

"The tough-to-forget part is the legal action he's threatening. Some vulture lawyer he's managed to hire is bugging me about an employment claim. Sexual harassment. The twisted, lie-packed, moneygrubbing accusation is that I fired him because he finally refused my advances after I'd used my job to make him have sex with the boss for several months."

"Certainly you didn't have him on the payroll?"

"Of course not. I did throw him some crumbs every now and then and had him cater an event for the radio stations and a Christmas party for the office. I always had him sign a contract. He was treated and paid strictly as an independent contractor. My old boss in the equipment business used to tell me 'never poop where you eat.' Well, actually, he said 'never shit where you eat.' Good advice. I've double-checked every deal with Bear Brian, and the paperwork states he's simply an independent contractor. This lawyer crap is an old-fashioned shakedown."

"Yeah, sounds like he has zero chance of winning."

"But as we both understand, there's a transactional cost for me to schlep though the courts, even though he'll lose. There's also the embarrassment factor; this scumbag attorney has already told me he plans a press conference and a media release. Worse, he'll have the EEOC in my knickers, and if I catch the wrong investigator, I can see problems—wouldn't they just love to show how fair and gender-neutral they are by pursuing a woman for sexual harassment? It would give them a pass for years to come, and being our cowardly, sound-bite-driven government, it's exactly the kind of statistic they'd sacrifice me for, no matter how innocent I am."

"I can't argue with your analysis. Pretty soon, you won't need me for advice."

"Honestly, what I dread the most is the *News and Observer* piece where I come off as a crinkly old bitch who has to hire young studs. How lovely."

"What contact have you had with Brian's lawyer?" Lisa asked.

"So far, a letter and then a longer letter offering a 'reasonable negotiated settlement.'"

"Fax me copies," Lisa said. "Give me a couple days to think about how we should approach it."

"Thanks," M.J. said. "Maybe I can recoup enough from selling the squirrel suit to pay my legal fees."

"Today is June sixth, 2011, and this is a called meeting of Stone and Stone, LLC," Joe droned, as serious and grave and ponderous as ever, as if he were a corporate titan on a podium, addressing hundreds of stockholders in a magnificent Manhattan ballroom.

"Joe," Lisa snapped, "can we just get to it? Why do you always do this?" Despite her earnest efforts to be tolerant and understanding of her husband's quirks, the whole Robert's Rules, dog-and-pony show was simply too much. Joe had appeared at her door after lunch and announced there'd be a "firm meeting" in his office, five o'clock sharp. Moments later, Betty had delivered a typewritten notice confirming the place and time.

"There's a correct way and a half-assed way," Joe said, and the calm, satisfied reply made matters worse. The firm's three thick files were stacked in the center of his desk, the files tabbed and organized, every paper and resolution in its place, twenty years' worth of boondoggle.

"There's a normal way and an anal-retentive way," she replied.

"New business," he said, ignoring her swipe. "Mr. Pichler phoned this morning while you were in court. They've received the nondisclosure forms we signed. He wants to discuss Lettie's medicine. I didn't take the call. Betty told him we'd be in touch soon."

"Okay. Why didn't you simply tell me?"

"I think we're at a point where we really need to stop and think. We need to either punt this and forget it or jump in whole hog."

"I agree," she said, nodding.

"If we jump in whole hog, it could be dangerous. It could also ruin us and the firm financially."

"I suppose," Lisa answered. "Do you think they'd really come after us?"

"From what I've seen, yes. In some form or fashion, yes, I believe they'll attempt to punish us if we cause them any problems. Maybe attack us legally, maybe otherwise. In fact, the more I've thought about it and the more we've learned, it wouldn't surprise me if Benecorp had a hand in Jane Rousch's disappearance. Remember the mysterious rental-car lady? Maybe she and her companion ended up dead and their car carefully abandoned in a parking deck because they were a direct connection to Lettie. They'd be a hellacious loose thread for Seth Garrison."

"True."

"Of course," Joe added, "I realize you're convinced that Lettie's alive. I'm not forgetting that possibility. Still nothing from the chat room?"

"Nothing. And I've sent tons of messages. I haven't told you, and it's a long shot, but I've checked by her trailer too. Several times, without any luck. But I know what I saw."

"I'm not trying to be a prick about it," Joe said. "I'm not saying you're wrong. Everything's on the table. We have to keep an open mind. If we pursue every alternative, then nothing can surprise us. I'm positive there was someone in your car who sounded like Lettie and claimed to be Lettie. No doubt. I believe you."

"So what do you think we ought to do?" Lisa asked. She was sitting across the desk from him. She was wearing her tanzanite ring and began rotating it around her middle finger. The blue stone scraped on each side as it turned. "I've thought and thought, and I'm not sure of our options. We could finesse, well, *counterfeit* trust or foundation documents, but I'm certain there's no chance you'd go along with that plan. We can hire a private detective to hunt for Lettie, assuming she's alive, and I really believe she is, but she could be anywhere. We don't have the first clue or lead. You could look in Topeka or next door in Chatham. It's frustrating as hell."

"I won't be a crook just because they are," Joe replied. He swiveled and took a walnut from a bowl he kept on the credenza. He cracked the nut in his palm, picked out the husk and dropped it into the trash can, then ate the meat straight from his hand. "As for a detective, you're right, where the hell would he search?"

"We don't have any leverage." She sighed. "Sooner or later, our ruse is going to end and they'll discover they already own the formula and we were posturing about Lettie's trust having a claim."

"Yep," Joe said. He rubbed his palms together over the trash can.

"I've considered trying to push this farther up the ladder." She quit spinning her ring. "What do we lose if we refuse to speak to Pichler, drop the iron curtain and tell him we want to talk to Garrison personally? Pichler's an apparatchik. He might not even understand the big picture, and he damn sure isn't in a position to make any kind of agreement or compromise with us."

"I'm with you," Joe said. "I've had the same thought. Certainly Garrison won't admit squat, but it'll buy us a few weeks, rattle their cage and maybe give us a small read on what he's up to. Who knows—maybe Lettie surfaces for good in the meantime."

"If he actually agrees to talk to us, that in itself confirms a lot."

"Along with the demand to hear from Seth Garrison, we also need to prod them a bit," Joe suggested. "Add some black pepper and habanero to their diet."

"How?"

"First, we let them know we're willing to file suit. A civil action to recover the Wound Velvet." He leaned forward, pressed his flat hands together under his chin, finger matching finger. A fleck of walnut husk was stuck on his wrist. "I'm realistic enough to know it's an uphill fight, but it'll make the point we're serious and here to stay."

"I've done the same math, Joe. What do we plead? Fraud?"

"Exactly." Joe broke his hands apart but stayed close to the desk's edge.

"Mutual mistake of fact?" Lisa added.

"Correct," he said.

Lisa was briefly quiet. "We're the two lawyers," she mused, "and Neal's the village idiot. I'd say it'll be heavy lifting for us."

"No doubt." Joe frowned, shifted in his chair. "But thanks to you, I friggin' asked him if he knew of any other assets, any estate holdings he wasn't revealing. He lied. He told us he didn't know any more than we did, yet there's no doubt he'd already been contacted by Benecorp and was their boy then. He'd probably struck a deal long before he claimed to us he was a babe in the woods." Joe took a breath, exhaled deliberately. He rubbed his neck. "For the record, I'm sorry I screwed this up, but who the heck knew? I was trying to be fair. I had no earthly idea Petty Lettie VanSandt had suddenly become Marie Curie. If I'd kept what she gave me, we'd be in the catbird seat right now."

"I don't blame you, Joe," Lisa said. "I agreed with your decision a hundred percent. You handed over a bunch of stray animals, a dilapidated trailer and a few thousand dollars. Attempted to do right by Lettie and her son. My asking was rote and routine, basic lawyering, nothing special. We were both in the dark." She twisted the TV ring a full rotation. "And hey, listen, I saw Lettie and talked to her and none of this estate bullshit is going to matter. She still owns the VV 108, simple as that. Neal transferred a big fat zero to Benecorp."

"Well, we've never mentioned it, and you've been generous not to remind me I might've pissed away a potential fortune, but . . . I thought I should apologize. I wish I could go back. I wouldn't make the same mistake again."

"Totally not your fault. No need to explain. We've all done things we'd like to take back."

"So, yeah, we allege fraud," he said. "If Neal claims he didn't know about the Wound Velvet when we did the deal, then it's mutual mistake of a material fact, and we ask to void my renouncement."

"Garrison will paint us as greedy, gold-digging lawyers trying to scrounge a buck from Lettie's simpleton son, and even if we win, what'll we get? We can't pinpoint what we're after. They'll hand over the formula for granny's lye soap or Kaboom shower cleaner, pure junk or complete garbage that doesn't work, and a year later they'll announce they've discovered the Fountain of Youth."

"I understand it's not an easy case. But I think we should pressure them, put the option of a suit on the table, at least let them know we aren't simply planning to roll over in light of what we've discovered. We tell Pichler we want to speak to Garrison, and that we're planning to file suit for fraud. If they stonewall, we drop the fraud claim on them."

"All right," Lisa said, didn't hesitate. "I'm a hundred percent committed."

"So I'll make a motion that we adopt the course of action we've discussed and dedicate all necessary firm resources. Do I have a second?"

"Damn it, Joe, you're such a twerp sometimes."

"A second?" he repeated.

"Yes, Joe, I second your motion."

"All in favor," he intoned, "say 'aye.'"

"What if I vote no?" she asked. "Just to aggravate you?"

"Then the motion would fail," he said, "and we'd forget about it."

"Aye," she said.

"Aye," he said, raising his hand to emphasize the vote. "I'll have Betty type the minutes."

"You do that, Warren Buffett."

"Another piece of new business," Joe added. "I think we need out-side counsel. Our own lawyers. You and I might have to testify. In fact, if this thing goes the distance, we absolutely will have to testify."

"Technically, Joe, only you'll need a lawyer. I don't have any claim to Lettie's estate. At best—or maybe I should say at worst—I'm only a witness. But yeah, I agree. If this escalates, we'll probably need a bat-talion of lawyers. Who'd you have in mind?"

"First, I say we see if Robert Williams will help us," Joe suggested.

"Huh. I love Robert and he's a great lawyer, but it's only him. His brother's not there any longer. He's solo. Don't we need lots of associ-ates and clerks and warm bodies in the trenches?"

"I said *first*. Nobody can look around corners better than Rob-ert. I've never seen him ambushed or surprised or blindsided. He's a swami like that. Savvy and smart. It'd be like having Nostradamus on our side."

"Fair enough. Good choice. Robert's a class act too. He'll be easy to work with. Even better, he's about the only man I know who can wear a double-breasted suit and not come off as Sky Masterson." She grinned at Joe.

"Next, what if we retain your party buddy Brett Brooks? I'm not a fan, personally, but he's got a powerhouse firm behind him and every judge in Virginia takes him seriously."

"No," Lisa blurted, the grin instantly gone. "Uh, no."

"Why?" Joe asked. "That was pretty knee-jerk."

"Because . . . well, Phil Anderson's a better lawyer and has a larger group of associates. Former state bar president, smooth operator in court, carries a big stick, never flinches." Lisa raked her hair forward, covered more of her neck. She shifted in the chair and pulled her skirt's hem closer to her knees.

"I thought about Phil," Joe said. "He's top-notch and fearless."

"And you won't make pissy cracks about him or demand to be pres-ent at every meeting or refer to him as my 'party buddy.'" She took another pass at her hair.

Joe laughed. "Me? Make 'pissy cracks'? You must be thinking of a different Joe Stone, the guy with the goatee, my evil, parallel-universe twin."

"Nope."

He tapped his foot, diddled with a thick brown rubber band, stared out the window. The phone rang and he ignored it. "Phil Anderson, huh?" he said when the phone finished and went to voice mail.

"It doesn't have to be Phil. But seriously, we don't need any degree of complication, no matter how great a lawyer Brett Brooks is."

"Okay. I'm sold. Robert and Phil Anderson it is." Joe stood up, leaned against his credenza and put his hands in his pockets. "Here's another idea. Tell me what you think. We've basically gone as far as we can in terms of an investigation. How about we bring the cops into the loop? Specifically, Toliver Jackson. I think it's time."

"Did he ever track down the e-mail from the library? To make certain it's legit and not Dr. Downs's vindictive handiwork?"

"He said he would. He also said it'd be a pain in the ass, so I haven't badgered him. But I'll follow up. I mean, given what's happened so far, I don't have much doubt Lettie sent it."

"If he could find just one tiny dirty link to Benecorp. Maybe he could run down the origin of the Jane Rousch money order, where it was bought. Or interview the dog guy, Don Beverly—somehow that's bound to be a part of this. Or, I don't know, think of something we haven't."

"I'm still a big fan of checking the hospital records," Joe said. "It can't be coincidence the rental car was so close by. But like you said, that won't be simple, either."

"Yeah, I'd definitely keep the records idea on the back burner for now. But we have a solid start for Toliver, enough that it should raise a red flag and get him interested."

"Do we tell him we think Lettie might be alive?" Joe asked. "About your leprechaun visitor?"

"Why not? I think we need to tell him everything. By all means, let's get her on the cops' radar so they'll be looking for her. Hell, as volatile as she is, maybe she'll get arrested somewhere. We'll see if he can locate any prints on her cardboard too. It's still in your desk in the Ziploc bag, right?"

"Yes. I'll give it to him." Joe smiled. "The absolute best would be Toliver interviewing Seth Garrison. I'd pay money to see that extravaganza."

"I'd bet on Toliver," Lisa said. "He'd take out his little notebook and drop a few Toliverisms on the king of Benecorp. 'Well butter my butt and call me a biscuit' is still my favorite."

"I'd vote for 'the dingleberry vortex.' As in 'you keep lyin' to me, you gonna find yourself deep in the dingleberry vortex.'" Joe mimicked the officer's speech. "It's simultaneously kind of childish and *Fahrenheit 451*."

"I'm guessing none of the criminals have any idea what he means. I'm not even sure I do. But it's been a signature line for years."

"So we're agreed on everything?" Joe asked. "We have a plan?"

"We do. Yes."

They voted again, two ayes.

"And if there is no further business, then I move we stand adjourned," Joe said, not a jot of fun or irony in the statement.

On the way back to her office, Lisa stopped in the hallway, stalled underneath the high ceiling and four-piece crown molding, and a banished recollection slipped loose, the memory of the warm Bahamian ocean, how she'd flitted to the beach and kicked off her shoes and started wading until the waves bobbed against her legs, her slacks soaked. She recalled the sand eroding with each pull of the tide, wallowing out holes around her feet and ankles, sinking her deeper and deeper into the bottom. Her mind allowed the image to mutate, and she imagined the ocean changing from blue to pale gray, and as far as she could see, the surface turned level and placid and the water transformed into hard concrete, and she was captured there, unable to move, locked in place from the thighs down, encased. She shook her head, cleared her thoughts and started walking again, and she muttered Brett's name and made a finger pistol, pointed an index finger at her temple, fired with her thumb. "Pow," she said.

CHAPTER NINETEEN

The Saturday following the Stone and Stone stockholders' meeting, Lisa was at the kitchen counter working on a favorite strawberry cake. Earlier, Joe had fixed them breakfast. He'd fried ham in the black skillet and cut the first honeydew melon of the summer—mushmelons, he called them—scraped away the center seeds and pared the rind from the fruit and then sliced the wet, green strips into fat chunks. She'd saved a bite of the salty ham and a piece of the honeydew and nibbled on them between cracking eggs and measuring flour and reading the recipe off a stained index card, written in her great-aunt's cursive, ruler-trained hand. She could see her lilies and snapdragons at the corner of the patio, giddy spreads of pink, orange, yellow and white atop yeomen green stems. Even though they'd agreed the Primland trip would be their anniversary present to each other, Joe had mail-ordered a Tiffany necklace and given it to her last night, a sterling silver key on a delicate chain—the key to his heart, he'd said, kind of silly and kind of sincere—and when she leaned over the recipe card, the key would swing forward and hang in the air. She'd surprised him with a custom-stitched saddle blanket, a bold "S" embroidered on each side, and she could tell he was happy to have it.

Almost every Saturday, Joe loaded Brownie into the farm truck and hauled trash and recyclables to the dump, the dog ecstatic in the truck bed, riding with stuffed garbage bags and large tubs of magazines and empty plastic containers. Joe carried the last bag to the truck and filled his travel mug with coffee and kissed her cheek. She was looking forward to some time alone in the house, baking and piddling, a footloose morning, but a few minutes later he returned to the kitchen and told her he couldn't find Brownie. The dog had been there for breakfast. He'd eaten, ambled outside and climbed into the sturdy house—shingled, insulated, and now with an orthopedic pad—Joe had built for him when he was a pup.

"He's not in his box, and I've looked all over the yard and the barn."

"Huh," she said. She was dressed in shorts and flip-flops, her hair gathered away from her face. She'd started beating batter for the cake, and she tipped the KitchenAid mixer back from its silver metal bowl. "Did you check the basement?" Pink batter coated the blades, and dollops dripped into the bowl. "Maybe he used the pet door."

"Yeah, the basement, the barn, under the vehicles. Everywhere. He's gone. Pancho and Lefty are in the hayloft. I even cranked the engine so he could hear me. Blew the horn. Yelled."

"Yeah, I heard the horn. Was he okay at breakfast?"

"He was stiff and slow, but no more than usual. I gave him his pills in a ball of cheese. He wanted to go out, and he went straight to his box. I saw him while I was cutting the mushmelon, right before you came down. He was just lying there in his house."

Lisa opened the door and stepped onto the porch. She called the dog's name several times. She walked to his box, stooped and stuck her head inside. "Did you hear anything, Joe?" she asked as she stood.

"Nothing. He hasn't been for a ramble in years. Usually, he eats and crashes in his house."

"I don't mean to seem paranoid, but I can't help wondering if somebody took him."

"Who would take him?" Joe asked. "And why?"

"Do I need to paint you a picture? How about the same people who are antagonizing Dr. Downs? A dog would be very minor given their history."

"Well, honestly, it did go through my mind, but it doesn't make any sense. What do they gain?"

"So, okay, two days ago we give Pichler the ultimatum and insist we talk to his boss, and now our dog vanishes. It's a coincidence?" She put her hands on her hips. "It's not as if we're swapping briefcases with Walter and the Dude, Joe. Benecorp probably sent people here to kill Lettie."

"The timing seems screwy, and it feels too soon and too small and too indirect for them. But, for sure, I thought of it."

She went with him, and they searched and hollered and drove the truck slowly to the highway, shouting "Brownie!" and "Here, boy!" from the windows, and they trudged to the creek at the border of their property and followed it for a mile in each direction, zigzagging for an hour through briars, mountain laurels, ditches and pine thickets. They didn't find the dog. They visited their neighbors, who were generous and sympathetic but hadn't seen Brownie. Their neighbor Taylor even offered to let them use his Gator if they needed it, so they could drive to the bottoms where he cut hay, cover more territory. They phoned the radio station, the pound, the newspaper, the police.

Before the noon closing time, they hurried to the dump. The recycling shed was a three-sided structure with an unpainted tin roof and rusted metal supports. As Joe eased the truck parallel to the shed, Lisa noticed a man and a woman were leaning over one of the huge recycling containers, methodically inspecting the newspapers, magazines, catalogs, inserts and store flyers. The woman was wearing tinted glasses, and the man was dressed in a red Lacoste golf shirt. They both greeted Joe as he walked past them, said a few words. A Volvo station wagon was parked by the shed, evidently belonged to the scavengers.

"What's up with the couple digging through the bins?" she asked Joe when he'd finished emptying the tubs and returned to the truck.

"Coupons. People come here and fish them out." He put the truck in gear.

"Seriously?"

"Yep. Sign of the times, I suppose. Though I understand there're experts on the subject who write blogs and articles, and they promote the idea. Makes it a little less embarrassing."

Lisa studied the man and woman. "Do you know them?"

"He's Colin Hanover. Used to be a supervisor at Tultex, before it closed. Nice guy from all reports. His wife's named Janie or Jamie or something close to that. They're here a lot."

"Damn," Lisa said. "How sad."

Joe released the clutch and steered them toward the green boxes, and before they stopped moving Lisa's BlackBerry sounded, mimicked an old-fashioned telephone ring. "Maybe that's news on Brownie," she said. She answered and said "Hello" and "Yes" and listened and tilted her head and shot Joe a concerned look and concentrated her lips into a thin, tense line. She asked the caller to wait a minute while she switched to speaker so her husband could hear. She took the phone from her ear and hit buttons from memory, three fast taps. "So you're with Benecorp?" she said.

"Actually, I report to Mr. Seth Garrison, who owns the corporation." The voice was on speaker.

"And your name?" Lisa asked. "What's your name? I didn't quite catch it."

"Elizabeth Briggs," the woman answered. "Am I successfully on speaker now?"

"Yes," Lisa said.

"Then good morning to you as well, Mr. Stone."

"Hi," Joe said.

"Mr. Garrison asked me to contact you regarding your request to discuss the VanSandt property. I wanted to schedule a time and circumstances that would suit you both."

"Why don't you just hand him the phone?" Lisa asked.

"Oh, no," Briggs replied. She laughed. She was condescending, haughty, the laugh a string of monotone *hahs* that translated to "I think you are a pitiful, dumb creature." "That's impossible for many reasons." She repeated the laugh.

"Could you do that again?" Lisa asked her.

"Pardon? Do what?"

"The laugh. It's the oldest wicked stepsister, right? Or Madonna, the 2005 version with the fake British accent?"

"I'm not positive I'm following you, Mrs. Stone. I didn't mean to insult you. But it *is* amusing you'd think someone as busy and influential as Mr. Garrison is standing here beside me, waiting for me to bring *you* to the phone."

"Okay, fine, when will he call?" Joe asked from across the truck.

"Mr. Garrison rarely does business over the phone. He would prefer to see you and Mrs. Stone in person."

"When and where?" Lisa was holding the BlackBerry between them, near the truck's roof so as not to break the connection.

"We have two options. We could schedule you for next week, the week of June seventeenth, for a meeting in Virginia Beach. We also have a week in the middle of July available in Florida. Key West."

"Why there?" Lisa asked.

"Mrs. Stone," Briggs sniffed, "Mr. Garrison is a Canadian resident and a citizen of the world. He's the eleventh richest man on earth. His itinerary for the next months is set. It does not bring him near Henry County, Virginia. However, Mr. Garrison does regret the inconvenience and would be pleased to pay for your travel and accommodations."

"So he really has agreed to meet with us?" Lisa asked.

"Hence my call," Briggs said.

"Why are you calling us today, on a Saturday, on my personal phone?"

"It was the next item on my list," Briggs told her. "I used your cell because I didn't expect to find you at your office. Your delightful assistant, Betty, gave the number to our Mr. Pichler. Here we all are."

"For sure, we'll be meeting with Garrison himself?" Joe asked. "Not some flunky, not his vice president of alchemy and jabberwocky." He nudged the truck forward. They were three vehicles away from the Dumpsters.

"You'll be meeting with Mr. Garrison personally," Briggs promised.

"There's nothing closer than the beach?" Lisa asked.

"No. As I mentioned, we're more than willing to underwrite your travel."

"We'll scrape together our pennies," Joe said. "Thanks just the same."

"I understand," Briggs said.

"Joe and I will check our calendars and see what we can do. Where would we meet if we choose Virginia Beach?"

"Mr. Garrison's helicopter would collect you at the airport and land you on his ship, where he's based."

"If we opt for Key West, we'll have to wait over a month?" Joe asked.

"Yes, sorry."

"And there's really no chance we could simply talk over the phone?" Joe asked. "Why not?"

"Seth Garrison has his own rules, Mr. Stone. I don't create them, nor am I able to modify them."

"Let me write down your number," Lisa said, "and we'll confirm something Monday. We're distracted right now—our dog is missing. You can imagine how upset we are."

"Certainly," Briggs said sweetly. "I'm sorry to hear it. I own two corgis myself. Best of luck to you."

"What do you think?" Lisa asked once she clicked off. She'd jotted the number in blue ink on her palm.

"I don't know—be careful what you ask for, huh? It's significant that he'll see us, but this feels like a wild-goose chase. A dead-end, exhausting detour. Like he's fucking with us. We drive the miserable five hours to the coast, he jollies us up and humbly pours us cups of expensive tea, charms us with stories about whales and seals, tells us a few lies about Lettie and off we go, no wiser than we were. What exactly do we gain? We'll also have to either be dishonest or admit we don't actually own the Wound Velvet, that he already has everything thanks to his contract with dipshit Neal."

"Yeah," Lisa said. "It's a long trip. If we could get him on the phone, it would be helpful. But this . . ."

"I guess we can think about it. Maybe we ought to stay a few days and make it a vacation."

"I'd pick Key West for a vacation, but I don't want to delay everything until then."

Joe pulled up to the Dumpsters, and the two of them slung the bags into a squat green container, heard glass break when the last bag banged against a metal side. The garbage stunk. A fly buzzed her ear. Crows had discovered a fetid slice of bologna and were tearing it apart, hopping and pecking on the pavement.

"I'm supposed to see Toliver on Monday," Joe said. "I'll ask if he thinks it's worthwhile. I tend to think we ought to go. Nothing to lose."

"If we're not here on Thursday, I'll have to reschedule my meeting with Montana and her new teacher. It makes me seem unreliable. I hate to miss the first appointment. I was planning to take her shopping too. Buy her some summer clothes. Her shiftless father's in rehab again."

"You've been doing that program for years and volunteered for everything under the sun. I hardly think they'll be upset. It's June. School starts in August. And you can buy clothes every day of the week."

"We'll have to see if Erica can house-sit and feed the horse and give Brownie his . . ." She stopped. "His medicine."

She and Joe drove directly back to the farm, and for a second time they searched everywhere they knew to look, kept at it, hunted along the creek, honked the horn all the way to the main road, crisscrossed the woods calling Brownie's name, crawled behind the square bales of hay and shined the flashlight, circled Foy Rice's pond, Joe with his hands cupped around his eyes so he could see into the shallows. Nothing. Lisa was so miserable she couldn't eat dinner, and soon after sunset, at nine-thirty or thereabouts, she dozed off on the sofa, woke near midnight and couldn't fall back asleep, then went upstairs and lay in the dark bedroom, hot and uncomfortable, the sheets and counterpane shoved aside, a random cloud occasionally smearing across the moon. Her cake was abandoned in its bowl, neglected, a lumpy pink swamp, the batter dried fast to the mixer blades, a chore to scrub.

She finally went under, a forced, translucent sleep too near the surface, some portion of her still tethered to her surroundings, but she didn't sense Joe leaving the room, didn't realize he was gone. At daybreak, she heard him downstairs shutting the front door, and she was quickly alert and pulling on the same shorts from Saturday, scooting into her flip-flops. She was starting the stairs when she spotted Joe coming toward her from the kitchen. "Found him," he said.

"Is he okay? Where was he? Is he hurt?"

"Come on," he told her, beckoning with his hand.

Lisa held the banister and clopped down the remaining steps. Brownie was in the den, lying on the rug in front of the fireplace, a favorite location during the winter months. He looked up at her and thumped his tail. He opened his mouth and panted, licked his black lips, sighed.

"He was at the far end of the pasture," Joe said. "Buried in a patch of broom straw a few yards outside the fence. I'll bet we came damn close to stepping on him ten times yesterday."

"Which end?" Lisa asked. "That doesn't make any sense."

"By the big oak that got hit by lightning. The split oak."

"He had to hear us, Joe. Is he hurt? Can he walk?"

"Yeah. He's weak, but he can walk. I came within five feet of him, and he didn't even stir. He didn't want to be found."

"Huh? Why?"

"It's what they do, sweetie. They wander off to die. He didn't want us to bother him. I'm sure he heard us. Hell, he could've walked back to the house whenever he wanted. I remember when my father's old bluetick did exactly the same thing. Daddy found him two days later in the corner of a tobacco barn and called Dr. Witt to put him down. Left him where he lay, and he and the doc walked to the barn and put him to sleep."

"Maybe Brownie was disoriented. He takes all that medicine."

"I suppose it's possible."

Lisa dropped to all fours and rubbed her nose across the dog's. "Hey, good boy." She scratched his head, stroked circles on his belly. "I'll cook him some eggs. And I'm going to call Dr. Withers. I don't care if it is Sunday; this is an emergency."

The vet was polite and understanding, especially given the early hour. "The theory," he said after Lisa explained why she was calling, "is basically anecdotal, but unfortunately it's frequent and recurring. We know for sure that many animals seek a quiet, confined place to die, especially cats. There's really no clinical data to support the notion, but from my experience there's an absolute correlation. I'd suggest keeping him inside or walking him on a leash. Make sure he has plenty of fresh water." Withers offered to drive to their farm and have a look at him, though he assured her there probably wasn't much he could accomplish medically. They finally agreed she'd bring the dog to his clinic early the next morning, and he'd see them before business hours, 7:30 on the dot.

Brownie was listless for the rest of the day. He did eat chunks of scrambled eggs when Lisa held them to his mouth, but he didn't show much enthusiasm for the food. "He seems so sad, Joe," she said. "I hope he's not suffering."

Monday, she and Joe were at the vet's a few minutes early, before the doctor arrived. They walked to the clinic's entrance with Withers, and Joe had to pick Brownie up and carry him when he balked at the threshold and stubbornly collapsed and refused to stand. Withers probed the dog's chest with a stethoscope, shined a light in his ears and mouth, then shaved his foreleg and pierced him with a needle to draw blood. Stung by the needle, Brownie yelped and jerked.

"He does seem to be declining," the doc said solemnly, confirming what they already knew. "I'm concerned the blood work won't be too promising, especially his liver function. We'll just have to do our best and make prudent decisions."

While they were talking, Brownie licked at the white, pallid spot on his leg, took two or three lethargic passes and quit. He lay flat and closed his eyes. The very tip of his tongue remained outside his mouth, a pink sliver against his black muzzle. At the end of the visit, he bit the vet's Milk-Bone treat, crunched it and broke it and partially ate it, but left the majority in pieces on the silver metal examination table, crumbs and dry tan bits. Joe stoically toted him back to the truck. Lisa let him ride in the cab, curled in her lap, his nose pointed toward Joe, a paw touching his thigh. Neither of them spoke, until Joe said he would take Brownie to the office, even if he had to carry him all the way from the truck and even if the dog had to piss on the floor.

Joe was finishing a call to a client and folding his cell phone shut when he walked into Toliver's office at the Henry County Sheriff's Office later that morning. The cop was seated behind his desk, studying a file and marking sections of a report with a yellow highlighter.

"Whoa there, Johnnie Cochran, what you holdin'?"

"What? Huh?" Joe asked. "And I'm white. The reference doesn't work. I'd be Shapiro or Barry Scheck."

"Where'd you find the fossil phone? That's a TracFone, isn't it? The LG cheapie from Walmart."

"So?"

"Seriously? You're sportin' the thirty-bucks-a-month TracFone from Walmart? You, the seasonal Mexicans, the food stamp artists and the wannabe drug dealers. I was kidding your wife not long ago about her BlackBerry, which is already nearly the same as a cassette tape, but this is feeble, even for you."

"All I need is a phone, Toliver. I have a computer at my house and office, I don't text, I don't play online games, I don't take photos and I'm not on Facebook or Twitter. Tell me again why I need an expensive phone and a draconian service plan? I don't even use the minutes I have. As we say in the legal world, the phone is a sword for me, not a shield. I rarely turn it on. I'm bothered enough as it is by people wanting free advice while I'm trying to eat dinner in a restaurant or buy a loaf of bread at the grocery store."

"Sure, Joe. You could have a horse and buggy too." Toliver grinned. "Wait, you sorta do. I saw you on your scooter last week. Easy Rider Stone. Still makes me laugh, especially now that you've put the basket on the handlebars. Me, I'm state of the art. New Droid. Amazin' technology. I don't have the luxury of switchin' it off. Crime don't take a holiday."

Joe adjusted a chair and sat down. "Did you ever look into that e-mail from the library? Supposedly sent by Lettie?"

"Yeah, damn, I went over there, and they stubbed up on me and really didn't want to help. It's fallout from the Patriot Act and all that shit. Can't say I blame them. I talked to Hal and told him it was for you and that we didn't need to know what anybody was readin' and we already had the contents of the e-mail and we're not Big Brother tryin' to pry into somebody's business. Plus Lettie's dead, so we won't be bruisin' her feelings. He finally agreed to check the sign-in log for the computers, and she was in fact there when the e-mail was sent. You want more information than that, you're on your own. He told me last Wednesday. I was plannin' to give you the news next time we crossed paths."

"Thanks," Joe said. "I don't have much doubt that it's authentic." He stood and leaned against the wall. He focused on the policeman. "I promised you I'd keep you up to speed if we discovered anything criminal in Lettie's situation. I think we're there now. I believe she was killed."

"Ah, okay. Gotcha." Toliver chuckled. "What you're actually sayin' is that you've chased this as far as you can, and as a last resort you want me to help you find something that you can't find by yourself. Do some grunt work. Misuse my authority for your advantage."

"To some extent, I suppose, yeah. But let me tell you what we have, and you tell me why you shouldn't be concerned. I know for sure Lettie invented a medicine or, well, a formula that is valuable. So valuable that the head of Benecorp, Seth Garrison, is hiring private, ex-military security and yanking strings to guarantee he has the rights to it."

Toliver widened his eyes. "Seth Garrison? There's a serious actor for you. Rich motherfucker too. The History Channel did a show on him. Have you met him? How do you know all this?"

Joe cocked his heel on the baseboard and detailed what he'd learned so far and how Toliver's earlier information about the rental car plugged into the bigger picture. He included Lisa's visit from a leprechaun claiming to be Lettie. "So you're right in a certain sense," Joe admitted after he'd finished. "We are stuck. We can go to Virginia Beach and meet Garrison, but I seriously doubt he's planning a confession, or that he'll do much more than a two-bit soft shoe and then maybe try to buy us off. We'd hoped we could count on your expertise. Hoped you might open a case and investigate it, or give us an idea how we can find an undeniable, direct, incriminating link. Or figure out who was in the backseat of Lisa's car and why."

The detective had been scribbling notes on his small, spiral-bound pad, listening and writing, but he didn't comment or ask questions. "Bunch of dead ends," he finally said. "Lot of smoke, no fire. Your idea of checkin' the hospital records in Charlotte is reasonable, but it still isn't a home run kinda solution. As for Lisa's plan, even if we could tie the location of the money orders to a city where Benecorp is located, so what? Plus, there's virtually no chance some rinky-dink convenience store kept their surveillance tapes this long supposin' we *could* trace the money orders somehow."

"Do you have any ideas?" Joe asked.

"Of course I do." Toliver made no effort to hide his satisfaction. "You want me to clue you in?"

"Absolutely," Joe said sincerely. "Please."

"You should've come in earlier. This is what happens when rookies and amateurs attempt to do police work. You end up frustrated and chasin' your own tail. Everybody watches *Barnaby Jones* reruns and *48 Hours* and figures, shazam, hey, ain't nothin' to this. By the way, you ever notice how almost every detective on *48 Hours* is a fat white guy with a mullet? Horrible dressers, most of 'em."

"I hadn't noticed," Joe said flatly, paying his dues.

"So here's what we do. We go to circuit court and get a warrant. We serve it on the phone service providers for our area. We narrow the focus to the few hours this Jane Rousch was supposedly in our area and review the calls that went through the cell towers. We see if any of the dialed numbers lead us to Garrison or Benecorp. I figure, especially after a strong dose of Lettie, that whoever was here called to report back. Routine warrant, easy to obtain. If it hits, we've linked Lettie, Garrison and the sheisty rental."

"Damn, Toliver. Sweet. Nice. Never would've crossed my mind."

"No shit, Joe. How perfect you just roll in here from the electronics wasteland too. I'm surprised you don't still have a bag phone. We do a call search once or twice a month. The lawyers usually don't hear of it 'cause it's so far removed in the chain of things. It rarely matters *how* we locate your guilty clients; it's what they say when we find them or the stolen property in their trunk or the DNA they give us that you spend your energy tryin' to keep from the judge."

"I'm assuming there'll be a ton of calls going through, even if we limit the time frame."

"Yeah. It'll take a while to search the records. You better hope this doesn't bog me down and ruin my stats."

"We could help," Joe volunteered.

"What did I just say?" Toliver asked.

"Right, yeah. You're the pro, we're the donkeys."

"Exactly."

"You think we should follow through and meet with Garrison?"

"Oh, hell yeah." Toliver almost squeaked the words and simultaneously made a nobody-can-be-that-ignorant face. "Absolutely. You never, ever pass up the opportunity to talk to a suspect. Never. Sometimes they slip. Sometimes you just catch a vibe, a feeling. Sometimes you can prove a little detail wrong later on. You should know this by now—all you shysters ever tell your clients is 'don't talk to the cops.' Why's that? Here, the fact this big-shot guy even wants to meet with you raises my antennae."

"How long before you'll have the records and an answer?"

"When I have them, okay? You can give me this Pichler's number, Briggs's number and the number at Dr. Downs's sister's. I suppose you could also locate the main numbers for Benecorp. Try not to fuck up that simple task. There'll be ten digits. We call the first three an area code. And let me have any new beyond-the-grave messages from Lettie. I'll send the cardboard she supposedly gave Lisa to the lab for a print check."

"Downs's sister?" Joe asked. "Why?"

"Because, unlike you, I plan to cover all the possibilities." Toliver licked his index finger and flipped through several pad pages. "Here we go. A little example of that principle for you. A freebie. Back in December, bunch of dumb-ass kids was pilferin' laptops from Walmart, so I'm there at the store watchin' the security video, and I see Lettie on the recordin'. This particular video is smack dab from around the time she officially went missing—had to be the night before the fire—and she's got a mound of crap at the register. Late, nearly midnight. Can't tell what it is, but with her just being found dead, I check the register tape and, no surprise, there's the camp fuel and matches and iodine for the meth, but why the hell is she buyin' a sleeping bag and toiletries? A plastic poncho?"

"So she can spend the night with her dope?" Joe speculated. "Monitor the brew? Maybe the poncho's like an apron or lab coat to protect her from the chemicals."

"Possible, I suppose, but she was so damn tight; she lived off metal scavenging and a little check from her dead brother's pension, right? She's springin' for a quality sleepin' bag?"

"She got around twelve hundred bucks a month from her brother's railroad pension. She was his beneficiary."

"Just something to keep in mind," Toliver noted. "May be nothing. Not easy to get a read on a crazy woman with a meth habit." Toliver shut his pad. "I'll be in touch when I'm done. Meanwhile, you might want to start ponderin' about some chaps in case you have to lay that high-octane moped beast down on the blacktop. Me, I'd suggest a pair with some major fringe."

That same afternoon, Lisa spoke with Burke Loggins, who was threatening to file suit against M.J. on behalf of his client, Teddy Bear Brian.

Loggins's secretary had phoned, then placed Lisa on hold, resurfacing several minutes later to apologize because "Mr. Loggins has went to take an emergency call in the library."

"No problem," Lisa assured her. "I'm sure an important lawyer like Mr. Loggins is extremely busy. I'm grateful he's clearing space to speak with me." Lisa had checked, and Loggins had a poor Martindale-Hubbell rating, the lowest grade the company used. "I just hate to run up his long-distance bill."

"Oh, heck, we're on his cell phone. We use it as the main line here at the office. He has unlimited minutes." The secretary paused. Lisa imagined her unwrapping a stick of gum to smack, or maybe readying her nail file. "Oh, okay, here you go. Mr. Loggins can talk with you now. Please stay on the line for Attorney Loggins."

"Mrs. Stone, Burke Loggins here. Look forward to doing business. Sorry about the delay on hold. Megacase in federal court starting to boil, and I had to take a conference call from the judge." The voice belonged to a sweaty, desperate, conniving and sketchy man, the words too gassed and falsely convivial, the rhythm a huckster's oily southern cadence, hawking tickets to a hoochie-coochie tent or peddling genuine Armani suits straight from the Italian factory at a 50 percent discount.

"No problem. Federal cases can be the worst."

"Tell me about it," Loggins said.

"So as I understand matters, you're planning to sue my client, M. J. Gold, based on various workplace claims."

"Hate to have to do it, but what choice has she left us?"

"I understand your position. Let me communicate ours." Her timbre changed. Lisa spoke precisely, sternly. "You and I both know you have absolutely no claim. Your guy never worked for Miss Gold, never—"

"Hey, now," Loggins interrupted, "we aren't conceding that. That hound won't hunt for you. She wrote him checks and hired him onto her payroll. Nosirreebob, we believe he was an employee."

"She also wrote checks to plumbers, the dry cleaners and her nieces and nephews for their birthdays. Be that as it may, we realize this is a shakedown."

"Mrs. Stone, are you accusing me of something dishonest? Unethical?" Loggins pumped his voice with indignation. "'Cause if you are, we may have other avenues to pursue. Are you saying I'm filing a bogus suit? We'll end this call right now and let a jury decide the merits of our claim."

"Hear me out," Lisa said calmly. "You have no case. No legal case. It'll never reach a jury."

"You'll damn sure learn different, I can promise you. My draft complaint has seven separate counts. They're all legit. Winners."

"Excellent. Add three more and make it an even ten. I have a saying: An aboveground pool will always be an aboveground pool, no matter how elaborate the deck and how expensive the chaise lounges."

"Yeah, well, this pool is dug deep in the ground with concrete around the edges."

"But, Mr. Loggins—if you'd just let me finish—please understand we *want* you to file your claim. We hope to make this a mutual and beneficial effort."

"You do? Well, you'll get your wish."

"All we ask is that we have some input into the press release, and that we know when you plan to hold the news conference."

"Why?"

"I don't mind telling you that Miss Gold sees mostly upside to this suit, especially since she has no financial exposure in the courtroom. As matters stand today, she's rich and famous, but famous only at a certain level. She wants her profile raised, and this suit, if it's drafted properly and colorful enough and handled correctly, will accomplish her goal. Right now, she's Montel Williams. Maybe Ricki Lake. She wants to be Oprah, if you catch my drift."

"Uh-uh. Not really."

Lisa spoke faster and enthusiastically. "Simply stated, she becomes one of the guys, rich and powerful enough to warrant her own handsome younger boyfriend. She's broken through the last barrier. You see movie stars and entertainment industry women who can call these kinds of shots, but not in the business world. She'd be the first female captain of industry with a bimboy, if we can control the press and spin the story in that light. And we think we can. We have press contacts who've been alerted. We just want them there for your announcement."

"Seems crazy to me."

"Really? Crazy like Donald Trump and Marla Maples? Richard Branson was absolutely ruined by his sexual harassment suit, huh? Quite the opposite, it makes these guys look like rich-ass swashbucklers who can do as they please. They're invincible. They can buy, manage and control beautiful people. And that, Mr. Loggins, translates into a perception of power, especially with other men."

"How would this be helpful to my client?" Loggins asked. "How would he be compensated for his damages?"

"He doesn't have any damages, okay? But at the end of the day, we'd be willing to pay you guys to be our Washington Generals. We of course will be the Harlem Globetrotters. But only if you take it all the way to trial. Part of the process, part of the illusion, is thrashing you in court. Not only does Miss Gold have sex with your attractive young client in exchange for a TAG Heuer and a trip to Barbados, but she also crushes him legally, which you and I both realize is inevitable. Settling would make her seem weak and undermine our long-term program. I'm definitely not asking you to intentionally tank the case. That *would* be unethical. Just make sure we get it before a judge, so it winds up dismissed. Don't white-flag it or withdraw it once it's filed."

"What kind of number were you thinking of for us to become involved?"

"Maybe five grand at the end of the trial. We'd pay it under the pretext of preventing an appeal."

"Have you lost your mind? We won't take less than a hundred thousand."

"You mean pesos?" Lisa asked. "Or maybe baht? Certainly not dollars?"

"We'll just file suit," Loggins barked. "Nothing to lose. We're playing with your money."

"True, but you're playing with your own as well," Lisa told him. "We'll absolutely wear your ass out in discovery. And in the end, two years from now and at the conclusion of all kinds of tedious work, you'll get nothing. We truly want this to go on forever. Miss Gold sees it as part of her advertising budget. Cheap publicity. You have to understand, she doesn't fear the publicity. She wants it. She didn't become rich by making orthodox choices."

"Bullshit," Loggins challenged her. "You think I'm that gullible?"

"What do you have after you file a suit that's a loser? You think your money's in the bluff. Normally, you'd be correct. But after you file, you're on the fast track to the sewer. Nothing but our beating you down and then humiliating you before a court on summary judgment. You'll never see a dime and you'll be tied up for years. Listen, maybe Miss Gold would kick in another grand or two to compensate your client for the pussy factor."

"Pardon me? That's real professional, Mrs. Stone. Nice mouth."

Lisa chuckled. "I just mean the embarrassment factor. He'll be a laughingstock and seen in many quarters as a pussy. Come on: A man gets a weekly allowance and travels around the world for free, and now he's suing the very attractive woman who made it possible? Have you seen Miss Gold? She's a pretty lady, and it's not as if there's some thirty-year age gap. And his job is to have sex? How do you think that'll play with the public? Or the men in Miss Gold's various heavy-equipment businesses? I can't wait to ask your boy Brian how he was able to produce erections under such awful duress. You'll come off as truly impressive too, for taking and promoting such a pathetic suit. The two of you will never sit on a barstool again without being ridiculed."

"How about twenty-five now? We sign a confidentiality agreement."

"How about you actually understand what I'm telling you? You have no value to us unless you go through with this, and we shape the media and the press runs with it and the whole production enhances Miss Gold's image. Why would we pay you to settle?"

"Fifteen?" Loggins wheedled.

"Six at the end, after the case is dismissed. Only then and not a dime more. Oh, and tell Brian to take his damn picture down from the plushie website. Miss Gold wants be seen as powerful, not as a character in 'Goldilocks.' I'll fax you some details for the press conference. We hope you'll mention my client's net worth. We've exaggerated it a bit, but I think it'll fly."

"The what site?" Loggins sounded confused. Lisa imagined him slumped against a desk in a two-room, strip-mall office, crestfallen and stymied, his cell phone at his ear, his name and occupation posted outside on the giant parking lot directory, sandwiched between the listings for a chain hair salon and a Dollar Tree store.

"FurNation," Lisa told him. "He's sexually aroused by dressing in a teddy bear costume. Truth be told, that's why my client dumped him. He needs to delete his account and stay off the site."

Loggins made a sound that was mostly a grunt.

"Mr. Loggins? Are you there?"

"Yep."

"Do we have an understanding?" Lisa asked.

"I'll have to, uh, run it past my client. Seems like a long investment for a small payoff. And hey, Burke Loggins doesn't have a big interest in being somebody's stooge. Not how I operate."

"Sure. And to make this happen, we won't try to humiliate you personally or anything, or chump you any more than is absolutely necessary—I probably stated the ridicule angle too strongly. We could negotiate those terms if need be."

"I'll be in touch," Loggins said, though he didn't even attempt to sound sincere, spit the words plain and rushed and dry.

Lisa hung up, dialed M.J. and informed her that she was fairly sure Bear Brian's whore lawyer had been buffaloed into abandoning the suit. "Once I convinced him you weren't afraid of the publicity, he lost his extortion leverage and we were in the clear. There's no chance he's going to hang around for two years while we go upside his head day after day and make him our courtroom bitch and media prop."

"Brilliant. What a relief. Wonderful. You realize I'd be mortified if this really hits the papers. Lord above, it would be awful. I was thinking of the opposite strategy, loading up and threatening him with blood in the streets if he did file the stupid paperwork and started yakking to the media. Thank our lucky stars Brian picked this clown to represent him. Of course, my sources tell me he was turned down by just about every reputable lawyer in Raleigh, so this parasite had to be at the bottom of the barrel. Bless you. Send me a bill."

"No charge, M.J. I'll put it in the favor book and then hold it over you for decades. That's what friends do." Lisa laughed. "Or you can treat me to the VIP experience at the Ice Follies or whatever they call it now. I'll follow up with Loggins in a day or two, keep pushing like we genuinely want him to file the suit. I'll have Betty fax him some bogus info and our fake press release."

"You, Lisa Stone, are the best."

CHAPTER TWENTY

Seth Garrison's helicopter was impressive, much larger than Lisa had anticipated. A Benecorp employee named Arch Harvey met them at the Virginia Beach airport and accompanied them across the tarmac and introduced them to the pilot, who was dressed in a crisp white shirt and dark blue captain's uniform and had very little to say, though he did shake hands with her and Joe. His name was Alden—she was never certain if this was his given name or his last name—and he had the demeanor of a man who positively lived for the bottom to fall out, was eager for a stall or turbulent weather or a mechanical hiccup so he could dose up on adrenaline and show off his talent. "Would you prefer the quick route or the tourist trip to the ship?" he demanded, the inquiry blasé and impersonal.

"How much longer," Joe asked, "is the tourist flight?"

"It's about sixteen minutes as the crow flies. So if I throw in some sights, probably closer to half an hour, maybe thirty-five minutes. Either way, you'll be on the ship in time for breakfast."

"What would we see?" Joe asked.

"A lot more ocean. A lot more beach. The city."

"Let's just get there," Joe said and looked at Lisa. "You okay with that?"

"Same trip would cost you four or five hundred bucks if you paid for it on some tour," Alden explained, still no inflection in his voice. "But it's your call."

"I'd just as soon take the quick route," she said.

"Fine by me," Alden noted. "I'll radio the ship and let Mr. Garrison know our ETA." He was looking toward Joe; it was impossible to see

Alden's eyes behind his dark glasses. "You planning on doing some bullet fishing? A short L-frame thirty-eight, right?"

Joe didn't flinch. He and Lisa had agreed on bringing the gun—who knew what might crop up? "Pretty difficult from a helicopter, even with 158-grain hollow points. My own reloads." He smiled slightly. "More sport in a fly rod too. Who the hell would want to shoot a fish?" Joe glanced at the horizon, spoke with his attention at a distance, elsewhere. The pistol was holstered on his belt, draped by his blazer. He was also wearing a tie and gray slacks.

"You might be surprised," Alden said, still impassive. "They'll collect your gun as soon as you board, or you can check it with me. Whatever you prefer."

"You seem trustworthy enough," Joe said. "You can hold it while we're visiting with your boss. By the way, what kind of helicopter is this?"

"Agusta AW109."

"It's quite a trick. You mind my asking how much it sells for?"

"No secret," Alden said. "You can find basic prices on the Internet. Around six million. This has some serious custom options, so add several hundred thousand more."

"My friend M. J. Gold has a private plane," Lisa remarked. "She says there's nothing to compare with flying under the right conditions. She claims it's addictive."

"I'll help you both in," Alden said, evidently done with the chitchat.

The passenger compartment was sealed off from the pilot's cabin, a separate, ritzy, flying room. She and Joe were by themselves, belted into comfortable leather seats with a polished wood console between them. Despite the console, they held hands for most of the trip. It occurred to her, as she looked down at the soft seam where water joined land, that for the very first time since Nassau, she hadn't immediately defaulted to thoughts of her infidelity as she'd admired her husband on the tarmac, counting on him to handle the situation with Alden, grateful he was his own man, feeling fortunate she was married to a badass who could build his own bullets if the store-boughts ran dry. It was a moment to mark: Realizing her affection for Joe hadn't served to merely set her cheating in vivid relief and amplify her guilt.

"I love you," she mouthed, and he squeezed her hand. The helicopter zoomed ahead, all business.

Once on the ship, she and Joe were greeted under the dying chopper blades by a crouched, older man with LEX, SECURITY written in block letters on his name tag. Chipper and talkative, he dutifully wanded them—apologizing in advance for the intrusion—and then steered them through a metal detector. Joe informed him that he'd "stashed a couple vodka mini-bottles in my boot for the encore," and Lex got the joke and laughed. He told them that Prince had performed a private concert for Mr. Garrison's last birthday. Lex also searched Lisa's purse, and the rummaging annoyed her, this man peeking into her belongings, opening a compact and taking the top off a lipstick tube, for crying out loud.

Seth Garrison was waiting for them in a conference room, and he was a polite host, met them at the door and thanked them for suffering the trip to see him. He was dressed in a black, collared shirt with the tail untucked, black jeans and black canvas boat shoes. Lisa knew from reading about him he was thirty-eight years old. His hair was black as well, thick and parted, surprisingly dated, reminded her of Emilio Estevez's clunky cut in *St. Elmo's Fire*. He wore a permanent three-day beard, the kind that came from a specialty razor, not inattention. There was an earring, too, a modest diamond. His watch was showy. His teeth were professionally aligned and chemically whitened, but his skin seemed appropriate for his age—no fillers or lifts as far as she could tell. He was slightly built, almost skinny, about an inch taller than she was.

"Please, have a seat. What can I offer you? Breakfast? Have you eaten already?"

"Just coffee for me, thanks," Lisa said. It was a few minutes past eight.

"What're my choices?" Joe asked.

"Do you like seafood? Our chef cooks a great seafood omelet."

"Sure," Joe said. "This would seem to be the ideal place for fresh seafood."

"Still only coffee for you, Mrs. Stone?"

"I'm good. Coffee's fine. Regular. Skim milk and half a packet of real sugar." She noticed that Garrison was not at all impressed or distracted by her appearance, didn't gawk or goober-smile or miss a beat in their conversation or freeze his face with hysterically fake apathy.

He used an intercom to send their order to the galley, also requesting a seafood omelet for himself. They settled around an oval-shaped table, she and Joe across from Garrison.

"I'm not familiar with how you do business," Garrison said. "Would you prefer to begin, or wait until we've eaten? I'm at your disposal."

"I'd say we go ahead," Lisa suggested. There was a large window behind Garrison, and she could see the ocean. The ship sat steady, with no pitch or sway. "We don't want to waste your time."

"I agree," Joe said. "But we'll leave it to you to set the agenda. What exactly is our business, Mr. Garrison?"

"Cool." He slid away from the table and crossed his legs. Oddly, he was wearing ribbed black cotton socks with the boat shoes. "It's simple, really. I'm interested in the late Miss VanSandt's VV 108. I want to own the rights. I thought I already did."

"You bought the rights from Neal?" Lisa asked.

"Yes. The whole enchilada." He shrugged. "But now I'm hearing we might not have what we'd hoped to purchase. I'd like to clean that up." He was amiable and relaxed.

"Our problem," Joe said, "is that we have no idea—"

"What the Wound Velvet is worth," Lisa finished. "We don't know what it does or why you want it."

"And I'm in no position to tell you." Garrison spread his hands, palms exposed. "I'm sure that doesn't come as a big surprise."

"No," Joe said, "but it does leave us at an impasse. The pig in the poke might turn out to be the grand champion."

A uniformed woman—probably eastern European, Lisa surmised—appeared and set the table with coffee cups, water glasses, cloth napkins and silverware. The ship's name, *Wave Length*, was sewn into the napkins.

"I understand," Garrison said, speaking as the steward went about her tasks. "If you in fact own the pig and the poke. Our lawyers have checked the records in Virginia, and it seems possible that you're bluffing us."

"Mr. Garrison," Lisa replied, "you aren't meeting with us over some minor tweak to an in-house program."

"True. You're bright people. You're smart enough to realize as much."

"Why, then, did your employee, Mr. Pichler, tell us a cock-and-bull tale?" she pressed. "Lie to us?"

Garrison smiled. "Ah, the cross-examination starts. Listen, I regret that. Mr. Pichler's a loyal employee and an excellent administrator. He is not a very good businessman or negotiator."

"You don't have to be a good businessman to tell the truth," Lisa pointed out.

"I agree," Garrison said. "Exactly. And we're together now so I can make amends and correct his error." The steward poured coffee for him, and he thanked her. "But can we please get back to my concern: Does some trust or foundation own the rights to the formula? A simple question. There's no need for much more discussion if we already own the VV 108."

"As best we can tell," Lisa said, "the asset was in fact transferred to you via the estate. We originally thought it was probable that Lettie had assigned it to one of her many projects. Turns out she didn't."

Her coffee was poured next, the skim milk and sugar packet brought on a separate saucer. The steward filled Joe's cup, then left.

"An honest mistake on your part," Garrison finally said. "I appreciate your letting me know. Thank you." He sounded sincere, not a speck of irony or smarm in the words.

"But that doesn't end our interest in the situation," Lisa said.

"Obviously not, since you drove all the way here."

"We think there're bigger issues," Joe said.

"Okay, but I'm not exactly sure where you're headed," Garrison replied, his expression cheerful, his tone still hospitable.

The steward reappeared and served Joe and Garrison their omelets, which came with fresh fruit and toast.

"What do you believe happened to Lettie?" Lisa asked. She focused on Garrison, made it a point to let him see her staring.

He sawed off a piece of omelet with his fork. "I believe she died in a fire. I understand the fire was related to meth production." He chewed and swallowed while she inspected him. He laid his fork across the plate, tines down. The metal on china caused a small squeak. "Why're you asking me?"

"We don't think it's so simple," Lisa said.

"The police are investigating her death as a homicide," Joe added. He hadn't touched his breakfast. Chunks of crab and curled shrimp protruded from yellow egg.

"A homicide?" Garrison repeated. "Why? How come?"

"I'm not sure we have all the facts," Joe said. "We do know that Dr. Downs has given the cops information that contradicts portions of Pichler's account. Downs believes she was murdered."

"Is your breakfast not up to par?" Garrison directed the question at Joe. "You're not eating."

"It's perfect," Joe answered.

"I don't know if my bud Downs happened to mention it or not, but he's crazy. Now, he's also a remarkable scientist, which is why I kept him around as long as I did and paid for his various stints in recovery, but make no mistake, he's thoroughly off the rails. It's very sad. There's an infinitesimal boundary between genius and lunacy, and it seems the best in the arts or sciences are those who can tightrope along the division and flirt with both sides and not tumble off into the void. I'm a fan of William James's theory of breaching the difficult barrier between the conscious and unconscious. There's a storehouse in our minds that we access only occasionally. Of course, James used peyote and nitrous oxide to open the door. Probably not such a great idea." He took hold of the fork and severed another bite of omelet. "Poor Downs has stumbled too far into the crazy camp these days. But I still like him and wish him well. He made a lot of money for us."

"He is fragile," Lisa agreed. "Still, there's no doubt Lettie wrote him and claimed that your company—in the person of a couple, uh, envoys in a rented car—paid her a forceful visit concerning the VV 108. More to the point, Mr. Garrison, the rental was under a fictitious name—Jane Rousch—and that same bogus renter returned the exact day Lettie was killed. The mileage on the first rental would take you right to Lettie's trailer and then back to the airport."

"I'm confused. If the name's a fake, how do you connect it with Benecorp?"

"Lettie e-mailed her pen pal Dr. Downs the plate number from the Benecorp visitors' car. Guess what? It matches the Rousch vehicle. Unfortunately, Pichler lied about that too."

Garrison stopped eating. For the first time, he didn't sound completely at ease. "And what do the two of you have to share about the mysterious Jane Rousch?" he asked, a small, muted strain of antagonism in his voice. He peered at Joe, then Lisa.

"Nothing," Lisa said.

"Nothing, huh?" he said, his eyebrows raised. "Not a thing? Really?"

"She didn't work for us," Joe said.

"No, she didn't," Garrison answered. "And do you have any information as to what has become of this Miss Rousch?"

"Why would we?" Joe asked.

"You tell me," Garrison said.

"I can tell you this much." Joe paused, poured cream in his coffee, stirred it with a teaspoon. "The final connection will be the call Rousch made to you after Lettie ran them off from her trailer and refused your offer. The cops are tracking that down as we speak. I don't guess you'd give us your private numbers and save the state some effort?"

"So if I'm understanding this correctly, after weeks of scamming me about the ownership of my formula and failing to gain any advantage, you're here to accuse me and Benecorp of killing Lettie VanSandt?" Garrison's tone was normal again.

"Not at all," Lisa said. "We're here to tell you about the evidence the police have compiled, and to confirm that you do indeed own the Wound Velvet. That's hardly a scam. The facts are the facts."

"From your reaction," Joe added, "I'm assuming someone called you from Henry County, Virginia, on September third."

"Maybe, maybe not," Garrison said. "But I will agree ours is a cutthroat business, and we and our rivals have historically been very guarded and under the radar in our movements. The Benecorp flag planted anywhere attracts attention, alerts our marketplace competitors and raises operating costs considerably. Our competition behaves similarly. Nothing unusual. As for Mr. Pichler, he wouldn't be privy to this segment of a project, this negotiation, so I wouldn't judge him too harshly if he denied it."

"You've answered my question," Joe declared. He still hadn't tried his coffee. His food remained in front of him, growing cold.

"No," Garrison said, "I haven't."

"If you're so fond of Downs, why're you harassing him with private thugs?" Lisa asked.

"Hello—because he's dangerous and he threatened me. The courts have already ruled on that issue. If I were spiteful or less than his friend, I would've filed charges and had him arrested. I elected not to. I chose merely to keep an eye on him. As I noted, he has a powerful mind. Who knows what injury he might dream up for me."

"Yeah," Joe scoffed. "You're pretty damn vulnerable. Especially to a criminal mastermind like Steven Downs."

"If you were familiar with his skills and his intellectual gifts," Garrison replied, "you wouldn't be so dismissive."

"So did you send your people to visit Lettie?" Lisa asked.

"I can promise you this much: I certainly didn't send anyone to do her harm, and I certainly had no involvement with her death. That's just ridiculous."

"What do you think Lettie's formula is worth?" Lisa asked. "Dollars and cents, I mean. I'm curious, and I can't see any harm in your telling us since we've conceded the Wound Velvet belongs to Benecorp."

"A reasonable question," Garrison mused. "But a difficult one. You see, Benecorp isn't really in the health-care business. Same as Exxon isn't in the petroleum business. Power companies aren't there to provide electricity. We're in the profit business, plain and simple. My objective is to make money. I'm not sure where the VanSandt discovery fits in that paradigm. Occasionally, we acquire projects to keep them on the shelf. If I had to speculate, though, based on the numbers I've seen so far, I'd say the VV 108 will probably go into production."

"I'm seriously considering a suit to get it back," Joe told him. "You know damn well you didn't come by the rights honestly."

"I see. So I have the local Henry County police to worry with, and now your threat of a suit. A pincer." Garrison slid his plate to the side. He removed a napkin from his lap and laid it—clumped and balled—on the table. "Is your bottom line money? A payment? Is that why you're here? I suppose there's always a cost to litigation. It's trashy to come right out and say it, and I assume it probably offends your extremely high professional standards, but would you like for me to price our situation?"

"No, we wouldn't," Lisa replied.

"No," Joe said curtly.

"How on earth would you possibly expect to win such a suit? Neal is Lettie's only blood heir, and you, a lawyer, signed away your interest under her will. I can't see how we're in jeopardy."

"Fraud," Joe answered. "Or mutual mistake of fact if Neal wasn't in on the smoke and mirrors from the beginning. We explicitly asked if there were any valuable assets he wasn't disclosing. We sent him a list of items. We asked him every which way from Sunday if there was anything in the estate not on the list. Doing your bidding, he lied to us."

"A lot of gaps and stretches there, Mr. Stone. And a big, ugly swearing contest. I'm confident Neal doesn't recall any such conversation. Your prospects seem extremely limited."

"We're anxious to take our chances," Lisa said. "I think a Henry County jury will believe us."

"You're positive we can't negotiate a fair settlement?" Garrison asked. "I hate to see this escalate. A Henry County jury will never hear this case. Diversity of citizenship will take us to a nice, neutral federal court. I know this because I'm frequently sued."

Joe leaned forward, closer to the table. "We can't strike a deal on a murder investigation, sir. Mr. Bushnell, the commonwealth's attorney, will make those decisions. As for the Wound Velvet, we simply want it returned to us. We're not happy about being screwed over. Who knows—once it's ours, we might even sell it to you if you're the right fit and the high bidder."

"Nothing's ever easy, is it?" Garrison stated. He sounded perturbed. He grimaced. "I hate entanglements. It's why I never venture too far ashore for very long, and then only when I have to. I prefer staying just beyond reach. I like international waters, outskirts, obscure ports, Indian reservations the states can't control and third-world districts at the margins of things. Your brand of stupidity is precisely why—for no reason, I'm being threatened with a bullshit criminal case by two lawyers who're angry they're on the losing end of a business deal."

"You can end half of your problem by giving us the Wound Velvet," Lisa said. "If you had no involvement in Lettie's death, the other half of your 'entanglement' will end well for you too."

"Please listen carefully," Garrison said. "Today, you and Mr. Stone can fly off the ship with half a million dollars—tax free, if you prefer—and we'll all part on happy terms. I'll gift you with a bottle of champagne so you can celebrate back in town. Or . . ." He paused, sipped water. "Or I can push the button and ensure your personal annihilation."

"How bright is that?" Lisa asked. "Believe me, if we were to go missing, Detective Toliver Jackson would be on your doorstep, no matter how far offshore you're anchored. You don't think we left without telling most of Martinsville where we are, do you?"

"Mrs. Stone, despite what you must think, I'm not a gangster. I'm not traveling around with a pistol strapped to my hip like your husband. I—"

"Right," Joe interrupted him, "you've got the hired help to handle the firearms for you."

"This is so terrible," Garrison said. "I don't understand it. Why would I harm Miss VanSandt? You've both worked yourself into a frenzy, and it's going to cost you dearly. I have no intention of touching either of you—how uncool. There's no need to be so paranoid and aggressive." He shook his head. "But if you bring this baseless suit against me, and if you claim I somehow had a hand in Miss VanSandt's death, you will bitterly regret it. You'll be ruined. I promise to annihilate you *legally*, in your own corrupt arena, with lawyers and judges and juries. I'm not going to have you kneecapped with a pipe or dump you into the sea. Or poison your food. What's wrong with you?"

"Let me ask you this," Joe said as soon as Garrison finished. "Would you settle with us for five million?"

Garrison studied him. "A lot of money. And as you mentioned, thanks to your false alarms, only half of my worries are eliminated by paying you for an asset you've already signed over to Neal. As to the other, do you have any influence with the local police?"

"None."

"Why five million?" Garrison asked.

"I wanted to see your reaction," Joe said. "Simple as that. This must be quite a discovery; you didn't even blink. Thanks for the offer. But we're not interested in bribe money, no matter how large the check." Joe finally took a bite of his food. "Probably the only chance I'll ever have to taste a fresh seafood omelet on a private ship." He chewed and began nodding. "Amazing. Even cold, it's delicious."

"Enjoy the moment and bask in your tiny little stunt. Perhaps Mrs. Stone thinks it's clever. I'm sorry we couldn't reach an agreement. Remember, please, my warning. Understand that the plans for your beat-down are already on my desk and foolproof and all the groundwork is in place. You'd have to realize this situation has been on my mind before today. Please don't push me. I never make idle threats. It's not in my nature." Garrison stood. "I'll have them tell Alden you're ready to leave. He'll return your pistol for the flight back so you'll feel secure. Good luck to you both." He walked away briskly, passing the steward as he left, and despite the goofy socks and disco hair and over-played departure, he made an impression on Lisa, left her convinced he could accomplish what he promised, or come damn close.

"Do you think they'd reheat this for me?" Joe asked her. "Or would that offend the chef? Maybe a to-go box is a better choice."

Concerned about eavesdropping, they didn't speak during the helicopter trip. Lisa emptied her purse, inspected the contents and felt and fingered the lining, pockets, bottom and flap. Joe carefully checked his holster and removed the bullets from his gun, gave them to Alden when they landed. "Souvenir," he said to the pilot, who looked confused. They changed rooms at their hotel, then sat on the carpet directly in front of a loud television, close together, and spoke quietly.

"I feel positive he's not bluffing us, Joe. But what does he have up his sleeve?"

"No way to tell," Joe almost whispered. "But for sure, the formula's a monster, and I'm positive he sent our old friend Jane Rousch and another henchman to take care of some ugly work with Lettie. Pichler wasn't high enough in the food chain to know about it."

"But this is still a mess. How the heck will we even know he's giving us the genuine formula if we win our suit? We don't even know the contents of the Wound Velvet, much less the proportions of each ingredient."

"Downs has some general idea, I think."

"Not really," Lisa said. "I quizzed him, and he doesn't know any particulars. And he's not the steadiest character on the planet."

"Yeah," Joe laughed. "Like how he's paranoid that Benecorp can hear everything he says and is constantly spying on him, so he takes all kinds of bizarre precautions."

Lisa laughed, too. "Maybe I should turn the microwave on and see if we can jam their satellite's listening capability."

"It's weird how Garrison said his defense was already in place. You think he ran in a Lettie impostor so you'd have to testify at a criminal trial that she's alive?"

"I can't see how that would injure *us*, not really," Lisa said. "And it would for damn sure hurt Benecorp—Garrison wouldn't own the VV 108 rights." She glanced at the TV. "I meant to ask him about Don and the missing animals, but he stalked away before I had the chance. Maybe that's kind of a signal to us, his fish in a newspaper, how it was so easy for him to make them disappear."

"Lord only knows what you can buy with his kind of money." Joe was silent for a moment. He leaned away from her, braced himself on straightened arms. He hinted at a grin. "Even scarier, he's one of the few men with a pulse you didn't delicious. Sounds strange for me to say, I suppose, but nearly every guy falls off the cliff when he sees you for the first time. It was like a comic book, where the superhero meets the supervillain and the heat ray or green lantern beam or spiderweb is battled tit for tat and they just lock up in a standoff. A tie."

"His last girlfriend was a super*model*. Or so say the gossip websites. I doubt an over-forty woman in Patagonia travel slacks is of much interest to him."

"Shit—you absolutely know you're still sexy. No doubt. I'll guarantee that you noticed his reaction too. After twenty years, I have a sense of what's passing through your mind."

"So do we file?" Lisa asked. "Do we sue a guy with metal detectors on his boat and a six-million-dollar helicopter? Tell me again why we're walking away from a comfortable settlement and provoking a shitstorm that might pay us far less?"

"We do sue him," Joe declared. "As soon as we hit Henry County." He fixed her with a look. "Because somebody needs to put things right. This SOB is a crook who most likely killed Lettie. Or tried to. He shouldn't be allowed to just sail away in his fancy boat without even breaking a sweat."

"Okay," she said, smiled. "I'm with you." She moved her knee so it touched his.

"But first, since we're going to wind up bankrupt and annihilated anyhow, courtesy of Seth the 'Sprockets' prince, let's go waste some cash and winging this town and limp home with zero sleep and a big fat hangover."

"Do you need to call a shareholders' meeting, or can we just get started?"

CHAPTER TWENTY-ONE

"This is about as big as it gets," Robert Williams declared after reading the Stones' draft of Joe's lawsuit against Benecorp, Neal VanSandt and Seth Garrison. Lisa had also outlined the facts before Williams studied the complaint, summarizing everything she and Joe had learned. "Jumbo."

Williams was behind the desk in his office, rimless reading glasses balanced at the bottom of his nose. It was June solstice, the twenty-first, and he was wearing a stylish summer suit. He'd been raised in nearby Danville, done a stint as a Harvard professor, then returned to the area and opened a general practice with his brother. Behind him, alongside diplomas and framed awards, was a photograph showing him installed as the first black president of the local bar. "What do you think, Phil?"

"I think if we can prove it, it's heavy-duty," Phil Anderson replied. A lawyer's lawyer and politely fierce in court, he'd driven from Roanoke for the meeting. He'd listened to Lisa as well—sat impassive and attentive—and then perused his own copy of the suit papers, taking longer than Williams to finish. "We'll all need agents and magazine-quality head shots if we win. But ultimately we're looking at an oath fest in front of a federal jury, and most people generally aren't sympathetic to lawyers trolling for money. Plus, we'll be a couple years before it's tried. The time and cost will be enormous, though I'm happy to do my part for free."

"We'll carry as much of the load as we can," Lisa assured him.

"Yeah, I'm certainly not expecting my friends and colleagues to pay me," Williams noted. "But travel and depositions and court reporters—it won't be cheap. Naturally, I don't need to tell you that."

"Appreciate the offer," Joe said, "but we intend to pay full freight."

"I'm not concerned about fees," Anderson insisted. "I'm not about to charge you. Let's not waste time arguing about it."

"The other problem I see," Williams said, "is that there's no hard evidence connecting Lettie's son to Seth Garrison. I'm sure Garrison won't admit the underlying deal, and I'm guessing the son won't, either. If it's fraud, we have the burden of proof at clear and convincing evidence. Never easy."

"If it's mutual mistake of fact," Anderson continued, "if we end up on that road and Garrison wasn't behind the curtain and there's no provable link on his part, we'll have to convince a jury that the two sophisticated lawyers who handled Miss VanSandt's affairs were equally as ignorant as her layperson son miles away."

"From the little bit I know," Williams added, "this Neal's on the simple side, and a jury's bound to feel sorry for him."

"Toliver has found the call that went from Henry County to Garrison," Joe said. "He told me day before yesterday. Unfortunately, the number Rousch—or whoever she is—used is a dead end. Still, the call from here puts Garrison and Benecorp in the loop, shows they were involved and had knowledge months ahead of my renouncing. We're supposed to believe that Neal just lucked into this? That Benecorp only spoke with him *after* he shows up in our office with his own damn waiver?"

"Strong inferences for our case," Williams agreed. "But we still have a lot of proving to do." He twisted in his chair, changed positions. The chair's swivel springs creaked, the sound worn and metallic. "I've seen worse odds, of course. One way or the other, we'll make it to a jury and have a shot. But to state the obvious, this will most likely be a life-changer for you and your law office. You're putting your reputation and credibility on the line in a fashion that will seem shady to the average person. Garrison will take your hide off in the press. He'll crucify you both."

"We understand this'll be a firefight," Lisa said. "That's why we asked the two best lawyers we know to help us. Truth be told, I'm more worried about Garrison's threat, his promise we're already sunk but just don't realize it." The air conditioner cut off, and the room became quieter, the floor registers finished until the temperature warmed a few degrees.

"Why, exactly, do you want to tackle this?" Anderson asked.

Lisa answered quickly. "With Joe, it's basically the justice involved. You both know how he is. He thinks Garrison should be punished, and he thinks Benecorp ripped him off and flimflammed him, and it's not in his nature to take a beating and do nothing. Honestly, if the VV 108 was worth a buck fifty, we'd still be right here with the complaint ready to file. That's just Joe."

"For Lisa," Joe said, "it's the money, plain and simple. She's betting that Lettie's alive and we'll be the forty percent owner of a miracle cure."

They all laughed. "The money *and* doing my level best to help my husband, whom I love very much," she said, her expression animated.

"You guys have any guesses what his dragon might be?" Joe asked. "How he plans to 'annihilate' us?"

"Did you take it as a physical threat?" Anderson directed the question to Lisa.

She shook her head. "No, he's too smart for that, though there was a moment on his boat when I was worried he might hurt us. We've been through it a million times and we're still stumped."

"Legally, holographic wills always cause complications," Williams said. "But that can't be the issue if he really said he'd annihilate you—we've all lost cases and had our hats handed to us. There must be something supremely personal about it if I'm understanding the context of his threat. Any skeletons Phil and I need to know about? Any weak spots?"

"Just the usual stuff," Joe answered. "We've run an honest practice, and beyond an occasional hangover and some high jinks in college, we're pretty ordinary. Unless horseback riding and hunting and showing up for work are crimes, I should be okay."

"Yeah, nothing comes to mind," Lisa said, though she was immediately scared a blush or splotch or blink might let on she wasn't being completely truthful. She held her complaint copy in front of her and bowed as if she were reviewing it. "Feel free to change or tweak whatever you want," she told Williams, eager to leave the topic.

"And we have absolutely no idea what this wound medicine is supposed to do?" Anderson asked.

"Correct," Joe said.

"No clue what it's worth?" Anderson asked.

"Correct," Joe repeated.

"Our threshold witness is a fired Benecorp employee with a documented history of mental health failings?"

Joe slid forward in his chair. "Sad but true."

"And *you* think it's possible Seth Garrison had a hand in Miss VanSandt's death?" Anderson was wearing a bow tie and a dark blue suit. He adjusted the bow tie, tugging on each side.

"Yep," Joe said.

"But Lisa's reasonably certain that Miss VanSandt's not even dead?"

"You got it," Joe answered.

"I saw her myself," Lisa said. "All this lawing and litigating is really just a tactic, as far as I'm concerned. An opportunity to push and probe Benecorp. I agree with filing the complaint, but I'm betting this suit won't matter one whit in the end. If I'm wrong, well, our suit still puts us where we need to be—in court."

"Hot damn," Anderson said. "We're off to a great start. Won't be long—we're all going to look like geniuses or total dumb-asses pretty soon. I'm glad the kids are almost through with college. At least that's taken care of if we go down in flames."

"Let's not forget"—Williams was smiling—"if Garrison did have Lettie murdered, he'll probably receive the key to the city and a reward for his public service. The day news of her death hit, Henry County sold out of fireworks and dancing shoes by closing time."

Less than an hour after Lisa returned from the meeting with Robert Williams and Phil Anderson, Betty buzzed to tell her there was a Mr. Robert Culp on the phone, a very panicked man with no file or record at the law office. "He said Mr. Stone normally handles his case, but since Joe isn't here he asked to speak with you. He sounds like he's scared to death."

"Oh, absolutely. Sure. Put him through."

A moment later, Dr. Downs was on her line. "Culp here," he said, sounding more stressed and harried than usual.

"Hi, Mr. Culp," Lisa said. "Are you safe? Is everything okay?"

"I'm at the Methodist church in Harrisonburg. In the pastor's office. They don't lock it. My sister's a member. It seemed like a safe place to call, but I'm still not convinced. I'm using the church phone."

"Listen—Joe and I really need you to hang in there. We've sued Benecorp. We've hired the best lawyers in the state to fight Garrison. We need you strong and focused. We need your help."

"Oh shit. Shit, Mrs. Stone. No."

"I know you aren't anxious to hear it, but it would make so much more sense if you'd let Joe and me bring you down here and put you in a safe place with our own security."

"I'm decompensating. I know I'm mentally sick. It's no secret. No mystery to me. That's the term, Mrs. Stone, *decompensate*. Like *renounce*. Another term. Joe Stone renounced the will. I don't think I can make it. My sister is giving me meds, and I'm still a wreck. Ships wreck, cars wreck, people wreck." He was anguished, sobbing and plaintive all through the skein of words.

"I can have Joe there in a few hours. Or I'll leave right now. He's in a deposition across the block. We can come and help you."

"I can't escape Garrison. He's been here. In my head and in my room at Amy's house. I said, 'Let me touch you and make sure you're real,' and he told me he wasn't real but I'd still be able to feel him."

"Seth Garrison was there, Doctor? In Harrisonburg?"

"I don't know. I saw him, but I'm falling to pieces. Even with my medicine. It's worse, you see, when you *realize* your mind has turned traitor. When you're aware of it and can't put the brakes on. I've heard from Lettie too. But she's dead, so who the heck knows." The crying wasn't as bad, the desperation in his voice wasn't as severe. "My mother, but that's not possible, either. I'm having to keep a log so I can follow myself. I have to write everything on paper so I can keep up with Downs. Ha! Writing all the time. No rest for the weary."

"What's your sister's number? I need to call her. Her cell or work number?"

"It's written in my notes, but I'll have to find it. It's definitely a part of my written history. Why won't Mr. Stone speak with me?"

"Sweetie," Lisa said sadly, sympathetically, "he's not here. He's not in the office. He wants to speak with you. He's worried about you. Remember how he's been checking on you? Calling your sister every few days? He's your partner."

"He's spying on me too," Downs wailed. "He wants my formulas. Formulae, actually. Is he in cahoots with Seth Garrison? But you already know that."

"No, Doctor," Lisa assured him, her tone as gentle and comforting as she could make it. "You asked Joe to help you and he did. We're your friends. Lettie assured you Joe was a good man, and he is. Joe and I absolutely believe that Benecorp is bad and that Seth Garrison is your enemy. We're here to protect you."

"I've passed the safe minutes. It's been too long. They're locked on to me now. I can feel it. I'm logging this in the record. Writing it down. Remember, Mrs. Stone, there's no escaping Seth Garrison. You can touch him whether he's there or not. Goodbye."

Lisa said "Doctor? Doctor Downs? Doctor?" but she'd heard a click and realized he was gone, that she was talking to an empty line.

She contacted Len Barrow's office and had his secretary pull Joe from a divorce deposition, emphasized to her it was an emergency. Joe gave her Downs's sister's cell information from his TracFone and promised her he'd be there as soon as he finished, probably in another thirty minutes. Lisa immediately called the sister, a James Madison University librarian named Amy Shepard, and found her at her job.

"Lisa Stone?" Shepard quizzed her. "Joe Stone's wife? From Martinsville?"

"Yes. We're law partners as well. I'm calling about your brother, Dr. Downs."

"Okay," Shepard said tersely. "I'm listening."

"I just spoke with him, and I'm extremely worried. He's in bad shape, very confused and frightened."

"Let me give you a preface, Mrs. Stone, so you won't think poorly of me. First, I'm assuming you really are Mrs. Stone. In Stevie's world, you need a scorecard to keep track of all the players and their alleged motives and multiple identities. As best I can tell, Mr. Stone truly is an attorney and Stevie sought *him* out, not vice versa. He seems concerned regarding Stevie's health. He calls periodically to check in, and he was kind enough to help return my van after Stevie stole it."

"So far, you're completely accurate," Lisa said.

"You also need to understand that I love Stevie very much, and that he's a genius. He earned a doctorate from UCLA when he was twenty. He was at the top of his class, and it came easy for him."

"I can tell he's bright," Lisa noted. "Eccentric, but extremely intelligent."

"*Eccentric* is charitable. Stevie has deep-seated and profound mental illnesses. I used the plural intentionally. He has been unstable for years and years, and we've done all we can for him. I'm his only sibling. But no matter the doctor, the medicine, the facility or the treatment, he always reverts to his old ways, and his sickness overwhelms him."

"I understand. It would have to be heartbreaking."

"So now that you have a sense of my perspective, do you know where he is? He's been missing for two days. We've alerted the cops, but it's not a priority for them. I need to locate him and have him committed until he stabilizes."

"Committed?" Lisa answered reflexively and immediately wished she hadn't.

"Yes, committed to a mental hospital. So they can treat his illness. Do you have a better idea?"

"No. No ma'am, I don't. Ten minutes ago, he was calling from the pastor's office at the Harrisonburg Methodist Church. Your church, where you attend."

"Thank you very much," she said formally. "I'll send my husband and the police over there."

"Mrs. Shepard, may I ask you something?"

"I suppose. I might not answer you, but go ahead."

"I understand your frustration with your brother and his circumstances, and from what I can discover, he's been a regular in the court system, lost his job because he made wild accusations against other employees and has landed in several mental hospitals. But a few moments ago he told me he'd seen Seth Garrison at your house, and he sounded believable. Totally sincere."

"Stevie is obsessed with Benecorp and Garrison. Perhaps you've seen the various court orders resulting from Stevie's bad acts directed at Benecorp. They're probably deserved, in a literal sense. In a legal sense. But, Mrs. Stone, Seth Garrison is a monster. If you're one of his minions posing as Lisa Stone, you can alert him and he can sue me for slander. He worked my brother like a beast of burden when he knew he was sick. God only knows how much money Stevie made him—that's why Garrison always paid for his rehab and kept him at Benecorp. Not—"

"So Garrison did pay for treatment?" Lisa interrupted.

"Please let me finish," Shepard said stiffly. "He doesn't care about Stevie, and these days Stevie's evidently connected to something important at Benecorp. Stevie has told me this, and I believe him."

"It's true. He is. Sorry to butt in, but there's no doubt about it."

"So Garrison has hired these awful people to bedevil my brother. Garrison knows—he absolutely knows—this will destroy Stevie, this following him and parking outside my house and the diabolical tricks they play on him." Shepard was angry, bitter, inflamed. "But there's nothing we can do about it, is there? My husband's brother is a lawyer, and he couldn't do a thing to protect Stevie. The police are no help, either. The thugs are within their rights to constantly lurk and linger on my street, especially given Stevie's threats. To answer your question, I'm positive Seth Garrison has not been in my house. I'm also positive that our deceased mother is not advising Stevie, and I was unable to discern the 'code' in alleged communications from people—both living and dead—that my mentally ill brother found in posts on various websites."

"Will you let us know how it turns out for him?"

"Thank you for your interest. I have to go; he's probably already on the move."

Lisa heard nothing for several days, and she tried to contact Amy Shepard on a Thursday, early in the morning. It was already hot and stuffy, the onerous summer heat stalled and languishing and shouldered up against the Blue Ridge Mountains, and Lisa was walking from their house to the Mercedes, and she thought of Downs and his sister, called Amy's cell number and heard a voice-mail message. She left her information and asked Amy to please get in touch.

Driving to town, Lisa came alongside a car on the four-lane, and a curly-haired lad, probably five or six years old, moonfaced and missing a tooth, watched her as she rode by his window, and she recognized him, had seen him a few days ago, the same boy, in the bulrushes by the small creek that meandered the public park, no shoes, no shirt, splashing the water, tumbling stones, kicking a mud bank, searching and hunting through the high grass, suddenly shrieking, "Crawfish! Crawfish! Crawfish!" and then, later, "Big lizard!" He'd explored the creek the whole time she was there, jogging after work, some fresh-air exercise once evening arrived and tempered the sun. A woman was driving him, and several other children as well, the brood in a bad-off, smoking blue Toyota, the rear bumper mangled and tied to the body with bungee cords. The boy waved at her, and she waved back, though they hadn't spoken at the park, and she guessed he was probably waving at everyone on the highway, even strangers.

Amy returned the call before Lisa reached the office, as she was turning onto Cleveland Avenue. "Stevie is dead," Amy announced, the sentence cold and sterile. "I hope you're all happy now. He hung himself in our basement yesterday. My twelve-year-old daughter found him. Nice, huh? He'd used a Magic Marker to cover my walls with calculations and equations."

"Oh my god, Mrs. Shepard. I am so very sorry. So sorry. He was a sweet soul."

"He's better off," she said flatly. "I hate to say it, but . . ."

"I completely understand my timing's not good, but I have to ask if you think Garrison was involved in this. I'm sorry, but your brother and I have a common foe in Benecorp. Was this suspicious?"

"We'd just located Stevie and were making arrangements for his treatment. Ironically, of course, Benecorp's security vipers have known exactly where he was every second of every day. My husband was upstairs when Stevie did it; there was nobody else in the house except our children. So, Mrs. Stone, yes, Seth Garrison killed my brother, but he was clever enough to do it at a distance and with the blessing of your inept legal system. He murdered Stevie one surveillance shift at a time, little by little. Early on in their torment, we found a speaker concealed in his room, the better for him to hear voices. I'll spare you a list of their other evils."

"Have you made arrangements? Will there be a service?"

"Not for you or anyone else, no."

"I'm so, so sorry. I—"

"Goodbye." Shepard cut her off and ended their conversation.

"I promise we'll try to do right by him," Lisa finished, alone in her car, the sentence almost sough at the end. She cried, not much, a tear from the corner of each eye, and her nose ran and her throat clogged with mucus, and she blotted the tears and parked and went to find Joe, didn't correct her makeup, wiped her nose with a wad of tissue as she trudged across the street and traveled several blocks. She stood on the sidewalk in front of Reid Young's law office, where—screw it—she lit a cigarette and smoked and occasionally dabbed her nose and eyes until she saw Joe through the plate glass, leaving, his briefcase at his side. She crushed the Marlboro Ultra Light with the toe of her shoe, twisted brown tobacco shreds—some burned black at the tips—from the paper and onto the rough concrete.

"Hey," Joe said as he pushed open the door. "I guess it's not a positive sign that you're waiting on the sidewalk next to Reid's office."

She gave him the news, and he hugged her and then looked her in the eye and said it was sad and pitiful but not shocking, and he told her not to be upset. "Poor Downs. In a strange sort of way, I'll miss him. He never really had a chance."

"Today, Joe, as soon as we can, we're hiring our own security. Off-duty or retired cops we trust. I don't care what it costs. We'd be stupid not to. Twenty-four-seven, Joe. You call Chris Lampkins and see if he'll help us schedule it."

"Okay," Joe said. "Though I'd like to think I can take care of us."

"Not when you're sleeping."

"I'll check with Chris."

"Such an evil thing to do," Lisa said. "Downs was so vulnerable. Garrison couldn't have cared less about being attacked—he just wanted Downs gone."

"No doubt."

"Pitiful," she added, repeating Joe's word.

Joe switched hands with the briefcase. "From a selfish perspective, it's fair to say our suit just became more complicated." He sighed. "With Downs dead, the e-mail from Lettie to him is going to be an even worse chore to prove at trial. Damn." He stared at the sidewalk. "Poor guy. Smart and crazy is an impossible combination. And Garrison knew exactly which buttons to push, didn't he?"

"He did," she said.

"You know," Joe said grimly, "bad shit happens in threes. Probably two still to come."

CHAPTER TWENTY-TWO

Brownie Stone died the next morning, on July 1.

A distressed, flustered, discombobulated, red-eyed Betty popped into Lisa's office, pushing open the door without a knock or any warning, and she insisted—her small hands flapping—Lisa needed to hurry down the hall and check on Joe, and Lisa was alarmed and immediately understood that whatever had happened was bad, bleak. She'd slipped her shoes off while she was proofreading a mobile-home-park lease at her desk, and she bolted from the room with bare feet, felt the polished wood and carpets and fine grit on her soles as she rushed to Joe's office. She was worried about a heart attack, a stroke, or some retaliation from Benecorp, or maybe word of her cheating had finally made it to her husband.

Joe was sitting on the floor, beside the chamois pad. Brownie was laid across his lap, the dog's mouth partially wrenched open and his lips drawn backward and locked in place. His tongue extended from a black corner and caught between his teeth so that—oddly—it was pointing upward, toward the ceiling, against gravity. Urine wet the very edge of his bed and had puddled on the oak floor. Joe was quiet. From her angle, the dog's muzzle seemed absolutely white, fluorescent, washed out by the electrical lights. One of Brownie's eyes was shut, the other mostly exposed, fixed and hollow, switched off, disconnected.

"Oh, Joe," was all she could muster, and she plopped down on the floor, right where she'd been standing, shoeless, despondent, crying, her knees pulled fast against her chest and encircled inside her arms.

"Came from the clerk's office . . ." Joe began but couldn't finish. He took a breath, shook his head, swallowed several times. "And I found him . . ." His voice fractured on the last word, and he stopped again. "Dead on his pad. I was gone an hour, probably less."

Lisa wasn't able to speak. Betty and their other secretary, Isabelle, filed in behind her, and Betty patted and squeezed Lisa's shoulder.

"He was rattling this morning," Joe said. "Hard for him to breathe." He wiped at his eye. "But it didn't seem that urgent. Nothing new. I should've taken him to Dr. Withers." Joe stood up and laid the dog on the pad, careful to keep the carcass away from the slight urine spot.

"I'm so sorry, Mr. Stone," Betty said. "He was a great dog. It won't be the same here without him."

"I'm going to bring the Jeep around front and load him," Joe declared. "I don't want to parade him through the parking lot like this. He'll have his dignity."

"Okay," Lisa said softly.

Joe left and returned and folded the chamois pad around Brownie, made a sling almost, and he carried the dog to the Jeep and placed him in the cargo area. Lisa walked behind them. Joe stepped to the side to make space, and she moved closer and put her hand on the dog's head and rubbed down along his neck, stopped at his stomach, all the warmth and life missing. "Poor boy," she said, still barefoot, still crying.

Suzy Loomis was passing by, and she braked her car and pulled to the curb and lowered the window and asked if everything was okay. "Brownie just died," Joe informed her, and she covered her mouth and her face sank. Almost everybody in Henry County knew how much the Stones loved their dog, and people later suggested his death was even worse than normal because they had no kids, almost as if they'd lost a child.

Their neighbor Taylor volunteered his Kubota tractor with a front-end bucket, and Joe used it to dig a deep grave near the split oak, the spot where Brownie had originally gone to die. The grave was atop a slight knoll, above a lazy stretch of slope and a field, the view clear in every direction, and in the late fall and winter when the leaves were absent, you could make out the creek at the border of the property. Joe squared away the corners with a shovel and posthole digger, stood inside the pit he'd cut from the ground, thigh-deep, and shaped the grave, shaved it neat, tidy. Lisa sat and watched, Brownie in a quilt beside her, completely covered. The quilt was old, a hand-sewn patchwork they'd inherited from Joe's Great-Aunt Macie, but it had two big, stubborn stains on it as well as a tattered corner, so they kept it stored in a chest, too valuable and too familial to discard, too soiled to spread at the foot of the guest room bed.

Lisa didn't want to see her dog's pained mouth and vacant eyes again, so she kissed him goodbye through the cloth, and Joe stepped into the hole and rested him on the soil bottom. They buried his metal bowl with him. DOG was stenciled in black letters across the bowl, the D chipped and dinged. Joe insisted on shoveling in the dirt by hand, scooped and tossed the mound of red clay from a plastic sheet until the opening was completely filled, the quilt's blues, indigos, yellows and violets disappearing bit by bit. He did use the Kubota's bucket to tamp the dirt, packed it flush with the rest of the earth, tight, secure, final. "We'll find him a marker," Joe said when he turned off the engine. "You'll have to help me think what to inscribe. You're better at that kind of thing than I am."

In the end, after a dismal July Fourth holiday, they settled on a small granite rectangle, ordered from the funeral home: BROWNIE STONE. FAITHFUL DOG.

CHAPTER TWENTY-THREE

"Damn it," Joe blurted. "Shit. I hate these infernal codes." His neck was craned, his nose almost touching his computer's screen. "The 'gotcha' puzzle they make you copy on Ticketmaster." He was in his office, a Friday, 10:00 a.m., a week after they'd buried their dog, another dry, hot, prosaic Henry County morning, yards starting to brown, the heat loitering and obstinate, not relenting even at night.

"It's 'captcha,' Joe." Lisa grinned. "It prevents wholesale buying and keeps the process honest." She came around the desk to join him. "What're you trying to order?"

"This is a total clusterfuck. Worthless."

"Oh, yeah," she said, reading the screen. "ZZ Top in Greensboro. You mentioned that. I definitely want to go. It should be fun."

"So is that an *o*, an *a*, or the number *zero*, and is it small or capital if it's an *o*? Of course, that's just the first little test. We still have to solve the hieroglyph at the end—looks like a giraffe's hind leg."

"Calm down. Try the New Words option. Hurry. Right there." She pointed.

He moved the cursor, clicked, and a new sequence appeared: warped, squiggled, pixilated letters that dissolved into a dark, muddled background. "Oh, yeah, that's so much better," he said sarcastically. He typed in letters, pecking the keys with his index finger.

"Change the middle *p* to an *r*," she instructed him.

He did and hit a key and the entry was correct and a set of arrows rotated in a circle and the message told him his wait would be seven minutes. "We're toast," he said angrily. "I preferred driving down to the mall and lining up at the record store. Or phoning in. This is criminal."

"Maybe not," she said. "We'll see."

"Perfect," he groused several minutes later. "Seventeenth row in the upper deck. And we have five minutes to accept those whiff-of-the-show seats. I wonder how many more codes I'll have to crack?" He folded his arms across his chest. "Our string of bad breaks continues."

"Those *are* in exile. Dang. Forget it. Hit Cancel. We'll just have to see what's available from the scalpers."

"Right—since we have so much extra money to burn these days," Joe said, though he wasn't mean about it, sounded more like he was in hopes of some commiseration from her. "Night-shift security at the farm is running us nearly nine hundred bucks a week."

"I know," she said. "But we can't spend the rest of our lives sitting at home. I'm sure better tickets will surface closer to the concert. It'll pan out." She nudged him with the heel of her hand. "You ready to go? I don't want to be late." She was due in Richmond at three-thirty to argue a case before the Virginia Supreme Court.

"Yeah. All set. We've got plenty of time."

"I don't want to feel rushed. It's stressful enough as it is."

"We're in good shape." Joe had helped her with the brief and listened to her rehearse her oral argument. "No way you'll lose; this appeal is typical insurance company obstruction. I can't believe they finagled a writ. They're just punishing you because you wouldn't discount your verdict. Like their candy-ass lawyer said, they 'plan to make you earn every dime.' They don't even bother to disguise it."

"I hope nothing happens. A hundred twenty thousand is a damn fair judgment. Forty of it's ours, which would come in very handy about now."

"You tried a great case, and you've written a perfect brief. You'll be fine. This'll be our rally cap."

"You don't have to go with me. I appreciate it, but you don't have to."

"That's a long stretch to be alone," Joe said. "Who knows what Seth Garrison has in store for us. I'm convinced we need to be careful and stick with each other. Your rule, remember? Plus, I don't want you falling asleep on the drive home."

"Thanks," she said. "You're a sweetheart."

Lisa had a hint of nerves at the beginning of her presentation, but she enjoyed the big stage, the ornate, commanding courtroom, the justices in stern robes, their lineage reaching back to John Marshall himself, the chief a woman, Justice Kinser, a petite, whip-smart lady from the western tip of the state who ran the show with a formal grace. Lisa was wearing a dark suit and rudimentary makeup. Her hair was twisted and pinned and caught in a bun. Joe sat behind her in the gallery, even though as her partner he could have joined her at counsel's table. The justices asked her only a single question, which she nimbly answered. Several of them seemed perturbed by the insurance company's lawyer, peppering him with questions, interrupting him mid-sentence, hammering flaws Lisa had highlighted in her filings. "Thank you, Counsel," Chief Kinser said at the end of the case. Their opinion would probably be finished and published by early fall.

Lisa and Joe were in high spirits as they left the Supreme Court building, and they decided to have a celebratory drink and an early dinner at the Tobacco Company before enduring the three-hour trek to Henry County. As they were walking through the city, about a block distant from the court's building, a disheveled man darted from a doorway and cut into their path, stood stationary with his arms outstretched so they couldn't easily pass him. Late in the afternoon, nearing five o'clock, it was still in the high eighties, yet the man was dressed in a soiled wool sport coat with elbow patches, a buttoned-to-the-neck flannel shirt underneath the coat. His pants seemed appropriate for the season, light-colored twill, though they were filthy and a front pocket was partially ripped from the rest of the fabric, flapped from his hip like an aberrant cloth ear. There was a dark stain coloring the pants' crotch. He had on tennis shoes with no socks. His hair was foul, unkempt, weeded with gray. A raised red scar—a straight line with stitch marks on each side—bisected his cheek. "Welcome, pilgrims," he greeted them.

"Hello," Joe said.

"Hi," Lisa said, trying to recall if she had any dollar bills.

"I have exactly what you need," the man declared, and he reached inside his coat pocket.

They'd stopped moving, and the stranger was ten feet in front of them. The quick dip into his coat alarmed Lisa, who gripped her purse strap more tightly and instinctively clenched her free hand into a fist.

"So what you got for us?" Joe asked.

Before Joe finished speaking, the man had already produced something wrapped in newspaper. "A mirror. And it ain't no bullshit mirror neither."

"A mirror?" Joe repeated.

"Yeah."

"A quality mirror?" Joe quizzed him. "As opposed to a bullshit mirror?"

"Amen." The man shuffled his feet, seemed to jog in place.

"Is it free or do we need to buy it?" Lisa asked. She loosened the fist, let her hand relax.

"Oh, I'll make you a fair price," the man answered.

"Can we see it first?" Joe asked.

The man unwrapped the glass and held it—his arm extended—in their direction. "Didn't I tell you? Ain't no bullshit mirror. Operates perfect. But you can't have it till you pony up."

"How much?" Lisa asked.

"Fifty dollars."

"Fifty's more than we can afford," Joe said. "It's kind of small. Fifty might be reasonable for a bigger mirror."

"Twenty-five," the man countered.

"I'll go ten," Joe told him.

"Or we'll buy you a meal at a restaurant," Lisa said. "Whatever you'd like. Most expensive steak on the menu. Your choice."

"I'll take the ten," the man said, tilting his head slightly. He held out an upturned palm. Joe took a ten from his wallet and gave it to him. The man then offered the mirror, which was tucked back in its newspaper. The man's hands were grimy; black arcs were embedded under every nail.

"You keep it," Joe told him. "I'm the kind of guy who actually needs a bullshit mirror. Yours probably has too much juice for me."

"I hear ya," the man said. "It's powerful."

"Can we pass now?" Joe asked, his tone firm but still friendly.

"Of course." The man stepped to the street side of the walk and invited them by with a grand sweep of his arm.

"Good luck," Joe said as they left.

Lisa spoke almost as soon as they cleared the stranger. "Jeez, Joe, I swear, the first—"

"Me too," he interrupted. "Same as you."

"I immediately tense up and wonder if it's a trap or—"

"A setup."

"Or if he has a—"

"Weapon in his coat," Joe finished. "Even though it makes absolutely no sense."

"I'm processing it and trying to tie it to—"

"Yep, Garrison. Bizarre. So was I."

"Maybe that's how he wants it to work," she said, "how he operates. Poisoning our heads."

"Has us spooked and second-guessing and seeing ghosts and shadows and threats—"

"Everywhere," she concluded. "Everywhere."

CHAPTER TWENTY-FOUR

Robert Williams personally delivered Seth Garrison and Benecorp's answer to Joe's civil complaint on July 14. When he came through the door at Stone and Stone, Lisa was standing in the waiting area talking to a solicitor from the Horsepasture Volunteer Fire Department about a donation. She instructed Betty to draft a fifty-dollar check for the department, and she and Williams immediately went into her office, and she buzzed Joe at the opposite end of the hall. As they waited for Joe, Williams mentioned the arid summer and the lack of rain, and she could tell he was anxious, uncomfortable, the pleadings evidently more than routine denials and pro forma defenses.

Joe arrived and sat across the desk from her, beside his attorney. "What's the word from Captain Nemo?" he asked.

"Happy Bastille Day," Williams said. He gave Joe a copy of the papers, then Lisa. She noticed Williams's cuff links when he reached toward her and his coat sleeve rode up his arm. They were gold and round, his initials—RAW—engraved in the metal. "Skip the answer for now and go straight to the counterclaim," he suggested.

"Is it bad?" she asked.

"I'd describe it as somewhere between a drive-by shooting and a full-blown jihad, but you decide for yourself. Start on page six."

Lisa flipped through Benecorp's filing. Joe had already located the counterclaim and was reading, holding the papers at eye level, the first five pages folded underneath the remainder, a corner staple binding the several sheets together. She began reading as well. Out of habit, she picked up a cheap plastic pen and used the dull, plugged end to keep her place on the page:

COUNTERCLAIM

Your Defendants/Counter-Plaintiffs affirmatively state and say as follows for this, their Counterclaim pursuant to Rule 3:9:

1. Defendants' previous pleadings are incorporated herein.
2. The Counter-Defendant, Joe Stone (hereinafter "Stone"), maintained a decades-long, attorney-client relationship with Lettie P. VanSandt (hereinafter "VanSandt").
3. As a direct result of this professional relationship with VanSandt, Stone became aware that VanSandt, an inveterate tinkerer and inventor, had created a "wound-cure" formula that had significant value in the pharmaceutical industry. VanSandt referred to her formula as "VanSandt's Velvet #108" or "VV 108."
4. That Stone, in flagrant breach of his duties as VanSandt's attorney and in violation of the Virginia Rules of Professional Conduct, embarked on a course of highly improper conduct to gain a share of the VV 108 formula and/or its ownership.
5. Specifically, Stone breached his fiduciary duty to VanSandt, exerted undue influence on her and repeatedly attempted to pressure her into granting him a share of the VV 108 property and/or its profits.
6. While this dishonest scheme was ongoing, VanSandt died unexpectedly in a fire at her home.
7. Prior to her death, VanSandt executed a will, drafted by Stone, that left the majority of her estate to her son and only blood heir, Neal VanSandt (a defendant herein), and a minor portion, $2,000 (U.S.), to the Henry County, Virginia, SPCA, a copy of which said will is attached as Exhibit "A." This document was executed mere days before her death in November 2010, and a copy was forwarded to her son. Since Stone drafted said will, he

was fully aware that he would not have any ownership of the VV 108 formula at VanSandt's death.

8. The will attached as Exhibit "A," the true last will and testament of VanSandt, was not probated as her final will. Instead, a purported holographic will, alleged to be written entirely in the hand of VanSandt, was filed by Stone himself in the Henry County Circuit Court Clerk's office on December 8, 2010. This document is attached as Exhibit "B." This fraudulent holographic will left the entirety of VanSandt's estate to Stone.

9. The holographic will is a forgery and fraud, created and submitted to probate by Stone so as to gain control of, and ownership rights to, the VV 108 property.

10. Counter-Plaintiff Benecorp is engaged in the creation, distribution and marketing of drugs, medicines and pharmaceuticals of all kinds and classes on a global scale. This is a highly competitive business, and the protection of marketplace strategies, product development and new technology is of the utmost importance to Benecorp. The company invests millions of dollars annually to insure this protection of assets, trade secrets, strategies and proprietary information.

11. By virtue of a patented system known as MissFit Matrix, Benecorp discovered a marketplace utility for VV 108.

12. Benecorp began confidential negotiations with VanSandt, which had not concluded at her death. Upon information and belief, as her long-serving counsel, Stone was aware of these contacts and advised VanSandt on the same, and, as stated hereinabove, thus became aware of VV 108's value to the pharmaceutical industry and specifically to Benecorp.

13. Upon VanSandt's death, Stone presented the forged will attached hereto as Exhibit "B" for probate and thus hoped to become the sole owner of the VV 108 formula.

14. VanSandt's son, Neal VanSandt, a nervous, legally unsophisticated man, contacted Stone to inquire about his mother's estate and was informed by Stone that Stone owned everything by virtue of the now-probated handwritten will.

Neal VanSandt was surprised by this and contacted legal counsel.

15. Benecorp did not wish for its competitors to learn of its interest in VV 108, nor, as a business strategy, did it wish to engage in a lengthy, public court battle with Stone to secure the rights to the VV 108.

16. Even though your Counter-Plaintiffs were initially highly suspicious as to the validity of this holographic will, and are able to prove at any trial of this matter that this handwritten document is indeed a forgery and not the true last will of VanSandt, they elected, strictly for economic and business reasons, to enter into a settlement with Stone in return for his disclaiming and renouncing any interest in the VanSandt estate in favor of Neal VanSandt. A copy of said settlement agreement is attached hereto as Exhibit "C." Benecorp then purchased the rights to the VV 108 from VanSandt's legitimate heir, Neal VanSandt, and, although not legally bound to so do, contributed $5,000 (U.S.) to the Henry County, Virginia, SPCA.

17. In conformity with this agreement executed by Stone, the negotiated sum of $750,000 (U.S.) was deposited in account number N120001443 in the Caribbean Fidelity International Bank, Nassau, Bahamas, in the name of Lisa Stone, the wife and law partner of Stone. A document establishing the transfer of said funds is attached as Exhibit "D."

18. Lisa Stone was physically present in the Bahamas on or about March 4–6, 2011, and withdrew the said deposit in full and complete satisfaction of this contractual agreement. Pursuant to the parties' understanding, the bank provided Benecorp with proof of Lisa Stone's withdrawal, attached as Exhibit "E."

19. Notwithstanding the parties' fully executed and binding agreement, Stone traveled to Virginia Beach, Va., in June 2011 and threatened Benecorp's founder, president and CEO, your Counter-Plaintiff Seth Garrison (hereinafter "Garrison") in an attempt to leverage and extort even further monies for himself. Specifically, Stone demanded an additional $5,000,000

(U.S.) in exchange for his not contesting the ownership of the VV 108 property, this despite having already received, via Lisa Stone, $750,000 (U.S.) as full and complete payment for his altogether fabricated claim and all his right, title and interest in and to the VV 108 property. Stone also informed Garrison he would "tell the world about VV 108," and thus potentially compromise Benecorp's marketplace advantage and proprietary interests. It was at this juncture that Benecorp hired a retired FBI handwriting expert to formally examine a copy of the handwritten will and determined with certainty that it was a fraud and forgery.

20. As a basis for his new $5,000,000 (U.S.) demand, Stone fraudulently and deceptively claimed the VV 108 had been, prior to VanSandt's death, transferred to a trust or other corporate entity and hence title and ownership did not pass to Benecorp by virtue of its purchase of all estate assets. This claim was first made to Neal VanSandt and subsequently to attorney Matt Champoux and finally to Anton Pichler, a Benecorp employee. With proper legal notice to Stone, and in keeping with company practices, this conversation with Pichler was recorded and will be produced at any trial of this matter.

21. In fact the VV 108 was never transferred to any trust, group, foundation, organization or corporation. As VanSandt's attorney, Stone knew this, and his representations to Benecorp and Garrison were knowingly false. The rights to the VV 108, under the legitimate will of VanSandt (Exhibit "A"), and/ or pursuant to Virginia intestate law, and/or pursuant to Stone's settlement agreement and renunciation in favor of Neal VanSandt, are, and have been for several months, the absolute, unencumbered property of Benecorp, owned by the corporation free and clear. Stone's knowingly false representations were simply designed to extort more money from Garrison and/or Benecorp.

22. Stone's current lawsuit is baseless and without merit and was filed simply in an effort to goad Benecorp into settlement, lest the details of the VV 108 become known in the global

marketplace, thus compromising Benecorp's strategic advantages.

23. Stone's conduct in (a) knowingly, intentionally and fraudulently presenting a forged will so as to gain ownership of the VV 108 property; (b) willfully, intentionally and deliberately breaching his settlement agreement with Benecorp without cause or justification; and (c) willfully and fraudulently attempting to extort money from Benecorp based on his knowingly false claim to Garrison (and others) that Benecorp did not own the VV 108 property, but rather a "trust" which Stone controlled owned said property, was/were, both separately and in combination, egregious, willful, wanton, reckless, dishonest and utterly outside the norms of societal acceptance. This conduct was done with actual malice toward your Counter-Plaintiffs and/or in conscious disregard of the Counter-Plaintiffs' rights.

WHEREFORE, in light of the foregoing, your Counter-Plaintiffs, Seth Garrison, in his individual capacity and as president and CEO of Benecorp, and Benecorp, a Florida corporation, hereby pray for the following remedies, relief and damages: (1) Your Counter-Plaintiff Benecorp seeks a finding and determination by this Court that it is the outright, fee simple owner of the VV 108 property, free and clear of any claim, demand and interest of Joe Stone and/or any other person or entity; (2) Your Counter-Plaintiffs also seek the return of $750,000 (U.S.), with statutory interest from March 5, 2011, for breach of the settlement agreement hereinabove described; (3) Your Counter-Plaintiffs demand judgment in the amount of $5,000,000 (U.S.) for common-law fraud committed by Joe Stone; (4) Your Counter-Plaintiffs demand $5,000,000 in punitive damages against Joe Stone; (5) Pursuant to the parties' agreement herein referenced, your Counter-Plaintiffs demand their reasonable attorney's fees and all court costs incurred in bringing this action; (6) As per Section 8.01-271.1 of the 1950 Code of Virginia, as amended, your Counter-Plaintiffs request sanctions against Joe Stone for the reasons hereinbefore set forth. A trial by jury is demanded.

"Fucking great googly moogly," Joe said. "What a hodgepodge of colorful lies. It's a bushel basket's worth of deceit and half-truths."

Lisa scowled at his reaction but didn't say anything. She dropped the papers on her desk and tossed the pen beside them. Adrenaline shot from her gut up into her throat.

"I also have a letter, Joe," Williams said somberly.

"It's straight out of Shysterville," Joe railed, ignoring him. "No, actually, I'm wrong: It's straight from a whorehouse in the slums on the outskirts of Shysterville. Fucking unbelievable."

"Their lead counsel," Williams continued methodically, "is a big-wheel Florida lawyer by the name of Edwin Nicholson. He's the real McCoy and lives up to his billing. He's won several high-profile cases. I hear he's extremely honest and totally aboveboard, which is surprising given his clients' tendencies. Their Virginia guy is Mack MacDonald from the Norfolk McGuire, Woods office. He's a serious player too. And McGuire, Woods is a resource powerhouse. Here's the second barrel: They've filed a bar complaint. They want your license suspended, Joe."

"We didn't expect them to retain the rookie from Legal Aid," Lisa said. "No surprise they'd hire top talent." She felt a crimp in her stomach. Her breathing lost its rhythm, misfired, picked up stray skips and surges. She inhaled through her mouth, licked her lips and drummed her clear-polished nails against a yellow legal pad, a client's phone number and several doodles on the pad.

"It's a complete, absolute house of cards, Robert," Joe insisted. "Bits and pieces are true, but it's a damn fiction. I never signed any agreement with them, and we never received one thin dime. Lisa took a Bahamas vacation with M. J. Gold, but she surely didn't come home with over seven hundred thousand dollars. American. I fucking love how they're so important and global they have to spell out that we're dealing in U.S. dollars."

"Well, as we all understand," Williams remarked, "it's not so much what actually happened that concerns me. It's what they can sell to seven strangers sitting in a jury box."

"And I didn't forge any will. That's crazy shit." His voice was ragged. "Sheriff Perry found the document. *He* gave it to me."

"Let's sort through it," Williams said.

"Exactly," Lisa agreed, still rattled. "They didn't just meet at the secretarial pool three days ago and start dictating random allegations they can't support. Think about what Garrison told us, Joe, how he claimed his plan was already in place."

Joe nodded vigorously. "You're right. You both are. Sorry. I'm not a very helpful client; I need to calm down. But fuckin' A, it pisses me off to no end."

"Let's recap the simple items first," Williams offered. He stood from his chair and paced while he spoke. "Okay, I'm sure they have phone records confirming that Pichler—and probably Garrison himself—spoke with Lettie prior to her death. They admit it. Give them credit, that's slick and neutralizes part of our case. They'll claim they were secretive about it because of their business requirements. The call from 'Jane Rousch' to Garrison and her visit to Henry County become significantly less incriminating. Classic strategy: Concede the issue and twist it to your advantage."

"They have me in the Bahamas," Lisa added. "Which was easy to track. It was no secret." She coughed into her fist.

"Thanks to Facebook," Joe griped. "Got to broadcast everything on Facebook or it doesn't really count. I remember her pal M.J. posted a couple times while they were there."

"Or perhaps they simply picked it up from talk around town," Williams speculated. He'd stopped wandering and was stationary, almost at the far corner of the room. "Once the will surfaced, you were both on their radar. Seems they started planning and building in precautions a long while ago. Keeping track of you. At any rate, they can prove Lisa was in Nassau—passport, customs, plane tickets. And you can bet the ranch they have the documents from the bank. No way they'd wing that kind of claim and not have the goods."

"Their 'goods' are street-vendor Prada," Lisa interjected. "Fake as fake can be. Counterfeit as hell."

"I assume M.J. will testify that Lisa didn't go to a bank," Joe said. "We should have a very credible witness." He looked at Lisa. "Did you two ever separate long enough for you to visit a bank and make a six-figure international withdrawal in a country that moves so slowly it's like the whole island's powered by two weak double-A batteries?"

"We never split. If push comes to shove, I have an absolute alibi," Lisa said, struggling to sound decisive. "Of course M.J. is a very close friend. They could impeach the hell out of her." She sucked in air, took a long and deliberate draw.

"I'll send formal discovery today so we can review whatever documents they claim the bank generated. Phil's already trying to track down as much as he can about the bank itself."

"That should be fruitful," Joe said.

"I'm also guessing they have you on tape telling Pichler a trust might own the Wound Velvet," Williams stated.

"Yeah, they probably do," Joe said miserably. "We never actually made the claim, never actually said more than it was a *possibility* but, yep, they probably have it. I called him back before I sent the nondisclosure agreement. Shit."

"Did they tell you the call was being recorded?" Williams asked. He was pacing again.

"I assume so. I think so. Pretty much every business does these days. 'For quality control and training purposes this call may be monitored or recorded,' right? I never paid any attention to it, but I was extremely careful not to misrepresent anything. We never said a trust owned the VV 108; we only said it was a possibility."

Williams remained at the far corner of the office. "They'll have a field day with the semantics, Joe. Especially if you initiated the contact and led them into this some-trust-might-own-the-wound-medicine discussion." He returned to his chair and took a seat, then leaned forward with his elbows on his knees, his fingers laced together.

"True," Joe said. "I realized at the time it might come back to bite me in the ass. There's a mention of potential trust ownership in the nondisclosure agreement too. I had to have some gimmick so I could tease out the information. Get a read on them."

Lisa was staring at the floor. She talked without bothering to look at her husband or Williams. "Given the unlimited digital magic that, hell, most teenagers have access to—and Photoshop and computer programs and state-of-the-art copy machines—creating Joe's signature on a settlement agreement would be child's play." She shook her head and finally looked up at Williams.

"Especially," Joe said morosely, "since they have a perfect example of my signature on the nondisclosure documents and the original renouncement I gave to dumb-ass Neal. I can't believe he'd go along with this and sell us down the creek. What a turd."

"Who notarized Joe's signature?" Lisa asked.

"A Helen Allyn," Williams answered. "Probably a Benecorp flunky who'll remember Joe just like it was yesterday. You allegedly showed her your Virginia driver's license—your ID number is written under her seal. I'll bet the number is accurate, but we'll still check."

Joe frowned. "It's a crying shame we live in a world where everything can be altered and reproduced and cut from whole cloth to the point that photos and documents are just another medium for skulduggery. It used to be good, old-fashioned lying under oath was the weapon of choice. But now . . ." He shrugged. "And, of course, the legal system really needed more ways for people to cheat."

"That leaves Lettie's will," Lisa said.

"I'll drive us over there," Joe said. "I'll tell Betty to call the clerk's office and have them pull the file."

"I have a sick feeling the file's not going to have great news for us," Lisa said. "Damn. I never saw any of this coming. It's amazing how imaginative these guys are."

"At least they didn't remove the case to federal court," Joe said as he was standing. "Not yet, anyway."

"I pondered on that, and I'm sure they did too," Williams replied. He'd also stood, and his hands were in his pockets. "If you're Benecorp, maybe you do decide to try the suit here in Henry County. We all know there's no bottom to the fall from a small-town pedestal. If your friends and neighbors think you've hoodwinked them and manipulated them, they stick it to you tenfold, especially if you're in an authority position—preacher, cop, mayor, local lawyer. It's personal. They're connected. You've screwed them and their community over, plus they're mad at themselves for getting duped. When they turn against you, it's vicious and rabid. The tar-and-feathers variety of unhappiness."

"God, this is just awful," Joe said. "Makes you realize how treacherous the system can be when you're on this side of the equation and it's your ass on the line. It isn't all so professionally clean and abstract. All of a sudden, it's a knife fight instead of a chess tournament." He glanced at Lisa. "You okay?"

"Yeah," she said, the response barely audible. "I'm fine."

"Listen," Joe encouraged her, "we knew this would be a brawl. They're lying, and we aren't. We understood it wouldn't be easy or quick. We're playing the game in our hometown with rules we've operated under for years and years. We'll whip them."

Lisa considered Vicky Helms one of the brightest, most efficient circuit court clerks in the state. She managed an office of nine other women, and every Henry County file was organized and in its proper place, every scrap of paper was accounted for, and every transaction was handled according to the Supreme Court manual, occasionally treated even better than the book required. The office collected fines, sold hunting and fishing licenses and received recordation taxes for deeds, and Helms had never been so much as a penny in error when the state audited her ledgers. County clerk was an elected position, and Helms was personable, attractive and mischievously funny, more of a cutup than the job title might suggest.

Lisa entered the clerk's office first, followed by Joe and then Robert Williams. She spotted Helms and instantly realized that the clerk was in a full-tilt tizzy. Helms sensed them and glanced up from a file and spoke as they were heading behind the front counter to where she was standing. "It's gone," she declared. "Flat gone."

The three of them crowded around her and focused on Lettie's probate file. Williams picked through each paper. The will was missing.

"You still have it on film, though, right?" he asked.

"Yeah, of course," Helms said. "Come on. I've already pulled it up on the terminal."

They walked into the deed room, which was filled with metal file cabinets and oversize, canvas-covered deed books that fit into slots along three walls. The books stretched from the ceiling to the vinyl-tiled floor; the oldest had the number 1 stamped on its spine and contained the county's earliest deeds, documents whose land descriptions made mention of rods, poles, creeks, gum trees, turnpikes, iron stakes and set stones. A row of computer terminals was located on a long wooden ledge near the wide entrance to the room, a chair underneath each terminal.

Helms pointed to a document on the screen. "There it is, but the original has disappeared. Of all people's to disappear, it had to be Lettie VanSandt's. Figures, doesn't it?"

Joe studied the document image on the screen. "No. Damn. It's a fake. It's close—probably on purpose—but that's not the will I brought over here. I've seen enough of Lettie's writing to know it's bogus. It's about a B-plus forgery. Good enough to look like somebody was trying, bad enough to make sure any decent expert could determine it's a con job."

"Well, Joe"—Helms bristled—"if it's on that screen, it's what you brought me."

"I'm not saying you made a mistake," Joe assured her.

"Well, what *are* you saying?" she demanded.

"Where do you keep the probate files?" Williams gently asked.

"In here, in a filing drawer. Probate has its own section. The third and fourth cabinets, halfway down." She gestured at the cabinets.

"So they're open to the public?" he asked.

"Unless the court seals something, every file in here is public record. Criminal, civil, probate, whatever. Except juvenile." She set her hands against her hips, tucked her chin. "That's the law, Robert. Same as in every courthouse in every jurisdiction in the entire state."

Williams reached out and briefly, gingerly touched her shoulder. "I know, Vicky," he said. "We're not blaming you. Not at all. We're just trying to figure out what happened."

"This office has never lost a document under my watch. Ever."

"Can people access the files without you knowing?" Lisa's tone was normal; she didn't baby the question. "I'm asking because we've never had any reason to learn the day-to-day details of how this office operates. We lawyers come and go as we please, but regular citizens? People not a part of the system?"

"If you know what you want and understand how to locate it using the index, you don't need one of us to help you. Only sealed files and

juvenile cases are unavailable. I've mentioned before at our confer-
ences that maybe the state needs a better system, a controlled access
or at least a sign-in, especially when we have all the historians and
genealogists and Civil War buffs handling priceless historical documents. They could damage them or, yeah, even steal them."

"So, anyone could walk in," Lisa said, "get hold of Lettie's file and
steal the original will?"

"In theory, yes," Helms replied. "Or a photo from a criminal file or
the separation agreement from a divorce case. It's not a fact we broadcast, and I hope you won't. It'll just give people ideas. That's the main
reason most everything important is duplicated by scanning it into
the system."

"Yeah," Joe said, distracted. He was using the keyboard to scroll up
and down the image on the screen.

"Maybe Lettie's will is missing, but we still have an exact copy on
record. Right there." Helms pointed at the terminal Joe was using. "For
that matter, Sandy Berger, from President Clinton's administration, he
made off with documents from the National Archives. As big an office
as there is. Remember that little fiasco? No system's perfect."

"We've all been scorched here, Vicky," Williams told her. "I promise
nobody's got an ax to grind with you."

"Sounds like Joe does," she said.

"No I don't, my friend," Joe promised her, now finished with the
screen and giving her his full attention. "Robert hit the nail on the
head: We've all been burned."

"You gave me Lettie's will, and I scanned it myself, Joe. I'm positive."

"All true," Joe agreed. "But then somebody broke into the system
and substituted a forgery. A forgery they want everyone to discover
as a forgery."

"Why take the original, Joe?" Lisa asked.

"Riding over here," Joe said, "it dawned on me that the original,
genuine will would have my fingerprints on it, as well as Lettie's and
the sheriff's. A paper fake in the file wouldn't. Even Benecorp couldn't
engineer that. Hacking the computers and inserting their forgery to
frame me only works if they eliminate the real will."

"Unfortunately, being local and having frequent access makes you a prime suspect," Williams said. "From a big-picture view, the missing document doesn't contradict their position because, well, you'd have the same fingerprint problem. They'll argue you gave Vicky the forgery and then destroyed the original since it didn't have Lettie's prints or DNA on it. Planting it for Sheriff Perry to find was part of a lawyer's clever scheme. Or even better, you didn't give Vicky the will the sheriff gave you. Switched them after he turned over what he found."

"How the hell would I learn she was dead before anybody else?" Joe asked. "I'd have to discover she's burned to a crisp, then sneak out and drop in my forgery. That doesn't make sense. Plus, Sheriff Perry could testify there was no switch—he'd read enough of the will he found to know it favored me."

"We need to see if we can discover evidence of the computer breach," Lisa said. "If we can establish how they did this, then Joe's off the hook."

"I'm not sure who's doing what to whom," Helms interjected, "but I can tell you every clerk's office in the state is linked into the system and so is the Supreme Court. There're a gazillion entry points and only basic security."

"We'll have to give it a shot," Williams said. "Even though they probably had George Hotz himself do the substitution and cover their tracks. Is there any surveillance video in here, Vicky?"

She formed a "duh" expression with her eyes and mouth. "We're lucky they let us burn the lights during business hours. The county's broke, Robert, and even if we weren't, I doubt the board of supervisors would fund a video system for us."

Williams smiled. "I needed to ask. I'll check the security entrance to the building, but unless we see Seth Garrison or Edwin Nicholson rolling through, I can't see where it'll do us much good."

"So from what I'm piecing together," Helms said, "you think someone stole the original and then hacked the system to put a forgery online?"

"Exactly," Lisa replied.

"But I read the scanned copy," Helms said. "Joe still inherits. Why go to that kind of trouble and not change anything?"

"Believe me," Joe said, "they've changed a whole lot." He looked directly at her. "Are you sure the scan image is the same as the will I gave you, Vicky? Identical?"

"I didn't study every jot and tittle. The scan looks very similar. But I'm a hundred percent certain that the paper you brought me is the one I entered into the system, and we had three independent witnesses confirm the writing—Delegate Armstrong, Debbie Hall at the newspaper and LuAnne from the bank. That's all I can tell you. I'm no expert on Lettie's handwriting—if it's fake, then it's fake, but I can't say I see anything obviously different."

"I understand," Joe said solicitously. "Like Robert mentioned, this isn't your mistake. You did your job perfectly. You always do."

"Well, thanks," Helms answered. "I hope this doesn't cause you any grief, Joe. I know you wouldn't do anything dishonest. You'd be the last person to steal from a court file. Not you. Never. That I could swear to from a witness stand."

Two weeks later, on a Thursday near the end of July, Lisa and Joe sat in her office and talked to Phil Anderson over the speakerphone.

"So I'm back, and here's the report from the Bahamas," he said with mock cheerfulness. "Rasta Phil. Mind you, I did turn down the hair braids at the straw market. I—"

"Wait," Lisa interrupted. "You actually went to Nassau? Robert told us you were investigating the bank; we didn't realize you were there."

"Tough gig, but somebody had to make the sacrifice," Anderson deadpanned. "My boy was home from college, and I used your case as an excuse to take him bonefishing. Hot as hell and not the best month to fish, but we still had an excellent trip."

"You shouldn't have done that, Phil," Joe said. "We absolutely need to reimburse you."

"If we make it to the finish of this mess and you're not in jail and still have a law license, we'll discuss it. In the meantime, we'll consider it a much-deserved vacation with my son. Hey, we won a couple hundred bucks playing cards, so there you go. An offset."

"Please send us your costs," Lisa insisted.

"Here's what I found," he said, ignoring her. "The bank is legitimate.

It's not Fort Knox or the Federal Reserve—it's the Caribbean and all that comes with it, but it isn't a complete front or a depository for hoodlums and dope smugglers. I hired a local attorney to hold my hand and make the introductions, and—"

"More we owe you for," Joe interjected.

"And he arranged for me to meet with the bank manager there in Nassau, an interesting fellow named LaMarr Pinder. I got the impression these people are accustomed to discreetly moving and parking some serious cash. They also make it a point to promote their confidentiality and offshore advantages, if you catch my drift."

"We do," Joe said.

"Since I already had the documents from the counterclaim and convinced him they were public record, he didn't have much problem confirming they were accurate and had been generated by his bank. Unfortunately, that means Garrison has a bank employee who will testify to the $750,000 deposit and the withdrawal on March fifth."

"No surprise there," Lisa said. "They'd never plead something so flamboyant and not have all their fake ducks in a row."

"The question is who really wound up with the $750,000," Joe noted.

"Exactly. The woman who allegedly withdrew the money had what appears to be your passport, Lisa. Pinder claims they checked it and made a photocopy. We'll compare the copy to your actual passport, but I won't be surprised if it's a basic match. Of course, when you Xerox only the main page of the passport with a black-and-white machine, darned if you don't lose most of the subtleties and built-in protections that could flag a counterfeit. Item next: They have your Virginia driver's license on file. Same story. A black-and-white copy. I'll fax you all this in a moment."

"If you're Seth Garrison," Lisa said, "coming up with quality counterfeit documents wouldn't be too difficult."

"Oh," Anderson said, "the lady who withdrew the money also had to provide them with a numerical password, which she did. The number came from Benecorp, so that's a nonissue in my book. Window dressing."

"What do we know about this woman?" Lisa asked. "I didn't sign anything there, so what about the signature?"

"Well," Anderson said, "we have the pleadings copy, and the name Lisa Stone appears on the signature line. Pinder refused to let me see his original. It is what it is. We'll need our own handwriting expert."

"It's forged," Lisa replied. "I didn't sign it. I never set foot in that bank. Never. But my signature is on literally thousands of documents in the court system. Twenty years of practice will do that. Anybody could locate an example and transfer it onto whatever they pleased."

"Sure," Anderson agreed. "The final piece of the puzzle is a security video. As you can imagine, if you've seen them on TV or during a trial, the tape from the bank is herky-jerky and blurred. Well, not blurred, but fuzzy. No resolution. My paralegal calls them Blair Witches. I often wonder why businesses even bother, given the poor quality. We see a dark-haired white woman with sunglasses and a hat enter and visit a teller, then she goes off camera to meet with Pinder. It could be Lisa. The video woman has the right size and build and hair color. It could just as easily be a thousand other women. I showed Pinder Lisa's photo, and he said, yeah, it was most probably Lisa who met with him. It happened months ago and they process a lot of transactions, so he claims he has no particular recollection. The clever answer. It's suspicious if he's too positive."

"If it was Lisa," Joe stated, "he wouldn't forget her."

Anderson chuckled. "True. I say that as her attorney and your loyal friend and a happily married man, and for no other reason."

"So it's very simple, isn't it?" Lisa declared. "Benecorp discovers the date I was in the Bahamas and films a look-alike pretending to collect the cash. They could've engineered this two weeks ago so long as the bank's in on the deal. The whole scheme requires a couple fake documents and a few banana-republic types and doesn't cost them a penny of the $750,000. More important, I'm sure our friends at the bank didn't do this for nothing; no doubt they received a handsome fee for their help."

"Alas, Mr. Pinder wasn't very forthcoming on those details," Anderson said. "And unfortunately it's a safe bet that a state court in Henry County, Virginia, will never manage to shake that information loose."

Joe made a whistling sound. "Wow. These fuckers can see into the future, can't they? There's another reason they didn't remove the suit—the feds might be able to lean on Pinder. Damn. An easy boat ride from Florida, but the Bahamas is another country. We'll see Pinder at trial, but we'll never see his bank's actual records."

"For me," Anderson said, "the most curious twist is the date the money hit Nassau—almost a month before Lisa arrived. Pinder confirmed that, seemed way too eager to talk about it, and Nicholson was happy to fax documentation of the transfer from Benecorp's U.S. bank. The money really and truly did go to the Bahamas, but well before Lisa got there. $750,000 was transferred while you were allegedly negotiating, but why send it so early?"

"It's simple, then," Joe said. "Lisa's right—they forge a few papers, film a lady no one can positively identify and claim she took money that Benecorp had already sent for some other reason. Most likely to conceal or launder. Or a tax dodge. Hell, I'll bet Garrison has money squirreled away on every island in the Caribbean. Lucky for him, Lisa happened to visit Nassau."

"Here's the problem," Anderson said, his tone constrained, worried. "I don't have to tell you this—you're both probably better trial lawyers than I am—but we're going to face a helluva job explaining away so many coincidences. We're stuck with some inconvenient facts—Lisa and the cash in Nassau simultaneously. Bank records from Pinder, even if they're fake."

Lisa spoke up. "If you're a crook, you think, act and plan like a crook. If the first deal's iffy and tainted, you naturally build in a safety net. He kept an eye on us in case this started unraveling—just like it in fact did. Having met him, I'd say he probably loved diagramming all the intrigue and monkeying around with his plans. He's a bit of a dork."

Anderson was quiet for a moment. A jag of static popped in the phone's antiquated speaker. "I hope you're correct," he said. "This won't be a cakewalk for us."

Joe bowed closer to the phone. "So we're clear, Phil, you're still on board with this? I need my lawyer to believe us."

Anderson answered quickly. "We both realize I don't have to believe you to be effective—we're lawyers, not priests. But, yeah, absolutely, I think you're telling the truth. You're the most ethical, honest lawyer I've ever met." He paused, laughed. "Of course most people would say that's not much of a compliment."

As soon as the call ended, Joe stared at Lisa, barely blinking. "I'm sorry I fucked up with the trust thing. It was a bad idea and played right into their hands. The one time in my career I skirt the rules, and look at the mess I've made."

"It was a reasonable strategy at the time. We had no idea. None. We've never been involved with something on this scale, with this kind of person, a man with this kind of power and influence."

"This is totally my doing too, my little red wagon. Thanks for sticking with me and supporting me; we've now officially got everything at risk." He sounded dispirited. "You're a good wife. I hope I haven't screwed us both."

Pained to see him so low and anguished, Lisa considered what she ought to say. "I . . ." was all she could muster before choking on spit and emotion and nerves. "I need to . . ."

"To what?" he asked.

"To . . ."

"I'm waiting," he said.

She came around her desk and stood behind him, leaned down and wrapped her arms around his neck, her cheek against his hair. "I need to make sure you know how much I love you and how hard it is for me to see you suffer and fret." She was close to his ear, so her voice was tame and subdued. She swallowed two quick times to push space in her throat. "You listen to me: I am positive, one hundred percent positive, that we will win this. We won't lose. Please don't worry. We're a good team, you and me."

Joe didn't move, answered without twisting toward her or changing his position, sat there punctured and listless. He was facing the empty chair behind her desk, staring at where she'd been. "You want to tell me whatever it is that's really on your mind?"

"I just did," she said. She tightened her arms and leaned more of her weight into him.

That night, a few minutes after nine, Lisa printed out a series of posts from #1 Chat Avenue and brought them to Joe:

ROBERTO100: what's it do, del?
DELLA STREET: Know soon! Pls. stay in touch.

ROBERTO100: danjerous.

DELLA STREET: Are you real?

ROBERTO100: u a dumass lk always.

DELLA STREET: Test. Who is Lee Orr?

ROBERTO100: dog warthen. test, y u not doing sh*t?

"There was no hesitation," Lisa told Joe. "She came right back with the ID on Lee."

"That's hardly the best security question," Joe said, still studying the paper.

"Actually it's not too bad, and it was the first thing that came to mind. It's her, Joe. We just need to find her."

"Next go-round, ask her whose cat she had last time she was in the office. Or her sister's address."

"She has a sister? I didn't know that."

"It's a trick question," Joe said. "And why the hell is she contacting you and not me?"

"Still no word on the prints from the cardboard you gave Toliver?" Lisa asked.

"We should hear soon. Usually takes around sixty days."

"It would flat erase our problems if we can locate her," Lisa said. "Most of our worries would disappear. The court case would be moot, and Garrison would have to surrender the VV 108. I'm still checking by her place, and I've started scanning the Token Rock site too."

"True. And *if* frogs had wings . . ."

CHAPTER TWENTY-FIVE

M.J. met Lisa inside the front entrance to the Village Tavern, a Winston-Salem restaurant they both fancied because of its grouper Hemingway and leather-bound wine list. They hugged and separated, and then M.J. blithely caught Lisa's wrist and led her away from the door, M.J. bubbly and chatty and merry, as if she were a twenties jazz darling showing her ingenue friend to a Prohibition powder room for gossip and a nip of flask gin. "Okay," she said, "I know you didn't call me completely worried and wrung out and use our Agent Ninety-Nine secret codes and drive nearly an hour to hear my happy news and zany reports, but we both realize I can be a selfish bitch occasionally, so there you go, but before we dive into your dilemma du jour, let me tell you about my recent good fortune, and while I'm blabbing, please act like you're thrilled for me and throw in a couple wows and reallys at the right spots, even though you're just marking time until we arrive at your issue which, truthfully, I'm sure is important and more pressing than what's on my agenda."

M.J.'s chatterbox greeting was still in progress as they walked past the hostess stand and three men wearing conservative suits and into the main dining room. They sat in a booth that connected to a wall, the bench seats, high backs and sturdy table all made of the same shellacked, dark brown wood.

"I can't wait," Lisa said as she was sliding across the smooth bench. "Let me guess: They've finally taught the royal stallions to ice skate, hired Yanni to compose the soundtrack and the touring version's coming to North Carolina?"

M.J. laughed. "Wouldn't that be spectacular."

A waitress brought water and silverware and menus and politely interrupted them by announcing her name—Alicia—and telling them she'd be taking care of their table. Lisa had no interest in alcohol but asked for a glass of chardonnay, the first choice that came to mind.

"I'll try a mojito," M.J. said. "No food right now, thanks." She smiled at the girl and returned to the conversation with Lisa while the waitress was still writing the drink order. "Okay, so a week ago I'm leaving the office and a red Mercedes SLK pulls beside me, right there in the parking lot, and this beautiful man, who claims he's never done anything like this, informs me he saw me walking to my car, random as random can be, pure luck of the draw, and he introduces himself and after I Google him on my cell phone and confirm who he is, I follow him to this happy-go-lucky bar in Chapel Hill called the Crunkleton and we hit it off. Amazing. As a bonus, I experienced my first mint julep."

"Wow. Seriously."

"His name is Craig Wilkins. He's a lawyer from Durham, a litigator. He's divorced. He has a kid starting college this fall, so I'm not potentially subject to any significant stepmoming chores. He was at our building interviewing a witness for a case, some woman down on the sixth floor. And believe it or not, he's a year older than I am. Actually, seventeen months older. So far, and it's only been three dates if you count the initial trip to the bar, he seems to be my kind of man. I understand it's still early and this could turn into Bear Brian, but I'm incredibly optimistic about Lawyer Wilkins. I've been in the best freakin' mood."

"I'm happy for you," Lisa said sincerely. "I am. Really. *Really.*" She grinned. "You absolutely deserve it."

The waitress delivered the wine and mojito and reminded them she'd be glad to bring food if they decided to eat.

M.J. tasted her drink. "Not bad," she said. "Thanks for letting me monopolize the conversation. I wish the timing were different for you—it's always hard to appreciate somebody else's jackpot when you're under a black cloud yourself."

"Actually, it makes me feel better. Lets me believe that karma or kismet or providence or whatever else will eventually do right by the people who deserve it."

"Tell me about your lawsuit," M.J. said. "I read the fax you sent. Can you do that in court—just completely make up shit?"

"What a gobsmack. Who the hell could've seen this coming? I never thought they'd go on offense. It's crazy. It's as if Seth Garrison can conjure up facts and a plausible case out of thin air. It's suddenly an absolute mess and tar pit."

"Thanks to my shiny new communications director, I learned last week we're not supposed to say 'tar *baby*.' This was totally surprising information for me. Every year, there's a new faux pas word. She gave me an avoid list to remember when I'm in public: pussy willow, pussycat, titter, Oriental and niggardly—meaning cheap, a word I'd never even heard of—are also definite no-no's in the corporate world. There're more on the list too. Some I'm supposed to skip because of the guffaws, others because I'd seem insensitive."

"Lord, you *are* giddy," Lisa said. "Were you at the bar before I got here?"

"Sorry. I'm just trying to be amusing and cheer you up. Lighten your load."

"We never could've imagined Garrison's counterclaim," Lisa continued. She kept her voice low, always concerned about eavesdropping. "I'm scared to death about what they might find in the Bahamas. I don't think Benecorp was following me while I was there—they didn't have any reason to, and I'm assuming they discovered my trip after the fact. But it'll be a legal and marital nightmare if Garrison's aware I wasn't with you twenty-four-seven, and you can bet your butt they've been busy in Nassau since the suit was filed."

"Have you checked with, uh, damn . . . his name's on the tip of my tongue . . . Brooks? Brett Brooks? Is there a chance he was in on the scam and gigoloing for Garrison? You think Brooks will complicate things—well, heck, I'm not even sure what you'd want him to do. Is it better if he lies or tells the truth? You're right. This is messy."

"The worst of it is, I can't stand to see Joe under all this pressure. This suit might crush us. He's worried sick, and it's killing me. His law license is on the line. He's *such* a good man, M.J."

"Here's my advice," M.J. said, her tone blunt. The giggles and cocktail gushing were altogether gone. "You should stick to your guns and don't bail the first time some predator takes a bite at your stock.

Stand your ground. Very little has changed in the big picture. Garrison didn't respond exactly how you thought he would, and he's blown serious smoke and done a fine job of firing back at you, but you're the best lawyer I know, and I know a bunch of them. Keep the faith. More to the point, what other options do you have?"

"Where Lettie VanSandt is at the very beginning of an equation, faith doesn't help. She's always plagued me and been a thorn, dead or alive." Lisa lifted her wineglass by the stem, then set it down without drinking. "I hate to ask," she said, focusing on the glass, "but if we have to—"

"I'm completely on board if I can ever help you," M.J. insisted. "Whatever—I'm your girl if you need me. I'll swear on a stack of Bibles I was with you." She leaned forward, her chin past the mojito, both palms flat on the table. "Not much scares me, Lisa. I've seen the junior version of Seth Garrison over and over and over, starting with the Craps Pirate and the repulsive little troll sales managers who'd offer to trade extra orders for a quickie blow job in a dealership toilet. I shot a man who needed shooting, but I didn't kill him even though I could've and damn well would have enjoyed it. To me, Seth Garrison is the exact same creature, except he has a fancy-pants yacht instead of a Sea-Doo over at the redneck marina. And you're the friend who looked after me when I was broke and an embarrassed failure living with my parents. So yeah, you give me my script and I'll read it." She relaxed, sat normally again.

Lisa continued staring at her wine, and she could see a slice of the restaurant reflected on the glass's pregnant side, was able to make out tables and chairs and the yellow-and-purple paisley in a woman's summer dress, the scene elongated and shrunken, capped by an overhead light distilled to less than a pinpoint, burning in the midst of the chardonnay. "I hope," she said softly, "I can sort through this." She didn't look at her friend. "Thanks. Thank you."

Still rattled and paranoid three days later, Lisa decided to visit Brett Brooks at his office, but she didn't phone or e-mail before leaving Martinsville, just traveled an hour to Roanoke with plans to appear unannounced, hoping to avoid intercepts and wiretaps and catch him cold, before he had time to prepare a lie or, perhaps, ask Seth Garrison for his marching orders. It was the beginning of August, and her car was blistering hot when she cranked the engine, didn't cool down—even with the controls dialed completely to cold—until she reached Bassett Forks. She nervously kept watch on the road behind her, accelerated to eighty-five when there was no other car in sight, parked at the Hotel Roanoke's lot, hurried into the lobby, had the concierge arrange for a cab, changed clothes in a restroom stall, crammed her hair into a hat, departed through a side door, used the pedestrian bridge to walk downtown and met her taxi next to an Italian restaurant.

Riding to Brooks's office, she let her head rest against the window glass, watched the city pass by cropped and unnatural, mostly the tops of high concrete buildings, thick black power lines and snatches of heavy, humid sky. She debated whether she should've simply driven herself to Brooks's address, whether her sneaking and plotting were wasted on surveillance that didn't actually exist or, if it did, was floating miles above in a satellite and wouldn't be fooled by her changing highway speeds and exiting side doors. She glanced at her driver, who seemed unusually poised and clean-cut. They stopped for a traffic signal. Shit, she even wondered about M.J.'s new beau, this lawyer who'd miraculously sprung from Zeus's head and tumbled into a parking lot. "Poor Downs," she mumbled as they accelerated and switched lanes.

Brooks's receptionist was pleasant, then firmly professional and finally irate. "Mr. Brooks is with a client," the lady said. "I've explained that, okay? You can wait until he's finished, and I'll ask if he'll see you without an appointment, or we can schedule something later, but I'm not going to interrupt him just because you're a lawyer and want special treatment."

So she was forced to wait in Brooks's reception area, wasting time on a leather sofa with squishy cushions, absently thumbing through a copy of *Garden & Gun*, then *Time*, the mailing labels precisely clipped from the magazines' covers, a precaution that she and Joe didn't bother with given how simple it would be for an unhappy client to locate their address. She was accompanied in the lobby by an elderly husband and wife who sat across from her, glaring, put off by the commotion, no doubt concerned she'd try to leapfrog them on the schedule. Lisa was nervous, embarrassed, unsettled, on the brink of seeing a man she'd been naked with not so long ago, then done her best to erase and forget, the biggest calamity of her life. She caught herself jiggling her foot and quit it. "Do you have a restroom?" she asked the receptionist.

Fifteen minutes later she heard Brett's voice migrating down the hall, and a frail man trailing a green oxygen tank appeared and shuffled through, leaving the office. She stood from the quicksand couch and Brett spied her as he reached the archway to the reception area, and his expression—pure delight, no disdain, mischief or guilt, nothing contrived—made her exhale and smile despite her frazzled mood, and she paused to adjust a necklace that was hanging cockeyed before walking toward him, didn't rush or kowtow, and he met her and wrapped an arm around her and cheerfully welcomed her and told her he couldn't think of anyone else he'd rather have materialize in his office on a dull Tuesday afternoon. "Why didn't you let me know Mrs. Stone was here?" he asked the receptionist, whose mouth narrowed and shoulders sagged.

"No worries, Brett," Lisa said. "She was very considerate and since you were with a client, I didn't want to interrupt you. I'm fine. She handled things as she should've."

"Oh, okay. Excellent." He turned to the older couple who'd been waiting along with Lisa. "How long you been here, Max?"

"Twenty minutes," the man replied.

"Longer," his wife added tartly.

"Here's the deal. Mrs. Stone is a rare bird and hotshot lawyer from Martinsville, and I very much need to speak with her, been trying to for weeks, so if you'll give me about ten minutes to take care of our particular business, your visit will be on the house, free as free can be. And, we'll pay for your parking."

The man grunted, but he was, like most people, charmed by Brooks. "We both know there's no cost to park in your lot anyhow," he said, suppressing a chuckle. "But we'll take the free meeting."

"Ten minutes," the lady declared. "After that, we start chargin' you. I'm keepin' track." She tapped her wristwatch, her finger bony and misshapen, the knuckles gnarled.

Brooks's office was enormous and remarkably meticulous, the furnishings expensive and vaguely retro, especially the chairs, the feel that of a discreet, high-end 1960s private lounge where scads of arrangements were brokered off the record and powerful people twisted arms and gunned dry martinis. There was a signed Dalí print—probably fake, like most of them, Lisa guessed—an original Chagall, and behind Brooks's sleek desk a LeRoy Neiman painting of a boxing match, vivid men in colorful battle, nothing too precise in the details, but the scene somehow exact and true, convincing.

"I like your office," she said. "I have a cheap reproduction of Blind Justice, a framed Monet poster and my diplomas on the wall. I didn't realize you're interested in art."

"Oh, hell, I'm really not." Brooks was sitting beside her in a chair, his legs crossed. He was wearing black cowboy boots with intricate tooling, the toes overlaid with silver. "I buy things when I'm in Vegas. Usually I'm about half in the bag when I visit the gallery, which is strategically located near the casino at Caesars. Melissa Robinson—a lawyer who *does* know her art—told me the Dalí's a counterfeit, that I overpaid by several thousand for the Chagall and the LeRoy Neiman is 'frat boy rubbish.' But I like them, so I bought them, and hang them here so I can take a tax deduction." He flashed a lopsided grin, pulled a cuff farther down the boot's shaft. "The Taubman hasn't been pounding on my door offering to take them off my hands, that's for sure."

"Thanks for seeing me," Lisa said.

"Happy to. Given the story in yesterday's Lawyers Weekly, I'm assuming I'm going to be disappointed as to the reason you're here. I'm guessing this is business, not Bahamian."

The reference to their trip caused her to involuntarily sit stiffer, her back jammed tight against the chair's support. "Strictly business," she answered immediately, stammering slightly. "Yeah," she added pointlessly.

"Ah, well, you can't blame me for asking. But there's no need to make you uncomfortable by revisiting that weekend. As they say in junior high, I'm pleased we can still be friends." Self-assured as he was, Brooks seemed slightly uneasy, clumsy, genuinely disheartened. He awkwardly slapped the chair arms with both hands when he finished speaking, and it made her like him even more. "How can I help with your dreadful lawsuit? What do I need to say about Nassau?"

"My problem is discovery, Brett. It's amazing how Joe and I sat and debated this, and it seemed so distant. I just knew we'd have hearing after hearing, skirmishes and grinding miniwars, and this would take years to resolve, and now, damn, we've got about three days left to answer under oath tons of questions that put me in a major bind, and as we both understand, there aren't any effective do-overs with interrogatories. We're locked in once Joe submits his answers. There's that pesky perjury concern too."

"I see your problem. Basic discovery and you're already in a straitjacket. I'm sure they asked you to list all witnesses and the names of all people with knowledge of events, the standard questions."

"The routine interrogatories, but given our answer to their counterclaim they've also specifically asked us to list who was with me in the Bahamas. Just like that, the case went from zero to a hundred."

"Well, technically, your husband's answering the discovery, and he's telling the truth as he perceives it, so he's covered."

"Yeah, but he's claiming I was with M. J. Gold. You don't have to be Learned Hand to see where that leaves us—they'll depose M.J. and me, and we'll have to lie. Maybe I will, maybe I won't. M.J. will claim she was with me and enjoy every minute of it—she's cold-blooded under pressure and doesn't have a very high regard for the legal system. But I figure there's at least a decent chance they'll learn you were there, so they'll get M.J. and me swearing on the record and then drop proof of you and me in Nassau, and suddenly we're in a world of hurt. I'm not only a liar but a cheater as well, and Joe gets hammered twice, legally and maritally. The final piece of my unfortunate puzzle is that while M.J. kept a fairly low profile the weekend we were gone, she used her credit card, and her other phones will show they were active in Raleigh, not the Caribbean. Our cover wasn't intended to . . . to fool anyone but Joe."

"Once they start digging, it won't be difficult to establish that we were together. Passports, immigration, TSA and airport security tapes aren't our friends. The seat belt fuzz and mini-pretzel constables might even recall us; it hasn't been that long."

Lisa cocked her head, puzzled.

"The flight attendants. They're so tiresome and redundant about the seat belts, as if they're going to do any good when you plummet from thirty thousand feet and bust the ground and the plane fireballs. It's a personal issue with me. Once, I dared unbuckle before the *ding* at the gate and almost was barred from my connecting flight."

"Oh," she said, barely listening to Brooks's practiced rant. "But right, they might remember us. I think strategically we have to proceed under the assumption they have the truth on you and me and can prove it."

"What can I do to help?" Brooks asked. "I'm happy to lie so long as I'm not under oath and don't jeopardize my license. I'm just not positive exactly what lie helps and what lie hurts."

"Well, basically, I'd appreciate it if you could stall and delay for as long as possible, should you become involved. We didn't expect to have to show our hand this quickly."

"Joe's clean, right? Hell, he's the most ethical lawyer there is."

"Absolutely," Lisa answered emphatically. "We have a few tricks of our own. Well, we have one trick. Maybe. If we can locate her in the damn top hat. Mostly, though, we need time to regroup and figure things out."

"I can definitely buy time if I'm subpoenaed or they attempt to depose me." He nodded decisively. "I know better than most not to believe the case that's tried in the press, but it sounds like they've got a couple big guns. If the will Joe gave the clerk is a forgery and benefits him, that's brutal, Lisa. I don't envy your choices when it comes to how to handle this."

"I hope I don't have to choose," she said. "More important, I needed to make sure, well, where you figured in all this."

Brooks recoiled. He scowled. "Meaning?"

"I had to make certain you weren't a part of some kind of plot. Sorry. The stress can make you crazy. You start hallucinating. You question everything."

"No need to worry about me," Brooks promised her. "I can't believe you'd even consider the possibility. I'd sure hope you could look back and tell my . . . friendship was completely genuine. Hard to fake head-over-heels. I'll do all I can for you."

Two days later he phoned Lisa on her cell. She was in her car, driving to see a disabled client about drafting a power of attorney, still making the occasional house call. "The damn process hound just arrived with a dep notice for me in your case," he said. "It's conceivable they sent it simply because my office prepared the renouncement, but I wouldn't count on it being so insignificant. I'd say that's a message from Benecorp, wouldn't you? And I'd also say you were tailed to my office. Sorry, Lisa." Brooks sounded concerned. "I threw the damn notice in the trash with him standing there, but we both understand I've now been served and the clock's ticking."

The morning following Brooks's call, the Stones met Phil Anderson and Robert Williams at Williams's conference room. Anderson had brought along a computer wizard named Derek Hansen so he could explain his opinions about the bogus VanSandt will in the clerk's office. When Lisa and Joe entered the room, he was busy with an iPad, and he looked up and acknowledged them only after several taps and slides on the tablet's screen. He initially focused on Lisa, stuck to the gaze longer than was mannerly and rotated his head several degrees clockwise, delicioused, not bothering to conceal his admiration. "Good morning," he said. He stood and stretched across a mahogany table to shake hands with her and Joe. He was wearing a seersucker jacket, khaki pants, a red tie and brown tasseled loafers. Lisa guessed he couldn't be more than twenty years old.

"Derek's the best in the business," Anderson stated after they were through with introductions and were all seated around the table, files and papers in front of everyone except Hansen.

"You're not what I expected," Joe noted, directing the comment to Hansen.

"My age?" Hansen asked, his tone neutral.

"No, actually, I'm pleased our expert is young—it's definitely a young man's game. Truth be told, I expected a skateboard and a backpack, maybe a piercing and sullen bad posture."

"That is the stereotype, isn't it?" Hansen replied. "But I'm not about that. Being a slacker's stupid, and it's even dumber to think your talents somehow justify antisocial behavior and hobo hygiene. You can be brilliant and bathe, can't you?" He was intense, spoke forcefully. "It's my own little crusade."

"How old are you?" Lisa asked.

"I'm twenty-two. But I've already graduated from Virginia Tech." He paused for effect. "The doctoral program at Tech. Strictly speaking, I'm *Doctor* Hansen. I brought a CV with me if you'd care to have a copy. How old are you, Mrs. Stone?"

"I was born in 1966."

"I wasn't asking as rhetorical payback. You're rockin' hot for your age." He turned toward Joe. "No offense meant, sir," he said, almost in a monotone. "It's a compliment, not a gambit. I have a steady girlfriend."

Joe smiled, amused. "None taken. After two decades, I'm accustomed to it. Plus, I agree with you."

"So tell us about the will," Williams said. "I'm anxious to hear how a fake could be substituted into the system."

"Sure. You hardly need me—this is a rung above *Computers for Dummies.* Here's the deal. The VanSandt document appears as a binary image on the terminal in the clerk's office. The software package is basic—Adobe PDF, probably the same program all of you run on your laptops. The very efficient Mrs. Helms has an RMS server there in her office. So does every other clerk's office in the state. Her whole package is provided by Richmond and, like I just mentioned, the components are uniform throughout Virginia perhaps with a few exceptions that don't concern us."

"Okay," Joe said. "I'm assuming, then, that you'd need to access her server, where, for lack of a better term, everything's stored."

"Correct," Hansen said.

Williams was sitting with his arms folded. "How do you do that? Gain access?"

"I can tell you how I did it," Hansen replied. "To obtain control, you simply need full administrative privileges. You need to be able to log on as a user who can access the entire system."

"Makes sense," Joe agreed.

"I obtained a roster from the Supreme Court's main website, sort of an organizational chart, then manually—yep, manually, ladies and gentlemen, that's how easy it was—entered a few shots at a password—"

"Wait," Lisa interrupted. "How'd you get into the system in the first place?"

"I used a rogue wireless access point to breach Mrs. Helms's system from her office, but if you have the password, you can use any terminal or computer in the network." Hansen waved his hand dismissively. "Seriously, Mrs. Stone, most ninth graders with an iPad understand the theory. This isn't complicated. I assumed the 'executive secretary' to the Supreme Court would be loaded for bear, so I did about ten variations of his name and birth date—which I found elsewhere online—and presto, I'm in the system. Pitiful security. Completely lame. If I don't luck into the combination manually, no problem—I've created my own program called Prospector that will automatically attempt thousands of variations of a name and numbers. Here, I didn't even need it."

"So," Williams said, "in effect you track down the people at the top of an organization via public information, then guess at their passwords to gain access? Or use your program to run different possibilities?"

"Precisely," Hansen said. "The whole security effort is such a sieve—I could've also manipulated the system to send a password to my e-mail. Really a beast there, guys: Everybody's e-address is their first initial and last name at Virginia Supreme Court. Clever and complex. It'd take years to crack that masterpiece."

Anderson smiled. "In a sense, there's not much out there to steal or access, Derek. Courts are all about transparency, and there's a great deal of redundancy in the system. It's like tapping into a phone book or a road map."

"Evidently." Hansen contracted his face, frowned, exasperated that people could be so haphazard with their security measures.

"The money question is: Can you tell when and how the fake was inserted?" Williams peered at Hansen. "Did Benecorp leave tracks? Can we trace it? Can you prove a substitution to a Henry County jury?"

"Yes and no," Hansen answered.

" 'Yes and no'?" Williams repeated.

"The system keeps log files that show who did what when, to put it in plain English."

"That ought to help," Joe said hopefully. "You just need to search the log files."

Hansen gave him a condescending glance. "Yes. Thank you. I have, of course. But if you're an administrator, you can erase the log files or change the date of activity."

"Damn," Joe muttered.

"Does the erasure itself show up or give us any clues?" Lisa asked.

"Not clues as you'd like to find them, but it does show up. Of course, it could happen in the ordinary course of things because of a full disc or a retention time limit or for other reasons, like a systems failure. I've found seventeen log erasures between the date of the LPV will being registered at Mrs. Helms's office and the day you discovered the fake. Any of those could be the door Benecorp opened and closed."

"But you can't directly tie it to Benecorp?" Williams asked. "It's just general, a possibility?"

"Let me put it this way, Mr. Williams," Hansen said, suddenly patient and earnest. "It's far more than a theory. I've considered your situation and talked to Mr. Anderson about it. While I'm testifying for Mr. Stone, at the very end I'll have my laptop primed, and I'll do the magic from the courtroom in front of the jury. Something kind of funny and spectacular." He rotated his iPad on the table and slid it toward the lawyers on the other side. "See, I hacked the system while I was sitting here waiting. I inserted a court paper from Supreme Court Judge Derek 'Dr. Overbyte' Hansen that sends lawyer Philip Anderson to the public stocks for six hours. I can do something comparable at your trial. Wham-bang and abracadabra."

"This is now in the system?" Lisa asked. They were all looking at a document with a big, hokey signature scrawled in red crayon.

"Of course. Go check. If we do this for real, I'll take the judge and the jury to Mrs. Helms's office and we'll pull it up on her own terminal, same as the alleged fake will."

"Damn," Williams said, allowing a grin to spread. "I'll drive over and confirm it. Better not alarm Vicky any more than she already is."

"Suit yourself," Hansen said. "Call me and confirm what I already know, then I'll erase my paperwork and scrub the log."

"Do you know a Sean Morris?" Williams asked. "From Brooklyn?"

"He goes by the handle Tribble. Yeah, I know him. He's a cyberanarchist and a bandit. Why?"

"Is he accomplished in this field, computers and so forth?" Williams pressed.

"Depends on what you mean," Hansen replied sharply. "He's a pickpocket. He and his nihilist pals think it's brilliant and urgent to unlock devices so they can defeat years of honest work and adapt phones and gaming consoles to their whims."

"Is he smart?"

"I guess you could say so," Hansen conceded. "In the same way Khalid Sheikh Mohammed is smart."

"He's their expert," Williams informed him. "You ready to take him on?"

"He's sloppy and brooding and a punk. If he's honest, he can't tell you squat, any more than I've told you."

"They've also listed a Dr. Han Liu from the University of Virginia as an expert," Williams said.

"Liu's a stuffed shirt and an academic glad-hander," Hansen sniffed. "Put it this way: He parrots what people like Tribble and Overbyte discover. His career consists of creating absolutely nothing. I'm not a fan. He's a commentator, not an innovator."

"I take it he'll be the polished, reassuring counterpoint to Morris," Lisa noted. "They plan to cover all the bases. These guys are shrewd."

"Oh, Liu will definitely be dressed for the role," Hansen remarked. "He adores bow ties. Maybe he and Phil are related."

"Speaking of which," Lisa said, facing Hansen, "could I offer you a tip? In terms of your wardrobe?"

"Seriously?" Hansen sounded uncertain.

"Yes," Lisa answered.

"If it's constructive input in a field I'm still exploring, input from someone with skill and experience, I'd more than welcome it." Hansen keened his head, seemed engaged, interested.

"Seersucker and khaki don't mix. I appreciate what you're trying for, and damn good for you at your age. I'm impressed. You're too young to go totally seersucker, plus it still has a *Matlock* echo for many of us, and unfortunately there's no true coat counterpart for your slacks, unless you go for a blazer, which is too pat and stock for a guy with your edge."

"Okay," Hansen said, completely focused on Lisa. He reached for his iPad and pulled it toward him.

"For the summer, invest in a nice poplin suit, tan or light brown. You can still use the same shirt and tie, but ditch the tassels. Also, don't scrimp on the socks and end up with droopy, fuzzy leg warmers. You can let the suit wrinkle and rumple, too, which would preserve what we like about you, keep your very unique Derek badge intact."

"Sweet. Poplin? Thank you. Where would I look for such a suit?"

"Give me your e-mail address, and I'll send you several options."

"I already have your contact info. I didn't come here unprepared. I'll shoot you my mine. How much will this set me back, a poplin suit or two? Coordinated shoes?"

"What're you charging us?" Joe asked.

"Phil informed me he bills at four hundred dollars an hour. I'll be charging you four hundred and *one*."

Everyone laughed.

"You should be able to afford the suit," Lisa told him.

CHAPTER TWENTY-SIX

"Seriously, Toliver?" Joe glared at the detective, pissed off.

"Hey, listen, man, what you want me to do? There're no free passes in my business. No exemptions. The gun pointin' to you isn't smoking, my friend, it's lit up like a forest fuckin' fire. You're on the receivin' end of a forged will you gave to Vicky, and we got pictures of Lisa collecting some serious bribery loot from a Panama-hat bank, supposedly on your behalf. There's large money in play and a dead woman. At least a missing woman. I'm supposed to ignore it? Do the small-town, good-old-boy whitewash?"

Joe just stared, didn't speak. It was near the middle of August, past closing time, around five-thirty, hot, an evening storm gathering, swollen, violent, gray clouds taking shape in the east, and Toliver had waylaid him as he was locking the office door, leaving for the day. They were standing on the sidewalk. A shifting, fitful breeze was about to become a wind. A scrap of dirty paper whirled and reeled above the ground, rose and rode and danced and dropped back into the gutter, done until the next gust. "How long have you been waiting to ambush me? Sneaking around here with your Mickey Mouse police tricks?"

"Don't be so damn sensitive. I drove here from Collinsville, saw your car, parked mine and walked directly to your door right when you were comin' out. I promise I haven't been hidin' in the bushes. I immediately told you my business, and you decided to flip on the imbecile switch and start fuming."

"Shit, Toliver, you clobber me at the end of a long day and announce all formal and Kojak that you're here to question *me* about 'the

VanSandt case,' and you act like you're here to cuff me on the spot. I told you about Lettie and Benecorp, remember? Now I'm being questioned because, what, you catch a call from Seth Garrison's lawyers?"

"Actually, no. Sheriff Perry got calls from Congressman Myers, the state police and the governor's office. But I was comin' anyway, long before the whores and political toadies partially paid their Benecorp debts and phoned the sheriff. I read the paperwork from the civil suit; that alone would send me for a visit. I have a report, also: No usable prints on Lisa's cardboard from the leprechaun. There were prints, but none of any quality. I also had 'em take a stab at that smidgen of letters and numbers, but no dice there, either."

"You're here to investigate me?" Joe locked the door but left his keys hanging. "Shit. Come on. You know me as well as anyone."

"I love it when people say that. How they *know* someone, and he or she couldn't have done it. Really? It's my favorite dumb-ass crime cliché. Nobody knows shit for sure. As long as you're human and have a heartbeat, you can lie, steal and kill. Every crook ever convicted has a mom and dad who loved him and believed in him to the last bitter disappointment. Your neighbors, they're always fuckin' shocked because they *know* the criminal and this couldn't be. People knew Bernie Madoff and Ted Bundy. A whole congregation knew Bishop Eddie Long. You and I both thought the world of Bonnie McNamee—no way she was embezzlin' from the PTA."

"So what do you want, Toliver?" The wind was gaining, blowing harder, less scattered. It caught the tail end of Joe's tie and briefly flipped it away from his shirt.

Toliver reached into his hip pocket and took out his tiny notebook. "Did you give Vicky a forged will?"

"No, I didn't," Joe snarled. "I gave her the will your boss gave me. Maybe you should talk to him."

Toliver wrote in his pad. "Okay, did you and Lisa receive any money from Benecorp?"

"No. Hell, no."

"Did Lisa go to the Bahamas?"

"Yes. So do thousands of other people. You'll need more pages in your little Oompa-Loompa pad to list all of them."

"But she didn't bring home any money from a bank there?" Toliver was still making notes when he asked the question.

"No, she didn't." Joe reached for his keys. "Are we done?"

Toliver made eye contact. "Of course, you did go meet with Garrison in Virginia Beach?"

"Yeah, at your urging. Hey, did you get any money from Benecorp? Did you steal the Wound Velvet formula?"

Toliver smiled. "Nope," he said calmly. "Anything else you want to tell me that we haven't already discussed?"

"Yeah—you can kiss my ass."

"I'll add that to my summary. It won't be helpful in sentencing when the judge asks 'Was Mr. Stone cooperative?' I'll have to tell him you were rude and used profanity."

"And what're you doing to actually solve the case?"

"Hell, I been busier than the trombone player in the Ringling Brothers band. Don't want my stats ruined. But I'm not inclined to share my info with a potential suspect, you see."

"Are you planning to harass my wife?" Joe demanded, still rankled. "To interview her?"

"If she'll see me, yes."

"I wouldn't count on it," Joe snapped.

"Well, I'll give it a shot," Toliver replied, putting away his pad. "Here's a nugget for you, courtesy of the guy who works for the county and hasn't had a raise in three fiscal years: What fool *withdraws* money—in cash—from a no-tell, fly-by-night bank? You transfer the dollars to the shady bank in order to conceal 'em and scrub Mr. Franklin clean as a whistle. If you wanted cash, why leave a trail? Demand a suitcase full of hundreds and be done with it. Why go to the Bahamas? The Bahamas are for cruise boats and parasailing, not dubious money schemes. You want to hide money, you're talkin' Cook Islands, Switzerland, maybe the Caymans. Odd, isn't it? Of course—too bad for you—your average Henry County juror ain't goin' to realize the difference. The Bahamas sounds exotic and rich to him."

"I suppose," Joe said cautiously. "But from the resistance we're seeing, I'd say the Bahamas still make the list of places to hide cash."

"So when I harass your wife, I'll explore that with her, why the deal was arranged in such a clumsy fashion. I'll also try to discover why she's leanin' on the counter there in the Bahamian bank."

"Pardon?"

"The lady in the surveillance tape, when the teller disappears to fetch the moneychanger from underneath the ceiling fan in his office, the lady kinda slouches against the counter. Leans on an elbow, very sorta sloppy and low-rent. Not poised, in other words. I've never seen such as that from Lisa Stone, and I've seen her more than most. Have you, Joe? Ever seen Lisa any way other than a hundred percent classy in public? The woman allegedly signin' for the money, when she was waiting there at the counter, she was all dressed for the role, huge polo match, rich-white-lady hat and them obligatory Jackie O glasses, but she was Baltic Avenue, St. Charles Place, tops. Evidently an excellent confidence woman, good at the grift, but definitely not your Park Place wife. Also, we never see her sign the first piece of paper."

"Huh. We've watched the tape until we know it by heart and, yeah, you're right. It's a shame we can't sell your theory to a jury."

Toliver grinned and hitched his pants. He was wearing a wide tie and a short-sleeve shirt, no jacket. "No 'we' involved, Kemosabe. I know it's not Lisa on the tape. Can't prove it, but I'm pretty sure of it. You, on the other hand, are still on my radar, with neon arrows directed at you. I put a giant star beside your name in my notes. An exclamation point too, in case important police people was to come checkin' behind me and examining my investigation. What a feather in my cap if I could pop a lawyer, especially the most honest attorney in the state." Toliver began walking away. He glanced over his shoulder. "I'll see you later. I need to beat the storm to my car. Lucky for me I was able to conclude my penetratin' interview with you before we got rained out. By the way, Joe, the posts from Roberto100 came from a coffee shop in Charlotte—only a couple hours down the road. Took the site a while to respond to my court order. If I was you, I'd check into that news, but what do I know?"

"Perfect," Lisa said. "You did well." It was noon, the day after Toliver Jackson's encounter with Joe, and she'd just taken a chair across from

Derek Hansen at the Fieldale Cafe. The restaurant was busy, noisy, and she hoped the talk and bustle would obscure their conversation. "Your suit's exactly what the doctor ordered."

"Thank you, though I *am* the doctor, so that would always be the case regardless of what I buy or how it looks." He grinned. "The e-mails with pictures were helpful. My girlfriend's also a fan. I bought two, in slightly different colors." He stuck his leg out from beneath the table and extended it toward her. "I didn't shortchange the accessories."

Lisa nodded. "Derek two point oh. Nice. But don't overdo it, okay? We want our rumpled genius, not some spooky popinjay."

"Point made."

"Did you bring your music?" she asked him.

He placed his iPad on the table, alongside a Bose speaker. "Who can I play in here and not be made to squeal like a pig at the end of a hill-billy's hunting rifle?"

"Anything is fine. Keep the volume sociable. I want to do all I can to keep our conversation private. I don't plan to say much, and I need you to keep your comments to a minimum as well, please."

"Okay. Esquivel is the choice." He raised the music's level until Lisa told him to stop.

She placed three sheets of paper on the table and gestured for him to pick them up. "See what you think," she said. While he was reading, a waitress came and Lisa ordered plate lunches for them both, fried chicken breasts, slaw, sliced tomatoes and macaroni and cheese, sweet tea to drink.

"I don't like coleslaw," Hansen said, continuing to read. The pages were handwritten. "Mayonnaise and cabbage—nasty."

"Sorry. I didn't want to interrupt you. Should I change it?"

"No. I'm fine." He finished the last sheet and smiled, scratched his cheek with his thumb. "Hmm. I don't know," he said. "Where's the rest of the team? Phil Anderson and your husband? Mr. Williams?"

She leaned closer to the speaker. "Not involved," she said under her breath. "Only me."

"Sketchy," he said, following her lead, almost mouthed the word without sound. "Illegal."

"Fight fire with fire."

"Why the deadline?" he asked. "So quick?"

She spoke more normally, but still stayed below the music, which sounded electronic and spacey, cocktail hour for the Jetsons, a sixties prediction of what would be hip and swinging decades into the future. "The law has something called discovery. It allows each side to learn the substance and details of the other side's case. It prevents surprises at trial and helps frame the issues. Unfortunately for us, once you receive what are known as interrogatories, you have only twenty-one days to respond. The responses are done in writing, under oath." She took the papers in front of Hansen, folded them and put them in her purse. She planned to shred them as soon as she returned to her office. "Phil wrangled a short extension from their lawyer, but we're down to only a few days before our answers are due. I hope we can get another delay from the judge, but even so, time is suddenly my enemy. Also, as part of discovery, you're able to request a deposition, a witness's oral statement under oath. The notices for deps have been served, and while we can use the excuse of busy schedules to cause some reshuffling, we're under pressure there too."

"I already knew what a deposition is," Hansen noted. He wasn't snide or haughty. His tone and expression signaled he understood the dilemma.

"So?"

He scratched his cheek again. "You're positive we'll win in court?"

"Yeah, as positive as you can be in a system that relies on seven random variables to reach an accurate result. But I need to have this before we show our hand. Need to know precisely *what* I'm winning or we'll be screwed."

"Okay," he whispered. "You can count Overbyte in. This should be much more fun than breaching Mrs. Helms's computer, especially at five hundred an hour, which strikes me as a fair wage given my tricky new responsibilities. And I'll need a letter from you confirming it."

"Sure," Lisa answered. "Deal. Do not mention this to my husband or our lawyers. Not a peep."

"The letter also should state it's kosher. If I take a fall, I'd prefer to have a warm body underneath me to cushion the blow."

. . .

The same evening, Lisa, feeling stressed and preoccupied, treated her elementary school student, Montana Triplett, to a Najjar's pizza and a child's manicure from the mall nail salon, so it was almost seven-thirty before she arrived at the farm, where she found Joe sitting on the front porch, still wearing his pin-striped pants and pressed white shirt, his collar unbuttoned. He was drinking the top-notch bourbon, the Van Winkle, just a highball glass and ice, no mixer, the brown liquor a rarity for him during hot weather, usually stored at the rear of the cabinet until the leaves turned color. He was in a sturdy white vinyl rocker they'd bought at Lowe's hardware, part of a matching pair on sale for ninety-nine dollars, and he'd removed her fern from its small table, dragged the table closer to the rocker and propped up his feet. His horse, Sadie, was in the front yard, grazing, let loose from the pasture, experienced enough she wouldn't bolt or cause trouble, happy to eat the clover patches and lush lawn grass.

"Good idea," Lisa said. "I'll get a glass of wine and join you. Okay?" There was still plenty of summer daylight in the sky.

"Okay," he said.

She kicked off her shoes almost as soon as she was inside. She shed her bra in the kitchen, draping it across a chair. She pulled her hair out of her face and fastened it with a plastic clip, then poured a glass of cold white wine from a bottle in the fridge she'd opened two days ago. She left a necklace on the counter, beside Joe's tie.

"How's the Van Winkle?" she asked as she was settling into the other rocking chair.

"The best. Even though it's too hot to be drinking it. I'm still under a roof, so at least there's no heresy in that regard."

"You look tired," she said.

"I am," he said miserably. "And I'm seriously worried they might whip us in this thing, Lisa."

"They won't."

"You keep repeating that."

"Because it's true," she answered.

"I'm like the doctor who discovers his own tumor," he said quietly. He was watching his horse. "All of a sudden it's not about billing codes and tee times. I can't believe the friggin' legal system's so wide open and so ... so ... such a street brawl that you can turn the law into a damn cudgel and just raise holy hell with it."

"Seriously? Really? Come on, Joe. We work off principles and documents and ideals that were created by men with wooden teeth, blunderbusses and knickers. Slaveholders whose state of the art was medicinal leeches. Men who'd for sure condemn a microwave oven as a witchcraft box but probably worship a remote-control model plane as a divine messenger. Men who'd never seen a basic tele*graph* or a black-and-white TV and set store by *Poor Richard's Almanack*. Guys who died from syphilis. It's a system that prides itself on being static and never changing. And even better, we trust the politicians to properly calibrate it."

"I doubt any system can keep pace with every advance and invention. And basic good ideas remain basic good ideas. You have a better suggestion?"

"I for sure could improve the moldy dinosaur we have. I could."

"Truthfully, I'm most concerned about losing my law license. The state bar investigator has referred my case to the district committee—the letter came this morning. They have a pack-of-lies affidavit from dipshit Neal to go along with the forged will, the video from the Bahamas, the fake agreement with Benecorp and a bullshit deposition from our pal Seth Garrison detailing how I tried to extort him, which dovetails nicely with the recording of me fudging about the possibility of a trust or foundation owning the formula. How would you rate my chances? The fucking hearing's set for October tenth. And against all that, I say, what, you have my solemn word I didn't do any of this? Please believe me? I know that's me lying on the phone, and the expert says that's my signature on an extortion agreement, and the will I handed Vicky is a fake, but hey, listen, I'm innocent. Shit. Good luck."

She set her glass on the stone porch, made certain it was steady, the rocks not completely level or smooth. "Okay." She exhaled, patting her hair. "Here's a plan, the best I can come up with. I know you'll throw a fit, but let's think about something unconventional. We have no chance if we play this according to traditional rules. None. You should realize that by now. It should be obvious. We'll get our butts handed to us even though you're innocent and Garrison's a damn scoundrel. We're heading into a fight with a rules pamphlet and some misguided sense of justice, and Benecorp is showing up with a bazooka. Hell, you'll be standing there lecturing them and wagging your finger, and they'll blow you to smithereens, Joe. Goliath has a Glock in this version, and no matter how virtuous and principled you are, you're naïve to think that honoring some impotent lawyer code will do anything for you, that the system can't be hoodwinked or scammed and you'll never lose so long as you stick to Lord Mansfield's noble instructions. You're standing in the martyr line, for no reason."

"And you'll correct this how? We're going to leap into the mud with them and become thugs and beat them at a game they understand and we don't? But, yeah, absolutely, you're right—I'd fucking prefer to be disbarred and be able to live with myself."

"Here's the plan, or at least the start. Don't interrupt me. Let me explain it before you have a conniption. The big picture is we replace Lettie *if*—and only *if*—we can't locate her." She pushed her hand in his direction. "Just let me finish. We agree that if Lettie isn't dead, none of this matters, especially if *she* exonerates you. If she says she wrote the will you gave the clerk's office and she's alive anyway, this nightmare is over and done with. There's no basis for a civil suit, no basis for you to lose your license, and the crux of Garrison's case—that you forged a will—is no longer viable. Everything will crumble from there."

He laughed. "While we're at it, let's conjure up the Green Hornet, Kato, a couple vampires, the Invisible Man, General MacArthur and a time-travel machine. We'll definitely kick their asses. This is genius—why would I be upset?"

"You don't have to be a dick, Joe."

"Who will we cast as Lettie's understudy?" he asked.

"Simple. We dupe a legal system that's been left behind technologically but makes forensic evidence a deity. We exploit an overwhelmed antique that's creaky and feeble, where we know all the trapdoors and pressure points. DNA and fingerprints and all the CSI marvels are gods—especially to juries—but we realize they have major clay feet and can be compromised a thousand ways."

"I'm all ears." He sipped his bourbon.

"Remember when Lettie was pissed at me because I wouldn't sue her neighbors for coaxing away 'her' finches and cardinals? Remember? She spoke to me only because you were on a hunting trip. She was furious because she couldn't afford birdseed and the Gardner family could, and they were using it to bait the birds and 'steal' them from her. She wanted an injunction—no more seed so her birds would return. Bedbug crazy as usual. I finally got tired of her mouth and told her the birds probably sensed she was part serpent and that's why they left. Not to mention the gang of cats at her trailer."

"So?"

"To be spiteful, she sent me a letter, and the gist was that I'm not worth a bucket of warm spit. In fact, I didn't even rate a bucket. She sent me a *thimble* of spit. Her spit. Covered and sealed with what looks like plastic wrap."

"Right. You showed it to me." Joe was balancing the glass on his thigh. "Another proud day for Lettie."

"We still have it in the file from that meeting. Betty's meticulous and a pack rat, especially where Lettie was concerned. She kept the letter, my notes, the spit."

"We'll clone her? Yes! Brilliant." He lowered his head, peered at her impatiently. "I'm liberated."

"I also have the elaborate curse she tossed on my desk a year or so ago. Among the feathers, sticks, dead flowers, beads, yarn and other voodoo is a braided section of her filthy hair." Lisa leaned closer and touched Joe's knee. "We have her DNA, Joe. What a huge advantage if we use it correctly."

"Correctly?"

"Here's the plan. We tell the court that Lettie's alive but in hiding, fearful of Benecorp. Look at what they did to her friend, Dr. Downs. This is all perfectly true. We arrange to have Neal tested. The judge can pick the lab so there's no room for cheating. If we drop a net on Lettie or she appears on her own, we're home free. If we can't get the real Lettie there, our spit and hair will match. Either way, the recorded will becomes a nullity, and the heart of the case disappears."

"Uh, I don't think they'll just let Barney and Andy drop off some samples down at the Mayberry malt shop. They'll want to see Lettie and her ID, the whole nine yards. Hell, the division of child support is more strict than that. I seriously doubt a lawyer as smart as Edwin Nicholson will sign up for your program."

"Exactly. We'd have to be very careful about how we arrange the testing. Only the judge and the technician would be present, along with Lettie and Neal. We emphasize she's mentally fragile and scared and that Benecorp is a threat to her—again, all true. Everybody else can watch by video conferencing."

"I'm sure Nicholson would happily agree to that condition as well."

"Let's consider another advantage we have: Who knows her better than you and me?"

"Probably no one," Joe said.

"Right. Which is why I could be convincing if need be."

"Great fucking googly moogly, Lisa. For heaven's sake—*you're* going to pretend to be Lettie? Seriously?"

"Possibly. Maybe. If I have to. It would be too risky to bring in a ringer; the fewer people who could screw us, the better. We have your will video, so I could replicate her tattoos. I've spent a lot of time with her, and only a handful of people really are familiar with her. I never said I had every detail nailed down. Point is, I'd give it a try if it's our best option."

Joe laughed derisively. "The most beautiful woman in ten states is going to transform herself into a hag and fool everybody?"

"Listen to me: Obviously we need to keep Neal and any Lettie impostor separated, even though he's such a nervous dunce he might not know the difference. We tell the judge that Neal's in league with Benecorp and Lettie's scared to be in the same room with him. Nobody else will've ever seen her before. Not the judge, not the lawyers, not the lab tech, not Garrison, not Pichler. She's brand-new to all of them. With the exception of the Henry County cops and the local politicians, who has actually spent much time with her hateful ass? We could send in just about anybody. As long as the DNA matches, we win. And we're really not cheating or being dishonest—Lettie's alive. I saw her. We've heard from her. If she shows up after we've used her hair and spit to influence the court outcome, well, we'll deal with any of her complaints then. Since you're her pal, I'm sure you could convince her it was for her benefit."

Joe raised his glass from his leg and swallowed bourbon. He took in an ice cube as well, and Lisa could hear him crunching it. "This truly is from the Wile E. Coyote playbook. Lord, next thing you know I'll be buying an ACME anvil and a length of stout rope and we'll be trying to lure Garrison into a narrow canyon." He stared at her. "No. Nope. No way. It's just asinine."

"Why?" she quickly asked. "It's unorthodox and risky, but it's not asinine." She leaned back in the chair and began rocking, made tight, compact strokes. "Go ahead. Tell me the flaws."

"The spit—you're planning on handing them a thimble and they'll simply accept it without any chain of custody or proof of when it was produced and where it came from?"

"I'm still working on that. We'll need some type of dental device or some fairly creative sleight of hand. Or help on the inside. I didn't say I had it totally figured yet."

"Putting aside the . . . the equipment and dexterity issues, I suppose you're planning to Magic Marker your tooth gold, and they'll be fooled by that? The school play, Raggedy Ann effect? Maybe add some big red circles on your cheeks?"

She paused, waiting a moment before she answered. A few tree frogs were beginning to chorus, a tractor-trailer's Jake brake popped and belched out on the highway, three-quarters of a mile away. A hummingbird buzzed by and hovered above an orange hibiscus bloom, needling nectar from its center. Lisa recalled—saw it in her mind, clear, bright, vivid—standing in the Nassau customs line, studying her own passport photo, waiting to be admitted, then walking through a checkpoint without turning around, the immigration officer's accented "enjoy your visit" and a three-man airport band's tourist music the soundtrack for her selfish failure. She shook her head. "How hard is it to have my tooth tricked up with some gold? People do that at the freaking mall. I'll wear a wig and a hat too."

Joe set his highball glass on the porch. He stood and stared down at her. "Are you making this up as you go along? You're planning to cover your front tooth with gold, paint yourself with tats and take a one-in-a-million shot at fooling an experienced lawyer and a judge—assuming we can keep Lettie's flesh-and-blood son out of the picture?" He stepped to the side and leaned against a post. "The best I see coming from this is *both* of us winding up disbarred. We'll both lose our licenses. Sweetie, Benecorp isn't the bear-suit mall lawyer you can jive and bluff. This isn't the usual cast of characters you've been able to delicious or outsmart your whole life." He eased his tone. "I understand you're the risk taker, but this is flimsy and insane. It won't work. It won't. I appreciate the . . . the effort, the offer, the fact you're trying to fix our problem, but there're way too many moving parts and way too many trip wires and way too many glitches we can't solve just sitting here on the porch bullshitting about it. Believe me, I wish it were viable, do I ever, but this is officially the worst idea in history."

"I'd rather take the chance than see something happen to you, even if it's a long shot and even if I risk getting in trouble too. Can't win if you don't play, and small odds are better than no odds at all. And it may never come to this. I think sooner or later we'll find Lettie."

"I know. I understand. But let's give the system a chance. I'm not sure how, but I believe sticking to the law will serve us better."

"I love you, Joe," she said, her voice fading. She dabbed at her eyes.

"I love you too. But that's not a reason to do something suicidal and stupid."

"You remember Lloyd Burnette?" she asked.

"Yeah, sure. The biker. Why?"

"He'd do anything for me, he admires you and he's reliable as can be. We saved him years in jail when I had the certificate of analysis pitched in his case. He never ratted on his buddies, though, even when it would've saved his own skin. He's solid. Close-lipped. He's legit now, does tattoos in Greensboro. They'd be temps, Joe, not permanent. He'd never breathe a word."

"No."

"We've invested twenty years into people, done right by them, been honest, helped them, taken jars of sourwood honey and boxes of tomatoes and sacks of corn as fees, carried tabs for years at ten bucks a month, never cheated or cut corners or failed to press as hard as we could for a client, and maybe now's the time to redeem those favors. Cash in the goodwill we've earned. I did Dr. Beasley's divorce. Three years it lasted, and he'd call all rattled, and I'd hold his hand and reassure him—never charged him an extra nickel. I feel positive he'd wrap my tooth after hours and off the record. Maybe he could build the container for the spit too. Those are the only ingredients. Some tats and a tooth—that would be a start."

Joe sat down again. "No. Period. But thanks. I appreciate your even considering it." He sighed. "So this was your ace in the hole?"

"Give it some thought, okay? Please. Think about this compared to where we are and what we can expect. I truly believe your reluctance is more about breaking the rules than not being able to somehow figure how to make this work. Try separating the two. We have the DNA. Her DNA. All we have to do is find a way to use it. And yeah, I'd love to come up with a plan that doesn't involve *me* if we can."

"I'll take my chances—my honest chances—in court and before the disciplinary committee. Maybe I can convert our goodwill there, where I'm supposed to. I'm not a hypocrite who jumps ship the first time we hit bad waves. I've invested decades in this system, and I've told hundreds of people it delivers fairness, and I'm not about to start acting like a scared punk. It would only make our situation worse, sweetie, your dishonesty." He had the bourbon again. "But you're quite a wife," he said. "Yes you are. I picked the right girl. Thanks for the offer." He sipped from the glass but suddenly stopped. He swallowed. He concentrated and looked at her hard. "Should I find it odd that you're so eager to do this, and you're the only person who claims to have seen Lettie? Quite an elaborate contingency plan for somebody who's certain she's alive. You haven't been misleading me, have you? Planning your own sting to rescue us?"

"Meaning?"

"This is permanently and positively a no. I want your promise."

"Joe—"

"Promise me as my wife and law partner that you'll forget about this. I won't have it, Lisa."

"Okay, okay. I'll forget about it."

"It's degrading too," he said disdainfully. "Degrading. You're a lawyer and a professional. Not a con artist or a boiler-room hustler."

CHAPTER TWENTY-SEVEN

"You need to please go and check on Mr. Stone," Betty said. It was another blistering August morning, two days after Joe had rejected Lisa's cockamamie offer to cure their legal crisis by blinging her front tooth and temporarily painting herself with dragons, mythical birds, Chinese symbols, scrolls, crosses, tigers, flames, Celtic script slogans and a multicolored cobra head.

"Why?" Lisa asked. She was at her desk, sneaking a cigarette and playing Plants vs. Zombies, a small reward for finishing a tedious land deed that had nineteen grantors, one-sixty-fourth fractional shares and a handicapped minor heir in South Carolina. She was at level three, the living dead dressed in sport jackets and red ties trudging from the margins of her screen. "What's wrong?" She looked up and waved a hand back and forth through the Marlboro Ultra Light smoke.

"I'm sure it has to do with a certified letter I signed for this morning. He took it real bad, Mrs. Stone. I can tell when he's upset and brooding."

"Huh. Certified mail is rarely good news. Yeah, thanks. I'll find out what's bothering him." She clicked Quit Game, stubbed out the cigarette and made the trip over the worn hall rugs to Joe's office. After all the time in their building, she knew the rugs' patterns by heart, the swirls, shapes, figures, lines and designs, had crossed them until every woven detail was familiar, lodged in her mind.

She didn't have to ask Joe anything, didn't have to recite why she was standing there in his doorway with a worried expression. As soon as he spotted her, he tossed the letter—a chunk of stapled pages—across his desk in her direction. "My reward," he said bitterly. "Joe Stone, the honest lawyer, receives his due. Thank you for being a true believer and honoring the system and refusing to compromise the rules. We appreciate your discipleship and dedication. Your 2009 Carrico ethics award."

"Betty said something came in the mail and upset you."

"That would be a fucking understatement, Lisa. Supreme Court Rules, Part 6, Section IV, paragraph 13-18: Bar counsel has certified to the Disciplinary Board that I am engaging in misconduct which will result in injury to others and that my practicing law poses an imminent danger to the public." He collected a rubber band from his desk, stretched it from his thumb, released it. It plunked against the wall and fell to the hardwood floor, close to the baseboard. "They're asking for an immediate suspension of my license. That shit doesn't happen unless they're figuring on a slam dunk. It's a done deal. Forget about October. August twenty-ninth is my date. Sweet, huh? I was district committee chair for six years. For six years I handled ethics complaints. Now I'm the friggin' respondent, the crooked lawyer, the threat to my community. And I'm going to lose—no doubt. They have the evidence. I have, what, my thin, flimsy words? Why the hell did I ever call Benecorp and fudge about the stupid trusts?"

"Whether you did or not, Joe, there's still the fake will, Neal's lies, video of an impostor in a bank supposedly collecting our money, incriminating signed documents and a deposition from a captain of industry who claims we tried to bribe him."

"Thanks for the helpful reminder."

"Robert and Phil expect to hear any day who our judge will be. They've already filed to extend the deadline for our discovery answers."

"Great," Joe snapped. "Doesn't help me one iota with this shit."

"I'm so sorry, Joe. God." She walked to him and crouched beside his chair. She took his hand, wrapped it in both hers. She was sideways to him, next to his hip and shoulder. He didn't look at her, stared at the far wall, angry and seething, a knot at the pivot where his jawline began curving toward his ear. He swallowed hard, and she could see it in his neck. "I've bombarded the chat room for the last week," she told him. "From nine o'clock until past ten, every three or four minutes, every night, not just Thursdays. I wrote 'Joe SOS' or 'Joe needs you ASAP.' Nothing. What a bitch."

"Thanks. If she's alive, we've absolutely got to find her. We'll get our clocks cleaned in court. I swear, now I'm worried that maybe she *was* hiding and Benecorp located her and finished the job. Or, shit, our luck, she got run over by a bus. Let's hire a private detective, even though it'll probably be a waste. I'll make some calls and set it up, but where in creation do you start looking?"

"Okay. I agree. Who knows, maybe a pro can find her—it's what they do. Billy Hamblin's always been pretty effective. Let's see if he's available. And we have the Charlotte lead from Toliver."

Joe didn't reply, didn't make eye contact, continued to peer straight ahead, rigid, fixed, resigned. "I miss Brownie," he finally said. "The room seems too big with him gone."

"I miss him too."

"Oh—I canceled our off-duty cops. I told Chris Lampkins we didn't need them anymore. The cost was putting us in the poorhouse, and I don't think Garrison would dare harm us now, huh? Why would he? No need—we're plenty dead as it is."

In response to a mass e-mail Lisa had sent, the entire Martinsville–Henry County Bar, except for three members, turned out in person to support Joe at his August disciplinary hearing, drove several hours to Richmond, most of them on the road by 5:30 a.m., a few there the day before, staying in hotels on their own dime. The three who couldn't make it because of such short notice sent long, favorable letters to the board. In all, thirty-six lawyers traveled from Henry County to the General Assembly Building, where the hearing was held in a side room adjacent to the main lobby. Mike Cannaday was suffering from cancer and clattered down the center aisle on his walker. "If they take Joe's license, they might as well take mine," he proclaimed, loud enough for everyone to hear, plainspoken as always.

More attorneys came from Roanoke and Salem and Danville, and Alan Black chauffeured a bunch from Stuart, a blue-moon rarity, as Patrick County was an extremely clannish place, especially skeptical of its "big-city" neighbors to the east. There were far too many people to fit comfortably in the space, so they lined the walls and spilled deep into the corridor. Joe didn't know his friends would be there—Lisa hadn't told him in case people decided not to make the trip—and he shook every hand, hugged several old friends and thanked them all, grudges and lost cases and local politics set aside for the day. Lisa could tell that he was moved, pleased, even gratified, and despite how strong the case against him was, seeing their colleagues buoyed her, gave her a dash of hope.

There was nothing from Lettie, nothing at all.

Bar counsel was a low-key pro named Kaye Slayton, and her presentation to the five-member board was methodical and powerful, a preview of exactly how the civil case with Benecorp would unfold. A pained Vicky Helms testified that Joe gave her the handwritten VanSandt will and that she personally scanned the document he brought to her. As she was leaving the witness stand, she volunteered that Mr. Stone never would've tried to do something dishonest, and Slayton coolly asked her again exactly who offered her the will. "Joe. Mr. Stone," Helms said, barely audible.

A handwriting expert from the state police declared the recorded will was a forgery. There was an affidavit from Benecorp's expert, too, confirming that the document wasn't prepared by Lettie VanSandt.

Then the panel saw the contract with Joe's purported signature, where he agreed to release the rights to an asset he owned only because of the fraudulent will. They watched a video of the money being collected in the Bahamas and were told that the respondent, Mr. Stone, had stipulated his wife was in Nassau on March 5, though he denied it was her in the video and denied receiving any payment whatsoever.

Over Phil Anderson's vehement objection, the board reviewed Caribbean Fidelity International Bank's paperwork and notarized affidavit, which showed $750,000 withdrawn from an account in the name of Lisa Stone. "This isn't a court trial," the chairman, Oliver Winston, reminded Anderson. "Our rules favor admission; the board members can give the evidence whatever weight they think it merits." Another of the board members, a bald, pinched, suspendered lawyer from Bedford, scowled. To his left, a bony woman with narrow eyes and an austere blouse furiously scrawled notes.

Following lunch, Anton Pichler was sworn in and then explained how Joe had misled him and Benecorp regarding ownership of the

VV 108. With Pichler still on the witness stand, Slayton played the recordings of Joe hemming and hawing about the possibility of a trust or foundation owning the rights to the wound formula. "It seemed like a double dip to us," Pichler noted. "We'd paid Mr. Stone once, even though we were suspicious of his claim, and here he's back at our door for a second round, demanding more money. It felt like a shakedown, really." The best Phil Anderson could do on cross-examination was highlight that Joe had never claimed *for certain* Benecorp didn't own the wound formula.

Kelly Richardson had rescheduled four cases so she could be at the hearing and was sitting beside Lisa in the front row, immediately behind Joe. "This isn't my cup of tea," Richardson whispered, her hand blocking her mouth. "I'm strictly a domestic relations gal, but this isn't sounding so hot for our side."

Slayton asked for a brief recess and left the room with the bar investigator, a retired cop from Grundy. Lisa assumed Slayton was reviewing her notes and trial outline, making sure she'd not forgotten any evidence or important testimony. She returned and instead of declaring she was resting the state bar's presentation against Joe, she announced that Seth Garrison would be her next witness, and although she did her best to sound nonchalant, there was a peculiar, jazzed excitement in her voice, a mixture of awe and top-this-stunt satisfaction, and damned if he didn't sweep in from a side door, Seth Garrison, Mr. G, the Benecorp king, an honest-to-goodness rich, reclusive celebrity, and he set the room on its ear, jaded lawyers, gigantic egos, men and women who'd tried death penalty cases, it didn't matter, they were all rapt and spellbound, impressed to see TMZ fame and mammoth wealth incarnate. Lisa noticed Christina Phelps from the public defender's office surreptitiously aiming her phone at Garrison so she could sneak a photo.

Garrison was comfortable testifying, relaxed, pleasant, not in the least haughty or condescending, a regular guy in an expensive tailored suit. He detailed how his company had determined the will was a fraud but, for obvious business reasons, decided to pay Mr. Stone anyway for a renouncement of all rights to the VanSandt estate. He identified his signature on the contract. He pointed to Joe's signature, claimed the notary, an administrative assistant with Benecorp, had met Joe at the Greensboro airport to witness the signature, this because the company had been burned before, and he wanted his people to verify the signing. He produced the records showing a payment of $750,000 into the Bahamas account and its subsequent withdrawal. "If Mr. Stone had honored that agreement," he said solemnly, "even as tainted as it was, we wouldn't be here today. To the contrary, we now know he learned just how valuable this formula might be, and he then began hounding us for more money. He lied to us. He claimed we didn't own the VanSandt wound medicine. He repeatedly told us it belonged to some trust, and we'd have to pay him again. It felt like we were being blackmailed."

Phil Anderson objected to the characterization, and the board chairman agreed.

"Sorry," Garrison said humbly. "I'm not a lawyer. I apologize. I'll just leave it at this: He came to us seeking further payment based on complete untruths."

"And then he sued you?"

"He did," Garrison said. "We were shocked."

"How much did he demand? The second time, when he incorrectly stated some fictitious trust actually owned the wound formula?"

"Five million dollars. Sitting there on my boat in Virginia Beach— five million dollars. I refused. Enough is enough."

"Thank you, sir," Slayton said. "And thanks for traveling here today. I realize you have a busy schedule."

"No problem," Garrison said amiably. Lisa noticed a dab of mousse and a decent cut had improved his *Breakfast Club* hair. Still, even in his commanding suit and spiffy white shirt, a touch of awkward, slide-rule geek bled through, made him that much more appealing despite his enviable success and reputation as a take-no-prisoners CEO.

Phil Anderson capped a ballpoint pen and walked toward Garrison, stopping midway between the witness stand and counsel table. Anderson tapped his palm with the pen as he spoke. "Assuming, Mr. Garrison, that Mr. Stone did in fact forge a will, and assuming he did engineer this secretive, highly irregular transaction in the Bahamas, and assuming for the sake of argument he later came to you seeking more money, assuming he'd done all these obviously corrupt things, why on god's green earth would he then sue you and put this deceit on the table and make it public for everyone to see? He'd have to be an idiot, wouldn't he?"

"Mr. Garrison isn't a mind reader," Slayton objected. "Any answer would be improper speculation on his part."

Anderson smiled. "My very first question, Mrs. Slayton, and you're already raising Cain."

"I don't mind answering," Garrison volunteered. "The same thought occurred to me several weeks ago, when we were sued. Seems like a fair topic to me, though I don't know the rules here."

"Well, okay," Slayton agreed. She glanced at Anderson, then the board members. "I'll roll the dice. Go ahead. You may answer. Objection withdrawn."

Garrison nodded. "You see, Mr. Anderson, so much of my business is about competitive advantage, and that means secrecy and lots of valuable information held tight to the vest. The suit was a bluff, a shot across my bow. Your client calculated I'd fold immediately and pay him off rather than watch this innovation dragged into the public arena. The lawsuit has put my competitors on high alert; Mr. Stone knew that would be a complication for us. The lawsuit has also cost me and Benecorp and our stockholders untold thousands of dollars because we've had to hit our brakes given the uncertainty generated by Mr. Stone's false allegations. He made a judgment I'd pay him off quickly rather than see these things come to pass. He was wrong, simple as that."

"Quite a gamble," Anderson replied. "If he'd really done all this conniving, he'd have to realize suing you was suicidal."

"Only if I chose the more difficult route," Garrison argued. "I could've negotiated a quick settlement and been on my way and no one is the wiser. Also he can still deny any wrongdoing and hope for the best with a jury in his hometown; he still has that chance remaining. In the final analysis, I was unwilling to be continually blackmailed, though that position has put proprietary information at risk and is costing my company money in delays. He didn't think I'd choose this response. He told me as much at our Virginia Beach meeting."

"You invited him to the beach?" Anderson inquired.

"Yes."

"Although you claim that at the time you thought he was trying to scam you?"

"We felt the original will wasn't genuine. We were highly suspicious of Mr. Stone's later claim that a trust or foundation owned the VV 108 asset. I invited him to Virginia Beach so as to get to the bottom of matters once and for all."

"But despite your testimony that you realized my client was a crook and an operator, you climbed right in bed with him, correct? You never called the police and said, 'Hey, wait, I'm being flimflammed'?"

"I was willing to pay Mr. Stone on the first occasion because the numbers and risk avoidance made sense. I think I've explained my position." Garrison leaned forward slightly. "It was a business decision."

"So your issue with the alleged second request for money wasn't about principle and ethics, it was about price? Mr. Stone, according to you, wanted too much?"

"I felt there was a small chance he might be telling the truth. When it became apparent he was lying, I concluded that no payment would make him go away. If we paid him five million, I believed he'd return a month later with more threats and dishonesty, hat in hand."

"And he wanted, or so you claim, five million dollars?"

Garrison paused. He stared at Anderson, frowned. "Sir," he said, lowering his voice, "I'm not 'claiming' anything. It happened. I have a recording of the meeting. Would you like to listen to it?"

Anderson was a seasoned lawyer. He kept his composure, didn't let on he'd been groin-kicked. "Perhaps after you finish on the stand," he said casually. "But let's visit another topic. You claim you were in negotiations with Lettie VanSandt before her death, correct?"

"Yes."

"How was that going?"

Garrison smiled. "Well, to be honest, she was very strong-willed." Several lawyers in the gallery chuckled. "We hadn't reached a comprehensive agreement, if that's the question."

"You sent representatives to speak with her?"

"Yes."

"These people traveled under fictitious names?"

Slayton stood up. "Why is this relevant to our hearing today? I don't think this is a proper question. Whether or not Benecorp had dealings with Miss VanSandt has no bearing on Mr. Stone's dishonesty and ethical lapses."

"But," Anderson responded, turning a half circle to face her, "it has everything to do with Mr. Garrison, who appears here today painting himself as some virtuous babe in the woods, who claims he was shocked, just shocked, to discover there was mischief afoot in his dealings with Mr. Stone. He claims he knew the will was a fake but paid six figures to make it go away. Strange, isn't it? Why not just notify the cops and be done with it? He suggests he was in bona fide negotiations with Miss VanSandt, but, lo and behold, he's running a shady racket packed with sketchy people and sham IDs. I think we're entitled to present the full picture of Mr. Garrison so this board can evaluate his credibility and compare his actions to plain old common sense. I would submit that when you do so, when you scrutinize what he's telling you, it doesn't hold water."

"Go ahead," the chairman said.

"Do I need to repeat the question?" Anderson solicitously asked Garrison.

"No," Garrison replied. "I'm happy to answer it. If I came off as sanctimonious, I didn't mean to. Making Mr. Stone disappear was a bargain for $750,000. I was worried about the money and Benecorp's interests at that juncture, not the principle. When I made the deal, I wasn't concerned with whether Mr. Stone should be punished by this panel or whether he should be allowed to practice law—that's your issue, not mine. As for our reps using confusing identities, I don't apologize for that. I didn't want to tip off every other drug manufacturer in the country we were attempting to purchase a formula that might be a blockbuster. I'm an aggressive, bottom-line businessman, Mr. Anderson, and none of this changes the fact that Mr. Stone used a forged will to gain money from me and then lied to me in an effort to leverage even more—very uncool. I'll admit I bargained with a devil, but I'll also tell you I finally ran out of patience with him when he crossed the line too far and started poking me with his pitchfork."

"The names, please, of the people who came here to meet with Miss VanSandt?"

Slayton objected again. "Seriously? He's admitted his company takes security precautions. So what?"

"He's admitted his company breaks the law," Anderson said.

"Not exactly," Garrison interjected, before there was a ruling. "I understand our negotiators used middle names and maiden names, that kind of thing. Confusing, perhaps, but I'm not agreeing we did anything illegal."

"How about we leave it at this," Anderson said. "Tell us the real names, and we'll move on."

"I'll do my best to locate the information," Garrison promised. "Miss Rousch no longer works for us, but I'll be pleased to provide you and the board with her name and address. I'm not certain where she is these days. We have thousands of employees, and we don't follow them after they depart."

"Does the notary who claims she witnessed my client sign the agreement still work for you, or has she evaporated also?"

"She's still on the payroll," Garrison said.

"She's my final witness," Slayton said quickly, darting her eyes at Anderson. "Helen Allyn. We anticipate she'll say she drove from a Benecorp company in Charlotte and met Mr. Stone at the Greensboro airport parking lot. Evidently, he wanted a large, explainable public place in case he was spotted."

Anderson stepped closer to the panel, who sat on a dais in leather chairs used by legislative committees when the General Assembly was meeting. He scratched his head, said nothing. The room was silent. "Was the $750,000 a legitimate payment in the sense it was listed on your company's books? Was it reported to the IRS?"

"Absolutely," Garrison answered.

"So why would Mr. Stone be rooting around in the Bahamas? There's a written contract in your possession, undeniable evidence of the deal, and you reported the payment to the government. Why would Mr. Stone go through all this rigamarole and allegedly send his wife to collect money in Nassau? What would he gain by that?"

Garrison wasn't ruffled. He answered immediately, his tone steady and confident. "We assumed he didn't want this on the local radar. It wasn't about taxes. Three-quarters of a million lands in your account in a smaller community, tongues wag. Also, he had to believe that if this arrangement went south on him, the privacy of a Bahamian bank might make it more difficult to establish he actually received the cash. We thought he was simply building a barrier between himself and the payment."

"Sounds slick when you say it, Mr. Garrison," Anderson replied, "but it makes no sense when you seriously think about it. Me, I'd just ask for cash dollars in a suitcase. Really difficult to trace cash handed over in an alley or at the Greensboro airport."

Slayton objected and the chairman sustained her, warning Anderson to ask questions, not offer editorials or his opinions.

Anderson twisted a small grin. He'd scored his point, and the mild rebuke was the price for doing it. "A final question, then: Where are Miss VanSandt's pets?" He was walking away as he spoke, his back to Garrison.

"Her pets?" For the first time, Lisa could sense Garrison was surprised. He added the classic, guilty protest, his voice half a register too high: "What pets?" He shrugged. "We donated five thousand dollars to the Henry County SPCA, more than the original will required. Does that answer your question? Beyond the donation, I have no idea about Miss VanSandt or her pets. Sorry."

Phil Anderson requested a brief break, and he, Lisa, Joe and Kaye Slayton met in a small room behind the panel's platform, the door closed, none of them sitting. "Did you sandbag me, Kaye?" Anderson bristled. "You gave me a list of your exhibits and evidence. What the hell is this about some recording from Virginia Beach? On Garrison's boat? You never, ever disclosed it."

"First of all, Phil, I'm not required to, not in a disciplinary hearing. I did you a favor by giving you our information. I try to be fair. I do more than is required, so you can climb down off your high horse. This recording is news to me. I gave you everything I had. It's not like I chatted with Seth Garrison every day. I was as surprised as you."

"Have you listened to it?" Anderson asked.

"No," Slayton answered. "I'll be glad to have the investigator get it from Mr. Garrison. We'll listen to it right now if you want. Together. It is what it is."

"Fair enough," Anderson said.

Anderson motioned for Joe to follow him, and he and Lisa left Slayton and huddled in a corner at the very front of the main room. They could see panel members milling around, the audience seats full of lawyers and friends. "So?" Anderson whispered, his head tucked, peering over his spectacles.

Joe was stoic, calm, almost beatific. "Sorry. There's no doubt our friend Seth has my voice saying 'would you pay us five million?' or 'would you settle for five million?' something in that ballpark, though I'm also damn sure the rest of the recording will have been doctored and patched together."

"You didn't actually ask him for five million, did you?"

"Only rhetorically," Joe answered, his voice emotionless. "I didn't really—"

Lisa interrupted him. "Joe sort of threw that figure out to gauge, to, you know, sort of peg just how valuable the formula was to Benecorp. We never truly tried to get paid. Hell, we never—I never—received any money in the Bahamas. This was Joe mentioning a number so we could see if this formula is as big as we think it is. Garrison never flinched. He offered *us* money, Phil, which we turned down flat. This is all crazy. I can't believe how conniving and . . . cunning this bastard is."

"Okay," Anderson said, "but I'm going to hear Joe on tape asking for five million dollars? Is that what I'm understanding?"

"Yep," Joe said. "Probably. You won't hear the complete conversation, and you won't be privy to the context, and the tape will've been edited, but you'll hear me ask for the money."

"Damn," Anderson replied. "Not helpful, to say the least."

Joe touched Anderson's shoulder. "You did a great job with Garrison. We made some progress. Thanks. Unfortunately, I've left us in a bind. Not your fault. Garrison has outmaneuvered Lisa and me. He was tuning in to all this and writing his story before we'd even thought about it."

The investigator returned with the recording, a CD, and loaded it into Slayton's laptop, and the contents seemed genuine, seamless and logical, beginning with chatter about breakfast and the stray sounds of a table being set with glasses and china and silverware, and next came a discussion about Lettie and a trust and the formula, and then there was Joe, no mistaking his voice or his demand, asking Garrison if he'd "settle" for five million dollars, and Garrison, righteously angry, warning them not to sue him or they'd regret it and making arrangements for the Stones to leave his ship. Finally, they heard Joe smugly carrying on about his seafood omelet, sounding like an asshole.

"I'll testify under oath that's been seriously spliced and manipulated," Lisa said the moment the recording ended. "It's as fake as the bank video, the contract, the cash withdrawal, the—"

"The will Mr. Stone presented to the clerk's office?" Slayton added, her eyebrows raised. "There sure is a lot of 'fake' involved in this case. We're almost, Mrs. Stone, down to the Richard Pryor defense: 'Are you going to believe me or your lyin' eyes?' Your husband brings with him a sterling reputation, and I'm aware he's highly regarded, but I'm sensing that even if we went back into the hearing and he confessed in front of a packed room, it would somehow be yet another 'fake.'"

"Are you going to offer this?" Anderson asked. "Play it for the panel?"

"This is an ethics hearing, Phil, so I want to be ethical. I learned about the recording the very same moment you did. I didn't conceal it, didn't sit on it for a tactical advantage. Tell you what: I won't play the CD unless Mr. Stone testifies and denies making the statement or claims it's being taken out of context."

"That's fair," Anderson conceded. "Thanks."

The hearing resumed a few minutes after three o'clock, and Helen Allyn was the bar's final witness. She identified Joe and testified she'd met him in the Greensboro airport parking lot and watched him sign an agreement. She didn't read the agreement, she stated, didn't pay attention to the contents, but she produced a UPS receipt from the overnight envelope used to send the papers to Mr. Garrison personally. She'd asked Mr. Stone for an ID, and he'd shown her a driver's license. Phil Anderson stood and wearily admitted the control number on the contract beside Joe's signature matched the number on his license. "I'll probably get scolded by my friend Mrs. Slayton," Anderson added, "but it makes no sense for Mr. Stone to sign an agreement and put this in the spotlight if in fact this was a scam."

"It makes perfect sense," Slayton shot back, "if this was the only way he could receive his payoff. At the time, no one knew the will was fake—except Benecorp, possibly—so why wouldn't Mr. Stone go through the motions of making this appear aboveboard? More to the point, Mr. Anderson is just assuming that Benecorp would agree to some illicit cash payment. I can certainly recall Mr. Garrison to refute that idea."

After Slayton rested the bar's case, Lisa, Joe and Anderson returned to the cramped side room, and as soon as the door closed behind them Joe said he wasn't planning to testify. "There's no need," he told them. "I'll come off as a dolt and a grifter." He stared at the floor, kicking at the carpet with the toe of his black wingtip. "Plus I'll get hammered by the boat CD. Shit." He shook his head. "You know, I wish everyone hadn't come to support me. Losing my law license won't be the worst part of this. Nope. It doesn't hold a candle to my friends seeing this debacle and leaving here thinking I'm a crook, twenty years straight down the fucking tubes."

"You at least have to deny it, Joe," Lisa urged him. "You can't just roll over. Sheriff Perry is here and can confirm *he* found the will at Lettie's and it left her estate to you. I'll swear the CD is cut and pasted."

"Phil's welcome to announce I deny all wrongdoing or some such, but I worry it'll only be worse if I sit there with nothing more than my word against tapes and documents—and hell, a very real set of phone calls to Benecorp—and trot out feeble denials and a string of 'yeah, but' hedges. 'Yeah, that's me talking to Pichler, but . . .' 'Yeah, that's me demanding five million, but . . .' 'Yeah, my wife was in Nassau the day the money was withdrawn, but . . .' No thanks. I'll keep the tiny speck of dignity I still have and not look like every other desperate defendant."

Lisa began crying, and Joe told her it was okay, hung his arm around her. "I can't believe this," she sobbed.

When—after less than ten minutes of deliberation—the panel gave its unanimous decision suspending Joe's privilege to practice law in the Commonwealth of Virginia pending a full hearing, his expression didn't change, held stable and inscrutable, and it was only after the chairman announced the panel found it prudent to also examine Lisa Stone's role in the dealings with Benecorp that Joe cinched his face and slammed the table with his fist and shouted "Bullshit!" and landed himself in deeper trouble, drew a warning from a capitol cop.

"Keep your head up," Joe told her as they were walking to their car. "I didn't do a fucking thing wrong."

She took his hand. "No, you didn't. I couldn't be more proud of you."

CHAPTER TWENTY-EIGHT

During the drive home from Richmond, around South Boston, near the stretch of fast-food joints and gas stations, Joe's cell phone sounded and he pressed the green Send button, accepted the call.

"So you took the Fifth," Toliver declared. "Didn't testify."

"Word travels fast," Joe said. He was driving, steered with one hand, held the phone in the other.

"Not really, chief. I was there."

"Oh, okay. I didn't see you."

"I was in the hall to begin with. Too many lawyers clogging the room. I finally made it in. Had a good view to see Seth Garrison come upside your head with a two-by-four. Pretty nasty."

"Yep."

"Yep," Toliver repeated.

"What brought you to Richmond?" Joe asked.

"I heard about the e-mail your fine wife sent. I told your lawyer I'd be a character witness for you. He thought I'd be helpful, though it seems we never got to that point. Besides, I'm still aggressively investigatin' this whole case."

"Oh . . . thanks for volunteering," Joe said.

"Bad day for the home team," Toliver noted. "Sorry."

"Oh well."

"How about I cheer you up? You ready? What do you call a criminal lawyer?"

"Beats me," Joe said.

"Redundant."

As soon as Joe finished with Toliver, Lisa called a Roanoke number, muttered "Pick up, pick up, pick up," while it rang.

"Hey," Billy Hamblin said when he answered on the fourth ring. "So? How'd the Richmond thing go?"

"Extremely poorly," Lisa told him. "Listen." She did her best to sound normal. "Any luck at all with my shoes? Certainly we have some news or a possibility. I'd really like to have them."

"No report," Hamblin replied. "Sorry. We're looking day and night for you. So far, nothing in stock at Charlotte or anywhere else."

"I thought you guys were the best personal shoppers in the business?" Lisa said impatiently. "How hard can it be to find a pair of blue Louboutins in my size?"

"We're on it, Lisa. We're doing all we can. I'm cracking the whip, believe me."

"Well, if we don't find them soon, I'll miss the party."

"Understood," Hamblin said. "Tell Joe I'm thinking about him. Sorry it didn't go well."

Three mornings later, despite not being able to practice law, Joe went to his office, and around ten, Betty brought him his mail, and she stacked his letters and magazines in a neat pile near the center of his blotter, didn't hand them to him even though he was sitting there watching her. On the bottom was an oversize envelope that was sealed with masking tape. There was no return information, the address was written in stilted, felt-tip print, and the postage was not metered—instead, two rows of mismatched stamps were stuck across the top-right corner, many of them in penny and nickel denominations. The postmark was from Greensboro, North Carolina. Joe immediately opened the envelope, and at first it seemed to be empty. He turned it upside down and shook it, and a half sheet of cheap stationery floated out:

> Lawyer Joe, S. Garrison tryed to kill me. I'm in danjer. Hiding.
> They stoll my med. Revelation 17:4 says the woman was dressed
> in purple and scarlet, and was glittering with gold, precious
> stones and pearls. She held a golden cup in her hand, filled with

abominable things and the filth of her adulteries. New site is
Wireclub/hobbys/drawing but use a nother computer. I will be
Tobysmom. Help! Remember the peekonknes.

Lettie

The writing was hers, as best he could tell, though several words
were shaky and sloppy. "Pee-kon-nes," he said, sounding the word.
"Pee-konknes." He read the letter again. "Shit. Pekingese. I can't spell
it, either." He called and left a message for Toliver, told him he had an
envelope and another letter and was in high hopes they could both
be checked for prints and DNA, the sooner the better—it was damn
urgent.

CHAPTER TWENTY-NINE

According to every Northern Virginia lawyer Phil Anderson and Robert Williams had contacted, Judge Dennis P. Klein was always—no exceptions—the smartest person in the courtroom, a nimble legal mind who, for kicks, taught constitutional law as an adjunct faculty member at George Washington University Law School and was all the more imposing because he still retained the residue of his native Brooklyn accent, chopped off an occasional vowel or whipped quickly through whole sentences if he became peeved or annoyed. He was unanimously regarded as a fair, thoughtful and scrupulous jurist, which is no doubt why the Supreme Court selected him to travel five hours from Arlington and preside over the case of *Joe NMN Stone v. Benecorp, Inc. et als.*

At the beginning of their motions hearing, Klein was professional and polite, mentioning how much he liked the Henry County Courthouse's architecture and thanking the bailiff for making him feel welcome in a new jurisdiction. Klein asked the lawyers for their names and wished them a good morning when they replied. "Let's take up this request by the plaintiff for additional time to answer discovery," he said after he'd finished with the preliminaries. "There's nothing unusual or difficult about the interrogatories, not that I can see. Why do you need a delay, Mr. Williams? In addition to the extension Mr. Nicholson has already graciously volunteered?"

Robert Williams stood. "Judge, perhaps I can short-circuit this. We just received some new information that will have a dramatic impact on our case. It will also determine whether we even require discovery. I'm not going to waste time squabbling about the interrogatories and requests for admission. Nor am I going to go through our original grounds for a modest delay."

"I read your motion," Klein told him, thumbing through the papers inside a stiff green folder. "So what's changed? I don't see anything new in here. Did I miss something recent?"

Williams stepped out from behind the counsel table. Joe was seated to his left, Phil Anderson at the opposite end. "Sir, we recently received a remarkable piece of information. We have every reason to believe Miss Lettie VanSandt is alive."

"The testator?" Klein asked. "The author of the will we're all here to debate?"

"Yes sir," Williams replied. "We're as flabbergasted as can be, but we hope to make her available to the Court and, of course, once that happens the complexion of this suit will change drastically. To state the obvious, much of why we're here becomes moot—neither Benecorp nor my client will own the VV 108 formula. If Miss VanSandt is alive, and we believe she is, then she is the owner of her Wound Velvet."

Edwin Nicholson walked to where Williams was standing. Anton Pichler and Mack MacDonald were still seated at the defendant's table. "Judge, the first we heard of Miss VanSandt's resurrection was around thirty minutes ago, and I have to say the timing and motives really cause my radar to alert. If Miss VanSandt is alive, I'm curious to know how the DNA from the female body found at her property matched up. I'm curious to know where she's been for months and months, and I'm really curious to learn why—exactly when the plaintiff appears to be in dire need of a delay—we suddenly hear this tale about wanting to check to see if she's truly deceased."

"Mr. Williams, what, precisely, does 'received information' mean?" Klein asked. "A thirdhand rumor she's living in a cave in Tora Bora? A sighting by a local at the Memphis Baskin-Robbins? Or did she appear in the flesh to you or your client?"

Williams smiled. He moved sideways, close enough to Nicholson that their shoulders nearly touched. "I understand the Court's concern. I certainly understand Benecorp's concern. Miss VanSandt has contacted both Mr. and Mrs. Stone. Mrs. Stone has personally met with her. A letter she recently sent to Mr. Stone has been analyzed by the state forensics lab in Roanoke, and the prints match those on Miss VanSandt's gun permit."

Nicholson shook his head theatrically. "Judge, as I understand matters, this fantastical report of a meeting comes from Mr. Stone's wife and law partner. His coactor in collecting my client's money from an offshore bank. As for the so-called print match, the new prints came from a half sheet of paper provided by Mr. Stone. The same Mr. Stone who represented Miss VanSandt for years and no doubt has files full of her paperwork. Am I the only person who thinks that's convenient? A little *scrap* of paper? Of course, none of our experts have had a chance to check the prints or the handwriting."

"So where is she?" Klein demanded.

"We're not certain," Williams said, but there was no hesitancy, no chagrin in his voice. "However, we plan to present her to the Court. In person."

"A death certificate and a DNA analysis confirm that Lettie VanSandt is deceased," Klein said. "How do you explain away those facts?"

Williams leaned forward and gestured at Pichler. "Judge, I think perhaps the issue of how her death was manipulated is best answered by the defendants. Or by Miss VanSandt herself."

"So you're planning to produce a person who claims to be VanSandt?" Klein asked. "Then what, we play twenty questions and compare old yearbook photos?"

"Here's our proposal," Williams offered. "And let me give the Court a brief bit of history and context. Miss VanSandt is eccentric, and that's putting it mildly. She was—well, is—a local character. She's very, very different. We now know that she believed the arrival of Benecorp's representatives was a biblical sign. If the Court would like, we can play a 911 call from Miss VanSandt that occurred as a result—"

"Judge Klein," Nicholson interrupted, "none of this has been raised in pleadings, it's all conjecture and hearsay, and we're just being ambushed. We had no notice of any of this."

"I apologize for that," Williams said. "I do. I will say, in our defense, that the state expert only provided the print report late yesterday, and it was done as a priority rush job. If the Court would prefer, I can put this all down on paper, and we can leave and give Mr. Nicholson time to review it and respond, and then set another hearing."

"Which would only serve to grant them the delay they're so anxious to have," Nicholson complained. "They're stalling because if they answer discovery truthfully, this nonsensical case will be dismissed."

"Let me hear what Mr. Williams has for us," Klein said. "I'm still on the skeptical side of the fence as well, and I'll certainly protect the defendants' interests if we somehow reach the point of my taking this seriously. I might simply listen to counsel's colorful narrative and be done with the whole issue."

"Miss VanSandt," Williams continued, "truly believed that the arrival of Benecorp on her doorstep signaled apocalyptic events. That's not conjecture. I have the recording here with me and will be glad to play it. We have the records custodian from the 911 office on standby if authenticity is a problem. We have an extra copy for the defendants."

"Okay, I have a lady who thinks the world's about to end." Klein folded his arms over his chest. "A lady you admit is not exactly . . . normal . . . in terms of her personality."

"She's afraid of Benecorp. Frightened. She feels threatened. She—"

Nicholson objected again. "How do we know any of this?" he demanded. "This is entirely cut from whole cloth."

"Judge, if we can't prove it, then we expect you will have no problem handling matters appropriately. As I volunteered, if Mr. Nicholson would like for us to jump through all the formal hoops, we'll be more than happy to. We can adjourn and I can write all this down for him."

"I'll note your continuing objection," Klein told Nicholson.

"Essentially, Miss VanSandt went into hiding. I'm guessing the defendants will scoff and object and complain about this fact as well, but we can also offer proof from several witnesses that Benecorp played very similar hardball with a man by the name of Dr. Steven Downs, a Benecorp employee who was instrumental in discovering the value of the VanSandt formula. Downs and Miss VanSandt were friends, and she had every reason to believe she would receive the same gross intimidation that Dr. Downs suffered. Benecorp constantly followed and harassed him, and we have the Henry County sheriff available to confirm this. Dr. Downs is now dead."

Judge Klein removed his arms from across his chest. "So you're claiming VanSandt fled because she was fearful of Benecorp?"

"Yes."

"And another individual by the name of Dr. Downs—who had a connection to her formula, or whatever you want to call it—was being bothered by Benecorp, which would justify her fear?"

"Precisely," Williams replied.

"I hate to interrupt," Nicholson said, wagging a finger to emphasize the important correction he was about to make, "but I'm far more familiar with Dr. Downs than anyone else here. He was the subject of numerous police interventions and court orders. He was unbalanced and had threatened Mr. Garrison. Mr. Garrison had him watched as a matter of legitimate self-protection. Dr. Downs is dead because, unfortunately, he took his own life. I have a cache of court orders and police reports I'd be pleased to share with the Court—simply put, Dr. Downs was dangerous and a threat to my client, and we have the paperwork to establish that. How Downs's years of misconduct have any bearing on Mr. Stone's dishonesty and fraud is beyond me. Mr. Williams's sinkhole keeps growing and growing. Soon it will swallow the entire room, all of us included."

"Have the bailiff pass your information to me," Klein said. "But at least we finally have a point of agreement: Dr. Downs, mentally ill or not, was of interest to Benecorp, and now he's deceased."

Williams continued the instant Klein stopped speaking. "And his death only confirmed Miss VanSandt's suspicions. Whether there is any legitimate reason for her being afraid really isn't our issue. We concede Miss VanSandt is erratic and very much her own woman. The point is, Your Honor, we can demonstrate that she was afraid. We can present you with evidence of the world as seen from her perspective, which will explain her disappearance."

"So when do I get to meet her?" Klein challenged.

"Here's our proposal," Williams answered. "We believe she is extremely paranoid at this point. She's very fragile. On the verge of full collapse. She would physically meet with the Court, but only the

Court. Fair or not, she believes Benecorp and Mr. Garrison mean to do her harm. She wants her whereabouts kept secret. So she will meet with you, Judge, at a Virginia location you and you alone select and communicate to us twenty-four hours in advance. The attorneys will watch and participate via closed-circuit video and audio. She will not, however, agree to being in the same space with anyone connected to Benecorp, even my esteemed colleagues. She especially does not want her son in the room with her, inasmuch as she feels he betrayed her and has sided with the defendants."

"How the heck will that accomplish anything?" Nicholson snorted. "Judge Klein, gifted as he is, won't be able to discern whom you've run in on him. He's never met this woman, nor have I. This is a wild-goose chase and a distraction. Come on, Mr. Williams."

"She can't disguise her DNA, and we propose to have her son in the building at the same time, along with a lab tech, and we'll do the DNA test there and then. We only ask that it be done immediately, while you watch and wait, Judge. We worry that if the saliva leaves your sight, Benecorp has the reach and resources to taint it. We also request that there be two labs, and that the Court select them both without letting us know their identities until after the tests are completed. Mr. Stone will pay all costs associated with the testing. He will pay for Neal VanSandt's transportation to the site."

"Now there's some judicial adventure," Klein said. "Sounds more entertaining than the usual picking fly dung from discovery pepper. What do you think, Mr. Nicholson?"

"I think it's wrongheaded and bizarre. Most important, if this woman is in fact alive, we should have a right to depose her, question her and have her subject to cross-examination at trial."

"Two points," Williams said. "First, if Miss VanSandt is alive, there won't *be* any trial, much less any cross-examination. Exactly what would you ask her, Mr. Nicholson? 'You sure we can't just keep your billion-dollar invention, ma'am?'" Williams paused, slightly bowed his head. He looked directly at Klein. "But to sweeten the bargain, we've already answered the majority of the defendants' requests for admission, document productions and interrogatories. In particular, we have admitted virtually all the document-intensive issues, such that the trial will be streamlined and Benecorp's evidentiary load will be lightened. We will agree that Mr. Garrison's testimony from the disciplinary hearing can be read to the trial jury by transcript if they would prefer to save him a trip to Henry County. We have admitted the authenticity of all bank documents. We have admitted that Mrs. Stone was in Nassau on the day in question. We have admitted the phone calls to Mr. Pichler are true and accurate recordings. We agree they can simply hand that information to the jury without any further foundation or proof. We will tender that signed and sworn discovery to the Court, but ask it not be considered formally filed and entered as a part of the record until we have a chance to produce Miss VanSandt."

"Have you answered or responded to every single item?" Nicholson asked.

"No," Williams replied. "We both know a few interrogatories simply aren't proper, and we can revisit those if Miss VanSandt doesn't appear. We've disputed a couple production requests, and several minor questions we just haven't gotten around to answering. But my goodness, we're giving you documents from Bahamian banks you probably couldn't establish otherwise. We're conceding entire chunks of your counterclaim. Stated differently, we're giving you ninety percent of why we're here today in exchange for a few weeks' delay. More to the point, it doesn't serve either side's interest to litigate a case for absolutely no reason. If Miss VanSandt is alive, we're spinning our wheels."

"So Judge Klein won't misconstrue your generosity, I think I'm accurate in saying that Mr. Anderson has visited the Nassau bank and spoken with the manager, Mr. Pinder, who confirmed the Bahamian end of the transaction. While we appreciate not having to get Mr. Pinder here in person, let's be clear that you're not giving us much of anything—we all understand that Mr. Pinder will vouch for the accuracy of the Bahamian documents."

Klein set both elbows on the smooth wooden ledge in front of him. He arranged his chin on two loose fists. "Does Section 8.01-271.1 ring a bell, Mr. Williams?" he asked.

Williams chuckled. "Oh, yes."

"Good. Good to hear. I'll give you your chance to bring Miss

VanSandt back to life, but if you don't pull that necromancy off, well, then you and your client will be looking at sanctions, both monetary and evidentiary. You'll pay all attorneys' fees and costs for Benecorp related to this grand detour, plus a punitive amount. Every dime, from mileage to lunch to tolls. I'll hold the discovery you've submitted in abeyance, but should Miss VanSandt remain unavailable, you and your client will pay all costs associated with any subsequent discovery hearings."

"We understand," Williams replied.

"One more ground rule," Klein added, still propped on his elbows. "Should this go awry, or prove to be a hoax, I plan to grant other 'appropriate sanctions' as the law allows in terms of the trial proper. You will start well behind the eight ball, if not underneath it."

"Acknowledged," Williams said.

"Note our objection," Nicholson added.

Klein took down his elbows and sat normally. "Now, Mr. Williams, I want you to file a formal written motion containing everything you just told me and ask for a delay. I also want you to file a formal written request for production from a person not a party and have it served on Miss VanSandt, or accepted by her at the time of her test. We'll see if she indeed consents. As you requested, this will simply be judicially supervised discovery, no more and no less. Since Neal VanSandt is a party, he's expressly subject to Rule 4:10, and it would seem he'll have to produce a sample, though he and his lawyer will have an opportunity to respond and be heard if he objects."

"Yes sir," Williams replied. "Understood."

"I'll simply postpone ruling on our other issues and the various motions until we see how this resolves," Klein said. He finger-scrolled through a smartphone, spoke while he was still reviewing the screen. "The big show will take place on September twenty-eighth at four in the afternoon. I'll confirm the labs, location and particulars the day before so we can arrange for the video."

"Judge, one final request," Williams said. "As odd as this may sound, even though this isn't being done in court per se, could you please wear your robe? My client thinks it might help calm and reassure Miss VanSandt."

"Why not?" Klein answered. "Would she like me to don a powdered wig and buckle shoes as well?" "Pahduhedwig" was how it sounded when he said it, the words and syllables rolled into one quick burst.

"What a bizarre day," Joe remarked as they were returning to their office from the hearing with Judge Klein. It was raining, drab, damp, the sky a uniform, foggy gray. The first cool pinch of fall was mixed with the wet air. "Hard to believe summer's gone. Found the first cocklebur in Sadie's forelock yesterday. My granddad always said that meant fall was coming. It was spring when 'the buds were the size of a possum's ear.'"

"Robert did a great job for us," Lisa said quietly. "And we seem to have a fair judge."

"What are the odds of pulling this off? Of her paranoid ass showing up?" Joe frowned. "We have a few weeks to get her to a precise spot at a precise time, and we basically have no reliable way to even contact her."

"But she's been more consistent and talkative on Wireclub. Three exchanges in two days, and she's supposedly on board for the DNA test. She agreed—otherwise I never would've allowed Robert to make our pitch to Klein. Oh—instead of walking to the coffee shop every five minutes to use their computer, I've recruited the manager to check the Wireclub site during the day and let me know if there're any new posts."

"He probably thinks you're having an affair or hiding money from me." Joe was driving. They were coasting into a red light, and he glanced across the interior at his wife. "At least I figure Lettie's actually out there somewhere—who else would've known about the lewd Pekingese joke? She told it to me at our office a month before she went missing. Of course, I'd feel a ton better if I could figure out *how* she's not dead. Either Benecorp bribed a lab employee or there's a colossal mistake or Lettie and Vic Frankenstein have been doing some grave robbing. At first I thought it was strange that Agent Hatcher delivered the items to be tested, but the sheriff told me he asked Hatcher to drop them off since the little wannabe was heading home to Roanoke anyway."

"Hatcher's a jerk, but why would Garrison stage her death if he really sent people to kill her?"

"Beats me," Joe said.

"How's it go?" Lisa asked. "The joke."

"You don't want to hear it," he said ruefully but managed a tiny smile. They were stopped at an intersection. Nearby, a sandwich shop had closed and left its building empty. A letter was missing from the restaurant's sign. FRI AYS SUBS it read, a blank where the D used to be.

CHAPTER THIRTY

"Glitches and gremlins," Phil Anderson quipped. "The logistics of the DNA test are proving to be an unexpected bear." He and Robert Williams were with the Stones in their conference room. "Lettie's big event is scheduled to go in a week, at four o'clock," he continued. "Nicholson and I conference-called Judge Klein this morning. Nothing's ever easy in our business, is it? Seems DNA comparison isn't quite as simple as a drug analysis or a Breathalyzer. Based on what Klein's clerk has learned, we're looking at two days minimum for the results, and the lab is stationary. The best they could do would be to send a tech to collect the swabs. The judge says the amplification alone—whatever that is—takes several hours. There's robot extraction and computers and all kinds of rocket-science mumbo jumbo. I've had my paralegal researching reputable labs and DNA techniques—we need to be aware of any vulnerabilities in the process—and he basically confirmed Klein's information."

"I'm embarrassed not to have known," Williams said sheepishly. "We, uh, just see the certificates in the court file. We check chain of custody and talk to the tech. They make it sound quick and routine."

"Yeah, I thought it was faster than forty-eight hours," Joe said. "I can remember the commonwealth's attorney asking for rush jobs, and I just assumed it would be a few hours, half a day tops. I didn't know, either. It's not on our end of things."

"This is a serious setback," Lisa said. "Bad news. Damn. The lab might spook Lettie. Will Klein still monitor it? Will he be there in person?" She squeezed her eyes shut, kept them closed. "And how in the world do we secure the samples and protect the whole testing procedure?" She opened her eyes. "We absolutely can't chance leaving the saliva unattended on some tech's desk for hours—Benecorp would have a field day."

"I hear you," Anderson agreed.

"So?" Joe asked.

"Here's the new program, pending your approval," Anderson said. "You gotta like Klein—at least he's creative and has a sense of humor. We'll only run a single test, not two. He'll use the state forensics lab in Manassas. So much for keeping the lab's identity under wraps. He'll be there to observe everything as we originally discussed. After the swabs are taken from Lettie and her son, each side can hire an expert or cop or whomever to babysit the samples, literally spend the night at the lab and monitor every step in the analysis. Since this intrusion itself will introduce a new variable into the state's security and the integrity of the thousands of samples already there, we'll have to pay overtime for the lab's own security to supervise our people and make sure they don't compromise anything. A lot of moving parts, but very doable. Believe it or not, Klein himself prevailed on the lab's director to make the exception for us."

"Why's that funny?" Joe asked. "Sounds nuts and bolts to me."

"Oh, yeah, sorry. Klein said to tell the resurrected Miss VanSandt that he'd be bringing his robe but not his pajamas. He doesn't plan to stay for the full two- or three-day testing process."

"Wow, better hold the pimp spot at the Comedy Corner," Joe remarked. "Hysterical."

"A high-water mark for a Virginia circuit judge, though," Anderson said. "What'd you expect? They aren't, generally speaking, a comedic group. And don't worry, I let on like he was the funniest dad-burned guy on the East Coast, made sure I outdid Nicholson with my belly laughs. I'm a full-service practitioner and a skilled sycophant. Cover all the bases for my clients."

"Lisa, can you make new arrangements with Lettie?" Williams asked. "Have you had any more contact?"

"It's always a crapshoot," Joe interrupted. "Lettie was pretty active for a while on Wireclub, and she agreed to the DNA plan; Lisa copied you both with that post. Now she's disappeared again. We've been sending up flares everywhere, even tried Token Rock's Facebook page. We'd always assumed Klein would run the test somewhere in Northern Virginia, so the plan is for Lisa to drive up the day before and scout things out and do her damnedest to find and protect our girl. It can't hurt to have Lisa on the ground where this is happening."

"You're the expert on all things VanSandt, Joe," Williams remarked. "You're her best friend. Hell, her only friend. If you can't manage her, it's a lost cause."

"Actually, she's very buddy-buddy with Lisa ever since she vanished. I'm off her favorites list these days for some reason."

"I realize," Anderson said, "that if she's as paranoid as I've be told, the last-minute change might rattle her. But the truth is—and the four of us understand this—there's rarely an important trial or huge case that doesn't have a crisis moment. A tree falls in narrow quarters, and we have to change plans and reroute the stagecoach through Tombstone. It's never routine, ever, no matter how many times you read the file and interview the client. You and Lisa need to convince Miss VanSandt that the run-up to court is frequently full of zigs and zags and amended pleadings and second acts and witnesses with mutating stories. We're fortunate here—we've got an engaged judge, we caught this early and we can correct the problem. I'm counting my blessings."

"Yeah," Williams agreed, "I hope this is the worst problem that comes along."

"So can I tell Klein you're signed off on this?" Anderson asked.

"Yes," Joe said.

"Not much choice," Lisa added unhappily.

"The video people will be here early on the twenty-eighth," Anderson noted. "They'll set up, connect everyone and check the audio and picture. Nicholson will be participating from Norfolk with MacDonald. Oh—the judge wants to move the time, to do it in the morning, so potentially there'll be only a single night at the lab before the results are ready. Klein also hinted the lab folks might be able to work past regular hours if they're close to a final report."

"Changing plans isn't great for us," Lisa cautioned him. "We need to keep as close to the original scenario as we can. How about we try to have Lettie there by eleven-thirty? That'll give us some margin of error if she needs persuading or is delayed. As it stands now, she's planning on four. We may never hear from her again."

"Eleven-thirty it is," Anderson said. "I'll shoot you the directions to the lab by e-mail. Robert and I will be here, at what, around eleven?"

"Fine by me," Williams answered. "Who do we send as our observer? Hell, who can we get there on such short notice?"

"Derek?" Anderson suggested.

"It's not so much about computers," Williams mused. "This is more in the subterfuge, black-arts department."

"Toliver," Joe said emphatically. "He'd be perfect. You agree, Lisa?"

"Yes. So long as he and Lettie don't cross paths and he's there just to safeguard the samples and watch the process. To mollify Lettie, we need this to come off as close to the original blueprint as possible. Lord only knows what she'll think if she sees Toliver sitting there with the judge. It's more likely than not she's had a feud with him some-where along the line, and we don't want another fly in the ointment."

"I'll contact him and see if he'll go," Williams said. "He's as good as we can hope for. And maybe we *should* have Derek in the vicinity too. I'm not sure how the test and analysis work, obviously, but it couldn't hurt to have him keep a cybereye on things."

"Okay," Joe said.

"This is it, guys," Anderson said. "All fair, all square, all in, all done before I drop the gavel and the bidding ends? No turning back after I confirm with Nicholson and the judge."

Joe hesitated. "Lisa?"

"Lock us in," she said.

Lisa went to bed early that night, frayed and fatigued at nine o'clock, and she didn't stir until the alarm buzzed at seven, woke with puffy eyes and red pillowcase marks lining her cheek. Joe was already in the bathroom, naked, his hair wet from the shower, standing in the mid-dle of the tile floor flossing his teeth, shaving cream dotting his ears, a red nick on his neck. His belly was slack, pooched, and he straightened and sucked taller when he saw her. "Looking sexy this morning," she teased him.

"Don't you know it. No way to keep it in check." He grinned. "When's the last time you slept until the clock went off?"

"I can't remember. It's been years. Maybe——" The bedroom phone rang, and she picked it up. Her expression quickly became excited, and she motioned in Joe's direction, frantic. "It's her," she whispered, almost hissing. "Hurry."

Joe took the phone. He'd left the bathroom and was standing in front of Lisa, a towel wrapped around his waist, watery tracks across the floor to where he'd stopped. "Hello?"

"It's me, Lawyer Joe. Lettie. Gotta talk quick before they can beam in on me. Listen, you need to meet me at Arnie Pruett's farm at five in the mornin' to carry me to the test. Five at Arnie's on the twenty-eighth, the day we go. Make sure you bring help and plenty of weapons." She pronounced the last word "wheapons."

"Okay. But Lettie, hold on, wait, don't say any——"

"And I need money. Send me a hundred dollars to the Western Union in Myrtle Beach. Under the name Sue Woods. Take the money from the case I won against them bastards in Salem. Them lightbulbs. *That* place. You with me? You understandin'?"

"Yep. Understood." Joe had turned the phone so Lisa could hear the voice on the other end. "Done," he said confidently.

"Five in the mornin'. Fingers crossed. *Adiós.*" There was a bump, as if she'd dropped the phone, and the call cut off.

"Was that her?" Lisa asked anxiously. "Could you tell?"

"It surely was," Joe said. "What a relief. What a friggin' relief." He did a little dance, flexing his knees and kicking his feet to the sides.

"Then we have fairly good news and also extremely troubling news—she's definitely alive and happy with the plan, but now Benecorp will be on her like nobody's business. They'll nab her when she tries to get the cash or meet at Arnie's. Two chances to derail us. She's walking right into their sights."

"Ask yourself," Joe said calmly, "why this paranoid, elusive, crazy-like-a-fox woman, who has been so scarce, who's only communicated by letter or the occasional chat room message, suddenly changes course and calls us and lays out her movements in detail. On our *home* phone, after alerting us to the fact she realizes the call's being traced and almost certainly intercepted."

"What's the number on the caller ID?"

"It's blocked, but that's not the point. Give her some credit. First, she hates Arnie, probably more than she hates anyone. She's barred from going on his property. He had her served with a no-trespass notice in 2010. That's a ruse. A decoy. It's the last place she'd pick."

Lisa nodded. "Ah, okay."

"As for the money, well, there is no money. The 'Salem bastards' would be the Salem True Value hardware store. She bought four economy lightbulbs there. The packaging claimed they'd last for a year. Lettie kept track of the hours she used a bulb—wrote it down on a calendar—and it burned out short of a year. Of course, then it was lawsuit or bust for her."

"Oh, yeah, I remember that fiasco."

"Salem is basically on the way to the lab. I have a feeling she'll be there, at the store in Salem, at five in the morning on the twenty-eighth. 'Fingers crossed' can also mean she's telling a lie, the way kids do, 'I had my fingers crossed behind my back.' She had to talk to me, because you wouldn't have known her history and picked up on her clues."

"All the free work and wasted time finally pay off," Lisa said. "The dividends have arrived." She smiled. "So what's the plan?"

"We send our private detective to watch the Western Union, just in case. At least Hamblin should be able to handle that, though he's been a hundred-and-fifty-bucks-an-hour waste so far. Next, we see if Trooper Harold will swing by the hardware store and take Lettie to Manassas for the test. I'll meet with him and explain the situation. There's nobody I trust more than Harold—he's steady and cagey and Dale Earnhardt in a police cruiser."

"I hope you're right, Joe. I hope you're not reading too much into her call."

"It was her, and she was trying to send us a message." He adjusted the towel. Water droplets speckled the floor, none of them quite the same shape. "I wish I didn't have to sit here like a knot on a log with my lawyers and could go with you to Manassas. Or with Harold. Those fuckers will have a wall around the lab, even with the distractions and misdirection."

"I'll walk over and share the good news with Robert. I'll make sure he and Phil realize how quiet we need to keep this. I may just drive to Roanoke and tell Phil in person rather than risking a call or e-mail."

"Lord, do I feel better. Yes. Now we're cooking with gas. Great googly moogly. We might actually pull this shit off."

CHAPTER THIRTY-ONE

On September 27, Lisa and Joe said goodbye to each other, and they hugged at the front door to their office of almost two decades, both of them apprehensive, and he insisted she take his .22 revolver along with her, stuck it in her purse beside the Mace, and she left their building with MapQuest directions for Manassas, a few minutes before noon. "Twenty-four hours, and we'll know," she told him over her shoulder. "Feast or famine."

"Be careful," he said. "Don't take any wooden nickels," he added, and she thought it was perfect Joe, corny and sincere and heartfelt . . . and damn smart advice.

She was positive that Garrison continued to track her, so she was careful about her appointment with Dr. Beasley, took precautions. After leaving Joe, she drove to Wild Magnolia restaurant, which was part of the same half-empty strip mall as the dentist's office. She went into the restaurant, found a booth and asked for a glass of sweet tea. She informed the server her husband would be there shortly, so she'd wait to order.

She wandered into the kitchen and while she was chatting with the owner—a garrulous, goateed fellow named Big Mike—and discussing the spices and seasoning in his voodoo shrimp, she abruptly apologized, grabbed her BlackBerry from her jeans pocket, pretended to study the caller's number and then staged a conversation with Joe. She listened and scowled and said, "I was worried about an injunction," and pointed at the red Exit sign, and Big Mike nodded it was okay, she could use that door. Walking off, she briefly smothered the cell with her empty hand and told Mike he didn't need to hold her table, and she was quick through the door and in the parking lot behind the building. She hustled past a large, humming heat pump and darted into the rear entrance at the dentist's office, locking the door behind her.

Dr. Blaine Beasley was round all over—round head, round glasses, round eyes, round hands, round frame, round ears. In college, his friends had nicknamed him the Planet. Following his 2007 divorce, he'd endured a stomach stapling and taken up with a horse trainer from Emporia, but neither lasted very long, so he was round and single again within a matter of months and now, at the age of forty-nine, he tended to his patients, played doubles tennis despite his gimpy knees and kept company with a bashful Georgia widow he'd met at the Martinsville Catholic church. When Lisa arrived, he was already in the treatment room, anxious and fidgety.

"Hey, Doc," she said cheerfully. "Ready to BeDazzle my smile?"

"I suppose. If you are." He fussed with the earpiece on his glasses, blinked. "You're sure about this?" He removed the glasses and began wiping the lenses with a handkerchief, the cleaning hurried and slapdash.

"The most important thing," she said solemnly, "is absolute confidentiality. No records, no reports, not a syllable to anyone, ever. Basically, as we discussed, your incredible favor might just help us correct some huge unfairness. We're really in a bind."

"You have my promise," he said. "There's nobody here but us. Office is locked. The staff's at lunch. For your fitting visit, your impression, we had you listed as a routine cleaning." He kept wiping his glasses, the white handkerchief practically flapping. "As far as I'm concerned, you saved my life. I truly believe that. My marriage was literally frickin' killing me." He put the glasses back on. "I know I was a wreck—and I'm still kinda embarrassed about how I acted during the divorce—but you treated me like, well, like family, and then got me an extremely fair result. If this will improve your circumstances, it's the least I can do. I can't imagine why it would, but I'm not a lawyer. I read that Joe has lost his license, and I'm guessing there's a connection somehow."

"Thank you," Lisa said.

"Have a seat. You'll be finished before you even realize it."

She slid onto an elongated vinyl chair, swinging her legs in last, crossing them at the ankles. The chair was orange, the room smelled antiseptic, the retractable light above the chair was harsh and clinical, already switched on. Beasley clipped a disposable towel around her neck and adjusted the chair until her head was tilted and slightly higher than her feet. She heard a motor whir while she was being positioned and a forceful, mechanical, pressurized pop when it cut off.

"Okay, I'm going to numb you," Beasley said. "Open for me." He was seated on a roller stool, and he planted a heel and jockeyed between her and a tray full of instruments, agile with the extra three legs despite his size, the movements second nature, ingrained. He came closer to her face, wearing a green mask. "Relax. Turn a bit my way. This is a dose of topical." He was confident and steady, all the senseless energy gone, his instruction to her calm, practiced, direct. He dabbed at her gum with a Q-tip, all around the tooth he'd be coloring, and she tasted a faint, bitter patch at the tip of her tongue. The very first cotton touch caused her to tense.

"There we go," he said. "Nothing to it."

"Yeah," she murmured.

"It works fairly quick," he noted. "In case you were wondering, your teeth look great," he added, killing time, waiting for the topical to dull her. "You're lucky."

Lisa didn't say anything.

"Little baby stick," he warned after returning from another swerve and slide to reach the tray.

She felt the needle pierce her skin and the lidocaine surge into her gum and trace along her tooth and its roots and fill the socket space, the painkiller cool, strong, rapid, and the dentist jiggled her lip and pressed and massaged and reset the needle and shot in more numbing, and it immediately pushed a path across her cheek and toward her ear, and she caught herself trying to bite down, and she squirmed and she sucked the best breath she could and shut her eyes, moved her hands from her lap to the chair's arms. Beasley tapped her gum with his sheathed finger, finished with the needle and dropped it on the silver tray, a *clank* interrupting the silent room when it landed.

"We okay?" he asked, though he was already reaching for the next tool.

"Umm-hmmmm," Lisa replied.

"Let's give the lidocaine a little time."

He waited a couple minutes, the room still awkwardly quiet, neither of them speaking, and then the analgesic took hold and spread, a creeping, tingling insulation that divided off a portion of her mouth and gum. He tested the effects, probing and pushing. She felt the pressure but nothing else, no sensation.

"You should be numb. Can you feel that?"

"Nuh."

He instructed her to make sure she kept her mouth open as wide as possible, and she watched as a gold veneer came toward her, disappearing into the light and her watery focus, her eyes stymied by the glare, her vision off-track, myopic, aimed at the ceiling.

She heard a tool scrape against enamel, and she noticed Beasley's concentration, his tightly pinched forehead above the mask. He inched closer, and she saw thick eyebrows connected by a scant black isthmus spreading across the top of his nose, the hairs magnified as if she were looking at him in an illuminated makeup mirror.

"I think we're good," he said. "Swallow, please." He suctioned her mouth with his free hand and wiped her chin with a gauze pad. "I'm going to have to shave the veneer a teeny-tiny bit." He used a small grinder that sounded like an electric bee when it touched the gold covering, then suctioned all around her mouth again.

She shifted her eyes to avoid the light.

Twice he forced the veneer into place and removed it and shaped it with the grinder. "All right," he finally said after he inserted the covering for the third time and pressed and pushed and pried. "Consider yourself formally grilled." He handed her a mirror. "How does it feel?"

"Fine. My mouth's numb, but that's about it." She smiled so she could see the tooth. "Thanks, Blaine."

"It's a temp and might feel a little strange. I didn't want to rough the enamel for the bonding any more than absolutely necessary, and I didn't want to damage your other teeth or gum trying to make it fit perfect. And it's not aligned like it should be, but you said that wasn't a big concern." Beasley checked his watch. "We're under ten minutes," he said. "Ahead of schedule." He was already walking out while he spoke, in a hurry, and she could hear his rubber-soled shoes squeaking on the floor as he waddled away.

"Fucking Seth Garrison," she mumbled, but not loud enough for Beasley to hear, and she trailed him down the hall, toward the door.

"That's it, I suppose," Beasley told her when they reached the exit.

"Blaine, please let me pay you," she said. "I brought cash. I can't let you go in the hole because you're doing me a favor. I realize gold's expensive, though you can have it back once I'm through."

He smiled. "It's not real gold, Lisa. And I'll charge you the exact same you charged me for all the mother henning and mitten tying and hours of midnight counseling. Or better yet, perhaps this will bring us even."

"More than even," she said.

"Promise me this, please." He leaned toward her. "You . . . take care of yourself, okay?"

"Definitely."

"And I can't help saying it, and it'll never go past these walls, but Lord help us all, don't raise Lettie VanSandt from the dead any longer than absolutely necessary." He twisted the dead bolt. "I'm sorry; I just couldn't resist." He smiled, and somehow even that was round. "Let's have one more quick peek at how everything fits before you leave— open for me." He clicked a penlight and aimed it at her mouth.

Wearing sunglasses, she stepped from Beasley's office onto the sidewalk and immediately spotted the truck, a white Ford F-150 with a trailer hitch and Harley decals displayed across the cab's rear window. She walked to the passenger side and climbed in. "Hey, Lloyd," she said.

"Long time no see, Mrs. Stone," Lloyd Burnette answered. His voice was deep, a salted, drawling baritone. "Can't say I'm unhappy 'bout that. No offense." He cranked the engine, and they drove toward the highway.

"None taken."

"Danville Holiday Inn? That still the plan?"

"Yes," she said.

"Okeydokey." Burnette was barely forty, but he looked considerably older, his face so lined and creased it appeared crosshatched in spots. "Fair to say I ain't never been to no motel with a woman looks as nice as you."

"Thanks for the compliment."

"The truth is the truth," he said, keeping his eyes directly on the road. "Your car safe at the mall?"

"I parked near the gym. It's open twenty-four hours a day, so people are usually around and the car won't be too noticeable."

"I shoulda knowed you were on top of that."

"So can you do the tattoos?" she asked. "I mean, how closely can you imitate them?"

Burnette's hair was pulled into a graying ponytail. He was wearing a black T-shirt from a motorcycle rally in Sturgis. The shirt was full and tight at his belly. "Well, I done my stencils. Some of them designs you want me to copy is quality. Some is crap. A few pieces I'll just do freehand. My big problem is havin' it not look brand spankin' new, 'specially what with me airbrushin' it. From the pictures you sent me, there's a few parts and designs that I can't see how they finish; as I understand it, I can just leave 'em blank. The nose rings is clip-ons, but you can't tell unless you was to yank on 'em or come right up to a person's face."

"On a one to ten, how similar will it be? Your best guess."

He chuckled. "The designs and the art, I'll give you an eight, maybe nine. If you or someone who don't know the trade was to look at it, you probably ain't gonna notice no difference. A pro'd see it. The color's the bitch. But I got some tricks, okay? I worked on my paints, and we'll wash 'em good, and the dragon—the dragon is real old, best I can tell—him we'll scrub with a little mineral oil."

"I appreciate your coming," she told him.

"No problem." He grinned. "Nice tooth."

"How long will it take you?" she asked.

"Good long stretch. Three hours, maybe four. I'll let everything cure and finish it early of a morning. I can spend the night in my truck and keep a lookout for you."

"No, please, I booked a separate room for you. I'd feel awful if you stayed all night in your truck."

"Like I said, I'll be in the truck. I wouldn't want somethin' happenin' to you, not on my watch, and I figure this is at least a little risky. Some favor that'd be, me lettin' you wind up in a bad spot."

"Thank you." Lisa was watching the car beside them, checking her surroundings, on alert for any kind of tail or surveillance. "Please, Lloyd, this stays between us. That's important. Not even Joe can know."

"What the hey, Mrs. Stone. Yeah. You done told me once. That's all the remindin' I need. I'm with the program."

"Sorry."

"Happy to help. You and your old man damn well done me good. I'd probably still be inkin' cons and learnin' gang tats if it wasn't for you. I owe you guys. You was court-appointed too. Most times, people in my situation get a lick and a promise. I ain't so much as smoked a joint since. Married to a fine lady. Bought me a house. My tattoo shop is keepin' me fed. I started a little seamless-gutter business on the side. I learnt my damn lesson."

"Glad to hear it."

"Not many people woulda give me a hundred bucks, either. Did you know that? I was broke as a joke. Mr. Stone was fearful I'd wind up in another mistake, and he handed me the cash last time I was in your office. October ninth, 2007. Day I walked free. Yep. Took me damn near three months, but I repaid it." Burnette held up the arm closest to Lisa. The date was tattooed on his biceps in elaborate script, an eagle perched on the O in October.

"Has it been four years?" Lisa said quietly.

"We're gettin' old," Burnette said. They passed a church and a convenience store made entirely of field rock. "Joe still pussyfootin' 'round on his little scooter?" He grinned.

"Uh, yeah."

"Damn, ma'am, that needs correctin'."

That night, after Burnette finished painting her and returned to his truck, Lisa couldn't sleep, but she didn't dare take a pill, not even a partial Ativan, was determined to be alert and focused for the DNA session. She stretched out on the hotel bed, wearing a tank top and pajama bottoms, underneath a coarse sheet, her iPod playing Donna the Buffalo songs, a dingy hotel mug full of hot tea on the floor beside her, and she leafed through an old photo album she'd brought along to keep her company, pictures of Joe and her from law school, Joe and puppy Brownie posing in front of a Christmas tree, a Mardi Gras party at Chatmoss Country Club, and several pages of Joe as a child, her favorite shot an off-center, black-and-white snap of him, knee-high to his grandpa, the two of them standing on a rural stoop, a screen door behind them, a wrought-iron *S* dead in the heart of the door, the 1960s, Joe the boy beaming, pointing joyously at a bag of rock salt and an honest-to-goodness ice-cream churn.

She called Joe and told him she was in Manassas at her hotel with nothing unusual to report. She mentioned the sweet photo of him, he and his grandfather getting ready to make ice cream, and told him he was adorable when he was a lad. She loved him; she told him that, too.

She dozed for a couple hours at most, woke when it was barely dawn and started the in-room coffee, jittery as she'd ever been in her life, and as she was reaching into the minifridge for creamer, she registered her cartooned arm and the crazy black and chartreuse nails she'd painted, her own arm foreign, a changeling limb. She checked her watch. "Please, Derek," she said aloud. "Come on." According to their schedule, he was supposed to have called before now, last night at the absolute latest.

Hansen had assured her he was smarter than Garrison's flunkies and that his call to her BlackBerry would be secure. He'd doctored the software in his own cell, and even if Benecorp somehow managed to penetrate his "moats and catapults," he promised her the crooks would be listening to gibberish. "We'll be long gone, and they'll still be campaigning in Eberron, lost and bewildered," he boasted.

Her phone rang at 7:15, but it was Robert Williams letting her know that Judge Klein's law clerk had heard—yesterday—from a woman claiming to be Lettie VanSandt, though even the caller's gender was up in the air, because whoever it was had used a voice modulator and sounded, according to the judge's mordant explanation, "like Satan in the fourth installment of a horror movie franchise, when all the original actors are gone and the budget's kaput."

"He seemed entirely skeptical," Williams said. "He also wasn't happy that a witness in a high-stakes suit had contacted his office, even just to confirm the time."

"At least she's still on schedule," Lisa said. "Thank heavens. But how the heck would she have a voice modulator? And why? That's weird. And suspicious."

"Not really. You can download the software onto your phone for free. My grandkids love it."

"That still doesn't explain *why*."

"Are we a hundred percent committed to this, Lisa?" he asked. "Is Joe positive it was her on the phone?"

"He is. And now she's contacted the judge, so we're as good as can be expected. We'll see how the day goes and hope for the best."

"My instincts tell me this'll end badly for us. I'm worried that Benecorp might've staged this and had a plant call so you'd seem devious and unreliable when your absurd tale falls apart."

"Hell, Robert, we're already so far behind, why would they bother?"

"Garrison's a schemer—we've certainly learned that much. At any rate, this stinks to high heaven. And assuming the state somehow botched the autopsy and the DNA match, and assuming she's still alive, she's such a blatant lunatic we can't count on her. She might think the Purple Whore has broken the last seal, or ever how all that unfolds, and disappear off the charts again. I'd say the odds of her acting rationally aren't in our favor."

"We're far too invested now," Lisa said. "No other choices left. She's alive and, yeah, she's crazy, but our best and only chance is getting her spit on a lab slide. Simple as that." Lisa glanced at her coffee. "No hard feelings," she said. "I understand completely if you want to withdraw, Robert. We don't want to drag you down with us if Lettie doesn't show."

He made a sound that was equal parts sigh and snort. "I bought the round-trip ticket. I'm planning on taking the whole ride, regardless of where it goes. Anyway, Klein will rain on you guys more than he will on me. I'm only the mouthpiece."

"I'm trying to be optimistic," Lisa said.

"If that changes, call me first, you hear?" Williams said. "Oh—also learned yesterday that Benecorp's expert determined the handwriting on Joe's letter isn't Lettie's. Just so you'll know."

"Handwriting experts are a dime a dozen and easy to buy," she said.

"Especially if you're Benecorp. Nothing new there. Doesn't mean a thing to me. Joe said it looked genuine to him. I saw her, and Joe talked to her, so their hired-gun flunky can say whatever the hell he wants."

She microwaved her coffee, and added more creamer, and lit a cigarette in the bathroom and switched on the wheezing exhaust fan to suck away the smoke, and then her phone rang again and the ID showed 800 in the area code, the word SEARS beneath the string of numbers.

"Hello?" she said tentatively, dropping the cigarette in the john.

"Mrs. Stone?"

"Yes."

"This is Overbyte."

"Overbyte? Is it safe to talk?"

"No worries—we're completely Bat-phoned and secure."

"How do I know it's really you?" Lisa asked.

"Esquivel, fried chicken, cabbage and mayo. Poplin suits. Nifty socks. You wore a peacock pin to the diner in Fieldale, different-colored stones in the tail. Satisfied?"

"How much are we paying you?" she asked.

"Four-oh-one. As in hundred per hour. Five now. I don't see why we couldn't just meet face-to-face like we did before."

"I have my reasons," she said. "The face part might be a bit tricky."

"Whatever," he said. "You're the ringmaster."

"Okay. So are you done?" she asked. "Please tell me you are."

"Done," Hansen answered.

"And?"

"Well, I have the classic good-news, bad-news report."

"Oh, damn, Derek, we're out of time. You were supposed to call last night."

"Hold your pee, okay? Quit freaking. I have the prize. Plus lagniappe I really didn't need to discover."

"Bad news first," she said. "How bad?" she added without waiting for him to respond. She searched the room for her purse, spotted it on the bathroom counter next to the sink.

"The bad news is that Hamburglar was caught. Not caught caught, but they know they've been hacked. There'll be digital footprints. To translate it for your purposes, imagine a couple of tower guards were shooting at me as I fled in my Aston Martin."

"But you know what the Wound Velvet does?" she asked. She grabbed her pack of Marlboro Ultra Lights from the purse, shook one from the opening, lit it, inhaled. She tossed the pack on the counter.

"I do," Hansen said emphatically. "But I have to hand it to Garrison, or whoever designed their system, it's a superior mousetrap. Of course I was rushed and in a hurry, thanks to your deadline. I'm embarrassed to have set off the damn alarms. It's clichéd, but I was to the 'cut the blue wire or cut the red wire' point and was tired as hell and running out of time, so I guessed, and the fifty percent probability didn't trend my way. Another week—or three days even—and I would've been invisible."

"Well, it's not the end of the world, as long as we have the disease. What does it cure?"

"If they can trace it to me, it might be the end of *my* world," Hansen complained. "This would be what you people call a criminal act. Let's not forget about the hired help when, crappy possibility number one, Benecorp's ninjas come hunting me with Tasers and garrotes or, crappy possibility number two, the feds show up at my apartment and the local news does the money shot of some mesomorph with a badge palming my head so I don't bang the Crown Vic's roof."

"Oh, okay, right, I see your problem," she said. "Sorry."

"I'm extremely well hidden, and I don't think they can pin me down, but these people aren't stupid. I used proxy on top of proxy and worked from an Internet café—two different locations, actually—so I *should* be safe, but you never know. Or they might suspect me because I'm on your payroll."

"We'll do whatever we can," Lisa promised.

"Which is basically nothing," he replied.

"Well, we can help you legally. Or hook you up with the best lawyers in the business. We'd certainly pay any attorney's fees."

"So you'll never believe what the VV 108 does." Hansen emphasized the last word.

"I'm waiting," she said.

"The project's called Werewolf. Want to guess?"

"No. Cut it out, please, Derek. Just tell me."

"Before Drew Carey dazzles you with the hot tub showcase, here's the bonus news. I found Miss VanSandt's dogs and cats. Well, I didn't actually locate them, since your big-hearted nemesis Seth Garrison killed them all. Every single animal."

"What? Why?"

"According to the file memo, Garrison at first thought the pets might have a genetic trait or something unique or some blood characteristic that was essential to the formula. He's a methodical bastard. Early on, they hit a few bumps replicating the Wound Velvet. They took soil, plants, tree bark, you name it. Canned soup, frozen meat, water from every spigot."

"How cruel," Lisa said. "And how typical."

"The guy who came for the animals is basically Garrison's security goon. Not his top muscle, but sort of a lieutenant. They debated just swooping in and rolling it Entebbe style and rounding up the critters, but decided they might not be able to corral them all and were afraid a neighbor or your local busybody might interfere or notify the cops, so they sent their hoodlum in a fake uniform and prepped Neal with the cover story. Once they learned there was no connection or value, Don—whose real name is Donnie Antonelli—shot the animals. Or as they put it, 'euthanized them with a sidearm.' A loose thread clipped for Benecorp. They dumped the remains in a landfill."

"We knew from the drop Beverly was crooked," Lisa said.

"I've been as busy as Ryan Seacrest on this. So come on, humor me. One guess. Garrison named it himself. Werewolf. Think."

Burnette finished touching up his tattoos before eight, and he shook Lisa's hand and wished her all the luck in the world. She noticed he was wearing a silver skull ring above his wedding band and that his thumbnail was mangled. "You be careful, you hear?" he warned her. "I'd say to send my regards to ol' Joe Stone, but I understand we ain't operatin' like that. Nope, I ain't seen you in years."

"We're in your debt, Lloyd," she told him.

M.J. arrived fifteen minutes later, behind the wheel of a rented Kia, and Lisa walked out and got in the car almost before it stopped moving. The Danville airport was a twenty-minute drive from the hotel. The flight to the Warrenton-Fauquier Airport in M.J.'s plane would burn an hour, longer than usual at 18,000 feet rather than 30,000, the ride at low altitude so there'd be no need for a flight plan, the airport selected because it was a few miles outside of Washington's Air Defense Identification Zone. Then they'd catch a taxi for part of the drive to the lab, and there'd be no record of the trip, no communication with a control tower, no formalities or paperwork. When Lisa looked across the small interior at her, M.J. was dressed for the part, wearing a trench coat, a man's fedora and black sunglasses.

"Wow," Lisa said. "You look like Jack Abramoff. Or Boris Badenov."

"I am *so* into this," M.J. replied. "I know this is serious business and we've got your whole livelihood on the line, but this is beyond exciting. Who woulda thunk it? I bought the coat at a London Fog outlet for thirty-five dollars. I've got an Amelia Earhart hat, leather with the flaps and whatnot, for the next leg, and the classic bomber jacket. The cab'll be waiting; it's already booked like we discussed. My office is keeping tabs on it in real time so there's no delay or hitch. We're monitoring the roads and traffic for any wrecks and construction. Your wig is behind me in a bag. We're off to the races."

Lisa managed to grin through the stress. "I'm happy you could find something suitable to wear."

"Clothes make the woman," M.J. noted.

"I need to call Joe one more time, so keep quiet." Lisa hit the preset, and he answered immediately. She wished him a good morning and told him she'd left her glasses on her desk, wondered if he'd noticed them.

"Yes," he said, meaning he had confirmation and believed that Lettie and Trooper Wilkinson were en route to Manassas. "Found them." The two words were buoyant.

CHAPTER THIRTY-TWO

When he came on the monitor set up in the Stone and Stone conference room, Judge Dennis Klein appeared professionally nonchalant, his expression dispassionate and dialed to zero, receptive to either side's thoughtful persuasion, a fair arbiter, the irony and zingers and showboat scowls put aside for the day's business. He was wearing his black robe, a red and blue rep tie visible at the opening near his neck where the robe's zipper ended. "So good morning, and here we are," he remarked and requested that the attorneys identify themselves again, a formality since they all could see one another on screen. Sarah Scales, a court reporter, was with Joe, Anderson and Williams, taking down what was said, mashing hushed keys on her stenographer's equipment, creating a record of every word and sound, even the *huhs*, *ummms*, *ers* and *ahs*. Nicholson and MacDonald had hired their own court reporter, and the judge swore in both ladies at the same time, putting them under oath to transcribe the proceedings accurately.

Neal's Richmond lawyer, Emmett Fulcher, had joined Nicholson and MacDonald in Norfolk. A week earlier, Fulcher had attempted to quash the Rule 4:10 subpoena requiring Neal to produce a DNA sample but lost the argument, barely made it to the courtroom podium before the judge stopped him and told him the law was against Mr. VanSandt. Fulcher had coattailed Benecorp's positions and pleadings, not anxious for his client to forfeit the considerable payment he'd received, and he and Neal were utterly allied with Garrison. Fulcher had a habit of chewing on an unlit cigar, and he stopped unwrapping a Montecristo during the introductions and held it beneath the table, temporarily out of sight.

"I am in a conference room at the Commonwealth of Virginia's regional forensic sciences lab in Manassas, Virginia," Klein announced after everyone had spoken. "I'm here to judicially supervise Rule 4:10 and Rule 4:9A discovery, specifically the taking of buccal swabs for DNA analysis from Neal VanSandt, a party to this suit, and a subject who purports to be his mother, Lettie VanSandt, this pursuant to a motion and representations filed by Joe Stone in the action styled *Joe NMN Stone v. Benecorp et als.*, Henry County civil docket number 11-1459. I am alone in the room save for my bailiff of seventeen years, Darrell Howell, and Julia Bard, a scientist with the state's lab. I asked the director here to pick a qualified person at random to perform the swabbing and analysis. Ms. Bard was the lucky winner." He smiled perfunctorily. "However, I'm informed that Director Harvey himself will keep a tight rein on this particular test."

Williams blocked his mouth with his hand, whispered to Joe. "We have a list of every employee in the Manassas branch. She's legit. She's been there for over seven years. Best we can discover, she's a straight arrow. We've had private security researching them all—nothing unusual has cropped up."

"Alas, we are the only three people in the room," Klein stated. "It's eleven-thirty-five, and the putative Lettie VanSandt hasn't favored us with an appearance. Neal VanSandt is present and waiting in the adjacent room. We've alerted security at the front entrance to watch for the alleged Miss VanSandt and accompany her directly here. They will serve her with a subpoena for this discovery. What was your last report from her, Mr. Williams?" Klein was visible on one monitor, the Benecorp lawyers and Fulcher on another.

"As of this morning," Williams answered, "we fully expect her to be there."

"Based on what?" the judge asked.

"My client, Mr. Stone, assures me that Miss—"

"Wait, never mind," Klein interrupted, "the lab director just stuck his head in and said she's cleared the entrance and is on the elevator. We expect her at any moment." He leaned toward his bailiff and murmured something that the microphone in the room didn't catch.

"Glad to hear it, sir," Williams said.

None of them spoke. Klein bounced the eraser end of a yellow wooden pencil against the court file. Anderson exhaled, plopped his elbows on the table and turtled his neck toward the monitor that displayed Klein and the lab conference room. Williams rubbed his eyes. Joe stood, then almost immediately sat down again.

"Judge, seriously?" Nicholson was the first to speak when the door opened and a security guard escorted in the lady who claimed to be Lettie. "Seriously?"

The woman who appeared on the monitors was wearing a floppy hat and giant sunglasses, and the scarf around her neck was bunched under her chin. Long, straight black wig hair fell from beneath the hat to her shoulders, hugged close to her cheeks. She was dressed in Lee blue jeans and a buttoned cardigan Christmas sweater—candy canes and Santa's sleigh—even though it was late September. Without direction, she immediately took a seat at the correct spot, in front of a camera and microphone.

"Judge, this is ridiculous," Nicholson complained. "She might as well be covered in a burka—this could be anyone. She should be required to let us have a full look at her."

"Judge, that isn't the deal," Williams said firmly. "That's not why we're doing this. We're concerned with what the DNA looks like, and that alone will tell the story. We have explained to Mr. Nicholson at length that Miss VanSandt is fearful of Benecorp and has taken measures to conceal herself to the greatest extent possible. Reasonable or not, she's afraid of Mr. Garrison. The DNA won't lie, whether it's collected from a buck-naked subject or a subject in a burka."

Klein scrutinized the lady adjacent to him. "Are you Lettie Pauline VanSandt?"

"Who're you?" The lady's voice was muffled; she'd dipped her head and almost spoke into the scarf.

"I'm Judge Dennis Klein. I'm the judge presiding over a case involving what purports to be the last will of a lady named Lettie VanSandt."

"Show me some ID," the woman insisted.

"Yep," Williams said spontaneously, "that's our girl. Contrary as ever."

"Judge," Nicholson responded, "I'd ask that the Court disregard that and caution Mr. Williams not to editorialize any further for us. He knows better."

·"Noted," Klein said. "Please don't do it again."

"My apologies," Williams said. "It wasn't calculated."

Klein rocked sideways in his chair, pulled the robe up past his hip and took out his wallet. "Fair enough," he said calmly. "Here's my state-issued identification card."

Phil Anderson covered his microphone with his hand and leaned away from the table. "Does that sound like her?" he asked Williams.

"Hell if I know," Williams answered. "I've never heard her voice. Unless you're at the 911 center or the sheriff's office, she's not real sociable. Is that her, Joe?"

"I'd say so," Joe answered. "It's impossible to be sure with the scarf trick and listening through a monitor. Plus, she's not saying much yet."

"Hand it to the Mountie," the woman instructed Judge Klein. "Don't try and touch me."

"Pardon?"

She didn't reply.

"I don't understand," Klein said.

"She means your bailiff," Joe volunteered into his mike. "She wants you to give it to the officer and have him hand it to her."

Klein shrugged. "Okay. Why the heck not?"

The bailiff passed her the laminated card and she inspected it for several minutes, front and back. She returned it to the cop. "Approved," she said.

"I'm gratified," Klein answered. "And now, ma'am, how about I take a peek at *your* credentials? Sauce for the gander is also sauce for the goose."

The woman dug into her front pocket, retrieved a sheet of note-book paper folded in quarters and slid it across the table in the judge's direction. Joe noticed she'd grasped it between her knuckles, didn't touch it with her fingertips.

"Is this for me?" Klein asked.

She nodded.

He unfolded the paper, pressed and smoothed it flat on the table with his palms. A driver's license was inside, but he ignored the license, moved it to the side and studied the paper. Finished, he focused on the camera and straightened a robe sleeve that had hung and wadded at his elbow. "Since counsel aren't in a position to see this, I'll read the contents aloud and then place the original in the file. Obviously, I'm sharing it strictly for informational purposes and without prejudice or any kind of factual impact as to its allegations. I'm reciting this verbatim from a typewritten document; there are misspellings and errors that won't be obvious when I read: 'My name is Lettie Pauline VanSandt. I agree for my spit to be tested. I am hiding because Seth Garrison wants to kill me. Same as he done to Dr. Downs. I am positive without no doubt in my mind that he sent Babylon's Whore to my trailer to kill me and steal my greatest invention. If he's her boss, then we know who that makes him don't we? I want this test to be over quick so they can't stick a lock on me. And track me. I need to leave fast.' *Fast* is entirely written in caps," Klein said drily. He picked up the driver's license. "Purports to belong to a Lettie Pauline VanSandt, date of birth August twenty-second, 1966. Customer number on the license is D88656021. We'll have it copied for the file as well."

"Judge," Nicholson interjected, "it would certainly be helpful in terms of authentication if you could retain the license for a few days so we could verify it's genuine."

"Actually," Klein said, "that's Ms. Bard's call. What's your usual procedure?"

The camera angle didn't completely encompass Bard. Half of her was cut off from the screen. "Normally I compare the ID to the person, and we make a copy, and that's it. We file a copy of the ID. We don't keep the original."

"You ain't stealin' my license," the lady exclaimed, her voice high. She pointed at the image of Nicholson on her screen. "Quit stallin', you pitiful excuse for a lawyer." She leaned toward Klein. She squirmed and twisted and wiggled her arms free and shed her sweater. A white, V-neck T-shirt was underneath. Tattoos lined each uncovered arm. She raised her chin, exposed her mouth, revealed her teeth. "Here's your ID." She pointed at the gold tooth, then held her arms high and displayed them for the judge. "I ain't stayin' here forever."

"Judge, how about the rest of it?" Nicholson challenged. "I mean, she seems willing to show us her most obvious features. We don't understand why she can't take off the hat, wig and glasses."

The woman looked away from the camera, addressed the judge. "Right there. Him askin' proves my point."

"Go ahead, Ms. Bard," Klein said. "We don't want to keep Miss VanSandt waiting. The Devil does indeed move swiftly, or so I understand." His gaze bumped up and down, studying the tattoos.

"Ha-ha-ha," the woman grunted sarcastically. "Real funny."

Bard tugged gloves from the opening in a cardboard container, worked them on, tore a paper package longwise and removed a cotton swab. "I'm required to check your mouth, Miss VanSandt," she said nervously. "Okay? Do I have your consent?"

"Don't you touch me," she squawked. "I ain't chancin' you anthraxin' me." She opened her mouth.

The tech approached her and crouched, and as she was stooping down, the woman jerked the swab from her hand. Bard stepped back, startled.

"Pick another one," the woman demanded. "From the spares. Let Klein pick."

"There's nothing wrong with that one," Bard said.

"Let Klein pick." The woman raised up from her chair but didn't stand, and she pushed closer to Bard and opened her mouth again. She stuck out her tongue, wagged it around, set her head at several different positions in quick succession.

Flustered, Bard tracked the woman's mouth as it moved, searched as best she could. "Please hold still," she requested, irritation in her tone.

The woman complied, kept stationary, and Bard knelt and peered up and continued her inspection.

"Okay," Bard said.

"By the way, that would be *Judge* Klein, please, when you refer to me in this judicial proceeding. Thank you." He selected another wrapped swab from the three packages remaining on the table and handed it to Bard.

"Open it slow," the woman demanded.

Bard made a point of positioning the package directly in front of the woman's face and methodically tearing the paper. "Is it safe to remove it now?" she asked, still peeved.

The woman nodded yes. "Give it to me," she said.

"What?" Bard asked.

"I'll stick it in my own damn mouth."

"Judge," Nicholson said, "that's contrary to the lab's standards and protocol. We object."

"I'm watching them," Klein said. "I'm here and this is being taped, so let's just please finish. Give her the Q-tip," he instructed Bard.

"Make sure you completely wet it," Bard said. "Move it all around your mouth and cheeks."

The woman took the swab, plunged it into her mouth, spun her wrist in circles, first one direction, then the other. She zipped the swab's stem crossways between her lips. She clamped shut and glared at Bard. "Enough?" she muttered through closed teeth.

"Yes," Bard told her.

"Be careful," Nicholson said as the woman was withdrawing the swab. "Watch her, please."

"Watch you lose what you tried to steal," the woman said angrily. She handed the swab to Bard, stood, scooped her sweater off the table, raised her scarf to conceal her face and shot for the door. She spoke through the cloth as she hurried from the room: "Tell my sorry boy Neal I'm ashamed of him. He damn well knows I meant to leave everything to Lawyer Joe."

"Either that was Lettie," Williams whispered to Joe, "or the best impostor ever." He shook his head, grinning. "Paranoid. Disrespectful. Tattoos. Gold tooth. Great, amazing call on the hardware store."

"Thanks," Joe said.

"From what little I can recall," Williams noted, "it does seem maybe she's gained weight or was padded, and her skin looked slightly different, smoother, the small section I could see."

"Or it could've just been the lighting and the camera," Joe offered. "I didn't notice much difference."

M.J. was waiting at a curb near the entrance to the forensic sciences building, and she tooted the horn of a blue Nissan sedan, lowered the window and raised her hand, waved. The woman, still all wrapped up, jogged toward her and stopped at the passenger-side door, forcefully opened it but didn't get in.

"Let's go," M.J. told her. "Come on."

"I don't think so."

"Huh?" M.J. said. "My plane's waiting. Hurry up."

She lowered the scarf so that it bunched on her neck again. She leaned inside and looked into the backseat. "I done my part, Attorney Lisa Stone, so now you tell me what they claim my formula cures other than wounds."

"Why aren't you getting in?" Lisa asked from the backseat. "We need to leave. Benecorp has this place swarming." She was hidden, lying with her head against the door, concealed by the seats in front of her.

"Quit fuckin' around and tell me."

"It doesn't cure anything, Lettie. Not really."

"Bullshit! We didn't have this circus because it don't work. You and me have a deal."

Lisa exhaled a long breath, almost a taunt. "I'm telling you the truth." She was still reclining, her feet closest to Lettie.

"Then how come Devil Garrison wants it? It's cancer, ain't it?"

"Hair." Lisa paused, and couldn't help but smile. "Your wound medicine grows hair. Quickly and permanently."

"It'll be a license to print money, Lettie," M.J. assured her. "Jackpot city, ladies. Market it in a combo pack with Viagra and you both can live happily ever after. I've already asked Lisa if it's too late for another partner."

"Hair?" Lettie mumbled. She removed the sunglasses, drew a bead on Lisa. "No shit. Hair? But it'll heal a wound too. I don't care what them peckerheads at Benecorp claim. It's a wound cure, best there ever was."

"Yep," Lisa said. "Hair. And pursuant to our *deal*, forty percent belongs to me and Joe."

"How come you're all dolled up to resemble me?" She puckered her mouth and slitted her eyes. "The trooper told me you'd be here."

"A possible diversion for Benecorp if we needed it. Simple as that."

Lettie began scratching her chin with a painted thumbnail. "That's a whopper of a lie. Somethin's fishy. Maybe it's just 'cause you envy me, but you ain't that sensible, no chance in hell, so I smell a big stinkin' rat." She added the glasses again. "You notice the address we're at?

10850 Pyramid Place. Pyramids is powerful objects. There's a omen for certain."

"An omen?" M.J. repeated.

Lettie gestured at M.J. "You I respect. A famous success story. Me and you should talk shop one day soon."

"Are you certain you don't want M.J. to fly you to Danville?" Lisa asked. "How safe is it for you here?"

"I made it by myself this far. Keep 'em guessin'. I'd rather count on my smarts than yours any day. You done such a brilliant job with Downs."

"Suit yourself, Lettie. Trooper Wilkinson is still here too. You could ride back with him."

"You need to drive me to a place in Falls Church. A house. It ain't far."

"Do you know how to get there?" Lisa asked.

"Got it wrote down, yeah."

"Fine with me. If that's what you want, sure." Lisa peered up at her. "You realize Benecorp's lined the block and we'll be followed?"

"No shit, Sherlock," Lettie said.

"For what it's worth, Lettie, congratulations. Good for you. Both for creating something so valuable and for outlasting Benecorp. I have to hand it to you. Pretty remarkable. Kudos."

Lettie didn't say anything but climbed in and shut the door. "Well, I reckon it was right decent of you to help me fight Devil Garrison. You and Lawyer Joe." She tipped back the hat and then tapped her gold tooth. "Did y'all take care of my animals?"

"I'm sorry—Garrison killed a lot of them. Some we saved. I hate to have to tell you. So you'll know, Neal played a big part in helping Benecorp destroy them."

"Shit. They was my buddies." Lettie wiped the corner of her eye, right above her permanent black tear.

"Joe and I took a couple cats. We named them Pancho and Lefty. And we did adopt out a bunch before Garrison had them killed."

"How 'bout Toby? He was the blind hound. What about him?"

"Not good news. I didn't know you named them. You told me you didn't."

"Just him," she said softly. "Only Toby. Had him the longest." She turned around and stared at Lisa. "How the fuck did you let that happen?"

"I'd be angry too," M.J. encouraged her, having fun. "You'd think your lawyer could do a better job safeguarding your important property."

"I'm gonna sue the piss outta Henry County for not protectin' them," Lettie declared. "Might put you in the suit too, Attorney Lisa Stone."

"By the way," Lisa said, "while we're still speaking to each other, how is it that you're alive, Lettie? Where've you been?"

They dropped Lettie near a cul-de-sac in Falls Church, where she hustled into a cargo van with a Virginia handicap plate and a TED NUGENT FOR PRESIDENT bumper sticker. During the trip from the lab, M.J. had aimed her phone across the seat and managed to video roughly thirty seconds of Lettie—who used the opportunity to blue-streak cuss Henry County for losing her animals—in case the court needed extra proof or there was a complication later on, and they'd persuaded her to leave another saliva sample, which she provided by spitting in the seat as she exited the car. Reminded, she'd bowed slightly to Lisa and almost immediately flashed her a middle finger.

Seconds after Lettie disappeared into the van, the rear doors opened and five identically dressed "Letties" filed out and scattered in different directions, three getting into other vehicles, one jogging away on foot, the last of the lot running into a small frame house with a crooked shutter and crumbling sidewalk.

"I'll be damned," M.J. said. "Being crazy and paranoid occasionally has its benefits."

"Sweet," Lisa said. "Pretty clever. I wondered what she had up her sleeve."

"Thank god she showed," M.J. said as the van and several cars pulled off.

"You're telling me," Lisa said. "I could've hugged her when I saw Harold walk her up to the front entrance. Even in the crazy costume, I was pretty certain it was her. I swear, it was like opening the letter and learning I'd passed the bar—I was that happy. And I loved the expression on the Benecorp creeps' faces when Lettie drove to the door in a state trooper's car. There's no doubt those two slugs pacing around the entrance were Seth's creatures. Probably his helicopter that kept flying over too."

"Welcome to the millionaires' club," M.J. told her. Lisa was still behind her, lying low in the rear seat.

"We're not home free yet. Let's hope Toliver can keep Benecorp's paws off the DNA sample. We've got our boy Derek ready in the parking lot, too, for whatever good it will accomplish."

Forty minutes later, M.J. turned in to a fast-food restaurant, switched off the engine and walked inside. She paid an advertisement salesman from a Virginia FM radio station—owned by Goldbricks, Inc.— two hundred dollars in cash and returned his keys. "Many thanks," she said. "No one at the station spotted me, and you folks are doing a great job there. Nothing beats a little undercover visit, though. You take care, and let me know if I can ever help you or our station in the future. Of course, as we agreed, my visit was strictly between you and me." She shook his hand, joined Lisa in a waiting taxi that returned them to the airport, and after sitting in the plane for more than an hour so Lisa wouldn't arrive back in Henry County too soon, they flew to Danville and then headed for the Wild Magnolia parking lot to see Dr. Beasley and get the Mercedes. The tattoos were gone when they landed, scrubbed off in the cockpit, a plastic bag of colorful rags and stained cotton balls ready to be thrown in the trash.

CHAPTER THIRTY-THREE

While M.J. was driving them to the dentist's office from the airport, Lisa nervously sipped a bottled water and waited until they'd been on Route 58 for several miles before calling Toliver at the state lab.

"Jackson" is how he answered his phone, a single gruff word, even though he had to recognize her number.

"Is everything okay there?"

"Hunky dory," he said. "I'm in position. Just hung up with your old man. He was full of advice and warnings and tellin' me to be on guard. Like I'm Fred Sanford, playin' checkers with Grady and dozin' off in my chair."

"Joe's Joe, right?" she said. "He doesn't mean anything by it. I'm sure he's worried to death. So am I. These characters are devious as hell, and there're millions of dollars on the line."

"Ten-four."

"Who's there for Garrison?" she asked.

"Nobody," Toliver replied.

"What? That doesn't make any sense, Toliver. Are you sure?"

"It does if he's here for himself. Sittin' right next to me, starin' at Miss Bard and the commonwealth's whizbang laboratory. She's keepin' us up to speed, the director double-checks every step she takes, I set up a video camera and Mr. Garrison has agreed not to use or display any electronic device includin' a cell phone, just in case he's got some kind of interference or mojo or transmission that might jam the equipment or skew the true results. Your science fair winner Derek's in the lobby, scannin' the ether for any potential trouble."

"How come you can use your cell phone?" Lisa asked.

"He doesn't care. I assume he thinks we aren't clever enough to jam up the test."

"And he's simply sitting there?" she asked, incredulous. "The reclusive Seth Garrison's twiddling his thumbs in a state forensics lab?"

"Actually," Toliver answered, "he's chattin' with me about boats and wise places to invest my money."

"Listen, Toliver, don't let him put you to sleep. He's a snake in the grass and as ruthless as they come."

"Ten-four."

"He's up to something."

"Couldn't tell you. But so far, so good. He says he wants to speak to you, then he's leavin' on a jet plane. He kinda sang it: 'Don't know when I'll be back again.' Acted it out with his hand being the plane and made a whistlin' noise for the takeoff."

"Huh?" Lisa was dumbfounded. "This is bizarre. Why would he leave? Are you positive it's Garrison? Did he talk to Joe?"

"Nope. Didn't ask to."

"Put him on. I'm anxious to hear from him. Can't hardly wait."

There was a pause, and Lisa could hear a muddle of voices and sounds and something beeping in the distance.

"Mrs. Stone, good afternoon. Nice to speak again." There was no doubt it was Garrison.

"Hello," she said, the surprise still shaping her voice. "What brings you to Manassas, which is neither a third-world country nor an Indian reservation? And isn't a port, either."

"Ah—excellent memory. I'm here to enjoy the show."

"But you're leaving?" Lisa asked.

"I'm afraid it's all over but the shouting. Congratulations."

"Okay," Lisa said noncommittally.

"Well played. That *was* Miss VanSandt, wasn't it?"

"Of course," Lisa said.

"Damn. How'd you convince the cops it was her DNA in the fire? Local favor?"

"I'm as puzzled as you are." She and M.J. were passing a sad-sack miniature golf course with peeling paint and mildewed carpets. M.J. was listening, rapt, dawdling along in the slow lane.

"It's a shame we can't open a negotiation," Garrison said. "Be done with all this hostile litigation and come to an agreement. We were victims too, you see. We thought Miss VanSandt was deceased, and we dealt in good faith with her son. Benecorp would be happy to make a generous offer to Miss VanSandt and dismiss the lawsuits and do everything in our power to ensure your husband's license is returned. We're innocent in this entire process. We were caught in a slipstream of bad luck."

"Where are Lettie's dogs and cats, Seth?"

"I have no earthly idea."

"The animals are important to her," Lisa said.

"While we're on the subject of unexplained disappearances, maybe we should ask your friend Miss VanSandt where Jane Rousch is. I suspect you might have some interesting information as well."

"Why?" Lisa asked. "How would she have any idea about your employee?"

"Still," Garrison said, his tone staid, restrained, pointed, "the VV 108 could theoretically do almost anything. Probably not much use to your new suitor unless he understands its properties. Benecorp would be an invaluable partner in that regard."

"We'll take our chances," Lisa said emphatically.

"You're certain?" Garrison asked. "I'd remind you that making use of information illegally obtained, say, for instance, by computer trespass, is going to land you in a world of trouble. Derek Hansen too. You only have half the loaf."

"I assume you're making up new lies and plotting new dishonest angles. I don't know anything about computer trespass, and I'd suggest you not try to intimidate Derek like you did Dr. Downs, who told us, by the way, why you want the formula. We know what it does. Of course, I'm betting you erased all his reports and work, didn't you? That left a footprint, though, and you'll play hell explaining what you deleted. It was Downs's discovery, and he shared it with us."

"Nonsense," Garrison snapped. "MissFit Matrix solved the VV 108. Downs had no involvement in finding an application for it."

"So you say, Seth. But how could we have learned it otherwise? And why would you delete his files unless it was because you wanted to steal what he'd discovered? Why'd you keep such a loose cannon on the payroll for so long unless he was a genius?"

"So what's the Wound Velvet's application, if you truly know?"

"As best I can tell, it makes people crazy for money, so crazy, in fact, that they'd slaughter animals and torture sweet, fragile scientists to death and try to kill a poor Henry County woman living alone in the woods. It makes people, especially people like you, lie and ruin lives and destroy reputations and never even give it a second thought. It's an anesthesia. Numbs your conscience. Powerful stuff."

"Bullshit," Garrison said. "You have no idea, do you? You and your merry band don't have a clue. Cool. You're still going to need me and Benecorp, whether you like it or not."

"Put Officer Jackson back on the line, please."

"You don't know, do you?" Garrison gloated.

"We'll see."

"A final variable, Mrs. Stone," Garrison said. "Before you turn me down and cause both of us needless problems, I assume you understand we're aware of your activities in Nassau. You realize that? And don't worry, I've stepped away from the policeman. He can't hear me."

"I never went into a bank, Seth. Sorry. Wasn't me. I never withdrew any money. You know that better than anyone since you filmed a totally fake video."

"It's not the bank that interests me. I noticed that your husband's lawyers avoided answering certain discovery questions. Many of the questions touched on who you were with during your vacation. There were a few other objections, but part of the fight was over something so routine. Odd, isn't it? And Mr. Brooks was uncooperative with us; he kept stalling and wouldn't set a deposition date after you went to such lengths to meet with him secretly."

"They're Joe's lawyers, not mine. As I recall, there was some issue about M.J.'s correct, legal name. We were waiting on that. Pretty simple."

"You still want to take the hard line with Benecorp? We both know the reasons for those omissions, don't we?"

"Maybe you think you do. I have no idea what you're talking about."

"I suppose, then, we'll just share our information with your husband. My courier is waiting outside your law office. What should I tell him to do?"

"Fuck you, Seth. How limp. So you're down to extortion, huh? Sad. You're a thug with a crowbar now."

"Probably be ugly when you see Mr. Stone. Very ugly. If I were you, I'd simply go ahead and confess to him. That's wise lawyerly advice, isn't it? Accept responsibility and demonstrate remorse when you're guilty? Hope for the best? Or maybe I'll just keep our surprise in the vault and let you wonder exactly when the bad news might surface. See how much you enjoy living under duress."

"Now *you're* bluffing, Seth. Badly." She laughed. "If you had the real goods, we'd already have seen them in some form or fashion. With all the cash on the line, I doubt you would've been sitting on that kind of leverage." She caught M.J.'s eye. "I might have a problem," she whispered, her hand over the phone.

"I received my information a bit late in the game, and it seems our case will end before I can use it in court. But I know that you and Brooks were together at the Ocean Club. I could tell you what you ate for lunch by the pool and how much champagne you had sent to your room. I have his signature on a credit card receipt from the restaurant. His checking account records showing a withdrawal he made from an ATM in Nassau. The rest I feel confident we can fill in. I hesitate to say 'flesh out' given the circumstances. The truth is the truth no matter how it's delivered or packaged."

"I don't know what the hell you're babbling about."

"Last chance, Mrs. Stone."

"As we say in court, Seth, what you think you know and what you can prove are two different things. I don't believe you have squat, and if you do, well, send it on to Joe. Of course, it doesn't matter how many receipts and dishonest wills and doctored tapes you cook up, you just lost millions. Millions, you little bitch. Let me speak to Officer Jackson. You and I are done."

"Your choice," Garrison said, seething. "I'll find Mr. Jackson for you."

"Please make sure you don't let him slip something past you," Lisa told Toliver a few moments later. "Stay put and stay on your toes, even if he leaves."

"Ten-four. Don't worry. You're startin' to sound like your old man." Toliver hesitated. "I'd say you and me are scheduled for a real interestin' conversation about a fire at the VanSandt property in the next little bit."

Lisa ended the call and snapped her head back against the seat. "Ah, damn, M.J., I think Garrison knows about Brett and Nassau. I mean, for crying out loud, can't I catch a break? I love my husband, and I'm remorseful as can be, and I've suffered over this for months, but I'll never be able to move on. One stupid mistake, and I realize it's my fault, I do, I'm to blame, no doubt, but my failing is . . . is immortal. Preachers or doctor dope or counseling or good-wife deeds or all the money from the Wound Velvet and this whole saga with Garrison—there's no way to fucking put a stake through it. I'm no better off than I was months ago. I just want my husband and my law practice and my farm, and I'm going to lose them."

"Like barnyard shit, my old regional manager, Rucker Lyons, was fond of saying. You can't rub it all off in the grass—some always packs into your boot treads—and then you have to pick it out with a paper towel and finish the job with a nail or rock or a knife blade, and no matter what you get a smear on your hand—can't help it."

Lisa snapped her head back against the seat again. She mashed her temples with the heels of her hands. "It's a very bad sign that Joe hasn't called me. You may have to pull over; I feel ill."

CHAPTER THIRTY-FOUR

"Why'd you lie to me, Lisa?" Joe shouted. He glared at her. "With a fucking straight face?" He was in their conference room, sitting at the table, alone. He'd brought along the wooden bowl of nuts he kept in his office. Busted brown walnut shells littered the table, and a skinny, pointed pick was lying among the shells and helter-skelter fragments.

"I . . . Joe . . ." Lisa stammered. She flushed red, from her collarbone to her hairline. Betty had told her that Joe was happy after Lettie's DNA test, celebrating with the other lawyers, but Lisa was on guard when she eased through the conference room door, worried about Seth Garrison's threat, cautious and wary, ready with tentative fibs and rickety explanations she'd cobbled together during the last of the ride from the airport. When she saw Joe, she didn't even bother. His snarl and ferocious yelling and the roped veins in his neck—as angry as she'd seen him in years—overwhelmed her and choked off any dishonest instincts. There was also a measure of relief, the junkie caught before she was compelled to rob another pharmacy, the jig finally up.

"Just flat lied."

She noticed a large yellow envelope on the table, the flap opened, released from its bendable clasp, a small section of a photograph sticking out. "I'm . . . sorry." She raised her hands, then let them slap against her hips. She cried, made no effort to hide the anguish.

"When were you planning on telling me?" he demanded.

"I'm so sorry."

"Twenty years, and this is the thanks I get. I can trust you about as far as I can throw you."

She didn't speak. It was odd, though, his mood—he was angry, bad angry, but his fuming didn't seem to quite square with what she'd done, wasn't popping the needle completely off the scale. There was still some give and margin in him.

"So?" he asked.

"It was . . . one error . . . a single—"

Joe stomped his foot to interrupt her. "It might've been one time, Lisa, but it was a doozy, wasn't it? How friggin' long did you think a spiteful lunatic like Lettie VanSandt could keep her mouth shut?"

"Huh?" Lisa dabbed at her eyes, smeared foundation onto her blouse's cuff. "Huh?" she repeated, stunned, confused.

"Brilliant answer, Lisa. 'Huh.' Lettie fucking called me, okay? She wanted to know why you were dressed to look like her, right down to the gold tooth. You didn't think that would send her into orbit?"

"Lettie called you," Lisa said deliberately. "Okay."

"I'm waiting for an explanation. What the fuck were you thinking? You promised me you wouldn't try this dumb-ass DNA masquerade. Promised. As my wife. As my law partner. Gave me your word sitting there on our porch."

"Technically, I only promised I'd forget about it. And I did, for days at a time."

"That's just the worst kind of lawyer bullshit. Pathetic. That's your excuse? Really?"

Lisa took a seat, leaving a chair between them. She raised her index finger. A speck of green polish was still on her cuticle. "Did Lettie also mention that she killed the Benecorp people? She shot Jane Rousch—or whatever her name is—and the man who was with her. Did she tell you that too?"

"Seriously?" Joe's expression unknotted a bit. He sat deeper in his chair. "Damn. How do you know all this?"

"She told me," Lisa said. "A few hours ago. During our drive to Falls Church."

"She confided in *you*? Confessed to Della Street?"

"Yes," Lisa answered, gaining composure. "She sees it as a hall-of-fame-caliber accomplishment."

"So what happened?"

"For sure, she believed the Benecorp people were apocalyptic. Poor Rousch showed up for the first visit in purple and jewels, and she and the guy with her attempted to make nice and befriend Lettie, and it turns out the woman was born in, yep, Babylon, New York, and it's Katy bar the door after that. Lettie tells them no sale, no way, no how. According to Lettie, they threatened her. Good cop didn't work, so they tried bad cop. They gave her a deadline. The guy opened his coat and let her see his gun. So far, this all seems reasonable to me. Very plausible. Most likely true." Lisa sniffed. She needed a tissue.

"Except the lady probably wasn't from Revelation," Joe said. His shoulders relaxed. He took the nutcracker from the spindle in the bowl's center and squeezed the handles together.

"Here's the ticklish part. Lettie claims that when the Benecorpers returned—the second trip from the Roanoke airport—she'd begun sleeping in her shed, armed and ready for doomsday. They snuck in at night, but even if you come through the Gregory tract that borders her land, you'll set off the dogs. Lettie swears they broke into her house, both with guns drawn. She shot them, Joe. Killed them. Got the drop on them because she was hiding in the shed. Her den window was missing and the space covered with cardboard, remember? She shot them from outside."

"Next . . . Benecorp manipulates the DNA to make it seem as if Lettie's dead so they can bargain with moron Neal and cut a deal for the Wound Velvet."

"Partially true, Joe. But think about that. It doesn't mesh."

Joe absently banged the nutcracker tongs together, the metal ends clicking rapidly against each other. "From what we've seen, they certainly have the capability to rig it, especially since none of this was a priority for anyone when she died." He put down the nutcracker.

"Lettie fixed the DNA, not Garrison. She shot Rousch and burned her in the building to give herself a cover. As far as the world—and Garrison—was concerned, Lettie VanSandt was a fried meth-head, six feet under. She tossed in the meth equipment as part of the misdirection. I've said it a thousand times: DNA's about the same as bird augury, just with better paperwork, if you plug it into a hidebound system."

"Still doesn't account for the match," Joe said.

"Lettie assumed nobody would waste any effort and money on her given the physical evidence. But to her credit she didn't take any chances. That night, she bought a new toothbrush and hairbrush. A razor. Remember the Walmart video and register tape? The toiletries? She dunked the toothbrush in the deceased Miss Rousch's mouth and brushed her hair—yeah, gruesome as hell. She also scraped and nicked the corpse with the razor. Then she planted everything for us to find nice and easy, just in case. Made them superhandy for us to locate. A high school sophomore knows which items the lab takes for comparison—you can learn that from an episode of crime show TV. She spent several hours cleaning and sanitizing, even wiped her nail polish bottles with Clorox. The body's DNA matched the samples the sheriff collected. Lettie was dead, but she wasn't. She'd escaped Garrison. Egomaniac that she is, she loved reciting this for me, went on and on about every detail, proud as punch."

"Okay," Joe said. "*She* drove the rental car and ditched it in Charlotte."

"Wore gloves and a shower cap—again, on the one-in-a-million chance the police happen to check the car. Garrison paid the charges and late fees because he damn sure didn't want an ugly loose end with the car company or the cops. That's why, on the boat, he kept pumping us about Rousch. He knew his goons were missing and something wasn't quite kosher. The odd circumstances had to be nagging him. Where was Rousch? Why was the car abandoned miles away from Martinsville? How were we involved?"

"Yeah," Joe said. "I remember." He still sounded upset.

"Lettie left everything to you. She figured you'd be a safe place to park the Wound Velvet while she sussed out why Benecorp wanted it and tried to stay alive and beat the Devil. She knew she could trust you. And then, because it's how you are—and I love how you are, I'm not complaining—Honest Abe Lincoln gave it away. Ironically, even though I was just being professionally cautious, I sort of waved a few red flags. As we both know now, Garrison substituted a clumsy forgery to frame us. I'm not sure if he did it before or after we sued him, but he had to realize there was a problem early on."

"Why didn't Lettie come to me with all this? I'm her lawyer and her only friend in the world." He rested his elbows on the chair's arms.

"She told me Lawyer Joe's too honest. It's fair to say you were a victim of your own blue-chip integrity and her not wanting to disappoint you. We both understand it's technically not self-defense when she could've escaped or phoned the cops and instead elected to blast people through a window. We both also understand that a Henry County jury *probably* would find her not guilty—you don't go snooping around a woman's house at midnight and expect a pleasant result, not here, not in Southside, no matter the niceties of the criminal code." Lisa tended to her nose with her bare wrist. "But she was afraid. She was afraid of how you'd handle it. How you'd react. What you'd do. She's not a lawyer, and she's paranoid and batty, so she was worried you might not help her or might even report her to the cops. She has such a low regard for me and my morals that it wasn't an issue."

"I'll be damned," Joe said. He scowled and shook his head. "How dumb can she be? I'd have fought tooth and nail for her."

"These were wicked people. They deserved it. This Rousch lady and her accomplice, they were armed; Lettie claims she kept their weapons as proof. I'm convinced they didn't return to Henry County to watch old movies and sip cocoa with her—at a minimum, they intended to hurt her and teach her a lesson. But she didn't have any interest in resolving the shootings through a proper police investigation and a trial, which would've put her in the public view and teed her up for Garrison. And also put her at risk criminally—the wrong judge or jury, and she winds up in jail."

"Where was she? Or where's she been?"

"Hiding. She mentioned a welfare hotel and a shelter in Charlotte. I know she used a computer there at the library. She also camped in the woods for long stretches, which explains the Walmart sleeping bag. After a while, she realized she couldn't manage this alone and jumped me that night in my car." Lisa leaned closer to Joe. "She swears she never saw all the messages we sent before your bar hearing. She always had to use a public computer and didn't want to risk being located through the Internet. She insists that she went weeks without any computer access. I do know she called you from the Charlotte bus station just as she was leaving for Salem. Used a college kid's cell. Her occasional wheelman and confederate is some dude nicknamed Goose, who breeds miniature goats and draws a disability check. He was her driver when she came here dressed as a leprechaun, and he helped her after the DNA test. According to his bumper sticker, he's a big Ted Nugent fan. She had a very inventive disappearance from Falls Church if you're interested."

"I'm interested in the man she killed. Where's he?"

"Bottom of Philpott Lake," Lisa said.

"Did you discover what happened to the strays?"

"Seth killed every damn animal after he had them hauled to Florida and then discovered they had no connection to Lettie's formula. I know because we hacked his computers. We played by Benecorp's rules, not lawyer rules."

"No shit? You hacked Garrison's computers?"

"Derek hacked Garrison's computers. We have to big-time take care of him if Benecorp comes hunting him."

"Ah. And you've learned what the Wound Velvet cures, I'm betting, the same way? We're thieves now too?"

"I have a clear conscience where Benecorp's concerned. Seth Garrison might as well have pulled the trigger on Downs, he absolutely screwed you at the bar hearing, and he killed those animals—think of Brownie getting shot thirty times over. Then there were his plans for Lettie. I didn't tell you about Derek because I wanted this to be all on me if it fell to pieces. My responsibility. You were completely out of the loop. Besides, I knew you wouldn't have any part of it, and it had to be done. No other choice."

"So it was her there with Klein, right? The genuine Lettie?"

"Right. Yes. Absolutely."

"So, okay, now the fucking million-dollar question: Why were you at the lab dressed like her?"

"If Lettie didn't show, I wasn't going down just sitting on my hands and whimpering. I was planning to walk to the front security entrance at the lab and hand them our hair and our spit on a swab. Simple and elegant. Fake Lettie and her tattoos would've been all over the security cameras, and there'd be witnesses who saw her. In a certain sense, it's Garrison's video trick turned against him. We'd have our own movie for the court. I used New-Skin on my fingers, the liquid bandage stuff, so I could hand over our hair and saliva baggies without leaving my own prints. Your old burglary client, Porter Owens, taught us that little trick."

"Pretty damn slick, I have to admit," Joe said. "Fits what we told Klein too. Lettie's scared, but she's there at the right place, doing her bit."

"Last night and this morning, I actually phoned you from Danville and was in a hotel there, so I had an alibi miles from the lab if push came to shove. M.J. flew me to Manassas after the tattoos were finished. Lettie's five a.m. True Value schedule meant I had to be ready yesterday. I had to prepare. Maybe Lettie doesn't show. Or maybe she and Harold get snagged on the way to the test. I was going to have a plan B, come hell or high water." She shrugged. "It wasn't ideal, wasn't Operation Overlord, but it would've given us a chance. It might also have bought us more time to locate the real Lettie. If we'd lost this case, we were ruined. We'd be broke, and my license was next on the bar's chopping block. If Lettie was a no-show, I just couldn't make myself sit on my helpless butt and let them take all our money and our livelihood and our reputations."

"So, if we're totaling your wrongs, you straight-up lied to me, broke the law with Derek and were ready to defraud the court if Lettie had disappeared?" Even though Joe was still agitated, he seemed to be relenting. He sighed. He tugged at his tie. He peered at the floor.

"Joe, listen." She changed seats, sat beside him, cautiously laid both hands on his thigh. "I need to . . ." She became emotional, stopped. She took her hands away from his leg. "To apologize. You're right—I've lied to you, and that alone weakened our marriage and makes me a bad wife. I can't take it back or change it. *Any* of it." Her voice was raw, hoarse, plain, frank. "I wronged you. I hope and pray you'll forgive me and at least be happy that we're safe from Garrison *and* on the verge of some life-changing cash. Soon you'll have your license reinstated and be a big lawyer hero. We won."

"It's not how dumb-ass your lie was, it's that everything we own is in the balance, and I can't trust you. It's crunch time, the biggest crisis of our lives, and I can't count on you to tell me the truth. That's the problem. I mean, I can accept your conniving with Derek and some of the other cut corners, but you didn't have to deceive *me*."

"I'm sorry I lied and let you down, but I love you and our farm and our little law practice and all our routines—our life together. When those things were at risk, I wanted them so bad I couldn't stand it. Please believe that. The bottom line, Joe, is that I did the very best I could to save us—you and me and our marriage and what we have together. I didn't care if it might cost me or if I might wind up in trouble."

"Evidently not." Joe smirked. "So what's the Wound Velvet do?"

Lisa didn't look at him. Her eye makeup was a smeared mess. "Hair. It grows hair. A 3.5-billion-dollar-a-year industry, and the billions are for products that don't work or don't work well."

"Perfect," he said. "I shouldn't be surprised. Damn. All this commotion and wheeling and dealing and lawing and maneuvering and plotting and three people dead . . . to grow hair. Won't save a life or cure any disease."

"I was flabbergasted when Derek told me."

Joe raised his eyebrows. "I'll bet poor stat-king Toliver's sick to his stomach. He's probably realizing about now that all he'll ever have is some unidentified remains at Lettie's to spoil his numbers. She'll never give him so much as the time of day. Only her lawyer has the story, and it's privileged. Damn—the March hare wins the grand prize. Where is she? Where's Lettie?"

"She refused to fly back here with me and M.J., but she had us drop her at a house in Falls Church so she could meet this Goose guy and put together a fairly artful getaway. She says she'll be in touch this weekend through the chat room; obviously, she's already phoned you. I suspect she'll surface for good when the will's invalidated and we can arrange a deal and this all becomes public—no need for Garrison to bother with her if he has no shot at the VV 108. Then she can be here every day, making us miserable again." Lisa darted her eyes down at the table. "What's in the envelope?"

Joe gestured dismissively. "Bullshit from a bullshitter. It's supposed to be pictures of you and your sweetheart Brett Brooks in the Bahamas. Delivered to me, in person, by none other than Downs's old buddy, Dillon Atkins, who was wearing an earpiece and a huge, smug, shit-eating grin. Sent from Seth Garrison, the same guy who had video of you in a bank, and contracts for a $750,000 deal that never happened, and fake documents with my name on them. The same ass-hole who had a forged will substituted into court records and spliced a tape of our conversation in Virginia Beach to make me sound like an extortionist."

"Can I see?" Lisa asked.

"If you want to," he said. "They're no more than a loser's last needle, his trying to fuck with us because we burned him at his own specialty."

"Well, good. Okay. I'm glad I don't have that battle to fight. So you're not pissed at me because you think I cheated on you with another man?"

"No," he said. "I'm pissed at you because you lied to me about your DNA scheme."

"That was awfully easy. Not that I'm complaining."

"Somewhere, sometime, for some reason, you have to choose and stick with it. Unless you dig in and draw a line, you can just chase your tail in circles and second- and third- and fourth-guess every damn thing. These days, you can't even believe what you see with your own eyes. I choose to believe in you and my twenty-year marriage, no matter what."

"Even though I misled you?" she asked.

"Yes. Despite that. It was dumb as shit, and you never should've lied, but it seems you were trying to take care of us. To help us. That part I get."

"Thank you for having faith in me when I probably don't deserve it."

"Well, there's faith, and there's also the fact that you called me on M.J.'s phone when you were in Nassau, and I saw her Facebook postings, and all that happened when there was no need for it to happen, no reason, no suspicion, no incentive for you to create a fiction. Plus, if this were true, I expect we'd have heard about it in court."

"Makes sense," she said.

"And it becomes really easy to trust you when the photos are another Seth Garrison scam." Joe reached for the envelope. She noticed he'd unbuttoned his cuffs and rolled his shirtsleeves partway up his fore-arms. "If you're Seth Garrison, and you keep manufacturing shit from your endless fraud factory, finally you get something wrong. You do too much. Try too hard." He pulled a photo from the envelope and laid it on the table. "I'm not certain about Brooks, but that's for sure you. Definitely you. Lisa Stone, wearing your UVA Law T-shirt. The beauty mark right below your neck. Your wedding ring. Your running shoes. The way you hold your head."

"Okay," she agreed.

"See anything else?"

"I'm flustered, Joe. Not really."

"The key," he said.

"What's the key?" she asked.

"Look at your necklace. I gave it to you in *June*. The key."

"Oh, damn. That's my anniversary present. My Tiffany necklace. The picture *is* fake. It is. The photo's from the park. Where I go to run. Somebody took my picture there and sort of switched several small things, but it has to be a fake."

"Don't act so fucking surprised; I might change my mind." He frowned at her. "Seth sent me a credit card receipt too. I assume it's equally as authentic."

"That's me inserted into a shot with Brett Brooks. I'll be damned. They Photoshopped me or whatever. It's not real."

"I don't know how the photo was produced—I'm not the digital expert—but that can't be you with Brooks in the Bahamas back in March wearing an anniversary gift you didn't get until June."

"I doubt many husbands would've studied the pictures so closely." She stared at the ceiling and briefly shut her eyes. Then she focused on Joe. "Probably only crazy, call-the-meeting-to-order Joe Stone. I'm so glad you spotted it. Oh, goodness. Bless you." She raked her hair with both hands. She glanced at the broken nut shells on the table. "That's what it would have to be."

He squinted at her. "I don't understand."

"Blind-ass luck and a husband who's patient enough to consider the fine print would be about the only hope when you're literally staring at adultery. That's what it would take. Twenty years or twenty minutes, there's not much you can do on your own. Nothing, actually. *Your* sweet, reasonable soul is my only chance."

"Well, your one atrocious lie was plenty. You've more than made your quota. By the way, how's Lloyd Burnette these days?"

"Oh, Joe, wait. I forgot. Your gift. I've already spent part of the Wound Velvet money . . . that we don't quite have yet. I wanted to mark putting this behind us, no matter how it went today. I wanted to do something for you after all we've been through. We can return it if you don't like it, if you're still mad at me or whatever, but please let me show you. It's a surprise. It should be at the farm. Would you at least let me show you? Please?"

CHAPTER THIRTY-FIVE

Joe followed Lisa's Mercedes to their farm, and she stopped near the barn, blocking the driveway. He switched off the Jeep's engine, and she came to his door. He rolled down the window.

"It should be in the stall," she said. "They were supposed to deliver it this morning. Trooper Harold helped me pick it out. Please just think about it before you say no. Maybe sleep on it. I understand you're angry, but I so want you to have this. If you're pissed about the money, I'll pay every dime myself, whether or not we ever see any Wound Velvet cash."

"In the barn?"

"Yeah. I'll wait here."

"Okay," he said. He was looking through the windshield, not at her.

"Are you still cross with me?" she asked.

He didn't answer. He left and shouldered the barn's painted oak door open and disappeared into the entrance, and she didn't hear anything and she couldn't see him, and then nothing happened, and plenty of time had passed, so she moved closer, walked to the fence and cocked her ear. She leaned over the top board, trying to spot him. Sadie trotted toward her from the bottom of the pasture, expecting grain or an apple slice. "Joe? Are you all right?"

A few minutes later, he walked to the gate, unlatched it and swung it open. He returned to the barn, and she heard the engine fire, louder than she thought it would be, and the noise spooked the horse, caused the mare to pivot and tear off across the pasture, snorting as she went, all four hooves in the air when she bucked. The cats fled, too, heading for the azalea bushes beside the porch. Joe was wearing his suit and polished black cowboy boots, and he drove the motorcycle through the breezeway and out of the gate. He never acknowledged her, and she watched him drive off, heard him accelerate. Before she lost sight of him, the throttle hesitated, and the bike wobbled. He put down a boot to keep from wrecking. She shut the gate so Sadie wouldn't get loose.

It seemed like he was gone for a long while, but when she heard the engine again, the sound approaching and gaining strength, she checked her watch, and it had been only ten minutes or so. She met him on the gravel driveway. He kept the engine idling, and locked his legs to balance the motorcycle.

"It's a Harley Heritage Softail," she explained. "Blue pearl and black. Classic lines and not too much too soon, as Harold put it. It really is beautiful."

Joe had on a helmet, a real biker's helmet, with colors that matched the motorcycle. He flipped the visor up.

"Do you like it? Harold said it was similar to yours, how you use the clutch and everything, so you should be able to learn it pretty quick. You already have a license—might as well take advantage of it."

"It's impressive. So are the ZZ Top tickets. Third row. I'm sure they cost a pretty penny."

"Well?" she asked.

"Driving over here from the office, I did some thinking," Joe said, talking more to himself than to her. "Fucking Lettie left me high and dry. Intentional or not, she damn near ruined me. After all I've done for her. So why exactly should I do her any favors?"

"You're preaching to the choir," Lisa told him.

"How much did this thing cost?"

"Around seventeen."

"Then, yeah, I'm keeping it. Thank you. We'll put it on Lettie's tab. It'll soon be a drop in the bucket for her. I'll consider it my executor's fee, over and above our forty percent of the Wound Velvet profits. And I've certainly earned it—twenty years of free advice and free work's worth far more than a motorcycle. All her bullshit aggravation. But we'll pay for the concert tickets ourselves."

Lisa allowed herself to hint at a smile.

"Get on," he said.

"I look a mess. I've been crying. And I don't have a helmet."

Joe patted the seat behind him, popping it twice. "Run down and get my old helmet. You can be the Great Gazoo for a change."

"Are you sure you can drive it with both of us riding?"

"I guess we'll find out. I've got ten minutes of practice under my belt, so what's the problem?"

She went to the basement and came back with the helmet and strapped it on. It was too big, didn't fit, slid down to her eyebrows and banged against her ears. It smelled of sweat and gasoline.

"Get on," he said again.

"Where're we going?"

"Toward the parkway. Beyond that, I have no fucking clue. We deserve a vacation. Might be a day, might be a month. Millionaires can do that."

She almost protested that she didn't have any clothes, and the house wasn't locked, and who would feed the horse and the cats, but she immediately thought better of it, and she straddled the seat and held him around the waist, ready for her first motorcycle ride.

He looped them through the yard and steered them toward the main road, and they left the farm, a couple dips and weaves on the gravel drive, and they almost spilled over completely when they hit the washboard bumps near the broom-straw field, nearly wrecked, but they soon got the hang of it, and Joe accelerated through the gears, took them smoothly up to speed on the blacktop, and she rested her chin on his shoulder and laughed, the wind whipping her face, a small tattoo on her upper arm, this one genuine, a secret she'd hidden in Lloyd Burnette's temporary dragon, permanent and inked into her forever, a bright red heart with a black outline and a single word in its center: JOE.

ACKNOWLEDGMENTS

Thanks to Charles Wright, Smilin' Ed Flanagan, Captain Frank Beverly, David "Hollywood" Williams, the very talented Ben R. Williams, Derek Bridgman, Dr. Michael Jones, Walter P. Miller, Wood Brothers Racing, Joe Regal, Chris Corbett, Eddie Hunt, Charles "the Baron" Aaron, Ruthie Reisner, Eddie and Nancy Turner, Edd Martin, Mrs. Ann Belcher, John B. Updike, Trooper R. E. Howell, Jr., and the wonderful, amazing Gabrielle Brooks.

I'm especially grateful to Sloan Harris, Heather Karpas, Liz Ferrell, Carrie Lee and everyone at International Creative Management.

My friend and editor Gary Fisketjon is the best in the business, and he once again made every single page better.

And grand prize, blue ribbon, over-the-moon thanks to my wife, Deana, alpha and omega, my sweet Bear.

THE MANY ASPECTS OF MOBILE HOME LIVING

In this masterful debut, Martin Clark proves to be the heir apparent of great Southern raconteurs and the envy of more seasoned novelists as he takes us on a frantic tour of the modern south. Hung over, beaten by the unforgiving sun, bitter at his estranged wife, and dreading the day's docket of petty criminal cases, Judge Evers Wheeling is in need of something on the morning he's accosted by Ruth Esther English. Ruth Esther's strange story certainly is something, and Judge Wheeling finds himself in uncharted territory. Reluctantly agreeing to help Ruth Esther retrieve some stolen money, he recruits his pot-addled brother and a band of merry hangers-on for the big adventure. Raucous road trips, infidelity, suspected killers, winning lotto tickets, drunken philosophical rants, and at least one naked woman tied to a road sign ensue in *The Many Aspects of Mobile Home Living*, one part legal thriller, one part murder mystery, and all parts all wild.

Fiction

VINTAGE CONTEMPORARIES
Available wherever books are sold.
www.vintagebooks.com